For The Good

of

The Country

Philip

Lamb

A CREATESPACE BOOK

Also By

Philip Lamb

Yellowstone Venture: Risking Bankruptcy to Escape Burnout

For the Good of the Country is a work of fiction. Other than the description of well-established historical events the names, characters, places, and incidents in this novel are the product of the author's imagination or are used fictitiously. Any resemblance to actual persons, living or dead is purely coincidental.

Cover designed by Kathy Kottwitz: Front cover taken from Architect of the Capital. Back cover modified the work of an unnamed talented civil servant and is in the public domain

To Joan
who took me as her
beloved husband

and

To all those asking:
"Who is telling the truth when
patriotism is the last refuge of
scoundrels?"

FOR THE GOOD OF THE COUNTY

TABLE OF CONTENTS

FOR THE GOOD OF THE COUNTRY

TABLE OF CONTENTS CONTINUED

PROLOGUE:

A NATION AT RISK

6 P.M., Wednesday, November 28, 1963

Crayton Langford and Jason Fields arrived early. They sat on the edge of their seats on the rail in the House Press Gallery. Both were accredited, though their credentials were suspect. Their press passes had opened many doors and read in bold print "N. B. C. PRESS." In fine print, The Nebraska Broadcasting Corporation described its holdings in Langford's hometown: KHAS Radio, KHAS TV, and The Hastings Daily Tribune. Crayton and Jason were students on the Washington Semester Program at American University. They were good friends, but opposites. Langford was from Nebraska, yet liberal; Fields from Minnesota, but conservative. They took themselves seriously and honed their skills on each other, arguing politics passionately, practicing for roles they were sure they would someday play.

Tonight, they were quiet, intense and focused. They were witnesses to history, irreversible, tragic, history. Kennedy was dead. He was murdered in Dallas, Texas. All Americans had lived his death. The nation was wounded. Soon, the man described as, "Big as Texas" would stand before them. Lyndon Baines Johnson was now President of the United States. He had claimed the office on Air Force One, just two hours after President Kennedy had died from an assassin's bullet that had blown off the back of his skull. With Johnson, Americans now understood the phrase, "The King is dead, long live the King."

William "Fishbait" Miller, doorman to the United States House of Representatives for fourteen years, took a deep breath: "Mistah Speakah, The President of the United States." Everyone in the chamber stood, but this was not the typical standing ovation, with boisterous shouts and thunderous applause. Rather, the clapping was hesitant, scattered and abbreviated. In near silence, Johnson proceeded to the Speaker's platform.

To Langford and Fields, Speaker McCormack's traditional "high honor and distinct privilege" in introducing the new President seemed sadly inappropriate. Conditioned by Kennedy, the Chamber tried to reserve judgment, but Johnson was the only obvious beneficiary of Lee Harvey Oswald's bullets. He had always been ambitious. Now he had his prize.

The nation had not had a Southern President since Zachary Taylor in 1848, thirteen years before the Civil War. "Forget Hell" was not just a Southern sentiment. Northerners remember as well. In total silence, Johnson began to speak. The world listened.

To Langford, his odious drawl was a slap at the nation. He was no Kennedy. Johnson was clumsy and uncomfortable. His gestures were mechanical and exaggerated. His disproportionate body went through motions completely out of sync with his words. Langford shook his head in dismay.

"Shut your eyes," Fields whispered. "Shut your eyes and listen."

Strangely, with his eyes closed, Langford found the President's words moving and reassuring. He could feel their sincerity. Not with "vigar," but with undeniable power, Johnson called on each Senator and Representative to join him. Together, they would enact the Kennedy Program as a living memorial to the martyred President. They were the right words for a tragic time.

"Thanks," Langford whispered. President Johnson was doing what had to be done. The nation could not be assured with one speech, but his words, and strength, and presence helped. Indeed, as Langford relaxed and looked around, he saw a setting that reflected tradition, confidence, and continuity. The nation had roots, deep roots, anchored in the bedrock of a glorious land. One hundred and eighty seven years of triumphs and tragedies, forefathers and famous sons, heroes and heroines, all spoke in a clear unmistakable voice; the nation was secure. The Capitol amplified that voice. The loss of one man, even if that one man was the President of the United States, could not threaten the nation.

Still, doubt remained. Maybe Kennedy was not the only target. Maybe there were other assassins. Perhaps Oswald was just the tip of a murderous conspiracy. Did it involve the Klan?

Castro? Communist? The Mob? Kennedy could be just the beginning. Who was next? Surely terrorists would anticipate this Joint Session of Congress. What a target – Johnson, the nation's Senators, Representatives, Cabinet Secretaries, and Supreme Court Justices all gathered in one place. How stupid! Sitting in the press gallery, Langford wondered if it was a shooting gallery. Was he safe? He thought he was. Johnson was the only target that made sense. Langford knew the line of succession, so would the assassins. Kill Johnson and chaos would surely follow.

How strange Langford thought, sitting comfortably with his friend in the Press Gallery wondering whether the man before them would be murdered. They were just spectators. His thoughts were obscene. It was the Roman Coliseum. No one knew the emperor. Was he here, in the chamber, or did he call the shots from afar? Would he let Johnson live or have him killed? If Johnson were eliminated, who would take his place?

Langford saw the answer. It was as frightening as the question. Fields had seen them, too, not the assassins but two constitutional land mines in the future of the republic. Congressman John McCormack, Speaker of the House of Representatives, was first in line of succession. He would be President if Johnson died. If McCormack died in the attack, Senator Carl Hayden, President Pro Tempore of the Senate, was second in line to the Presidency.

Incredibly, but in adherence to protocol, all three – President Johnson, Speaker McCormack, and President Pro Tempore Hayden – were on the Speaker's platform within a few feet of each other. A huge American flag, hung vertically, would serve as the backdrop for whatever was about to happen.

As Johnson stood before the House trying to reassure the nation, McCormack and Hayden sat behind him, to his right and left in tall brown leather high back chairs. McCormack, the wispy, white haired Speaker was slumped to his right, sound asleep. His glasses sat cockeyed, low on his nose. Occasionally, without regard to Johnson's speech, his right hand would wave spastically across his face in pursuit of a real or imagined fly. Carl Hayden, President Pro Tempore of the Senate sat to McCormack's left. Unlike McCormack, Hayden was awake. Behind dark rimmed glasses his lifeless eyes were open; so was his mouth. He was eighty-six and drooling. If anything happened to both President Johnson and Speaker McCormack, Carl Hayden, former sheriff of Maricopa County in Arizona Territory, would be President of the United States.

Langford and Fields, and all the students on the Washington Semester Program, had had a seminar with Speaker McCormack (and one very protective aide). They spent an hour with him. It was long enough. The seminar, held in The Speaker's Capitol Office, ended with the Speaker, like now, sound asleep. A few of the more sympathetic students thought McCormack's non-responsive answers that rambled on about his childhood and the grand old flag, had more to do with his poor hearing than his mind. Langford, a bleeding heart, was nevertheless, a hard-nosed realist. He knew better. McCormack was only seventy-two, but already hopelessly senile.

Carl Hayden was Arizona's senior senator. He had been an Arizona Congressman for over fifty years, since statehood in 1912. World War One, the war, over there♪ over there♪ wasn't over, over there; it hadn't even begun when Hayden was first elected to the House. He was born much earlier, in 1877. When Hayden was a boy, Wyatt Earp, his brother Virgil, and Doc Holiday had fought the Clanton Gang. The Tombstone Epitaph covered the story, and called it "The Gunfight at the O.K. Corral." In 1886, Geronimo, leader of the Chiricahua Apaches, surrendered to General Nelson Miles, Commander of the Department of Arizona Territory. Hayden was from the Old West, another age, another century.

Why were these noble relics still in service? The answer was simple and not uncommon. Like many senators and congressmen, Carl Hayden and John McCormack were cornerstones of a whole power structure not only in Washington, but also in their home states. Without them, it would collapse. They had to be kept in office. John McCormack and Carl Hayden were necessary props. Jobs were at stake. Their office staffs still had mortgages and bills to pay. Their supporters still believed in the policies McCormack and Hayden no longer remembered. They were fronts for those policies. They issued press releases they never read. They cast votes they didn't understand. And every few years their names appeared on the November ballot, and they and their teams were reelected.

Time had passed them by, but so had death. They were used and would be until they died. The question of Presidential succession was real. It wasn't a classroom exercise. It wasn't a Hollywood script. Kennedy had been killed. Oswald had been killed. His motives and co-conspirators (if any) were unknown. Johnson's health was suspect and McCormack and Hayden were unfit.

John Kennedy's assassination spotlighted the succession problem. Its solution became an urgent national priority. President Johnson stood alone between the nation and a constitutional catastrophe. He had already had one near-death experience. In 1955, he had had a massive heart attack, "as massive a heart attack as you can have and still live," he used to say. Now, eight years later, the people, their Senators and Representatives, friend and foe, prayed for his safety. They prayed that neither an assassin's bullet nor the stress of the Presidency would kill him. They prayed for time.

The sixties were not the sleepy days of a young nation growing strong in splendid isolation. The times were dangerous, and the country rich with impassioned crazies. The Ku Klux Klan spearheaded Southern resistance to the civil rights movement. Four kids in a Birmingham church were their latest victims. The United States was at war with international communism. The cold war was heating up again in Vietnam. It was said Russian ICBMs, launched from hardened silos, could reach Wichita, Kansas, in 15 minutes. The Cuban Missile Crisis screamed its lesson. The nation could not afford to be without an effective leader, not for a week, not for a day, not for a minute.

Afford it or not, President Johnson stood before the nation with no Vice President. The Constitution made no provision for backfilling the office. If Johnson died, the United States and the free world would be without effective leadership – not for just a minute, or a day, but months or years. How would the nation move beyond McCormack and then Hayden? The Constitution not only had no procedure for backfilling Vice Presidential vacancies, it had no procedures for removing incompetent Presidents. Impeachment was reserved for treason and other high crimes and misdemeanors, not incompetence.

In other nations faced with similar problems, the military might "rescue" the country in a *coup d'etat*. Would that be required here? Was a military junta in our future? Were contingency plans already in place? Would the generals promise free elections when the country was ready? It happened all around the world, why not here?

In the United States the Constitution is expected to provide the answers. However concerning incompetence, the Constitution said only that if a President couldn't "discharge the powers and duties of his office, the same shall devolve on the Vice President." Remarkably it failed to answer the question, who was to make a determination of incompetence and under what conditions. Nowhere in the Constitution or the laws of the land was that question even considered, much less answered. In 1787, at the Constitutional Convention, John Dickinson, a delegate from Delaware, warned his fellow delegates they had to address it forthrightly. They never did. The question – who has the authority to declare a popularly elected President unfit to serve - had never been answered.

Now lawmakers were in a race. The question had to be answered. The Constitution had to be amended. Dickinson's hypothetical concern loomed before them as a Constitutional crisis. The question of succession was real. The question of incompetence was in the wings. Maybe the danger was magnified by the nation's grief and outrage, but it was clear and present. Kennedy was dead. Oswald was dead. Johnson was vulnerable not only to an assassin's bullet, but to his heart condition. McCormack and Hayden were unfit. The Constitution was flawed, perhaps fatally. The long arduous process of amending the Constitution needed to be done overnight. Until an Amendment was in place the nation was at risk.

THE TWENTY- FIFTH AMENDMENT, A PRESCRIPTION WITHOUT WARNINGS

John McCormack's and Carl Hayden's colleagues moved with a sense of urgency. To be adopted an amendment would have to be passed in identical form by a two-thirds vote of both the House and the Senate and then ratified by three-fourths of the fifty states.   The House and Senate Judiciary Committees began the process immediately commissioning studies, and calling on experts from the academic, legal, and medical communities.   Hearings followed.   Just as the need for filling a Presidential vacancy had been obvious to the founders, so the need for filling Vice Presidential vacancies and addressing the problem of Presidential disability was made obvious by history.

The case was overwhelming (Prologue End Notes).   It began with Alexander Hamilton, mortally wounded in Weehawken Heights, New Jersey, and ended with the assassination of John Kennedy in Dallas, Texas.

The United States had been incredibly lucky.   It had been playing Russian roulette for 175 years, beating all the odds.   It could have been burned badly.   For thirty-seven of those years, in time of war, peace, prosperity, and depression, the nation had had no vice president. Fortunately during those times no president died. It was just luck.   The need to fill Vice Presidential vacancies was obvious.

The need for replacing incompetent presidents was less obvious, but with study it was even more compelling.   Presidential incapacities were closely guarded secrets.   Like alcoholic or senile congressmen, only multiplied a thousand fold, presidents are the tips of icebergs of powerful interests.   Vested interests (if not national interests) dictated denial and secrecy.   Even limited hindsight, however, documented that at least nine of our thirty-five presidents, one in four, had been incapacitated while serving as president.   Presidents Harrison, Taylor, Lincoln, Garfield, McKinley, Wilson, Coolidge, Roosevelt, and Kennedy all were medically incapacitated during a portion of their presidencies.   For some, the incapacitation lasted only hours, for others it lasted years.

No matter its duration, never during any of these "incidents" did a vice president have the gall or the courage to assume the duties of a stricken president.   Even when presidents were mortally wounded, vice presidents waited.   They didn't have to wait long with Presidents Kennedy and Lincoln, who died within hours of being shot, but President McKinley lived eight days after being shot and President Garfield lived for two and a half months.   It made no difference. Vice Presidents always waited until death confirmed the incapacitation. Similarly when a president was terminally ill, they waited. It took cholera only five days to kill President Taylor, but pneumonia took a month to kill President Harrison. Franklin Delano Roosevelt's case was even more difficult. No one can say when heart disease, hypertension and arteriosclerosis incapacitated Franklin Roosevelt. We only know when it killed him – April 12, 1945 toward the end of World War II.

As one might imagine, early precedents did not serve the nation well when presidents suffered incapacitation but failed to die. Rather they dictated that the Vice President would not assume the presidency while the President was still alive. Consider President Wilson's Vice President Thomas Marshall. When President Wilson returned from an exhausting campaign promoting the Treaty of Versailles in September 1919, his health was failing. On October 2nd Woodrow Wilson suffered a debilitating stroke. He never fully recovered but his condition was hidden from the country. For seventeen months Thomas Marshall sat on the sidelines while Wilson's second wife, Edith Bolling Galt Wilson and his trusted friend "Colonel" Edward House acted as ad hoc co-presidents and "winged it" until Wilson "completed" his term in March of 1921. He died February 3, 1924.

In the summer of that same year (1924) President Coolidge watched his sixteen-year-old son die of an infected blister he had gotten playing tennis at the White House. President Coolidge was crushed. He could not be consoled. His depression was clinical, severe, and incapacitating. He slept for fifteen hours a day. Vice President Charles Dawes did nothing. President Coolidge served his full term until President Herbert Hoover replaced him in March 1929.

For all of its existence, the nation had no way of determining a sitting president's fitness for office. With the recklessness and fecklessness of youth, the United States had stood on the world stage without any insurance. A stroke, Alzheimer's, depression, cardiac infarction, alcoholism, senility, any one of a thousand illnesses common or rare, threatened not just the competency and life of the President, but the democratic character of the nation.

Maybe this wasn't a critical problem in the early years of the Republic after our first presidents got us off to a good start. But the problem grew. The competency of the president was as important as the role he played in domestic and world affairs. By the latter half of the twentieth century, the President of the United States was the most powerful man in the world. Domestic and world affairs were inseparable, and communications were instantaneous. The world had grown small and interdependent, just as the Presidency had grown powerful and independent.

In the twentieth century the "miracles of modern medicine" compounded the problem. Life and death had to be redefined. Life existed if an electro-encephalogram could identify some brain wave activity. The absence of such activity became the legal definition of death. Life could be prolonged until it was no longer worth living. Organs could be "harvested." Transplants became common. Donor cards, especially for motorcyclists, were encouraged.

As long as loved ones had hope that a cure might be found, "vegetables" were preserved. Since no expense or effort would be too great to save the life of a president, his odds of joining the living dead were magnified. The system could no longer count on death to end a constitutional crisis. Like justice, it was no longer swift and sure. It was obvious that a dead president could no longer discharge the powers and duties of his office. But it was equally obvious that being alive was only a necessary, but hardly sufficient condition, for a president to discharge the powers and duties of his office.

According to the Constitution, only impeachment could remove a living elected president, but the grounds authorized by the Constitution were extremely restricted. Only "treason, bribery, or other high crimes and misdemeanors" were mentioned. Incompetence didn't make the list. Yet it was a fact of life. Presidents have been depressed, comatose, drunk, and dying. During those times, even in the nuclear age, the nation could do nothing, but wait and hope. It was a prescription for disaster.

With Kennedy, Johnson, McCormack, and Hayden the nation would wait no longer. After nineteen months, Congress proposed the Twenty-Fifth Amendment (See Prologue End Notes). On February 23, 1967 it was ratified and incorporated in the United States Constitution. No longer would the nation play Russian roulette. Vice Presidential vacancies would be filled, and incompetent Presidents could be replaced.

Section One of the Amendment answered the question: When does the Vice President become President? The Vice President becomes President when the President dies in office, or resigns, or is removed from office.

Section Two made the line of succession from the Vice President to the Speaker of the House to the Senate Pro Tempore to the Secretary of State and through the Cabinet almost obsolete. It directs the President to fill Vice Presidential vacancies. "The President shall nominate a Vice President who shall take office upon confirmation by a majority of both Houses of Congress."

Section Three was almost revolutionary. It allows a temporarily disabled President to pass his duties to his Vice President until he feels the disability no longer exists – at which time he could reclaim his duties.

Section Four is absolutely revolutionary and is the framework for this novel. It allows the Vice President to become the Acting President, even against the President's will. The Vice President becomes the Acting President when he and a majority of the Cabinet assert the President is incapable of discharging the duties of his office. If the President contests that assertion, he can resume his duties unless the Vice President and a majority of the Cabinet again assert his inability to perform his duties. If the latter assertion of inability is supported by a two/thirds vote of both Houses of Congress, the Vice President remains Acting President of the United States. If it is not, the President resumes the powers and duties of his office.

The Twenty-Fifth Amendment was not used in the Johnson administration, but it was in the next two Republican Administrations. On October 10, 1973, Spiro Theodore Agnew, Richard Nixon's Vice President, was forced to resign as part of a plea bargain that found him guilty of accepting bribes and income tax evasion.

Using the provisions of the Twenty-Fifth Amendment, President Nixon chose Gerald Ford to fill the vacancy. Both houses of Congress confirmed his appointment on December 6th of that year. Just nine months later, Nixon himself was forced to resign and again the provisions of the Twenty-Fifth Amendment governed. Gerald Ford became the first un-elected President of the United States. With Congress controlled by the Democrats, President Ford nominated Nelson Rockefeller as his Vice President. Rockefeller was a liberal Republican and acceptable to Democrats. He was confirmed by a majority of both Houses of Congress.

Sections Three and Four of the Amendment, dealing with disability, were not immediately used, but as early as the Reagan Administration they gave comfort to the nation and its leaders. When John Hinckley shot President Reagan in an attempt to win the love of Jodie Foster, the President underwent dangerous surgery. His doctors successfully removed a bullet lodged in his chest just inches from his heart. If that surgery had not gone well and President Reagan had required a long recuperative period, Vice President Bush could have been made the Acting President at Reagan's request. When Reagan returned to the White House, aides have written he suffered from posttraumatic shock depression. The depression lasted about a month and was debilitating. If it had persisted, President Reagan could have appointed Vice President Bush Acting President. If he refused that option and the Vice President and a majority of the Cabinet felt he was unable to discharge his duties, they could have begun the process of assuming those duties, even over the President's objections.

In hindsight, the nation also took comfort in the knowledge that should Reagan's Alzheimer's have struck earlier, during his Presidency, the nation would not have been hopelessly vulnerable. In the latter part of the nineteen nineties, American political leaders looked with dismay at the health problems of Boris Yeltsin and their impact on Russia. They smugly concluded that, at least now, with the Twenty-Fifth Amendment that could not happen here.

ACADEMIC INSIGHTS

As a result of its early history, the Twenty-Fifth Amendment received generally positive reviews. There were, of course, outstanding questions concerning Section Four, that addressed incompetence and the involuntary removal of the president, but they were of interest only to a handful of constitutional scholars. That interest peaked in 1996 at the Annual Meeting of the American Political Science Association. At the San Francisco Hilton, in a very small seminar room that was still too large for the attendees, Harry Shapiro (Indiana State University at Terre Haute) and Richard Thurman (University of Nebraska at Kearney) discussed Thurman's paper on "Probable Conflict Resolution Scenarios Matching an Overly Ambitious Vice President Versus an Incompetent, but Recalcitrant President."

After forty-five minutes, for want of interest, the two friends adjourned the seminar to the Hilton Lounge. There, after a couple of double Martinis, they were alone and their analysis was sharper if less scholarly and more repetitive.

"The streets of hell are paved with good intentions," Thurman muttered again, "Good intentions," he repeated. "Want another, Harry?"

"It'll be a God Damn Civil War," Shapiro announced again.

"Civil my ass," Thurman guffawed. "There won't be anything civil about that war, my friend. When the winner gets to divvy up a three trillion dollar pie there ain't gonna be nothing civil about it. Mud and blood, no holds barred."

"You are right, Richard. You are so right," Shapiro agreed. "Mud and blood, no holds barred."

"Did you say you wanted another?" Thurman asked. "It's my round."

"Sure," Shapiro answered. "Why not?"

"Did you hear that arrogant Anglophile, Wells?" Richard asked. "Now there's a scholar."

"The esteemed Doctor Anthony James Wells of Haaarvard University," Harry intoned. "I did indeed." Then leaning back, Harry assumed his best "William Buckley" Wells pose and mimicked the learned doctor: "I can understand your founders not recognizing the value of the Parliamentary system, but surely, gentlemen, after nearly 200 years your Congress could have rectified their error. They did, after all, with Kennedy have the perfect opportunity. Don't you think?"

"What a jerk," Thurman was contemptuous. "Like the Congress could rewrite the entire Constitution and have it ratified overnight. You know that bastard is a full bull drawing twice my salary and I teach two summer sessions."

"Rich, you know they did the only thing they could. The Congress I mean." Harry was deadly serious. "They made themselves the judge of any dispute between the President and the Vice President. What else could they do?"

"It'll be a god damn war." Thurman stated. "You think it will happen in our lifetime, Harry?"

"You can bet on it, Harry. You can bet on it."

Prologue End Notes

- On July 11, 1804, Aaron Burr, Vice President of the United States, shot and killed Alexander Hamilton. Burr was charged with murder. He fled south, all but officially vacating the office of Vice President until the charges were dropped. For several months President Jefferson had no Vice President.

- On April 20, 1812, in the latter days of James Madison's first term, his Vice President, George Clinton, died. Clinton, a seven term Governor of New York, had also served as Jefferson's Vice President. For the remainder of his first term, Madison had no Vice President.

- In Madison's second term his Vice President was Elbridge Gerry. But the man who made gerrymandering famous died November 23, 1814, leaving Madison again with no Vice President.

- President William Henry Harrison won the campaign of 1840 with the slogan, "Tippecanoe and Tyler, too." He was inaugurated on March 4th, 1841. It was a chilly day and Harrison caught a cold that turned into pneumonia. President Harrison died one month later. He was the first President to die in office. His Vice President, John Tyler, was awakened at his home in Williamsburg, Virginia at 5 A.M. on April 5, 1841, to learn he was President. For three years and eleven months of his four-year term, President Tyler had no Vice President.

- President Zachary Taylor, "Old Rough and Ready," died after less than a year and a half in office. On July 4th, 1850, Independence Day, he attended a celebration at the partially completed Washington Monument. It was terribly hot; he drank lots of water and was stricken with "cholera morbus." He died five days later on July 9th. Millard Fillmore succeeded him. President Fillmore had no Vice President.

- President Fillmore, a Whig, was not nominated by his Party in 1852, and a Democrat, Franklin Pierce, won the Presidency. Pierce's Vice President was too ill to come to the inauguration, but was sworn into office by a U.S. official in Havana, Cuba. A few weeks later, on April 18, 1853, he died at home in Alabama. For almost his entire Presidency, Pierce had no Vice President.

- On April 14, 1865, while attending a play at Ford's theater, Lincoln was shot. He died the next morning and was succeeded by Andrew Johnson. President Johnson escaped impeachment by one vote. He had no Vice President.

- James Abram Garfield was shot July 2, 1881, by a mentally ill office seeker, Charles J. Guiteau. At first, doctors thought the President would live. He was sent to the New Jersey seashore to recover but grew weaker. Chester Alan Arthur, Garfield's Vice President, was reluctant to assume the duties of the Presidency until Garfield died. He waited patiently for two and a half months. Garfield died September 19, 1881. Arthur had no Vice President.

- Grover Cleveland and his Vice President Thomas Hendricks won the election of 1884 and were sworn into office in March of 1885. Nine months later, on November 25, 1885, Hendricks died. Cleveland served the remainder of his term without a Vice President.

- In his first term, William McKinley's Vice President, Garret Hobart, died November 21, 1899. In his second term, President McKinley was shot by Leo Czolgosz in Buffalo, New York. He died eight days later on September 14, 1901. His Vice President, Theodore Roosevelt, succeeded him. Roosevelt had no Vice President for the remainder of that term.

- President William Howard Taft, a three-hundred-pound heart attack waiting to happen, lost his Vice President, James Sherman, October 30, 1912. For the remainder of his term he had no Vice President.

- On October 2, 1919, after suffering a physical collapse while campaigning for the Versailles Treaty and the League of Nations, President Woodrow Wilson suffered a severe stroke. He did not die. He remained President. He was incapacitated. His second wife of four years and his good friend, Colonel House, assumed most of his duties. Thomas Marshall, Wilson's Vice President, considered declaring the President incapable of discharging his duties, but felt he lacked constitutional authority for such a move that might well split the nation. The Versailles Treaty was defeated and the stage was set for World War Two. Thomas Marshall, a man of considerable ability, is now remembered only for suggesting that what the nation needed was a good five-cent cigar.

-       August 2, 1923, amidst growing rumors of corruption in his administration, President Warren Harding died. Calvin Coolidge, "Silent Cal", succeeded him. President Coolidge had no Vice President for the remainder of Harding's term.

-       At Warm Springs, Georgia on April 12, 1945, near the end of World War II, President Roosevelt, Commander-in-Chief of the United States Armed Forces, died from a cerebral hemorrhage forecasted by hypertension and arteriosclerosis. Harry S. Truman succeeded Roosevelt. President Truman had no Vice President for the remainder of Roosevelt's term.

-       President Dwight David Eisenhower suffered a coronary thrombosis in September 1955, and still chose to run for another term. In 1957, he suffered a mild stroke. Nixon stood in the wings.

-       President John Fitzgerald Kennedy was shot and killed November 22, 1963. Lyndon Baines Johnson succeeded him. President Johnson had no Vice President during the remainder of Kennedy's term. Hubert Horatio Humphrey served as Johnson's Vice President in his second term.

THE TWENTY-FIFTH AMENDMENT
OF THE UNITED STATES CONSTITUTION

Section One: In case of the removal of the President from office or his death or resignation, the Vice President shall become President.

Section Two: Whenever there is a vacancy in the office of the Vice President, the President shall nominate a Vice President who shall take the office upon confirmation by a majority vote of both houses of Congress
.

Section Three: Whenever the President transmits to the President Pro Tempore of the Senate and the Speaker of the House of Representative his written declaration that he is unable to discharge the powers and duties of his office, and until he transmits to them a written declaration to the contrary, such powers and duties shall be discharged by the Vice President as Acting President.

Section Four: Whenever the Vice President and a majority of either the principal officers of the executive departments or of such other body Congress may by law provide, transmit to the President Pro Tempore of the Senate and the Speaker of the House of Representative their written declaration that the President is unable to discharge the powers and duties of his office, the Vice President shall immediately assume the powers and duties of the office as Acting President.

      Thereafter, when the President transmits to the President Pro Tempore of the Senate and the Speaker of the House of Representatives his written declaration that no inability exists, he shall resume the powers and duties of his office unless the Vice President and a majority of either the principal officers of the executive department or of such other body as Congress may by law provide, transmit within four days to the President Pro Tempore of the Senate and the

Speaker of the House of Representatives their written declaration that the President is unable to discharge the powers and duties of his office. Thereupon Congress shall decide the issue, assembling within 48 hours for that purpose if not in session. If the Congress, within 21 days after receipt of the latter written declaration, or, if Congress is not in session, within 21 days after Congress is required to assemble, determines by two-thirds vote of both Houses that the President is unable to discharge the powers and duties of his office, the Vice President shall continue to discharge the same as Acting President: otherwise, the President shall resume the powers and duties of his office.

CHAPTER ONE:

ANDREW HOLMES STANTON

2:00 A.M., Monday, New Year's Day.

"It just breaks my heart. I love him so much. I honestly do, but he's not the same. I don't think he ever will be." Howard could hardly hear her, but he knew what she was saying. Virginia sat on the couch in his office, her face pressed into the Kleenex she held in her right hand. Crayton Langford, chief of staff, held her left hand. He said nothing.

Howard Lipsack, Langford's deputy chief, had never seen Virginia cry or exhibit emotion of any kind. Even her laugh was a just a single syllable issuance that let you know it was time to return to the topic at hand.

Virginia Hastings, special counsel, was brilliant, decisive, and tactless. She was also attractive in a disciplined manner. She was not married, never had been, but she was in love. So were Howard and Crayton. They all loved a dear old man, Andrew "Andy" Holmes Stanton, the President of the United States.

Andrew Holmes Stanton was seventy-eight years old. He had survived his sixth year in office. Danielle "Danny" Rebeau Stanton, his beloved wife, had not. She had died in August. They had been married for thirty-nine years. She was the only woman he had ever loved. She died of cancer. Commentators said it was expected and that that should make things easier for the President. They were fools. Her growing dependence mirrored his own and wore him down until he realized he didn't want to live without her.

Danny's death followed by only four months the death of the President's best friend, Matthew Lee Thorn. Matt was Stanton's vice president and, other than Danny, his closest confidant. It had been a devastating year, but it was over. To observe its passing and welcome in the New Year, The White House had hosted a small New Year's Eve party of Washington notables. The new year had to be better.

Virginia was still crying softly when Lincoln Smith, press secretary, joined the post mortem "party." Howard gave her another Kleenex and she wiped her eyes before looking at Lincoln.

"You saw it, too," he said.

"Yes," she nodded.

"Saw it, heard it, felt it," Howard said.

"Do you think we were the only ones?" Lincoln asked.

"Hell, no, the whole world was there. Did you see Secretary Ramirez trying to comfort Gretchen?" Howard asked. "They both ended up crying. Stanton kept calling her Danny."

Lincoln was despondent. As cautious and diplomatic as the press secretary was in public, he was outspoken, insensitive, and blunt in private. "Is he just old or crazy, or old and crazy?"

"For Christ's sake, Lincoln! You piss me off." Crayton was on his feet and in Lincoln's face. "Crazy? His wife died. His best friend died. He's alone with the toughest job in the world. He hasn't had time to grieve. The day after Matt died, the press was hounding him for a replacement, and those bastards in the House and Senate were floating trial balloons, telling him whom they'd accept and whom they'd reject. Before he could bury his wife he had to referee the debate over vetoing health care. Cut him some slack, God Dammit."

"I'm sorry. I am sorry, you know that, but I'm not the enemy here. I love him as much as you guys. I can cut him some slack, but will the Republicans? Will the Chancellor of Germany? The Prime Minister of Israel? The Army of God? The word's out. He's old and he's slipping. They are going to test him, and if he can't cut mustard they'll eat him alive. You know I'm right." Lincoln softened. "He needs help. He needs our help."

Upstairs, President Andrew Stanton sat on his bed reflecting on the night. He slowly untied, then loosened his right shoe. Tonight was the first night he had felt halfway decent since Danny died. Four months... maybe time, he thought. It was good to have the girls home. Thank God he didn't have to spend Christmas alone with all these people. He had danced with each of his daughters and knew they enjoyed it. So had he. They moved like their mother, and he could see her in their smiles and hear her in their laughter. For the first time without remorse he could remember how good their lives had been. He and Danny had two wonderful daughters and so many good years. Gretchen, the oldest, favored her mother while Nicole was obviously his girl. They'd be leaving in the morning. He tried not to think about it.

He wondered whether he had had too much to drink or the drink was interacting with the pills. He doubted it, but he had to be careful. Back from the Vietnam, as a freshman congressman, second youngest ever and Washington's most eligible bachelor, he drank too much. It affected his performance. He could have done better. Now, over a half-century later, he still felt the need to be cautious. It had been a slip when he called Gretchen "Danny," but a natural one. When he and Danny and the girls were all together in California, he always confused the girls; calling Nikki, Gretchen; and Gretch, Nikki. Maybe Danny wasn't involved; he couldn't remember, but always the girls. It was a family joke. He was like his dad. Harold Stanton never could keep Andy and his brothers straight. It was a natural mistake.

"Do you think he had too much to drink?" Howard asked.

"I don't know, I don't think so, but with his pills, who knows. I actually thought he was doing better," Virginia answered. "Dancing tonight, he had his old grace and energy. He looked taller. The whole scene reminded me of his first inaugural ball in California. He and Danny were beautiful," she paused, and then darkened. "I can understand a slip, but he introduced her as Danny. You should have seen their faces, particularly after he turned his back. Only Elizabeth Anne took it in stride. Hell, she even refreshed his drink. "

"We'd be lucky if they just thought he was drunk." The Chief sat forward on the couch. "But this isn't doing us any good. It's 2 A.M. Let's call it a night. Tomorrow we'll have him call everyone who might have been a witness. Make sure his calls are all business. He can thank them for being here tonight and then

ask them to give him an honest hearing on the Omnibus Crime
Bill, or whatever. Maybe it'll work. Let them think he just had a
bad night. Show them he's back at work, still in charge, doing the
nation's business. Time will help. It always does."

President Stanton decided he was getting better. It had
been rough, first Matt, his lifelong friend, and then Danny, the only
woman he had ever loved. He had never known such pain, such
despair. Four months had passed since Danny's death. He had
screwed up the Security Council, Cabinet meetings, Council of
Economic Advisers. How many times, he wondered. Just the fact
that he now cared said he was getting better. He was sure of it. He
had to. The country couldn't wait any longer.

Dreading the night, President Stanton readied himself for
bed. He followed his same routine, forgetting nothing, hoping tonight he might sleep. Undressed, he looked at himself in the mirror. He was old. Where he used to see himself, he now saw his
dad as he looked after he had retired. Would he ever recover? He
brushed his teeth, returning his toothbrush to the cabinet below all
the pills. "Not tonight," he muttered. "Not tonight."

He turned out the bathroom light and knew there was only
one more. He got slowly into bed. It was too big. He thought
about reading, but knew he was only postponing the inevitable. He
rolled over and turned out the last light. His mind stopped register-
ing sights and sounds. Under cover of darkness, the demons were
released. One after another they came, then together: what he had
said, the way they looked, the demands, his exhaustion, tomorrow,
the decisions, the meetings, the cameras. It was no use. The night
was slipping away. He had to sleep. Like every other night, he got
up, went to the bathroom and opened the medicine cabinet. He
took the sleeping pill with warm water, hoping it would act faster.
He prayed the pill would shut down his mind. He arranged the pil-
lows again so he could still hold her. They had slept like spoons
sharing a pillow between their legs. He missed her hand in his, the
soothing rhythm of her breathing, and the warmth that radiated
from her body. He wanted so badly to hear her..."Relax Andy, let
it go..."

"Oh Danny, Danny," he cried softly. "I can't do this, Danny."

CHAPTER TWO:

THE PARTNERS

1:30 A.M., New Year's Day

"He's getting worse," Elizabeth Anne announced. The Roosevelts had just returned from the White House. It was one-thirty A.M., but Elizabeth Anne Roosevelt wasn't ready for bed. Her heels hammered out a staccato beat as she paced the parquet floor of their master bedroom. She had things to say. Her husband, the Vice President of the United States, lay dressed on their bed in his stocking feet. His hands were locked behind his head.

"Who's that?" he asked innocently.

"Don't screw around with me, Bill. You know who! Dammit, why do you do that? The President of the United States, Andrew Holmes Stanton, that's who. He's lost his mind. Why do you bait me? You know it infuriates me."

"I'm sorry," he said. William Butler "Bill" Roosevelt, Vice President of the United States, was rarely as intense as his wife. Tonight was no exception. "I don't know whether he's worse or not. Maybe he just had a bad night. I suspect tomorrow morning he'll wish he had gone up to bed about an hour before he did." Roosevelt paused. "You know, I think he does fine with issues and decisions. It's the lapses, when he's in another world that makes you think he's worse. Tonight, with Gretchen, I don't know where he was, but I guess he was with Danny."

"It's been four months. I tell you, he's no better," she continued. "If anything, he's worse, but I'll tell you one thing, and Daddy agrees with me; as time goes by, people are going to be less and less forgiving. Either he gets better or he's out and if he's out you're in."

"Out? What are you talking about, Elizabeth? He's the President of the United States, a darn good one. He's more popular now than at anytime during his presidency. Your father is a hell of a businessman, but I wouldn't say he's exactly got the pulse of the public. You know, President Stanton and I disagree on just about everything, but that doesn't stop me from seeing that the American people love him. I had my chance in September when he asked what I would think about serving as Acting President. You told me then the public wasn't ready. Well, I'm telling you now, the public is still not ready."

"They may love him now, but just wait. The word is going to get out. This is Washington. Nobody could criticize him right after Danny died, but I'm telling you, he can't hide behind her shroud forever."

"I swear, Elizabeth, you are a work of art."

"You know I'm right," she insisted, moving to the foyer. She picked up the phone and hit speed dial number one for her father, the "Commander." No one answered. She left a quick message and returned to their bedroom.

"Don't you think you're being just a little bit hard on him?" Roosevelt answered. "I suppose his support might erode, but the people are going to stand by him until they see it for themselves."

"They'll see it," she said. "They'll see it soon enough."

Vice President Roosevelt and his wife Elizabeth Anne made quite a team. Both were forty-six; tall, athletic, and telegenic. He was ambitious but patient, while she was driven. He was intelligent and principled. She was brilliant, pragmatic, and as James Croft's sole heir she had means. Roosevelt's assets were less tangible. He was heir to the Democratic Party's most venerated political dynasty yet he was openly conservative. In college, he had considered switching parties, but politics was in his blood and he knew the name "Roosevelt" had magic. It was money in the bank. It was still twenty points in any Democratic primary in any district, in any state in the country. Conversely, it was still poison in the Republican Party.

With the new year the Roosevelts would be married sixteen years. There had been ups and downs, but by and large, it was a good union.

Roosevelt was a Congressman from the Seventh District of New York when he met Elizabeth Anne Croft. They met in Telluride, Colorado, on a skiing weekend. She was staying at the family compound while he was staying with friends. Elizabeth was a striking woman, above average in height, well proportioned, and obviously athletic. On the slopes, at a distance, she was beautiful. Up close, she was attractive, but in a business-like manner. She moved with more purpose than poise. She had flashes of beauty, but only when she was caught off guard and that was rare. Normally she was hard and calculating. She was only thirty then, but already juggling a half dozen companies and contracts in her father's empire. After her brother died, she was his heir apparent.

James Croft Jr. died with two companions, piloting the company's Lear Jet, on the way home from a hunting trip. FAA investigators were unable to determine, with certainty, the cause of the crash, but felt drugs might have been a contributing factor. (In college, James Jr. had been arrested on two different occasions for supplying recreational drugs to his fraternity brothers. With Croft's resources he was never convicted, but even Croft's resources failed to identify his supplier.) The FAA report postulated pilot error as the most likely cause, particularly in light of the ideal flying conditions and the lack of any discernible equipment failure. While there was no mention of drugs, James "Commander" Croft was in a rage. He ordered his own investigators to bring him the unvarnished truth, no matter the costs.

Six weeks later he had their report. He shared it with no one and never spoke of his son's death again. Rather, he turned to his daughter with new respect; asked her to quit medical school and began grooming her to take over his empire. After all, she was now the only surviving child of James and Anne Croft.

James Croft had made money any way money could be made. He made lots of it. In his early years, he was involved in pyramid schemes of every stripe in every part of the country. In each, he managed to exit just before the bubble would burst and the authorities would shut it down. In the sixties, his wealth was already a matter of public speculation. He didn't rest. With leveraged buying, he moved in and out of dozens of traditional industries – buying, dividing, holding, and selling. He didn't miss a step. Invariably, his intelligence operatives out-performed his competitors'. With insiders and informers, the Commander knew his opponents' strategies even as they were being formulated. Snitches, turncoats, informers, insiders, and operatives, Croft paid

them all well, and gave them a free hand. He had complete deniability, but total information. There were lawsuits, of course, but
his legal team played hardball better than anyone. If they ever lost,
the records were sealed and no one the wiser. By the mid-
seventies, James Croft was regularly listed by Forbes as among the
wealthiest men in America.

In the last three decades, he had concentrated on government contracts. As always he was not a gambler, not a big risk
taker. Croft sustained a competitive advantage that was the subject
of hushed rumors and wild speculation. The Commander dominat-
ed his own cabal of moneyed men, directing their "bundled contri-
butions" for best returns. He maintained a low profile, but was extremely well connected in both parties. His connections were not
only with policy makers in the Congress, but decision makers in
the bureaucracy. In back rooms, his generosity was legendary and
handsomely rewarded. When government contracting officers resigned or retired, they found a home in Croft's far flung empire.
His lobbyists were a Who's Who of former senators, representatives and White House insiders. He always knew a little more than
his competition about the big picture, how weapon systems were to
interact, time frames that were desired if not required, and funding
decisions that had yet to be formally announced. When his companies won contracts, which they regularly did, there were lawsuits, but nothing was ever proven. On those occasions when he
lost a bid, his friends on Capitol Hill would convene Congressional
hearings to examine an obviously flawed process.

Elizabeth Anne Croft married William Butler Roosevelt
just four months after they had met. The Commander considered
Roosevelt his finest acquisition. When asked where they were going for their honeymoon, Roosevelt announced he and Elizabeth
Anne were going to the Senate if the good people of New York
would have them. It was a marriage of convenience, fame and fortune, yet it worked. It worked for both of them.

With Croft's money, William Roosevelt became an irresistible force in New York politics. Even though he was "inexperi-
enced" and had never run for a statewide office, Roosevelt won his
seat in the Senate. The race was close, but never in doubt. Roosevelt and his new bride moved to Washington. Their new home
was Morgan House on Embassy Row. Croft owned Morgan

House. He had used it to wine and dine his Washington "friends."
Now while Roosevelt immersed himself in his senatorial duties
and cultivating his colleagues, Elizabeth Anne continued the Croft
tradition, wining and dining Washington's power elite. She became a much-respected member of that very exclusive club.

For six years they devoted all of their energy and intellect
to cultivating Washington. They were distracted only slightly in
Roosevelt's second term when "Little Jimmy" was born. James
Croft marked his christening by giving Morgan House to Elizabeth
Anne.

James "Jimmy" Butler Roosevelt was an only child. Bill
thought he needed a brother, or a sister, but Elizabeth Anne said,
"No." She was adamant. Jimmy was a perfect child. Having another baby only risked failure. Parents of two children were only
part-time parents for at least one child. Inevitably, two children
meant sibling rivalry. It could be horribly destructive. They
would quit while they were ahead. He didn't argue the point; it
was her call.

Roosevelt won his second Senate term in a landslide so
great that when he declared for a third term he had only token opposition. While he was obviously popular among New York
Democrats, on the national level he was suspect. To national
Democrats, his victories, like his life, had been too easy. They
found the Croft connection corrupting. Whether they described
him as driven by the polls or by principles, he was too conservative
for many of them. The fact that Republicans regularly described
Roosevelt as "moderate and reasonable" also hurt his standing
among Democrats. He was an experienced yet untested politician.
It was said he had convictions, but not compassion. Roosevelt had
no gut reactions –only, well-constructed position papers.

The beginning of Roosevelt's third term in the Senate coin-
cided with President Stanton's second term in the White House.
Stanton had not wanted to seek a second term, but was convinced
to do so by Danny and the leadership of the Democratic Party. Only he, they argued, could keep the White House and give the Democrats a chance at recapturing the House and retaining the Senate.

Andrew Holmes Stanton and Matthew Lee Thorn won a second term in the White House, but they had had no coattails. The

Republicans not only retained the House, they won the Senate. Commentators quickly predicted gridlock.

Before the election, when the Democrats controlled the Senate, Roosevelt had been Chairman of the Government Operations Committee. After the election he was just its ranking minority member. For Elizabeth Anne and William Roosevelt, this was a down time. Their marriage suffered. Jimmy spent more and more time with his grandfather. The future looked depressingly like the past except that Bill's power and influence were greatly diminished. They debated a run for the Presidency, but given his standing among Democrats, it seemed more like a waste of time and money than a long shot. His career seemed to have run its course. It would end, they feared, as his predecessors had, in a hotel ballroom decorated in red, white, and blue. Roosevelt would stand before a crowd of disillusioned supporters and supporters in denial. Over their vociferous objections he would concede defeat. His concession speech would break no new ground. It would be trite and humiliating. He would thank his supporters, compliment his opponent, and then note with forced conviction that while he had lost, the principles for which they had fought had won.

CHAPTER THREE:

A TRAGIC YEAR

Fourteen months into his second term, President Stanton and his best friend, Vice President Matthew Lee Thorn, were playing tennis. Stanton had lost the first set, and insisted on an immediate rematch. It was a glorious afternoon. They were tired, but having great fun. Their game, normally respectable, was becoming slapstick. Their wives watched, giggled, and heckled their two old men mercilessly. When Andrew fanned a lob, but ran around and got it on the bounce with a dink shot that barely made it across the net, they were howling. Matt's heroic efforts to get to the ball ended when he stumbled, did a graceful roll, and lay spread eagle on the court. The girls were hysterical. "Game, Set, Match," Andrew shouted, arms and racket extended, on his way to "leap" the net. Matt didn't get up. He never got up. He called for Jean, and then with his head cradled in their arms, his eyes fixed first on Andy and then on Jean he said only, "Andy, you take care of my Jean," and then weaker, "Don't worry, Jean, it's easy for me."

"Matt, Matt, Oh, my Matt. Please don't do this," she begged. Death had never been so personal.

President Stanton was devastated. Matt was his best friend and other than Danny his only true confidant. They had known each other for sixty-five years, since boyhood days in Oak Ridge, Tennessee. As kids they lived the lives of Tom Sawyer and Huckleberry Finn. They were neighbors. Stanton was older, but only by a couple of years. After high school they went their separate ways but both served in Vietnam. Thorn got there first as a grunt. Stanton came later as a Second Lieutenant. Their whole lives were intertwined. After Vietnam, when Stanton represented the Fifth District in the U. S. House, Jean ran his Nashville Office. Matt was a political reporter for the Nashville Tennessean. Stanton was best man at Jean and Matt's wedding. Danny was the last to join the foursome, and that was over thirty-nine years ago. They had rich lives and took pride in each other.

The Vice President lay in state for two days. At his funeral, the President, Jean, and Danny sat before the congregation. A small lectern was to their left. There were many eulogies. The networks covered it all with respect and very limited, whispered commentary. The First Lady and President Stanton spoke last. Danny, whose breast cancer was no longer in remission, had thought long and hard about death. She spoke simply and directly.

"Our Matt," she began and then looking softly at Jean, "your 'Thorny', lived a wonderful life. His was as rich and as full as life can be. Our lives, not only his, but yours and mine as well, are all too short. Matt knew that. He wrote each chapter, each day, of his life from the first, now to the last, so well that we need to overlook nothing to know this was a good, good man. Throughout his life Matt had the unconditional love of many of us, but it was to Jean he gave his unconditional love. She was the cornerstone of his strength. Now that he is gone, who will be there for her? And who will help us? His memory helps shows us the way, but his memory may not be enough. It's not enough for me. It's not enough for Andy. It may not be enough for you, Jean. We need each other. We need you, Jean. We have chapters yet to write in our own lives. They will either add to or detract from what we have already written. I pledge to you, I am here for you now, for as long as I have breath in my body. Please, Jean, be here for me, and especially for my Andy."

Danny moved from the front of the congregation back to her chair next to Jean. She took Jean's hand from Andy's as he stood and moved to the lectern.

Commentators whispered that President Stanton was crushed by the death of Matthew Thorn. But as he had throughout his life, Stanton composed himself and did what had to be done. In a sure voice, President Stanton remembered his friend. He spoke of boyhood pacts and Congressional oaths, of "blood brothers" and returning veterans, of newlyweds and old couples, and public triumphs and private tragedies. He remembered elections won and elections lost. He told of their service in Congress, and how that service ended with their decisions to champion civil rights and oppose the war. He talked of their years in the private sector and then of their return to national prominence. He recalled and praised again Matthew's greatest public triumphs: The Market of the Americas, and The Status of Jerusalem.

Mainly, President Stanton spoke simply of their friendship; how it included their wives and children, and how it had grown from shared experiences to trust, respect, admiration, and pride. He illustrated Matthew's character and strength when he buried his only child, Steven, Stanton's godchild. He told the congregation how he and Danny had called upon that strength as they struggled to deal with Danny's cancer.

Toward the end, he shared with the congregation his dependence on his friend, the Vice President. He confessed he would be lost without him. President Stanton concluded by telling his dead friend, "I miss you, Matt. No one will ever replace you in my heart," then he added, "nor, I fear, in the counsels of this nation." To the congregation and the nation he said, "Matthew Thorn leaves a legacy of good friends, good works, good counsel, and good will. We must all... working together... fill the vacuum his death has created. God help us... God help us all."

With the eulogies over, network anchors turned to their White House and Congressional commentators for speculation concerning Vice President Matthew Thorn's replacement. With a Democratic President and a Republican Congress, the question was complex. Whoever the President nominated would have to be acceptable to the Congress. The nomination was further complicated by the fact that Stanton was in his second term and could not succeed himself. The next Vice President would surely be a leading candidate for the Democratic presidential nomination. In effect, they speculated, the Republican Congress might well be choosing the Democratic nominee for president. They concluded the situation was ripe for mischief.

The commentators agreed the President's first choice would be another good friend, Robert Evans, the two-term Governor of New York. They also agreed that Evans would never win Congressional confirmation. Though time would be required to produce a compromise candidate, strangely, one name was already being floated. That name, they reported, was William Butler Roosevelt, the Democratic Senator from New York.

Three weeks after Matthew Thorn's death, the nation had a new vice president. He was not President Stanton's first choice, but he was an acceptable choice, not only for the President, but also for the Republican Congress. Stanton found Roosevelt bright, energetic, and principled. Stanton hoped he was capable of growth and compassion. Commentators found Stanton's choice analogous to President Ford's choice of Nelson Rockefeller. Rockefeller had been acceptable to a Democratic Congress because Rockefeller was a liberal Republican. Roosevelt was acceptable to a Republican Congress because he was conservative Democrat.

Republicans were delighted. The Democratic nomination for president, which would have gone to Matthew Thorn without a fight, would now be wide open. They knew Roosevelt was ambitious and, as Vice President, would be emboldened to seek the presidency. They also knew he would be opposed. Just as the conservative right dominates Republican primaries, liberal activists dominate Democratic primaries. The conservative Roosevelt would not win his party's nomination without a fight. The Democrats were in for a bloody, divisive donnybrook. Since elections are won by whichever party can race back from the extreme and capture the middle, for the first time in sixteen years, the Republicans had a good shot at the White House.

Roosevelt had served as Vice President for a half year when Danielle Stanton, the President's wife, died. For the second time in a year, the President was lost. Roosevelt tried to be supportive, but the President could not be consoled. At one point, the President considered asking his Vice President to serve as Acting President, in accordance with the provisions of Section Three of the Twenty-Fifth Amendment. He needed time to compose himself. Roosevelt suggested they move cautiously. By the next day, for various reasons, both thought it not a good idea. The President was aware that he and Roosevelt had significant policy disagreements. And he knew that he could not stand by, should Roosevelt, as Acting President, make decisions or choose directions with which he disagreed. For his part, Roosevelt spoke of the dangerous precedent they would be establishing if he, an unelected vice president replaced a much loved elected president. The decision would not have public support and would weaken the nation. Roosevelt also suggested that a formal invocation of the Twenty-Fifth Amendment was completely unnecessary; both he and Elizabeth Anne were ready to assist the President any way they could.

The President was impressed. With agreement, their conversation turned light and they revisited the issue. The President speculated the presidency might become a part-time job. Unscrupulous presidents might shirk their duties and pass hard decisions to their vice presidents, or turn over their duties whenever they "wanted a little time off." In the same vein, the Vice President suggested some future president might abuse the appointment to enhance the prospects that his vice president would succeed him. Their conversation lasted almost an hour. It had been frank and friendly.

By New Year's Eve, four months had passed. The President had had good days and bad. Early, his staff had given him the benefit of the doubt; feeling sure, in time, he would be better. Now their doubts were doubled. Each day they assessed whether he was any better or had taken a turn for the worse. On his good days, they thought he was just about "his same old self." On bad days alarmists worried – not too privately – that he was clinically depressed. New Year's Eve was a bad day.

Elizabeth Anne was right; the word would get out. One way or another, the word would get out. She would do what she had to do. President Stanton didn't have much more time.

CHAPTER FOUR:

DAMAGE CONTROL

9 A.M., Monday, January 1st.

"Happy New Year, sir." Crayton Langford, President Stanton's chief of staff, shuffled the papers he was carrying, and took a seat opposite the President.

"Thank you, Crayton. I believe it will be. I honestly do." The President, who had just said "Good-bye" to his daughters, was remarkably upbeat.

"Mr. President," Crayton began hesitantly. "Mr. President..."

"Yes, Crayton. What is it?"

"I'm afraid, sir, we need a little damage control. You need to make a few calls." Crayton bit the bullet and told the President about his "slips" the night before.

With a sigh the President responded, "So you think I should make some calls? How many, to whom and on what pretext?"

"Not many, sir. I think you could share your New Year's resolution with them. You know, not to let another session of Congress pass without the enactment of the Omnibus Crime Bill. We get two birds with one stone. They see you in charge, and you let them know your number one priority for the upcoming year."

"Crayton, I know you and the staff have been worried. I've given you reason to be." The President spoke slowly. "Scenes like last night must be upsetting, but I want you, all of you, to know I'm getting better. I know I am. It's so clear. For the first time last week, with the girls here, my memories of Danny brought me joy, not pain. Let me tell you that's a big, very big change."

Tears welled in the President's eyes. He wiped them away. "I'm still a bit of an emotional basket case, but give me a little time. I can still do this job."

"Yes, sir," Crayton mumbled. He could have handled this conversation easily with anyone else, but not the President of the United States.

"Let me have the list," the President directed. Crayton took it from the top of his stack of papers. It had been his first priority.

"The Speaker and Chairman Wills? You do earn your keep, don't you, Crayton?" The President punched his phone: "Millie, get me the Speaker, please."

After the calls, for the remainder of the day, President Stanton, his chief of staff, and the director of the Office of Management and Budget began reviewing "final" budget proposals with the Cabinet Secretaries. The budget would form the financial basis for the State of the Union the President would deliver to the Congress, January nineteenth. It was a productive and reassuring day. The New Year was off to a good start.

Ronald Hodges had been with William and Elizabeth Anne, since they first moved to Washington fourteen years ago. Hodges was employed at Morgan House when Croft suggested it be the Roosevelt's home. The Commander had only one "condition." He suggested they give Hodges a try, noting that he had been a long-time loyal and discreet employee. When Roosevelt was appointed Vice President and the family moved from Morgan House to the Vice Presidential residence at the Naval Observatory, Hodges moved with them. When asked, he liked to say he was just a family keepsake, but he was much more than that.

For Hodges, New Year's Day was just another workday. If the Roosevelts were in, he was on duty. This morning, he knew they would have visitors. He found the Vice President and Mrs. Roosevelt in the kitchen having coffee and scanning the Post. They found no mention of President Stanton's problems.

Hodges waited for them to look up. "Mr. Vice President, I guess we're both going to be working today, sir. Secretary Reynolds and Secretary Kelly are here to speak with you."

"Now, Ron?" Roosevelt was incredulous. "Good God, the Rose Parade hasn't even begun."

"Yes sir. I'm afraid so. I asked them to wait in the library."

"Thank you, Ron. Tell them I'll be along shortly. "

"Ron, tell them we'll be joining them," Elizabeth Anne directed. Then turning to Roosevelt she added, "You don't mind, do you, dear? Paul and Robert are old friends. They know we have no secrets."

Paul Reynolds, Secretary of Commerce, was one of four Republicans in the administration. President Stanton appointed him in his first term to demonstrate his commitment to bipartisanship and to curry favor with the business community. Reynolds was an insider in both Washington and Wall Street, but mainly he was a survivor. His varied career showcased a talent for prophetic moves. Paul Reynolds was an old hand at changing horses in midstream. Today he paced about the library in the Vice President's residence trying to stay focused.

With Reynolds was Robert Kelly, Secretary of Transportation. Kelly, the former CEO of Kondraki Construction, was driven. He was a gambler. He had reacted to childhood poverty and abandonment with ambition and guts. Robert Kelly played by his own rules. He made quick decisions and never looked back.

Early in the administration he had been considered a comer, but now his career was on hold as the Justice Department considered allegations that during Kelly's tenure as CEO his giant construction company had engaged in subcontractor fraud and labor union kickbacks. Critics called for an independent counsel especially in light of Kelly's prior, though apparently limited, connections to Croft Industries. Though the connection with the Vice President's father-in-law flamed interest, the "scandal" was still a tempest in a teapot. Secretary Kelly denied any wrongdoing and claimed the charges were politically motivated. President Stanton stood foursquare behind Secretary Kelly, insisting his administration was committed to the highest ethical standards and would take all appropriate action dictated by the facts.

Both Reynolds and Kelly moved toward the Vice President and Mrs. Roosevelt as they entered the library. "Gentlemen," the Vice President shook each man's hand. "You're getting the new year off to a fast start. Maybe you should slow down. Ron, bring us some coffee, please."

"Mr. Vice President, Mrs. Roosevelt," Kelly was trying to be restrained, but it wasn't in his nature. "You were at the White House last night. You saw the President. We all did. That makes us responsible. We have a duty. We can't let this continue. America is cruising toward a catastrophe. I can't help but think we must..."

"He's right sir, ma'am," Reynolds interrupted. "With President Stanton at the helm we're on the Titanic. It's only a matter of time before he ...before we ...the country, pays a terrible price. He has two more years. Unless we act, the United States will be in mortal danger that entire time. Maybe we'd be lucky. But for two years?"

Two years and nineteen days to be precise," Kelly stated. "We've got to act. The Constitution requires it. If the President can't discharge his duties 'the same shall devolve on the Vice President.'"

"Gentlemen, please have a seat." Vice President Roosevelt organized his thoughts. "I want you to understand my position. It is my sincere hope that you are both alarmist, but I have indeed seen what you have seen, and it is frightening. A bad night, even a week, a slip here or there can and should be overlooked. But you're right. What we are seeing is a pattern, a pattern of deterioration that is not likely to be reversed. The President is old; he's going to get older. He has suffered great losses and time has not eased that pain. The President appears, at best, to be coping, but only with a greater and greater reliance on drugs. I fear he may, in fact, have developed some serious chemical dependencies. The Constitution has a solution, but you must understand it is just politically impossible at this time."

"No, no," Kelly interrupted. "We must seize..."

"Wait Robert, please. Hear me out," the Vice President insisted. "The Constitution has a solution. You and I and six additional Cabinet Secretaries must declare the President incapable of discharging the powers and duties of his office. I think finding like-minded Cabinet Secretaries is very possible, but I do not think the American people would accept a declaration of incompetence at this time. The Constitution gives the government many many powers, but it can exercise those powers only when it has the support of the American people."

"Are you saying we can do nothing?" Reynolds asked with a hint of exasperation, looking toward Elizabeth Anne for support.

"No, of course not," Roosevelt answered. "All I'm saying is elections are the cornerstones of democracy. We will be overturning an election, removing their president. The people must be with us. They must see the need for themselves and know our motives are pure."

"What can we do then?" Kelly's exasperation was obvious.

"We must be ready to move the instant the American people are ready to accept the legitimacy of that move," the Vice President answered.

"What Bill is saying is we must begin right now," Elizabeth Anne was emphatic, prepared, and on a roll. "Not tomorrow, now! We must find six other Cabinet members who will stand with us when the time is right. Our efforts must be quiet, discreet. The President, and particularly his White House staff, must not be alerted. We must pick the most likely prospects, know their concerns and choose intermediaries who will maximize our chances of success. Jason Fields is going to be our point man on this." Then, looking directly at her husband she added, "There will be no additional contacts with the Vice President. He must maintain deniability."

"I suppose I agree with that," Vice President Roosevelt acknowledged. "I hadn't given it much thought." Then in a decisive tone he continued. "What I do know is, even though we must begin now, you must understand we are creating only a contingency plan. It will be activated only if and when the American people are ready and I will be the judge of that. Is that understood? Secretary Reynolds? Secretary Kelly?"

"Yes sir," Both men answered without hesitation.

"I also want it understood," Elizabeth Anne glanced at her husband and then continued. "You will make no contacts with anyone concerning this without specific prior approval of Jason or me. You will make no notes, no diaries, no journals, no recordings, and no memoranda of understanding. Nothing will be e-mailed. Nothing will be written on a computer or note pad. No messages will be left. There will be no record of any kind. Absolutely none! I hope you've got the idea. Any authorized contacts will be in secure rooms with no witnesses. This isn't paranoia, its prudence. Things could get very ugly."

"Gentlemen, it's trite, but true, the power of the presidency is awesome," Vice President Roosevelt spoke with obvious conviction. "President Stanton may be crippled, but his staff, his very competent tough staff, will be fighting for their lives. Under the cover of "National Security" they will have every tool of war at their disposal. And make no mistake - this could be war, and we'll lose it if we fail to maintain the element of surprise. We have only two advantages: The President's debilitating condition, and surprise. Only if we confront the President with a *fait accompli* can we expect success."

Elizabeth Anne moved to the Vice President's desk and picked up the phone. "Jason, would you come to the library, please?"

Jason Fields, the Vice President's chief of staff, managed Roosevelt's first Senate race and had been a close confidant ever since. As a strategist, only Crayton Langford was in his league. In conservative circles, the former Republican had no peers. He played hardball and he was their best. When he joined the Vice President's team, he joined as captain, chief of staff. Jason Fields knew the Republican Congress; he knew its leaders and followers, the saints and sinners, their states and districts, their friends and their foes. He knew their strengths and weaknesses, their dreams and nightmares. If they had skeletons, he knew where they were hidden. Most important, Fields knew how to use every bit of knowledge he possessed. Insiders joked a DNA test would prove LBJ was his father. Roosevelt's campaign to save the nation was in good hands.

CHAPTER FIVE:

GROWING STORM

1:30 P.M., Tuesday, January 2.

Containment of the President's problems ended the next afternoon. Arnold Bradley, chief of the Washington Bureau of The New York Times, called for Lincoln Smith, the President's press secretary. He wanted to give him the opportunity to comment on an article The Times would be running in the morning edition. Lincoln took the call.

"I'm sorry, Link," Bradley began. "You know I have great sympathy for the President. I lost Beth over a year ago and I still have trouble...but then I'm not the President."

"You've got a story, Brad?" Lincoln's mind raced through all the headlines and stories he had imagined concerning the President's behavior since Danny's death. He held his breath.

"It's just this. We have unnamed sources who say that in the weeks following the First Lady's death, the President had to be regularly sedated," the reporter stopped there, and waited on Smith.

"That's it?" Smith asked dismissively, hoping his need for time was not transparent.

"No, it's not," Bradley could smell evasiveness. "We will be reporting the President was using Valium, for depression, anxiety, and sleeplessness."

"Look, Brad, I'm not in a position to comment on any medication the President might be taking. I can confirm that the President found it difficult to sleep after Danny's death, but I don't think that's much of a story. You know how devoted they were."

"Lincoln, my sources are good. The President was taking ten milligrams of Valium, three times a day. That's an unusually heavy dosage, twice the recommended level." Again, Arnold Bradley waited. Over the years he had dealt with a dozen press secretaries. Lincoln Smith was among the most forthcoming, but thus far his call had only elicited that the President had loved his wife and had taken her death badly. This was confirmation, of a sort.

"I told you, Brad, I don't know of any medication the President may, or may not, have taken." Lincoln paused not so much for effect as to assess risks. He rolled the dice. "If I knew, my position would be 'it's covered by the doctor/patient privilege.'"

"For Christ's sake, Lincoln, we're not in court. Stanton isn't the accused, but he is the President. Just after Mrs. Stanton died, the President was dealing with the threat of nuclear war between India and Pakistan. That much Valium can screw you over, or to quote our medical authorities, 'produce incidents of disorientation, confusion, and memory lapses.' I think the public has some legitimate interest here. Don't you?"

"You're right, Arnold. I'm sorry. I told you I don't know if the President was taking any medication or not. I do know he was depressed and had trouble sleeping, but I did observe that he found relief in work. I think it helped him forget, not for long, but for a little while." Smith gave up on games. "I'm sorry I can't be more helpful. I'll make some inquiries and get back to you if I learn anything."

As Lincoln hung up he bolted for Langford's office. There would be other calls; Johnson at the <u>Post,</u> Nelson at <u>The L.A. Times</u>, lots of them. He had to be ready. Seeing the urgency on his face, Langford's secretary waved him on in.

"It's hit the fan, chief. Just the tip of the iceberg, but it's hit the fan. He knew too much. Someone is out to get us. Either his doctors are talking or they've gotten hold of the President's medical files. This is mean; no holds barred. It's dirty. Christ, maybe someone has been going through his medicine cabinet. I don't know where it's coming from, but we better find out and I mean now."

"Slow down! What the hell are you talking about?" Crayton had no idea what was happening, but he knew this was serious. Lincoln was cool. Lincoln was control. Now he had lost it.

"Crayton, I'm serious. We've got problems." Lincoln was breathless. "We don't have a chance unless we know who's behind this. I'm sorry. I've just had the damndest conversation with Bradley at the <u>Times</u>. I didn't handle it well, not at all."

After the press secretary and the chief of staff reviewed Arnold Bradley's call, they understood it was not a fishing expedition. Bradley had facts and details never meant to be public. They had a leak, not the kitchen variety, but a malicious leak meant to harm the President.

"Why now?" Langford asked. "Why now? I know New Year's Eve was bad, but he's getting better. Yesterday was a great day. He was focused, sharp, in command. You should have seen him with the Secretary of Defense. His lapses are rare now. They've never affected his judgment, not from the first day. At most, we only had embarrassing pauses and some quiet tears. We just take a break until he's ready to go again."

"Where are we vulnerable?" Smith asked. "What do I need to know? I can think on my feet as well as the next guy, but I don't want to be blindsided on this. It's too important. We could get calls for resignation."

"I don't think so, Link. We need to make four points: One, whatever problems the President had, they didn't affect his performance. Two, they're over. Three, they are over. And four, THEY ARE GOD DAMNED OVER!"

"That may be, but in the 'info-tainment' world this is news. And that world is competitive. Reporters are going to smell blood and blood sells like nothing else. I need to know the case against the President. What lapses are we talking about? I've got to know what I'm up against. I saw the President New Year's Eve. How many other incidents have there been?"

"I don't know, Link. I haven't been keeping book on the President. You're with him almost as much as I."

Lincoln pressed his case. "I'll lose my credibility, chief, if I have to come running to you with every question. Those guys are not stupid. If we have to cook up answers, one at a time, for each question, we won't get a sympathetic hearing. You know that. They'll suspect the worst and you'll see it in their reporting."

"I understand your need, Link. You'll have to hold them off, at least until tomorrow afternoon. I'll survey the staff, the Cabinet, and anyone else who has regular contact with the President, but I want to handle this. It has to be done discreetly, damn it, or we'll be the source of our own problems."

"It's not going to be easy, chief. I'm still a reporter at heart. Those guys are going to dig. They're going to smell pay dirt."

"I know," Crayton consoled. "Some of your reporters are better connected to our staff than I am. Just remember, Link, sympathy is on our side. The President is loved. He's loved for his compassion and he just lost his wife. If he weren't devastated, he wouldn't be the man they love, we love." The chief stopped, and then pointedly complimented the press secretary. "Link, what you told Bradley, you were right. He is back at work on the people's business. He finds it therapeutic; it gives his life meaning. For now, it is all he has."

Crayton's "in house" investigation took more time than he had ever anticipated. Memories are "amorphous." They merge and fuse, shrink and grow, or fade and die. His investigation violated that old adage of letting sleeping dogs lie. Questions are reminders for memories forgotten, but they not only resuscitate them, occasionally they reincarnate them into forms totally alien from their original character. The mind is a fertile field.

Stanton's chief of staff had wanted to low-key his investigation, but he didn't have time to do it alone. The hounds were gathering. Crayton had to involve his staff. He had no choice. There was too much to do. Stories had to be uncovered, confirmed, and put into context. Witnesses needed to be found, interviewed, and challenged. Dates had to be verified, patterns discerned, and explanations explored. At best, his investigation would only approximate the truth.

As reports were accumulated and organized, Crayton's concern multiplied. Together, in one file, all the individual anecdotes, descriptions, and evidence of Presidential "lapses" were impressive and troublesome. He reminded himself repeatedly that the incidents had taken place over four months. Further he knew the file contained a great deal of duplication, the same event as seen from a dozen different perspectives. Nevertheless, it was there. Cabinet and Security Council meetings had been cut short, conferences postponed, and public appearances canceled. Aides related how they made last minute substitutions and changes in the President's schedule because "he just wasn't ready," or "wasn't up to it" or "needed more time." And then there were other numerous occasions in which the President was inattentive, or confused, weeping or was red-eyed. In the wrong hands, the file would be devastating.

The investigation documented that as time went by, the President's staff expected him to be better and their scrutiny had intensified as they checked out that theory. It was as though he had had a stroke and his family, the White House staff, couldn't help but look for signs of trouble. Simple things - if the President forgot a name, the date, or needed a reminder – were seen as significant. The President was under a microscope. What they normally overlooked, did in fact overlook with each other, they now took as evidence that the President was still having trouble. His every movement and utterance was examined. The way he carried himself, the energy in his voice, the strength of his handshake, all helped to paint a picture.

The White House staff was worried, not for the country, but for the President, a man they universally admired. People see what they looked for, and now, after four months, the President's staff looked for problems. Large or small, real and imagined, "his problems" were attributed to "his condition."

The staff needed to know what Langford knew, knew beyond a shadow of a doubt. The President was better, much better and getting better every day. The problems he had documented, that the staff had seen, the real ones, were, by and large, dated. They occurred shortly after Danny's death. In recent weeks, the President had had a few flashbacks, but they were now rare and inconsequential.

With Howard, his deputy, Crayton mapped out a strategy for reassuring the staff without incurring the danger of "protesting too much."

Then together, behind closed doors in the press secretary's private office, they gave Lincoln Smith a copy of the "Incidents File." It contained not only the investigation report, but also its appendices, working papers, calendars and transcripts. In private the three worked until midnight trying to anticipate and answer any and all questions Lincoln would face. When they concluded, if they were ahead of the curve, their lead was miniscule.

The first course for the media's feeding frenzy was served Saturday night when <u>The New York Times</u>, Sunday edition rolled off the presses, hit the streets and the net. Arnold Bradley's article: "President in Mourning; Nation at Risk" was page one. It confirmed whispered suspicions that good taste had suppressed in the early days after the First Lady's death. Despite the late hour the story was spread, geometrically. By morning it had exploded. It was ground- breaking and it was legitimate news. <u>The Times</u> had made it so.

Thousands of reporters, editors, producers, anchors, commentators, and talk show hosts had their story. Sunday morning news junkies found it on all stations. At first reporters simply quoted or paraphrased Bradley's article. Depending upon their cycling of the news, the President's condition was the lead story every five, fifteen, or thirty minutes. It was repeated, again and again and again.

By midmorning the respected weekly news programs produced "in-depth" discussions of "President in Mourning; Nation at Risk." Off the top of their heads, regular talking heads boldly examined the "Stanton Story," put it in context and gave it perspective. Radio and television talk shows interviewed their own experts (and men on the street) about the relationship between grief, depression, drugs, and competence. Several featured noted physicians who examined the efficacy of drug therapy and responded to questions not just from "the round table," but also from listeners around the country. Enlightenment was not the only goal. While many questions concentrated on the potentially dangerous side effects of drowsiness, disorientation, confusion, and hallucinations, many others solicited a discussion of the impact of diarrhea, loose stools, difficulty urinating, dry mouth, and sweating on presidential performance. Sexual dysfunction was mentioned often, but only in passing.

By midafternoon Sunday the expertise of America had been mobilized and brought to bear on the question of Stanton's fitness for office. Senior statesmen, freshman senators, distinguished scholars, and brash reporters along with geo-politicians, pollsters, pharmacists, and psychiatrists of every stripe speculated gravely about hypotheticals. Those with the least credentials spoke with the most authority.

"What if...? What if...?" they asked. "What if the nation had been confronted with a real crisis while the President was drugged?" They were imaginative and tireless in their speculation. They anticipated crises, from terrorist attacks to thermonuclear war. Their questions suggested answers they never spoke. They didn't have to.

At the same time, less prestigious radio and television "call-in" talk show hosts worked hard to engage, hold and expand their target audience. They, too, interviewed experts, men on the street. Like the physicians and psychiatrists, these "experts" were asked about the relationship between grief, depression, drugs, and competence. Without hesitation, disclaimers, or facts they championed their opinions. When the more outrageous hosts, in an off-handed, yet transparently calculated manner, introduced sexual inadequacy, callers were queued up around the nation to give their opinions. After all it was an important topic. Sexual dysfunction was a potential side effect of a lot of drugs. Could a president be a president if he were concerned about his manhood? Wasn't he supposed to be the commander-in-chief of the most powerful nation on the face of the earth? The presidency was now, indeed, the talk of the nation. For the media, it was a bonanza. Not since the days of Bill and Monica, cigars and a blue dress had ratings hit such highs.

When the story ended its first week's run, it was serialized. Daily polls asked listeners or viewers to cast their vote: "Should President Stanton resign?" "Are drugs affecting President Stanton's performance?" After these solicitations, anchors would hypocritically, yet piously, announce that "these are not, we repeat, are not scientific polls" followed by an announcement of when the results would be available. Each network bannered regular segments with the same catchy title and promotional music. Special segments were prefixed with "Breaking News." All the segments were supplemented with a film sequence. One in particular was used by all the networks, again and again. It juxtaposed film of an energetic, jubilant President and First Lady celebrating an election victory, with a film of the President, a bent old man, burying his wife. The old man repeatedly and tenderly touches the flag-draped casket. As he turns away, he staggers and has to be supported by friends. A close-up shows his face distorted with grief and wet with tears.

The camera then follows a clumsy knot of mourners bearing the President across green grass to a black limousine. We get glimpses of him, through tinted glass, his face buried in his hands. The limousine is followed down Pennsylvania Avenue. The film ends as the black wrought-iron gates of the White House close behind the President. It looks like a sanitarium.

In its second week, when the story appeared to be fading, new revelations surfaced. On Tuesday, Nelson with the L. A. Times, asked Lincoln if it would be fair to characterize the President's behavior at his October 11th Cabinet meeting as anguished and confused. On Wednesday, Johnson with The Washington Post, asked Lincoln to comment on a December 3rd National Security Council meeting, "Did the President end that meeting by saying, 'I'm sorry, I can't go on with this any more?'"
At the same White House news briefing, Lincoln was asked to explain how the President of the United States could have repeatedly mistaken his daughter for his wife. They had their sources.

At first, Lincoln tried to disarm questions by speaking of the President's loss and his special relationship with Danny. When questioned about "incidents," he answered they were taken out of context or were inconsequential. Lincoln never admitted the President had had bad days, but constantly emphasized he was better. The incidents they asked about were always in the past. How could they be otherwise, the reporters grumbled.

"Never has the President been distracted from the people's business! Never!" Lincoln hammered. "It's been his one refuge from grief."

The daily White House news briefings, always a sparring match, were ugly now. Each round of questions moved the standards of decency lower. Offensive, insensitive questions that simply would not have been asked in an earlier time became common, so common they became acceptable. The briefings made great "theater," mud wrestling with meaning. They were carried live, and always ended with unanswered questions shouted at the press secretary as he retreated to the inner sanctum of the White House.

"President Stanton postponed his trip to Saudi Arabia; will he postpone the State of the Union?"

"Is the President under psychiatric care?"

"Is the President drinking alone?"

"Does the President still see his wife?"

It was, in fact, the President's confusion at the New Year's Eve party that changed the debate. No longer did the media speculate about what might have happened in the past, but rather what could happen in the future.

While people regularly voiced outrage at the press and asked, "why can't they just leave him alone," public opinion polls showed growing concern about the President's ability to do his job. They had no doubt he was a good man, but was he still a capable man? Was Andrew Holmes Stanton, President of the United States, still capable of discharging the powers and duties of his office?

More and more presidential spokesmen suggested that the State of the Union would answer any and all questions about President Stanton's competence. Newsprint and airwaves were again filled with speculation on the import of the speech. The State of the Union was hyped and sold like a Super Bowl. Competition for audience share among the networks was fierce. They all advertised broadcast teams of all-stars from many disciplines. Each featured panels of psychiatrists and bereavement specialists assembled for instant analysis. They would look beyond the President's words; at his appearance, carriage, confidence, strength, delivery, and demeanor. By the end of the State of the Union, maybe even before, they would be ready to render judgments on his fitness for office.

CBS and Fox News, anticipating the results of their own experts' analysis, impaneled constitutional scholars to discuss constitutional options for dealing with an incompetent president. The President's State of the Union was completely recast. The health and well-being of the Union was secondary to the health and well-being of Andrew Holmes Stanton, President of the United States.

CHAPTER SIX:

THE STATE OF THE UNION

7 P.M., Tuesday, January 23rd.

Howard "Fixer" Gonzales, doorman to the House since the Republican takeover, took a deep breath, "Mistah Speakah, The President of the United States." Everyone in the House of Representatives, on the floor and in the galleries, stood and welcomed the President with their applause. Democrats went much further, cheering and shouting their greetings, to bolster their beleaguered President. The Republican majority was polite.

"It starts now," ABC anchor Peter Clark whispered to an audience of millions.

"Yes, Peter, the President is already addressing many of the questions that have been raised since the First Lady's death." Sandy Rhodes was Peter's favorite White House correspondent. He, too, spoke in hushed tones. "The President looks great. He's working the chamber like a campaign ropeline. And nobody can do that better than this President."

"Yes, Peter, the President looks comfortable, very much at ease with himself. You can see it in his carriage and especially in his face. He's relaxed. The President has moved into the House as though he were coming home." Ann Nelson, M.D. in psychiatry spoke with great authority and, at least a little ambition. She had written two well-respected books, Posttraumatic Stress Disorder and The Insanity Defense, and one best seller, Sometimes I feel Like a Nut. She was hawking "Aging Well"– a mental health pilot for ABC's "20/20." She needed airtime. Along with its instant polls concerning the President's performance, ABC was asking its viewers their reaction to Dr. Nelson.

"Perhaps the House is home to the President," Peter responded. "He did begin his political career here. That was a long time ago, but maybe it's fitting that it is here that he will be judged."

"This is indeed Judgment Day," Doctor Nelson noted. "In the President's mind, this is Judgment Day."

"In this case the jury is the American people," Peter added. He could work with this woman. She certainly was attractive enough to host her own show.

The President of the United States had reached the well of the House. He moved directly to the Speaker's platform shaking hands first with the Vice President and then with the Speaker. The Speaker asked for quiet and then introduced the President. Again, as is the custom, the House erupted into the required applause and shouts of approval.

The President made no immediate effort to calm the crowd, but rather seemed, simply and wholeheartedly, to enjoy their greeting. Just before it had run its course he asked for quiet. His timing was excellent.

"This is his time," Peter announced. "He'll never have a better chance to answer his critics. Here he gets to speak directly to his jury, the American people. He'll try to tell them he's still in charge and working hard to protect and promote their interest. Let's listen."

The President was superbly prepared. He thanked the Speaker and then turned to the chamber and to the American people. Nothing in his manner was contrived. He spoke with joy and passion, not for effect, but because he believed. His voice and his body were one with his message. Time and time again, he was interrupted with applause. At first, it was partisan, on cue, but shortly, it was real and spontaneous.

President Stanton was a true democrat. He loved the people. He trusted and admired them. It showed. Working for them gave his life meaning. He knew them, for he knew himself, the good and the bad. He was sad when they failed, but angry when they failed to try. He took pride in their strength and industry, but warned them of their capacity for evil and error.

The President celebrated the people's goodness, but called upon them for greatness. He warned them life was short. It must not be wasted. This was their time. This was their chance; this was his chance. They must not miss the opportunities it offered. They should, could, would, and must be models for future generations. They could show the way. They could leave a legacy of greatness, grounded in giving, caring and goodness. If they worked together as a community, using all the tools available to them, they would realize their potential. Again and again, the chamber erupted with approval.

Around the nation, people who couldn't avoid the State of the Union, now listened and even nodded in agreement. This was the man they elected and this was why. He was back. And he was ready again to lead them and bring out their best.

They were guaranteed success, the President argued. It was completely in their hands. They, and no one else, had the power. All success demanded was the simple act of caring. Not the thought, but the act; not just empathy, but action and effort. That was the legacy, that was the model, and that was the way. The wealth of the world was not theirs to squander. It had to be used to benefit all God's children and all God's grandchildren. "We must be wise," he urged. "We must care, and we must share!" Again the chamber exploded.

The President stood back, his arms still outstretched. He was smiling, delighted that they saw the future he saw. The applause was deafening. "Amazing," Peter Clark murmured. "Just amazing."

President Stanton looked around the chamber from right to left and then to the galleries. He seemed to make eye contact with dozens of individuals. Then he saw her, where she always sat. Standing now, smiling and applauding like all the others. She wore the blue dress she wore at every State of the Union. He could see the necklace that held the locket he had given her when they first dated. He was transfixed. She blew him a kiss. He grinned, waved, and spoke clearly to her, "Thank you, Danny. Thank you for being here for me. I'm all right now." He knew he'd never see her again, not like this. It was over. He was better. "Good-bye," he whispered. "Good-bye, Danny."

"My God, Sandy, did I hear that right?" Peter Clark, like every other broadcaster, began his career shoving microphones at "famous" faces. Now he was caught off guard. "What the hell was that?"

"You're on the air, Peter," control cautioned.

"I don't know what it was, but it wasn't an exclusive," Sandy responded. "Good-bye, Danny" is tomorrow's lead in every daily in the country. What in the world could be going through his mind?"

"That, gentlemen, was a classic flashback." Dr. Nelson announced with all the authority her sexy voice could carry. "It's over now, watch."

The President turned back to the chamber. They were still standing, but stunned and silent. Had they heard? Yes. Oh, God, yes. He could read their faces. How could he tell them they had no need to worry? How could he tell them that he was now ready to dedicate his life to his only remaining love, his country? He recoiled from the shock he saw. He had no answer. None would work. He glanced up to the gallery, but just for a second. He knew she would not be there.

"Ladies and gentlemen, please excuse me. I had concluded my remarks and wish only to say I look forward to working with you, all of you, to meet the needs of this great nation. God bless you, and God Bless America." The President turned, shook hands with the Speaker and his Vice President and moved quickly to the floor. As he continued toward the exit, his friends still reached out to him, but this time their eyes were filled with tears.

CHAPTER SEVEN:

POSTMORTEMS

7:55 P.M., Tuesday, January 23rd.

As President Stanton emerged from the House he spotted his chief of staff, "Did you see it, Crayton?"

"Yes sir, I did." Crayton answered. "I think...

"I think my grand slam went foul. I want you to get the staff together tonight in my office. We've got a lot to talk about. Ten-thirty, okay?"

"Yes, Mr. President, we'll be there. Mr. President, can I suggest we include Congressman Stevens? He's a good, good friend."

"No, Crayton, not tonight. Just Virginia, Howard, and Lincoln. I don't want anyone pulling any punches."

"Yes, Mr. President, We'll be there. Ten-thirty." Crayton didn't care for "spontaneous" postmortems, but in this instance they needed to move quickly.

President Stanton was already losing ground. The networks had only seven minutes for instant analysis before the "Republican Response." Anchors, commentators, and pundits filled those minutes. They asked attention-grabbing questions and answered with qualified speculation. With delight, masked in solemnity, they asked: "Are President Stanton's self-inflicted wounds mortal?" "Can President Stanton survive?" "Can this President, who once commanded the respect of the entire world, now, command only its sympathy?" To these and other similar questions, the answers: "Time will tell;" "Only the American people have the answer;" and "President Stanton holds the key;" were pronounced just as gravely as the questions had been asked. Only on CBS did Professor Emeritus Samuel Turner of Harvard suggest that Section Four of the Twenty-Fifth Amendment could come into play. He was cut off before he could explain. All the networks promised a ninety-minute special, analyzing the State of the Union after the required Republican Response. Worried that they might lose their audience during that response, all of the networks ran captions continuously urging their viewers to stay tuned for "Presidency in Crisis."

Home from the State of the Union, Elizabeth Anne Roosevelt hugged her husband and suggested a nightcap. She was radiant. It had been a wonderful evening. She had "ousted" President Stanton, and her husband would be the next President of the United States. At last, the people had now seen for themselves. The time was right.

Immediately after the White House New Year's Eve party, Paul Reynolds, Secretary of Commerce, and Robert Kelly, Secretary of Transportation, had suggested to the Vice President it was time to invoke the Twenty-Fifth Amendment. They minced no words: "If the President wouldn't voluntarily step aside, he would have to be pushed." The Constitution required the Vice President and a majority of the Cabinet to certify the President's incompetence before he could be removed. Eight of the fourteen Cabinet Secretaries would have to sign on.

In response to the Reynolds and Kelly's initiative, the Vice President directed his staff to quietly contact other "likely prospects." He suggested if the President's condition deteriorated, the nation needed a contingency plan that could be implemented before the nation was put at risk. Before the State of the Union they had the unconditional support of six Cabinet members. Two more had hedged, but stated emphatically they would be with the Vice President if the President's condition became obvious. It was obvious tonight. It was time to move. Everything was ready.

Vice President Roosevelt was apprehensive. He knew what he had to do, and it pained him. Elizabeth Anne had predicted this time would come, but her giddy excitement disappointed him. Even though he felt ready, the thought that he would soon be president was overwhelming. She was right, of course; this was his chance, probably his only chance. But that bothered him. It wasn't supposed to happen this way. He was a Roosevelt. He wanted his motives to be pure, or at least to be seen that way, but they were suspect even in his own mind.

Roosevelt was convinced he could be a great president. He was groomed for the office, he dreamed of it, trained for it. He knew the country needed him; that wasn't the problem. The problem was his party. Democrats needed to see him as president before they would seriously consider him as their candidate. This was his chance. Hell, he thought, Teddy became president when McKinley was killed. What's the difference? When Danny Stanton died, so did the President.

"I'm going to tell him," Roosevelt stated.

"And spoil the surprise?" Elizabeth Anne laughed. "You're crazy. It'd just give him more time to fight you. You're not serious, are you?"

"Yes, I'm serious. I'm going to do it. First, it's the decent thing to do. Second, it will give him the opportunity to resign and leave the presidency with dignity. And third it will make governance after he's gone much easier. He'll probably thank me. He knows his time's up. You don't know him, Elizabeth Anne; he loves this country. He'll do what's right." He paused, and then continued, "It'll be a lot cleaner if he simply declares himself no longer up to the job, and asks me to serve out his term. The country will appreciate his candor. In fact, from President Stanton, they'll expect it."

"You're right. Very presidential, my dear. Very presidential." Elizabeth Anne was serious now. "You're right. It won't cost us a thing. If he's going to fight us, he'll fight us. But this way, he'll have a chance to see we've got him beat. His only choice is to bow out gracefully. You're right again," she concluded.

"He did consider resigning in September," Roosevelt mused. "Why wouldn't he want it now? Maybe I should have pushed him then."

"You know, William Roosevelt, you need me more than you realize. If you had taken over last year, you could have served only one full term. By waiting, you just might be the second longest serving president of these United States."

"What?" Roosevelt was stunned. "You knew that last fall, didn't you?" Roosevelt challenged. "That's why you argued the people weren't ready. You were so convincing. I don't know whether I'm amazed or appalled."

"Face it, honey. You need me." Elizabeth Anne purred. She slipped out of her aqua blue dress. "No person shall be elected to the office of the president more than twice, and no person who has held the office of president, or acted as president, for more than two years of a term to which some other person was elected president shall be elected to the office of President more than once," She recited the relevant section of the Twenty-second Amendment, verbatim. "Passing on the President's offer in August means you can now serve the remainder of his term plus two full terms of your own."

"You are incredible, Elizabeth Anne. Absolutely incredible."

It was ten-thirty. The President moved slowly around the Oval Office. He wasn't tired. He thanked them individually for coming in and being with him for so many years. Was he calling it quits? His tone worried them. Virginia Hastings, Howard Lipsack, Lincoln Smith and Crayton Langford were known as "Stanton's hard core." They had been with him since California. They were wonderfully comfortable with each other and with the President. They never forgot he was the President, but he was their friend. Without exception, they admired him. He had never let them down, not until now.

In their minds, throughout his long career, Stanton had been on the right side of every issue. In the fifties, he was outspoken in his opposition to McCarthy. He ridiculed the idea of monolithic communism. In the early sixties, he lost his Senate seat because of his stand on open housing. Later, he quietly (too quietly in his mind) resigned his cabinet position over Vietnam. As president of the University of California, he opposed Proposition 13. Later as governor of California, a State of extremes, he consistently found reasonable positions. With extraordinary leadership, he built majority coalitions to support those positions. He was extremely persuasive. He had a rare balance of passion and patience. His persistence was legendary. Given time, he found relevant analogies for every audience. With easily understood logic he'd take them from their own beliefs to the position he was promoting. His was not the tortured logic of partisans defending party positions; rather he was a principled pragmatic with a vision of a better world.

Gathered in the Oval Office, Stanton's staff waited on the President to take the lead. They wanted the truth, but feared they had been ignoring it. Even before Danny and Matt died, former staff members from California days would pull them aside and asked if the President was all right. They were surprised by the question. They found it curious, even strange. He was in command. They worked with President Stanton daily. They hadn't seen him grow old.

The President half sat on his desk, one foot on the floor, his arms folded across his chest. "Virginia, gentlemen, I'm sorry, but we have a monumental decision to make. We had a lot riding on the State of the Union tonight, and I blew it. The people had heard my critics for weeks, but reserved judgment. They waited for me and gave me the benefit of their doubt. They had to see for themselves. Well, now they have."

"Mr. President, it was an incredible speech. Even the Republicans..."

"Wait, Howard," the President insisted. "Let me finish. I needed to answer my critics and show everyone that their concerns about my competence were without merit. I did pretty well for a while, but with seventeen words I confirmed their worst fears. Hell, I fueled them. The people tuned in wanting reassurance. Instead, they heard their President talk to his dead wife. There will be calls for my resignation."

The President stood up and moved about the room. "Whatever my answer, it must be for the good of the country." He paused and looked from one to the other. "I trust your counsel more than my own, but I have one piece of information you don't. Despite what you heard and saw tonight, I am better. There will be no more flashbacks, that's over." The President hesitated and then continued. "I guess you should give that assertion as much weight as you think it deserves. Even if you believe it completely, that alone does not dictate the answer to the question of resignation. The people, the Congress, the Cabinet, the military, and the international community must have confidence in me. I'm sure it's been shaken. Maybe it can be restored. I don't know."

"Mr. President, how do you know you're better, that there will be no more flashbacks?" Lincoln Smith was more accustomed to answering questions than asking them. He proceeded gently, "How can you be sure?"

Stanton turned to the whole group. "I'm sure, but I don't know how to convince you. If I did, maybe I'd know what to say to the American people. I don't want to sell you, or them, a bill of goods." The President took a deep breath. "Let me try to explain. We all have memories. Each of us can visualize a special Christmas. We even hear our favorite carols, and feel the chill as well as the excitement. If I listen, I not only can hear Salvation Army bells, I can see the volunteers, their tripods, and buckets. So can you. You hear the sounds, you know the colors, you can see your breath and you know you're fumbling in your pockets for the right amount. Some memories we have in common; others are unique to each of us. We recognize people, their voices and faces, because we can hear them and see them in our minds. We all heard Martin Luther King's dream and, if we listen, we can all hear it now. We can hear it, feel it, and share the dream. That's good. It's wonderful. Our memories are real."

Lincoln and Virginia as well as Howard and Crayton exchanged glances. They weren't sure where President Stanton was going with this, but they could see his mind at work. He was in command.

The President continued, "We occasionally see and hear the famous, but more often it's the familiar, our families. 'I can see him now.' 'I can just hear him say.' Those are not just phrases; they are facts. Long before Danny died, I saw her and heard her many times when she wasn't there. When I was too hard on the girls, she'd tell me to lighten up. When I tried to rush a decision, she'd tell me to slow down, and when I was about to lose it she'd tell me to take a deep breath. I wish I had listened. In my flashbacks, I didn't see aliens or talk to Martians, I talked to Danny."

"But you thought it was real," Howard's emphasis on real made his point.

"Yes, I did. There were a few times, they never lasted more than a minute, when Danny seemed more than a memory. I missed her too much. It was never dangerous. Danny never said anything to cause anybody any concern. She didn't tell me to invade Canada. In fact, she never told me anything she hadn't told me a thousand times before. She told me to be strong, to take care of myself and be good to the girls. Danny and I were married thirty-nine years. We talked all the time, but in the latter years we didn't need to. I knew what she was going to say and she knew what I was going to say. It was just comforting to hear the words."

"How do I know it won't happen again?" The President repeated Lincoln's question. "I'm almost afraid to tell you. It won't happen again because Danny's telling me I'm fine and I need to get back to work. In fact, if you listen you can hear her, she's telling you, as she always did when we got bogged down, that it's time to move on and do what's right for the people. I thank God I'll always hear her, in my mind and in my heart, until the day I die; but I know what's real. Sometimes it's hard to accept, but I know what's real."

Stanton laughed and broke the tension. "Tomorrow morning, I expect Danny will tell me to lay off the donuts. I should, you know." Then summarizing, he added, "You don't have to worry. It won't happen again. I know what's real. What I need to know is what's right."

"Mr. President, we need to move fast. Can we meet in the morning?" Crayton pressed. "All the choices may not be ours. Secretary Wirtz tells me he's had some cryptic conversations with members of the Vice President's staff. They said they were not speaking for the Vice President, but wanted to talk off the record about 'decision points' and the Presidency. He waved them off, and they never got back to him, but he thinks something may be afoot."

"The morning's fine, Crayton," President Stanton responded. "Virginia, I want to know the law on this. Howard, I want your best work. I want a resignation statement, and I want a statement explaining why I've rejected resignation and chosen to stay in office. Lincoln, either way, you're in for a hell of a week. The press is going to pound on you until we give them an honest, simple explanation of my State of the Union. We'll work on that together. It'll be interesting what sound bites come out of this. Let's make it nine- thirty. Thank you all. You've all got a lot of work to do, and I need a good night's sleep."

CHAPTER EIGHT:

A PRESIDENTIAL DECISION

9:30 AM, Wednesday, January 24th.

"Good morning, Mr. President. Did you sleep well?"

"Good morning, Virginia. Yes, I had a good night's sleep. Good morning, everyone. Howard, do you have my resignation statement?"

"Mr. President," Crayton answered for his deputy. I told Howard to forget that statement."

"You what???"

"Please let me explain, sir," Crayton answered. "If you insist, we can produce a resignation statement in ten minutes. You asked us to give you recommendations that considered only one factor, the good of the country."

"Mr. President," Virginia Hastings continued, "that sounded like a heavy assignment, but it was not. The question of who is to be president of the United States for the next two years is limited by the Constitution. There are only two choices, you or Vice President Roosevelt."

Howard, checking Crayton, took over. "We have two concerns, Mr. President: First, are you better? And second, if you are better, can you reclaim the confidence of the American people?"

With a deep breath, Crayton interrupted, "Let me speak frankly, Mr. President. Your State of the Union gaffe, coming on the heels of other slips, frightens us. We know you believe you are better, but we still have doubts, and so must the American people. We are convinced your difficulty with Danny's death hasn't affected your decision-making so far, but we fear it still could. We know your problems have, at least temporarily, affected your ability to lead. Like you, we long for the past when you had Danny and an exceptional Vice President. But this is the reality. For the next two years you or an Acting President Roosevelt will lead the United States of America. It's that simple; which of you will make the better president?"

Crayton paused. He surveyed his colleagues and then continued. "Your team is experienced, tested, and proven. We are members of that team, Mr. President. We're obviously prejudiced, but I assure you, putting our country first is not difficult. We believe your policies and philosophy of governance are in the best interest of our country. Vice President Roosevelt doesn't share our philosophy or our policy commitments. He may be principled, but he's a cold, ambitious man totally lacking compassion. He may love our country, but we're not at all sure he cares for its people. Even if you are weakened, Mr. President, we are of one mind; for the good of the country you must complete your term."

"Lincoln, don't you have a part to play in this production?" Stanton asked.

"No, sir, I'm the director," Lincoln laughed. I told them what to say."

"Good job!" was the President's amused response. "That was just what I wanted to hear." Then more seriously he asked, "Will we have much difficulty convincing the American people that the country is in good hands?"

"I think they want to believe in you, Mr. President," Crayton answered. "That always makes it easier. We'll just have to show them, in dramatic fashion, that you're taking care of business. We need policy announcements, program initiatives, town meetings, one or two international visitors, and one damn good fireside chat."

"Will the networks give us time?" Stanton asked.

"I think so, sir," Lincoln answered. "They're asking a hell of a lot of questions to turn around and say it's not newsworthy."

"Mr. President," Virginia interrupted, "I think you may have a more immediate problem. The Vice President has asked to see you this morning."

"That's true, sir," Crayton nodded. "I asked Millie to put him off until this afternoon. He's scheduled for two."

For a moment the President was reflective. "You know, at one point, right after Danny's death, I talked to him about the possibility of making him Acting President. He seemed interested at first, but we slept on it, and the next day we both concluded it wasn't such a good idea. What does he want, Crayton?"

"I don't know, sir. He wouldn't say. It could just be a courtesy call to offer support, but after Secretary Wirtz's comment, I wonder."

"Mr. President, Crayton, I think we've got to prepare for the worst," Virginia Hastings was not an alarmist, but she was always prepared. "During my research last night, I became painfully aware of Section Four of the Twenty-Fifth Amendment. It authorizes the Vice President and a majority of the Cabinet to assess the competence of the President and assume control of the government if they conclude he's unable to discharge the powers and duties of his office. It has never been used, but it's there, just waiting for a vulnerable president and an ambitious vice president."

"Virginia's right, Mr. President. You've got to play it coy, sir," Howard warned. "Make him show his hand."

"I think I've already seen his hand." The President paused. "Aaron, Secretary Chadwick, called a couple of days before the State of the Union. He insisted on being put through, but then just seem to want to chat. It was a strange call. He said all the usual stuff, I said all the usual stuff, and then he assured me the American people were fair-minded and reserving judgment. I thought it was just a courtesy call, but then kind of out of the blue, he said something like, he wouldn't be rushed, but the speech was truly critical for my Presidency and the nation. He ended it by wishing me well, several times, enough to make me uncomfortable and then hung up. I didn't make much of it at the time, but I know he said he wouldn't be rushed and now I think it was a warning."

"I think you're right, Mr. President, and I'd like to be in on your meeting with the Vice President."

"Why's that, Crayton?" The President asked with just a hint of defensiveness.

"I have no doubt you can handle the Vice President, sir. I just believe we shouldn't make it easy for him. He's got to know what he says will be on the record. I don't want to give him any wiggle room."

"Maybe we're all making too much of this, but I believe Crayton's right, sir. If we get into a pissing war, I want to be able to tell the press who said what with no questions asked. You need a witness, sir. We don't want to give that son of a bitch any deniability."

"Hold on, everybody." the President cautioned. "I appreciate your loyalty, Lincoln, but let's reserve judgment on the Vice President, at least until we hear what he has to say. I've asked you all for the benefit of the doubt. I think we should extend the same to Roosevelt. We'll know soon enough." The President thought for a moment, and then asked Crayton if the Vice President was in his office.

"I believe so, sir."

The President reached for his intercom, "Millie, get the Vice President. Tell him his two o'clock has been canceled. I want to see him now."

The President saw their questions. "You don't have to prepare an offer to help," he said. "On the other hand, an attack takes time and runs on a schedule. It's easier to defend against an attacker who's off balance."

"Crayton, you stay with me," the President stated. "Thank you all. We'll post you immediately."

Before they could leave, Millie Wilson, the President's secretary stepped into the Oval Office. "Mr. President?"

"Yes, Millie."

"Mr. President, the Vice President says he needs just a few minutes. Could he see you at eleven?"

"Of course, Millie. Tell him eleven is just fine."

CHAPTER NINE:

ULTIMATUMS

11:10 A.M., Wednesday, January 24th.

"Mr. President."

"Yes, Millie."

"The Vice President is here, sir. May I send him in?"

"Yes, Millie, send him in, please."

William Butler Roosevelt, Vice President of the United States, moved into the Oval Office very much like a man with a mission. In his left hand he carried a slim leather briefcase. The President stepped around his desk and shook hands with his Vice President. Each took measure of the other. In appearance, the President could have been Roosevelt's father. While they were approximately the same height, Roosevelt had a military bearing and appeared taller. Despite his age, the graying Stanton looked in good shape. In his college days, he had played second base for the University of Tennessee and set the SEC record for double plays turned in a single season. He still had an easy, natural carriage.

"Have a seat, William," President Stanton directed. "Would you care for coffee?"

The Vice President sat in the right high back leather chair facing the President. The President remained standing. From the back wall, Crayton came forward and took the chair next to the Vice President. For just a second, Roosevelt seemed startled. He had not wanted an audience, but he was okay with one; his conscience was clear. Though he was not at ease, he felt what he was doing had to be done.

"No, thank you, Mr. President, my stomach's a little upset as it is." Roosevelt leaned forward and spoke respectfully, but directly, "Mr. President, you have a record of public service that's unequaled by any living American. Indeed, it even stands you in good stead with all the great men and women of American history. For years, you'll remember America suffered for want of a positive role model. Today, you are that model. Your life, your record must not be tarnished."

"I appreciate your comments, but I suspect they're only prelude. What exactly are you suggesting?" the President asked.

"Mr. President, I'm afraid you are endangering your legacy. Last September, you asked me what I thought of your stepping down and appointing me Acting President. I told you I didn't think that was necessary. Now, sir, I do. Please believe me, Mr. President, I don't say this lightly; you are at a crossroads, where you can cap your life's work with a selfless act of resignation, or you can diminish or destroy it by resisting what is now obvious."

"What is so obvious to you is still a little obscure to me" the President prodded.

"Sir," the Vice President spoke with respectful empathy, "your grief has taken a heavy toll. Everyone would understand."

"Just when would you suggest I resign?" The President inquired. Stanton felt like Tom Sawyer attending his own funeral, except in this case, he was expected to participate.

"It should happen quickly, sir," Roosevelt sensed success. "You should take the lead, Mr. President. The people must see you leading and doing what's right for the country."

"You didn't tell me when," the President stated.

The Vice President shook his head slowly. He sat on the edge of his chair rocking slowly back and forth. Leaning forward, he brought his hand to his cheek and then slowly pressed it up to his forehead and then back to his cheek. Vice President Roosevelt looked up at the President. He appeared to be agonizing over the decision. Finally, very slowly he said, "Immediately, Mr. President. It should be done immediately. To wait, sir, with the media frenzy exploding around us, is to be pushed."

"Am I being?" the President asked.

"Being what, Mr. President?" Roosevelt sensed trouble.

"Being pushed, Mr. Roosevelt? Am I being pushed to resign?" The President spoke each word emphatically.

"I'm giving you my best advice, sir," the Vice President knew he sounded defensive. He wanted Stanton to believe resignation was his choice, but Roosevelt also wanted him to know it was his only choice. "The media will destroy your presidency. A number of your Cabinet Secretaries, and I, believe you must resign your office to save your presidency."

The President stiffened, and now stood directly above Roosevelt. "And if I don't resign, Mr. Vice President, will I still have your support and the support of my Cabinet?"

The question was a lightning strike. The dance had ended. Roosevelt had hoped, even expected, President Stanton would work with him. He had given the President the opportunity to end his presidency as a patriot, doing what was right for the country. Stanton was making this very difficult. Persuasion looked impossible. The President had considered resigning before, when everyone understood his grief; why not now, when everyone knew it was necessary? Roosevelt had had no choice; the President had forced his hand.

Crayton waited for the thunder and watched as the Vice President reached for his brief case and stood facing the President. They had more than eye contact. Theirs was a clash of wills backed by extraordinary self-confidence. Their anger was controlled, one abused but certain, the other misunderstood, but adamant. Neither gave. The Vice President removed two letters from his brief case and handed them to the President. "It would be best if you resigned, sir."

The letters were addressed to Senator Albert Frank, President Pro Tempore of the Senate and Congressman Louis Mathis, Speaker of the House of Representatives. Other than the addressees, they were identical:

> **We, the undersigned, including the Vice President of the United States and a majority of the Cabinet, do hereby provide our written declaration that Andrew Holmes Stanton, President of the United States, is unable to discharge the powers and duties of his office. <u>That being so, Vice President William Butler Roosevelt shall immediately assume the powers and duties of the office as Acting President.</u>**

**William Butler Roosevelt, Vice President of
   the United States
Aaron F. Chadwick, Secretary of the Interior
Marc F. Collier, Secretary of Defense
Lee J. Fong, Secretary of Education
Robert D. Kelly, Secretary of Transportation
Harold R. Kruegman, Secretary of Agriculture
Helen G. Ramirez, Secretary of Housing and
   Urban Development
Paul W. Reynolds, Secretary of Commerce
Charlene J. Tuckman, Secretary of Energy**

President Stanton glanced at one and tossed the other to Crayton. They both recognized the invocation of Section Four of the Twenty-Fifth Amendment. Virginia had warned the President and Crayton, but no one could have prepared them. They had understood going into the meeting, that Roosevelt might make such a declaration: yet they were no more prepared for it than a parent is to hear his child has cancer.

President Stanton tried to mask his emotions, but it was impossible. He understood the horrendous implications. Their declaration stated he was not fit to be President. Once delivered to the Speaker and President Pro Tempore, the record would be written, there would be no turning back. If he contested it, they would do battle before Congress. The will of the people, an election, could be overturned. He could be replaced, his policies and programs reversed and abolished. Legal or not, it was a *coup d'état*. It was ironic, he thought. Two Democrats, each using all the powers of the presidency, would fight for the office and a Republican Congress would choose the winner.

"Do you know what you're doing?...What you're doing to the country? You're not ready, Mr. Roosevelt," Stanton exploded. "You have a name, you have money, but where is your experience? Where are your convictions, your compassion, and where is your judgment?"

"Mr. Vice President," Crayton couldn't resist, "the President was about to give me his decisions on the Conscription Bill and the Final Status of Jerusalem. Would you like us to delay so you can make those decisions? Or do you want us to go ahead and make the tough calls so you don't hurt yourself at the polls."

Roosevelt ignored Crayton, and spoke directly to the President. He was remarkably controlled. "I know exactly what I am doing, sir. I am doing what is best for this country. The question is, do you? Will you resign or will you be removed?"

"You're wrong. There is another option. I will not resign and I will not be removed. You will withdraw this abomination. Anyone can see I handled my grief badly, but no one can say I have handled the affairs of this nation badly. What decisions do you fault? What duties, what powers have I neglected? Mr. Roosevelt, if you fail to withdraw your declaration you, and perhaps I, will be destroyed. Our contest will unleash ambitions no one can control. There will be no rules. The prize is too great."

"Mr. President, I wanted to make this easy for you and the country. I still do. I will hand deliver this declaration to the Speaker and President Pro Tempore tomorrow. You have twenty-four hours. Good day, Sir."

With his ultimatum delivered, Vice President Roosevelt turned and left the Oval Office.

CHAPTER TEN:

STRATEGY

1 P.M., Wednesday, January 24th.

"How did it go?" Elizabeth Anne met her husband in the foyer. She knew the answer just looking at him.

"Not well, not well at all." Roosevelt mumbled. He was unhappy with himself. Why had he failed? It seemed so obvious that the President should resign. "I just never thought he'd resist."

"He won't resign?"

"No. More accurately I should say 'Hell No!'"

"You're positive. You showed him the declaration?" Elizabeth Anne knew the answer. "It doesn't matter. This time tomorrow you will be President."

"Acting President, Dear," he corrected. "Stanton didn't miss a beat even when I showed him the declaration. I tell you, he may be crazy, but he is tough. He is not bluffing. He'll go down fighting. He thinks he's right. He believes we're going to tear the nation apart, but he's going to fight. He says were going to unleash forces over which we will have no control, but he's going to fight. And he challenges my judgment. God, this is going to be tough."

As they entered the dining room, Roosevelt was much annoyed to find his father-in-law finishing lunch.

"Hope you don't mind, we went on without you," Croft announced. "Lunch was really special. I offered Maggie a job again, double the pay, but I think she's holding out for the White House."

Margaret Arnold had been with the Roosevelt family for forty-two years. She was on her second generation of Roosevelts. She loved William; she had been his nanny, but if it had not been for little Jimmy she would have quit a long time ago.

William sat opposite Croft, next to Elizabeth Anne. Margaret brought him French onion soup and a chicken salad croissant. He needed to talk, but hesitated; Croft should not be present. He was not just a benign old man, doting over his grandson. He was a powerful player with his own agenda. Nothing escaped him. Roosevelt had never really seen him work, but he had seen the results. Croft had his ways; his modus operandi was intimidation and retribution. Whenever they were together Roosevelt had to continually remind himself, he, not Croft, was the Vice President of the United States.

"We need to go back to the Cabinet," Roosevelt said. "We've got to hold our eight and go after some insurance. If Stanton is true to his word, they'll all have to sign on again. That's not going to be easy. We practically guaranteed them he'd resign. Hell, a number of the Secretaries wanted to believe that they were doing their old friend, the President, a favor; just giving him a gentle nudge, an excuse to do what he needed to do. They may not sign on this time."

"The hell they won't," Croft exclaimed. "Christ, Bill, you've got'em by the short hairs. They walked out on that limb with their eyes wide open. There's no turning back. Your aides need to pass the word. They don't have any choice. They've already pissed off the President. You're the only game in town. Their future is with you or they don't have a future. If they waver or even whimper, they've got to know you'll burn them."

"I don't think you understand," Roosevelt lectured. "These are men and women of honor trying to do what's right for the country. They value their integrity. They have a future with or without me, and they know it. They are where they are because each of them has superb ability as well as their own power base."

Croft only shook his head. Roosevelt hated talking politics with him. With the Commander, every fight was a street fight that had to end in total victory. Roosevelt believed, in politics, you had to work with people. Your worst adversary on one issue could be your strongest ally on another. He had been sure, with Stanton, this fight didn't have to be in the gutter. It could be fought with credit, if not victory for both sides.

It was just that sort of thinking that kept Croft underground. He couldn't talk to his son-in-law. Roosevelt, he thought, might not be a liberal, but he was hopelessly naive. Elizabeth Anne was different. She had proved herself in a way only Croft understood. He knew she was willing to do what had to be done without any bullshit. She had proven that.

In the last three weeks Croft had been tempted a number of times to cram the honorable Secretaries Reynolds and Kelly down Roosevelt's throat and give him a lesson about the real world. They were his boys. He resisted. Roosevelt was stupidly principled. Now, certainly, was not the time to tell Roosevelt how his early champions had come to see him as the nation's savior. Croft would be patient and wait for the day when his son-in-law would be president. Then his naiveté would be priceless.

"What's next?" Croft asked innocently.

Elizabeth Anne outlined the days ahead. "Assuming the President makes no move to resign, we deliver the declaration to the Speaker and President Pro Tempore tomorrow noon. Then, if Bill's right, two seconds later, the President will slap into their hands his own declaration that he's just fine and ready to carry on with the nation's business. Unfortunately, nobody has to cosign with the President. All he has to do is assert his competence. Then as soon as we can, but no later than four days, we've got to go back to the Congress with at least eight Secretaries and repeat our declaration. At that point, the issue is fully joined and the decision lies with Congress. They have twenty-one days to determine the competence of the President. It will take a two-thirds vote to remove Stanton, but with a Republican Congress that's not a big hurdle for us. They thought he was crazy when the people elected him."

"Am I right that the Constitutional presumption is with the Vice President?" Croft asked.

Roosevelt's glance at Croft failed to disguise his surprise.

Elizabeth Anne continued the charade. "Well, Daddy, I am impressed. That's right. While Congress is deliberating, the Constitution makes William the Acting President."

As head of the Roosevelt's domestic staff, Ronald Hodges had moved in and out of the library attending to the needs of the Roosevelts and their guests. Now he sought the Vice President's eye.

"Yes, Ron, what is it?"

"Mr. Vice President, Jason Fields, and Brad Curtis are here to see you. Should I show them in?"

"Yes, Ron," Elizabeth Anne responded.

"Well, we've got to be going. Come on, Jimmy," Commander Croft called for his grandson. "It's you and me, buddy."

"We'll slip out early, Dad. I'll be by for him no later than ten," Elizabeth Anne promised. "You be ready, Jimmy."

Croft stood, shook hands with Roosevelt and took his leave. At the door, he couldn't resist, he turned and winked at his daughter, "Remember, son, take no prisoners."

In the moment between Croft's exit and Jason's entrance, a livid Roosevelt turned on his wife. "Listen to me, Elizabeth Anne. Your father is not to be involved in this. Is that understood? He dirties everything he touches." He spoke low through gritted teeth.

Elizabeth Anne stiffened and looked at him squarely. "You're a little late, dear." Her tone was as condescending as she could make it. "I'm not sure the high road leads to the White House."

"Gutsy bastard, isn't he?" The President's tone reflected a grudging admiration.

"He didn't blink," Crayton answered. "I didn't think our Vice President had it in him."

"Well, we are in a fight. As best I can tell there are three rounds and we've already lost round one. Look at that list. That's my Cabinet," the President slumped in his chair and studied the declaration.

"Any surprises?" Crayton asked.

"One...two... maybe three. Hindsight can sure bite you in the ass," the President laughed. "Three of the four Republicans in my Cabinet join Roosevelt. Can you believe it?"

"I believe it now," Crayton responded. "Wish we had listened to Howard."

"He wasn't very high on our efforts to establishing our bipartisan credentials, was he," the President agreed. "But we were proactive then, trying to forge a partnership for America," he said sarcastically. "Now we're just circling the wagons to save my Presidency."

"We're doing more than that, sir; we're looking after the nation. America's future is best served by you serving out the remainder of your term." Crayton's matter-of-fact statement was reassuring.

"What a God-awful precedent," Crayton continued. "If we lose this fight, America will suffer not only from a loss of leadership for the next two years, but for the foreseeable future. Roosevelt will not only overturn the election, he'll pervert the Twenty-Fifth Amendment." Crayton became reflective, "I was there at its inception. The Congress was worried about a President with his skull blown off. The Twenty-Fifth Amendment was adopted to remove an incompetent president, because he flat couldn't do the job. It was never intended to remove a president who's doing the job, but struggling with some personal problem."

"Well, Crayton," the President sighed, "that may be, but we both know I'm vulnerable because I let Danny's death affect my Presidency. We contained it for a while, but the people saw it for themselves. I blew The State of the Union - that's a Constitutional duty. I'm better now, but if I can't convince my own Cabinet of that, then I suspect the people may be out of reach. If that's the case, we won't stand a prayer. Only the American people can save my Presidency if this goes to Congress. I hope I can convince them it's worth their while."

"Well, enough of that." The President slapped his thighs with both hands and stood erect. "Get the team in here, Crayton. We've got a lot of work to do!"

"They're on standby, sir," Crayton hit the intercom. "Millie, tell them to come in."

"I want you in here too, Millie," The President directed. "Bring your pad, we're making history and I don't want anybody freelancing about what we did here."

"Jason, Brad," the Vice President greeted his Chief of Staff, Jason Fields, and his deputy chief, Brad Curtis. "Thank you for coming. Have a seat." The Vice President motioned them to the library table where Elizabeth Anne waited impatiently.

"Can I have Margaret bring you anything?" Roosevelt asked.

"No thank you, Mr. Vice President," Fields answered for both of them and took a seat opposite Roosevelt. Elizabeth Anne motioned for Brad to sit next to her.

"William met with the President this morning," Elizabeth Anne began. "He says he won't resign. We need to review our strategy. We must leave nothing to chance."

Before she could continue, the Vice President interrupted to review, in some detail, his meeting with the President. He felt it important they understand the President's resolve.

"So that's where we are," he concluded, "in uncharted waters. I don't believe President Stanton has any intention of resigning. He'll fight us every step of the way."

The afternoon sun had brightened the library, but marked the passage of time. Elizabeth Anne's impatience grew. "In sum, William gave Stanton twenty-four hours and now Stanton's going to use it." Elizabeth Anne showed no intention of reading Roosevelt's body language. "Where do we go from here, Jason?" she asked.

Fields didn't answer immediately. He and his staff had been working on contingencies for months. He was well prepared and confident. He laid it out quickly. "After we deliver our declaration to the House and Senate you will be the Acting President of the United States. I suspect that will last about two minutes. By that time, the President will reject your declaration and reclaim his office. We must act just as fast in reasserting your claim."

Jason took off his glasses. "You must understand our time is now. We have a majority now. It may or may not last. Minds can change and commitments broken. We must do everything we can to hold our majority together. We must insist that private commitments be made public so they cannot be retracted after a little presidential arm-twisting. First, of course, we've got to make damn sure we still have a majority of the Cabinet willing to sign again, your declaration that the President is incapable of performing his duties. As soon as we do that, you will again be the Acting President. You will stay in that position for up to twenty-one days until the Congress declares either you or Stanton to be President."

"If the issue is laid cleanly and quickly before the Congress, we'll win." Brad Curtis took over. "It was just fourteen months ago that this Congress unanimously approved you as Vice

President. It is a Republican Congress. Stanton's rolled over them time and time again. They hate him. And let's face it; they don't believe you can win the Democratic Party's nomination. They think you'll go for it, but they're confident you'll be challenged and beaten from the left in a nineteen-sixty-eight-style donny-brook. That will leave them in the center to take over the White House. It's been a long time for them. They're hungry. They won't let this opportunity pass."

Jason nodded in agreement. "We're in great shape if it goes to Congress," he summarized. "And it will go to Congress if we keep a majority of the Cabinet."

"Our first step," Brad began, "should be to meet with our eight cosigners. We should meet them as a group and then indi-vidually. We need to assess them, who's hanging tough and who's having second thoughts. We've got to stress to them there is no turning back."

"There are a couple of Cabinet Secretaries who are going to be pretty upset with us," Roosevelt stated. "I told Elizabeth Anne, we practically guaranteed them Stanton would resign. We sold them on the idea that they were doing their old friend a favor; let-ting him do what he wanted to do despite the objections of his staff. I tell you, this isn't a given. There's no guarantee they'll sign on this time."

"You're right, we oversold resignation and we can apolo-gize, but it doesn't matter," Jason emphasized. "They need to know we're going to win this thing. We're going after insurance. We're talking to the rest of the Cabinet, and we're going to win. Either they're with us or against us. They have got to see them-selves sitting pretty in your administration or being burned badly by it."

Roosevelt winced hearing Jason spout Crofts' words, but feared he was right. Stanton was right, too. He was losing control. Once they learned President Stanton was going to fight, not all of the eight original signers of the Declaration of Incompetence would automatically re-enlist. They would have to go after them hard and they'd also have to go after each of the six other Cabinet Secretaries.

"We've got to remember, when we meet with the supposed Stanton loyalists, they may feel they're on a sinking ship," Roosevelt stated. "If it is properly presented, they may grab at a life-line."

"You're absolutely right, sir," Fields stated. "We have a real chance to pick up some additional support. These guys are winners. All their lives they've been grooming themselves for the next job. They don't want to see their 'promising careers' go down with Stanton. I think we could be surprised."

"Pleasantly, I hope," Elizabeth Anne cautioned.

"Brad and I have tentatively divided the Cabinet into five groups: (1) strong supporters, (2) those leaning in favor, (3) the undecided, (4) those leaning against, and (5) those opposed. After our meetings we'll get together and reassess our evaluations. The four of us will concentrate our efforts on the undecided and those leaning for and against. Each Cabinet Secretary will have Brad, Estelle or me as a twenty-four-hour-a-day contact person for rumor control and general handholding. All media contacts and statements will be cleared through Conrad and me. I'd like both Estelle and Conrad in on all future meetings."

Estelle Cohen was the Vice President's Special Assistant for Legislative Affairs. Conrad Tate was Roosevelt's Press Secretary. Both joined Roosevelt's team when he was the junior Senator from New York. Even then, they saw him as their ticket to the center ring. While they were both ambitious they were also extremely loyal to the Vice President.

"Does Conrad have releases ready to accompany the declaration?"

"Yes, Mrs. Roosevelt," Jason answered. "They're ready for your and the Vice President's review. In fact, Curtis told Conrad and Estelle to be here at five. I suspect they're outside now."

"When do we meet with the Secretaries?" Roosevelt asked.

"We should be ready with our eight signers tomorrow at eleven," Curtis answered.

"After that," Jason took over, "starting at eleven thirty and going for the rest of the day, Brad and I will be meeting with them, one on one, to pin them down. If there are any negotiations, I assure you, they will be preliminary. Brad and I will make commitments for ourselves only, none for the Vice President other than those of a general nature."

"Expand on that, Jason?" Elizabeth Anne's question was asked to reassure the Vice President.

Jason looked directly at the Vice President. "As we discussed," he indicated Elizabeth Anne, "we'll try to get through each session, by telling the Secretaries that we'll ask you to look into something, or consider them for this or that appointment, but we will not commit you positively to do anything. However, you know the Secretaries. They're pretty savvy folks. They may want guarantees, particularly the second time around. We'll try to steer clear of anything controversial, but we're going to be flying by the seat of our pants. When in doubt we'll check it out with you, sir."

"That's fine, Jason, but I do expect, as you conclude each of your meetings, you will excuse yourself and brief me on any and all understandings or problems. At that point you will bring the Secretary to my office and I will either seal their endorsement or thank them for their consideration." Roosevelt paused and then stated with obvious conviction: "So long as we maintain our focus on the President's incompetence and the danger that represents to our nation our efforts will be honorable."

"Yes, right, sir." Jason agreed. Then with a quick glance at his deputy he continued. "And from your office, we will take the Secretaries to Conrad's office where they can work with him on press releases, statements, and appearances."

"Good, very good!" Roosevelt pushed back from the table and stood. "Now, Elizabeth Anne and I must excuse ourselves. My former colleagues in the New York Congressional Delegation have made us their guests of honor at the Empire State's Annual Dinner. At my suggestion, they invited the Cabinet not only to meet the delegation, but also to meet a select group of New York notables."

"Jason," Elizabeth Anne wasn't quite through, "get Estelle and Conrad in here. Go over, in detail, what we know about each of our Secretaries. The Vice President and I will try to keep the Cabinet under wraps tonight."

        "Millie, tomorrow at noon, the Vice President will deliver to Congress this document," President Stanton handed his secretary the declaration. He gave her a moment. "It says that I am no longer fit to be President."

        "What! He's going to give this to Congress! He must be crazy!" Millie Wilson had trained herself to show no emotion. Normally she didn't. Her job was to record and occasionally execute the decisions of others. "I suppose he thinks he can do better," she scoffed.

        "That's it in a nutshell, Millie. Pardon my pun," the President laughed. "That's why we're meeting." Stanton paused and then looked directly at his secretary. "Millie, it's extremely important that everything we do is accurately recorded and portrayed. Our actions here will become precedents for the nation just as surely as the procedures used in the impeachment trial of Clinton were established by the precedents found one hundred and thirty years before in the impeachment of President Andrew Johnson."

        "I understand, sir." Millie had regained the composure her position required. "Please proceed."

        President Stanton was comfortable with his staff. They all knew, understood, and respected one another.

        "Mr. President," Virginia Hastings began, "it seems to me there is a baseline of information here that we should all understand. Very simply there are fourteen Cabinet Secretaries; eight constitutes a majority. We can assume, to keep a lid on their proposed coup, the Vice President's people recruited Cabinet Secretaries in a certain order."

        "Not alphabetical?" Howard quipped.

        Virginia ignored the interruption. "They started with those they believed to be most sympathetic to their cause and worked down the list until they reached the magic number. Apparently that achievement coincided with the State of the Union. They had only one misstep, Secretary Wirtz. Finally, we can also assume once they had eight, they shut down their recruiting rather than risk blowing their cover."

        "What's that mean, Virginia?" Crayton asked.

        "It means, even in the Vice President's calculations, the remaining six Cabinet members are not likely to be predisposed to the Vice President's position. Conservatively, we should be able to pick up at least four or five of them. And that means we need to turn two, or at most three, of the Secretaries who signed the declaration. Do that and we'll end this nightmare."

"I agree with Virginia," Howard stated. "But it's simpler than that. If we can turn just one of the eight, Roosevelt's going to have to recruit another Secretary from the bottom of their list, from among those least likely to be attracted to their cause."

"Good, that's good," Crayton interrupted. "If we can turn just one of their supporters, or even move him into the undecided camp, then they'd have to go after some tough targets. That's dangerous. They could overreach, make some mistakes, serious mistakes that could scuttle the coup."

"Whom should we go after?" Lincoln asked.

"We do have to move quickly," the President stated. "Look at the signatories. Let's go through them. Who can we convert, Crayton?"

Crayton leaned forward in his chair holding a copy of the declaration. "The one that surprises me, or at least disappoints and concerns me the most, is Aaron Chadwick. He's a wonderful leader. If we could turn him around, it would be over."

Aaron Chadwick, Secretary of the Interior, was the brightest star in the Stanton Cabinet. He was highly regarded by his colleagues and in fact by the President and his staff. While he reserved judgment and held his own counsel, once Secretary Chadwick made a decision, he was a powerful advocate. His not so secret ambition was to be on the Supreme Court. As a young man fresh out of law school he had clerked for Associate Justice John Paul Stevens. He loved the court and counted several justices as good friends. Given his legal training, reputation, respect for procedure, and passion for fairness, he was an obvious candidate for a future appointment. Strangely, given his reticence and aversion to sound bites, he was a media favorite.

"Chadwick is my biggest disappointment, too," the President stated. "I'd love to talk to him. You know, I think he tried to warn me, but he never talked to me about his decision. That's not like him. It's got to make him uncomfortable. I don't think I can change his mind, but I'm sure he'd hear me out and if I could plant some doubts, he'd reconsider. Changing his mind is not beneath him. He's more wedded to the truth than consistency. If nothing else, I believe I could learn a great deal from him. He's a straight shooter."

"Okay, Chadwick's on my list. Let's move on," Stanton directed. "What do you think about Collier?"

"You know," Crayton began, "a Republican at Defense is normally good cover for a Democrat in the White House, but Secretary Collier has been a thorn in your side from the start. He's rarely been with you and recently he's been all but disloyal."

"I should have demanded his resignation after the budget review," Stanton grumbled. "He not only challenged our priorities, he was damn insulting."

"What are you talking about?" Lincoln insisted.

"At the Defense Department's budget review, just before the State of the Union, Secretary Collier described me as 'a dangerous Pollyanna,'" President Stanton answered. "He apologized later."

"Ya, in private," Crayton noted. "His comments were public, his apology private. I'm afraid Marc Collier's policy differences with you, sir, are so great he'll never be brought around. You shouldn't waste your time."

"You're right," Stanton agreed.

"How about Fong?" Virginia asked. "He's been with us since California."

"Another Republican," Lincoln said as though that explained everything.

"You don't see Binder's name here. He's a Republican," Howard observed.

"He's where he wants to be. I don't think Fong is. Treasury's a stepping-stone to big money on Wall Street. Secretaries of Education don't go anywhere. Maybe Mr. Lee Fong went fishing for an appointment with a future," Crayton speculated.

"Lee's smart, but you're right – he's always had his own agenda," the President stated. "Nevertheless, I think I should talk to him. We have a history."

"Okay, you're going to talk to Chadwick and Fong. How about Kelly and Reynolds?" Virginia asked.

"There's no point in doing one without the other," Howard noted.

"I don't think there's any point in talking to either one," Lincoln stated. "They march in lock step to a different drummer. I don't even recognize the tune, much less the drummer."

"Lincoln's right," Crayton agreed. "I don't know what Reynolds wants, but Kelly would insist on a pass from Justice and you won't get one without the other. You don't want to go there. The word from Justice is Kelly's problems aren't going to go away until he does. And I mean for a long, long time, jail time."

"There's supposed to be a lid on that investigation, Crayton. What goes?" the President asked.

"We have friends at Justice that don't want you backing Kelly too enthusiastically," Crayton answered. "They didn't say much, honestly, just enough to keep us out of trouble," he added.

"You'd think Justice would know better. Telling us anything could get us in more trouble than telling us nothing, but that's not our concern today, is it? Do we have any friends at Housing?" the President asked.

"I think Helen Ramirez is your best shot. She doesn't have an agenda." Lincoln knew the Secretary of Housing and Urban Development from his days as a press secretary for the Department. "She's a civil servant in the best traditions, rose through the ranks. She has expertise, but she doesn't have an agenda. Helen respects elections and political leadership. Her only concern will be your competence and the nation's welfare. You can address those."

"You're right," the President was upbeat. "Helen could be our break."

"Since we're talking about women, how about Charlene Tuckman?" Virginia asked. "Women put you in office, maybe they can keep you there."

"Even in a nursing home I'd still be a father figure to the women of America," Stanton laughed. "Unfortunately that won't help me with the Secretary of Energy. I may be wrong, but the Charlene I know is hell-bent to be the first woman vice president. She wanted the appointment when Mathew died. For her, I'm not just over the hill; I'm irrelevant, a lame duck. Roosevelt's her best shot and she knows it."

"You're right, sir," Crayton nodded. "Secretary Pruett showed some restraint; but Charlene was shameless in her pursuit of the office. I could tell tales."

"Another time, Crayton," Stanton smiled. "There are ladies present."

"You haven't considered the Secretary of Agriculture," Millie stated, looking at her notes. "It's not my place, but I think Mr. Kruegman is truly an honorable man."

"I think you're right, Millie," President Stanton sighed. "Having Harold Kruegman and Aaron Chadwick join the Vice President hurts because I respect them both. I want to meet with Harold, too."

"Mr. President, I don't think you have time," Virginia reviewed her notes. "Thus far, you'll be meeting with Secretaries Chadwick, Fong, and Ramirez. Add Kruegman to the list and you're well into tomorrow afternoon. Additionally, you know you also need to at least touch base with the six non-signers. They need to be told to sit tight until you have a chance to meet with them."

"Maybe the time constraints aren't as tight as we think," the President stated. "We know tomorrow noon the Vice President is going to deliver his declaration to Congress that I am no longer fit to be President. Immediately thereafter, I'm expected to declare I am fit. We also know, as soon as he can after that, the Vice President will want to reaffirm his declaration. But listen, after his initial Declaration, we control the clock. I can wait a few hours, even longer. I am going to talk to these Secretaries and then when I'm damn good and ready I'll tell Congress I'm fit to serve out my term."

"Of course, it's so simple," Crayton exclaimed. "There's a down side, I suppose. The longer you wait to respond, the longer Acting President Roosevelt goes unchallenged. People may think you can't get your act together or don't really want the job, but if we can beat the news cycle we're home free. We've got at least five more hours. That helps, but we've still got to move fast."

"Then it's agreed," the President summarized "we'll move as fast as we can, but we don't go back to Congress until we've had a breakthrough. Millie, get me Aaron Chadwick."

The Empire State's Annual Dinner was held at the National Press Club's ballroom. In an innovative move, The New York State legislature sponsored the event and funded it generously. They hoped it would unify their Congressional delegation and make it more effective in representing and promoting the State's interest in Congress and with the Executive Departments. Drawing upon New York State's musical and culinary resources, the dinner had become one of the gala events of the Washington social season. Invitations were highly coveted.

William Butler Roosevelt, Vice President of the United States, and Elizabeth Anne Roosevelt were greeted like stars at a Broadway opening. They were among the last to arrive and spoke only briefly to newsmen. Roosevelt ignored several pointed questions concerning the President's health, and spoke only of the special place in his heart for the people of New York. Elizabeth Anne smiled, waved and said only how much they were looking forward to the evening. Before entering the ballroom, the Roosevelts were announced to the other guests. As they were escorted to the head table they received a standing ovation.

Over the course of the next twenty minutes the ballroom slowly organized itself like an orchestra warming up for the overture. Guests, secretly celebrating their own presence at such an august gathering, delighted in the company they were keeping and readied themselves for a wonderful evening. The distinguished, of course, kept their proper places while waiters, wine stewards, and "climbers" moved from table to table. The latter certified their success by being seen as widely as possible. Their narcissism, already burning out of control, was fed by overhead screens that replayed the grand entrances of their fellow notables. Above the din, snippets of their comments to the press could be heard.

A sea of people saw the head table as a distant island for the chosen few. An inconspicuous cordon of Secret Service agents made them almost unapproachable. For Elizabeth Anne, it was a splendid isolation. She watched the crowd and talked casually with Mark O'Brien, New York's senior Senator. O'Brien sat to her left. To her right, Elizabeth Anne knew, was the next President of the United States.

"Isn't that Mrs. Chadwick?" Senator O'Brien asked indicating an attractive woman appearing on the overhead screen with a much younger man. "Who's the fellow?"

Elizabeth Anne looked at the screen in time to see Sharon Chadwick, Secretary Chadwick's wife, maneuvering in line to be "ambushed" by Peter Wallace of ABC's Washington affiliate, WGET.

"She looks like a woman with a mission," Elizabeth Anne whispered to the Senator as she looked at the screen.

"Mrs. Chadwick, you're looking forward to the evening?" Wallace had been asking a variation of this question since WGET's live coverage began. He extended his microphone to her and tried to look interested in her reply.

"Oh yes, Peter. This is always a wonderful evening. The Secretary and I had such a lovely time last year; I can't say how much he'll miss not being here, tonight." Sharon Chadwick begged for the follow-up.

Wallace nodded appropriately, but appeared distracted as he tried to spot his next celebrity. Returning his attention to Sharon Chadwick, he adjusted his earpiece in time to hear control's cue: "And where is the Secretary tonight?"

"And where is Secretary Chadwick this evening?" he asked.

"Unfortunately, Peter, at the last minute, the Secretary was called to the White House, so my escort tonight is our eldest boy, David. He's on leave from the Navy. Nathan, our youngest is with his grandmother tonight."

"Good to meet you, David," Wallace shook hands with the strapping young man and then turned back to Mrs. Chadwick. "It looks to me like the Chadwick family has solid bench strength. Thank you for stopping by. Have a lovely evening."

"Oh Christ," Elizabeth Anne spoke softly to no one. Exercising considerable control she smiled at the C-Span camera that was permanently trained on the head table and turned toward her husband. "Bill," she touched his sleeve, "Aaron Chadwick isn't here this evening. He was called to the White House." Her whisper was an accusation.

"I told you Stanton would fight us," he replied with a mandatory smile.

"You didn't offer him the Supreme Court, did you?" she hissed.

The Julliard String Quartet began its program with Mendelssohn's Quartet in D Major, Opus 44. "No Dear, I didn't." Roosevelt took a deep breath and tried for patience. "It's not relevant. The only issue is the competence of President Stanton. It most certainly is not who will be appointed to fill the next Supreme Court vacancy."

Elizabeth Anne strained to hear her husband's "measured" response.

"The issue, you pompous ass, is who will be the next President of the United States." She turned abruptly toward Senator O'Brien and joined in the applause for the Quartet. "Aren't they just marvelous?"

Initially, Roosevelt was amused. He was no longer surprised or shocked by his wife's intensity. He squeezed her hand playfully under the table and learned they were having more than a little spat as she jerked free. Her silence was becoming quite annoying. Passing time, Roosevelt wandered about his mind concluding at one point the Empire State's Annual Dinner was aptly named, not only for its host, but also for its length. The evening dragged on and on. He fiddled with his dinner and studied the program like a boy in church trying to calculate when he would again be free. When the Julliard finally began Beethoven's Quartet in E minor, Opus 59, No 2, Roosevelt called for their limousine.

As they pulled away from the lights at National Press Club, they spoke the words they had rehearsed in silence.

"Bill, you are right, the issue is not about a Supreme Court appointment, but it is also not about your honor. It is about the future of this nation and who will be in charge of that future. You and I honestly believe President Stanton is incompetent and the nation is therefore at risk. Very simply you must decide what you are willing to do for the good of the country."

"I'm sorry, Elizabeth Anne, but that's what you don't understand or won't accept. I have made that decision. I decided early on that I would do everything in my power to make my colleagues in the Cabinet understand that President Stanton is no longer competent to serve as President, but nothing more. I will not deal with any extraneous issues, just the President's competence. To do otherwise is to begin a bidding war that in no way serves the interest of this nation."

"That's all well and good, but the Cabinet is composed of men and women who are mere mortals." She resisted saying, "unlike you." "Do you think the President's men are above a bidding war to stay in power?" She paused, hoping to give him time for thought and then continued softly. "Dear, you've said many times what an excellent choice Secretary Chadwick would be to fill the next vacancy on the Supreme Court. That hasn't changed, but it could tip the balance for or against you. Crayton will use it. Chadwick's a leader. You can't afford to lose him."

"Chadwick is a leader," the Vice President agreed, falling silent as he tried to second-guess what rules, if any, would govern the President and his men.

As they approached home, Elizabeth Anne took Roosevelt's hand and suggested that she'd go on alone to pick up Jimmy. Roosevelt agreed. The last person he wanted to see tonight was James Croft.

Commander James Croft's Washington estate was two miles from the Naval Observatory off Nebraska Avenue near Tenleytown, the highest point in the District. Elizabeth Anne Roosevelt arrived late. She was obviously in a foul mood.

"What's the matter?" Croft asked.

"Cut the crap, Dad. You know very well what's the matter." Elizabeth Anne's frustration had reached a boiling point. "If you don't, I'm afraid your snitch is grossly overpaid."

"Snitch? What's gotten into you, Elizabeth Anne? What are you talking about?"

"It's eleven o'clock," she sneered. "Surely Hodge's faxed you his daily digest."

"Is that it?" Croft asked incredulously. "You're upset because Hodges and I talk. We're old friends, for Christ sake!"

"Old friends, my ass. He's been your paid mole in my household since William and I moved to Washington."

Elizabeth Anne paused, stared at her hands, and visibly softened. "That's not it. That's not it at all. I'm sorry, Dad, I'm just ready to explode. We're so close, so close, but we could blow it. Tonight was just awful. William wants to be President, but he won't pay the price. He doesn't understand he's got to fight for it."

"I don't need a report from Hodges to tell me that," he laughed. "I've seen and heard it for myself. Your husband wants to be President, but he doesn't want to dirty his hands. I had to bite my tongue this afternoon; you were there. But this is nothing new, Elizabeth Anne, William is William. What happened tonight?"

"He's so pigheaded," Elizabeth Anne complained. "For years he's said, time and time again, to anyone who would listen that Chadwick should be on the Supreme Court, but now when he needs his support will he tell him? Oh no, that would be wrong. Our William will speak only of the competence of Stanton, nothing more. What a crock."

"Why are you worried about Chadwick?" Croft asked. "He's with us. He signed the Declaration."

"Secretary Chadwick missed the dinner tonight," Elizabeth Anne was still agitated. "His wife 'let it slip' that he had been called to the White House."

"So they're already working our list?" Croft asked. "They started tonight, with Chadwick," she answered. "Do you think that the President's men will miss the chance to stroke that monstrous ego? I'm sure they've already told him he's their only choice to fill the next vacancy on the Supreme Court."

"The problem is Chadwick has real influence with the rest of the Cabinet," Elizabeth Anne continued. "If we lose him, we lose everything."

"Then we won't lose him," Croft insisted. "Tomorrow at eleven you're meeting with the signers, first as a group, and then individually."

"Hodges does give a complete report," Elizabeth Anne teased gently.

"You've got to be in on Chadwick's meeting with the staff, Elizabeth Anne. He's got to know that if he's on our team, he's on his way to the Supreme Court. And if he's not, if he's a turncoat, he's got to know he's going straight to hell. This is hardball like he's never seen before. We've come too far. This is the presidency. A three trillion-dollar budget is at stake. We're playing for keeps. He's got to know that."

"I'll be there," Elizabeth Anne agreed. "When I'm through, Chadwick will believe William signed off on the whole package. I'll make sure of that."

"You've got another job. After the meeting, you've got to make the decision. Croft spoke in shorthand that needed no explanation. Elizabeth Anne was not just his daughter and heir. They were in business together and they were cut from the same cloth. "I can take care of it, make it look like an accident, but it's your call. If he's with us we don't touch him. If he's not, or even if he's a wild card, he's gone."

"If it's a go, when can it happen?" Elizabeth Anne questioned.

"Earlier is better, but it's got to be within four days," Croft answered.

"How can I let you know?"

"I'll start setting things up now. The team will be on standby tomorrow morning. After you meet with Chadwick tomorrow, you'll know what needs to be done. Give me a call. If we've got a job to do, just tell me you'd like me to drop by for Jimmy. Got it?"

"Sure," Elizabeth Anne responded. "That'll work. That's good."

"We'll do what we have to, Hon; Stanton's not going to beat us."

"You know, Dad, there are a lot of factors that argue for a hit. If the number of Cabinet Secretaries drops, from fourteen to thirteen, then the number of Cabinet cosigners we need on the declaration drops from eight to seven. We get two birds with one stone." Elizabeth Anne was nothing if not analytical.

Croft thought back to James Jr. He had been such a weakling, a drug-abusing coward. He wondered if she had been as analytical then as now. She was truly his daughter. He couldn't dispute her logic, but there were not just two birds for one stone, there were three: Once in office, after they explained to the good "President Roosevelt" how he came to be President, he would be theirs. Commander Croft could not contain his pride, "Elizabeth Anne you and I are going to make history. Nothing can stop us."

"I love you too, daddy."

CHAPTER ELEVEN:

AARON CHADWICK

7:00 P.M., Wednesday, January 24th.

Aaron Chadwick envied his wife. While she was on her way to a gala evening at the Empire State's Annual Dinner, he was on his way to the White House. He had no doubt what was on the President's mind.

Secretary Chadwick had been a holdout for the President. He had resisted repeated overtures to invoke the Twenty-Fifth Amendment until the State of the Union.

For the Chadwicks, President Stanton was a dear family friend. In many ways Andrew Stanton reminded Aaron of his father. That was especially true as the President struggled to survive Danny's death. Jacob Chadwick had lost his wife, Gloria, three years earlier. He too could not be consoled. Time did not heal all wounds. Aaron had watched his father's grief slowly destroy him. At the end of a year Jacob Chadwick was disoriented, confused, and clinically depressed. To Aaron, President Stanton seemed to be on that same road.

The most difficult personal decision Aaron Chadwick had ever made was to insist his father give up his home and move to an assisted living facility. It had been the right decision. His father was doing a little better.

The most difficult political decision Secretary Chadwick had ever made was to sign the declaration stating President Stanton was no longer able to discharge the powers and duties of his office. The verdict was still out on that decision.

"Aaron, thank you so much for coming in. Do sit down. I won't keep you long." President Stanton was strangely at ease.

"President Stanton, I'm so sorry...," Secretary Chadwick began

"There's no need, no need for that, Aaron," Stanton interrupted. "You did what you believed was right. I know that and I respect that. The fact of the matter is after Danny died, I gave you, and the others, plenty of cause to question my ability."

"Mr. President, my decision to sign the declaration was the most difficult I've ever made. You must believe my only concern was for the welfare of our nation.

"I know it was, Aaron, but you're not out of the woods yet," the President smiled. "That's why I needed to talk to you. Tomorrow after the Vice President delivers his declaration to Congress, I will personally deliver my rebuttal. At that point either you'll reconsider your position and decide that I have the ability to complete my term or you'll reaffirm your declaration and the issue will go to Congress. As a respected leader in the Cabinet your decision will influence a number of Secretaries. You have a heavy responsibility."

"I gather you're not going quietly into the night?"

"No, I will not," the President replied. "My motives are the same as yours, Aaron. I have no hidden agenda. I love this country. If I thought I couldn't handle this job, I'd step down. I don't know whether you know this, but I considered it in August. Maybe then, right after Danny's death, I should have, but not now, Aaron, not now."

"You think your difficulties are behind you?"

The President stood and picked up the photograph of Danny and the girls he kept on his desk. A moment later he looked up and spoke softly and directly to his friend. "I'll always miss Danny, Aaron, just like your dad will always miss Gloria, but I'm not Jacob. I need you to remember that and judge me as you see me."

"I did think you and my dad were very much alike," Secretary Chadwick stated.

"We are, but we're not twins. When your folks retired they not only sold their business, they sold their home and went on the road. Together they were fearless." The President paused. "It's true, Danny was the center of my universe; but for your dad, Gloria was the universe. When she died, he had nothing else. That's not true for me. It was Danny who insisted I run for a second term. We made promises. With her help I won that election. The people entrusted me with this job. I have work to do"

"But can you still do the work?" Aaron probed.

"You've got the right question, Aaron. It's the only question. Please, please remember that. The question is not who will make the better president, although I believe I would. The question is simply whether I am competent to do this job. If I am, then the Constitution directs you to respect the sanctity of my election and let me complete my term."

"What about the State of the Union?" Aaron asked.

Again the President smiled. "I had a flashback, a very vivid memory. It was regrettable and I embarrassed myself. On Friday I'll tell the American people my loss has never affected my judgment concerning their future. Then I'll ask for understanding. I'm sure they will respond positively. They have vivid memories of Danny, too. If anything, our memory of her, acts as a North Star, a moral compass for the nation. I think they'll understand, don't you?"

"I'm sure they'll want to, Mr. President. So do I, but what we all saw was still very disturbing."

"I understand, Aaron." Secretary Chadwick was making no commitments. "All I ask of you is to reconsider your position, make a decision, and play the leadership role that the rest of the Cabinet has come to expect."

"On that you have my word," Aaron responded.

The President shook Secretary Chadwick's hand and guided him toward the door. "Actually, Aaron, I have one additional request. It's very important. Call it a Presidential directive, perhaps my last. Whether this all results in my removal or retention, the nation will need a complete record of your decision making. I'd ask you to include not only our discussion here tonight, but those that are sure to follow. I'll do the same."

"I'll do my best, Mr. President. Is that all, sir?"

"Yes, Aaron, thank you again for coming in."

"Good night, Mr. President."

"Good night, Aaron."

Millie Wilson was on the phone when Aaron Chadwick left the Oval Office. "I know it's important, Lincoln. I know...I know what you've got. Yes...Yes, you've made it perfectly clear, but Jean Thorn is still holding for him. I know he'd want to talk to her."

Secretary Chadwick couldn't help but wonder what the President's press secretary had that was so important. Chadwick had an awesome duty. He wished for an easy answer. Lincoln had to be working on the press release to accompany the President's declaration of fitness.

Millie put her hand over the receiver, "Good night, Secretary Chadwick."

"Good night, Millie."

"Yes, he's leaving right now. Lincoln, I'll tell the President he can't be long...Just get it set up and I'll send him down. Should I call Crayton?"

Lincoln's office in the West Wing was on Aaron's way out. As he approached he heard President Stanton at the end of his seventh "State of the Union." He slowed, not too obviously, and looked at his watch. He could hear excited voices.

"There! There! Stop yours. Now, rewind this one...Stop...No forward... Right where the applause begins. Ya, right there. Look at that!"

"Jesus, they're identical...Everything."

"Look at Danny here at the sixth. Now Elizabeth Anne the other night."

"I can't believe it. She could be her twin. Look at the dress. Her hair. Christ! Even the necklace."

"That's not all. Run them both together."

"My God! You've got to be kidding. It looks like their lip-syncing."

"Anybody think that could be a coincidence?"

Aaron had heard enough. He didn't need to see the tapes. He needed to think.

The President arrived late but on the heels of his chief of staff. Just off the phone with Jean Thorn, he was obviously upbeat.

"What took you so long?" asked an excited Lincoln. "I sent everyone else home, they wanted to stay, but I thought we should do this in private."

"Is that the way you address the President of the United States and his chief of staff, Mr. Smith?" Crayton asked mildly amused.

"Obviously my days are numbered," the President joked. "And here Millie had convinced me that Lincoln had the miracle elixir that was going to save my Presidency."

"Did she tell you?" Lincoln asked.

"No, she just said I was to report to you, in your office, immediately. No respect there either, I'm afraid. I came on the run," the President laughed.

"I'm sorry, Mr. President," Lincoln toned

"Well, can you?" the President asked.

"Can I what, sir?" Lincoln asked.

"Save my Presidency, Lincoln. Save my Presidency."

"I'm not sure I can do that, sir, but then again... this might. It just might." Lincoln responded.

"Well don't keep us in suspense, Lincoln," Crayton urged. "You have our attention. What have you got?"

"A little background," Lincoln suggested. "You see I was trying to see, excuse me, sir, what set you off at the State of the Union. It was such a magnificent speech and you delivered it beautifully. It was obvious to everyone that you were in command, speaking directly from your heart. You were connected with the American people and they were connected with you. But then you saw Danny and even spoke to her and it was over. Not just over, but destroyed. You had taken us all to such heights and then you dropped us. Just eloquent ravings."

"Come on, Lincoln," an exhausted Crayton was losing patience. "What have you got?"

"No, go ahead, Lincoln, I'm interested," the President intervened. "In fact, I'm fascinated. I believe you had just arrived at the point where my "State of the Union" had been outted as - what was it? Ah yes, the eloquent ravings of a madman. Please, go ahead."

"I'm sorry, sir. But you see I had to know what you had seen. And now I can tell you. You saw Danny. I've seen her too."

"What in the hell are you talking about, Lincoln?" Crayton was at the end of his rope.

"Look, look here," Lincoln directed their attention to two large pull down screens as he hit the play button on the control console. "That's Danny at last year's State of the Union address. See Vice President Thorn behind you there, Mr. President. Watch, it'll just take a moment. This comes toward the end of your speech."

President Stanton, Crayton Langford, and Lincoln Smith watched the First Lady stand, applaud, and blow a kiss to her husband as he received a standing ovation from the United States Congress. She looked so beautiful, so healthy, and alive. She was obviously celebrating her husband's triumph. As the applause continued, she waved again, and then again she blew him a kiss.

"I don't know how much more of this I can take, Lincoln," the President interrupted. His voice was choking and he made a preventive swipe at welling tears. "You do have a point?"

"Yes, sir, I do." Lincoln stopped the first tape and started a second. "Please look at the second screen," he directed.

Again President Stanton, Crayton Langford, and Lincoln Smith stared at the First Lady standing, applauding, and blowing a kiss to her husband as he stood before the United States Congress.

"The focus is pretty bad," Crayton commented. "What's the point?"

"Let me sharpen the focus," Lincoln said. "Please look again."

"Oh, my God," the President was stunned.

"What is this, Lincoln?" Crayton demanded.

"That, sir, is Elizabeth Anne Roosevelt as she appeared last Tuesday at the President's State of the Union."

"How did you do that, Lincoln?" President Stanton asked. "Is it doctored?"

"No, sir, it is not."

"Altered in anyway?" Crayton pursued.

"No, that's the tape, just as it was recorded Tuesday night."

"Any explanation?" the President questioned.

"Only two that I can think of, Mr. President, either this was a most unlikely coincidence or it was a deliberate premeditated impersonation of your dead wife."

"And you believe the 'why' is obvious?" Crayton asked.

"Yes, I do. I believe this charade was a cynical attempt to produce a public presidential flashback as a prerequisite for invoking the Twenty-Fifth Amendment." Lincoln was emphatic.

"Well, it worked, didn't it?" a temporarily contrite President Stanton asked.

"What can we do with this?" Crayton asked. "Can we use it?"

"I don't see how," Stanton responded. It hardly vindicates me. Everyone heard, saw. I spoke to Danny and she had been dead four months."

"Lincoln persisted, "But it unmasks them. Their motives aren't pure. They're power hungry, ready to do anything."

"I don't know about their motives, but their means are despicable," Crayton agreed.

"I still don't see how we can use this," the President stated.

"Discreetly," Lincoln commented. "Very discreetly."

"It would play well only to the congregation, the faithful," Stanton observed. "For me, it is both disillusioning and reassuring. I never would have suspected that Vice President Roosevelt would resort to such tactics, but now that I do, I'm ready to defend my Presidency with every ounce of energy I possess."

"It helps to know what we're up against," Crayton spoke resolutely. "There may come a time when we can use these tapes. They could energize our supporters and perhaps even convert a fence sitter."

"Perhaps," the President acknowledged. "Perhaps. I don't like war analogies, Lincoln, but let's just think of them as part of our arsenal."

"They'll be there, Mr. President. "I'll put it together." Lincoln was already thinking of several investigative reporters who would find the "coincidence" newsworthy.

"Thank you, Lincoln." The President moved toward the door.

"Yes sir. Good night, Mr. President."

"One more thing, Lincoln," President Stanton stood in the doorway, "I don't want them used without my authorization. Understood?"

"Yes, sir," Mr. President.

CHAPTER TWELVE:

PERSUASION

8:30 A.M., Thursday, January 25th.

Andrew Stanton was having his second cup of coffee. Despite all the turmoil surrounding his Presidency, he was comfortable with himself, almost happy. His conversation with Jean had been absolutely wonderful. They had been friends for over fifty years. When he was first in Congress, she was in charge of his Nashville office. That was nineteen fifty-six, he mused. They had shared so much and had so much in common.

Jean had called to tell him she was coming to Washington. His first response was to insist she stay at the White House. Then he found himself telling her everything, particularly that he might not be in the White House. He wasn't diplomatic, he wasn't presidential, and he wasn't guarded. He was himself and that was just the way she liked him. Maybe he sounded bitter, after all he spoke of treachery, betrayal, duplicity, and crushing disappointment, but Jean understood. She understood everything. She was his confidant, like Danny.

Jean not only reminded Stanton of Danny, she reminded him of Danny's words. At Mathew's funeral, as Danny struggled with her own cancer, she had asked Jean to be there for her "and especially for my Andy" when her time came. Jean assured him that she was there for him and would always be. She was coming to Washington next week. President Stanton was looking forward to her visit. It hardly seemed possible that Matthew had been dead almost a year now.

President Stanton was not looking forward to this day. He was meeting with Harold Kruegman, the Secretary of Agriculture at nine; Lee Fong, Secretary of Education at ten; and Helen Ramirez, Secretary of HUD at two. The American people had chosen him to be their President, but now, to stay in office, he had to win the approval of his own appointees, prove to them he was competent. It was exasperating. Worse, it was demeaning.

"We said we would insist that their private commitment be made public. That way they can't be retracted after a little presidential arm twisting." Elizabeth Anne quoted Jason Fields' briefing almost verbatim. She was arguing for the immediate delivery of the declaration to the Speaker of the House and the President Pro Tempore of the Senate. "We're ready. We need to do it now!"

"I said I'd give him until noon," the Vice President reiterated.

"For Christ's sake, Bill, he's already given you his answer. You said it yourself. He said 'Hell No!' What more do you need?"

"You're not listening, Elizabeth Anne. I gave him my word."

"Bill, if you screw this up... I swear."

"It's just three hours, Elizabeth Anne. It won't cost us a thing."

"Okay, okay. I hope you're right."

Andrew Stanton met with Harold Kruegman privately. The President had decided that he alone would make his case to the Cabinet Secretaries. No one could do it for him and no one could do it as well. It was, after all, his competence that was in question.

Unfortunately, the Secretary of Agriculture had made up his mind. Harold Kruegman came from a large family farm in south central Nebraska. Once his service in the administration was over, he expected his children would put him out to pasture just as he had his father, and his father had his grandfather. It was the natural order of things.

"Mr. President, you've done a marvelous job. The country is strong and united. The economy is robust. Even our farm families are sharing in the prosperity. Your place in history is assured."

"Harold, I was elected to serve a four year term. I am perfectly capable of fulfilling that commitment and meeting my responsibilities. When Danny died I was devastated, but I never let it effect my decisions. You know that. We pushed the Fairness to Farm Families Act through Congress just after Danny died."

"Andrew, you can be remembered as a great president if you end it now. Roosevelt will be just a caretaker. He can handle that."

"Harold, this nation will not fly on autopilot. I'm not ready to be remembered. I have work to do. We made commitments."

And so it continued for nearly an hour. Both men were polite, but neither listened. Harold Kruegman was a good man. He had not come to his decision lightly and would not be dissuaded.

As with Secretary Chadwick, the President concluded the meeting by asking Secretary Kruegman to make a complete record of their conversation. They agreed on one thing: the precedent they were creating should be well understood.

The President walked Kruegman to the door and returned to his desk. The President hit the intercom. "Millie, come on in here, please. I need to summarize my meeting with Secretary Kruegman before Fong arrives."

"I'm sorry, Mr. President, Secretary Fong called while you were with Kruegman. He cancelled his ten o'clock."

"What? He cancelled?? Did he offer an explanation?

"No, sir, none. He did say he was terribly sorry."

"Sorry is right, my god!" the President snapped. "That's just great. I guess we'll have time to write that summary, Millie, as well as my obituary. Come on in here, please. I need to see a friendly face."

William Butler and Elizabeth Anne Roosevelt greeted each of the eight Cabinet Secretaries as Hodges brought them to the library. The atmosphere was unavoidably conspiratorial. No one was interested in the light brunch available at the far end of the room. While Lee Fong cornered Brad Curtis, most of the Secretaries crowded about Aaron Chadwick and Harold Kruegman. They spoke in hushed tones. Conrad Tate and Estelle Cohen moved quickly to squelch any group dynamics.

"May I have your attention, please?...May I have your attention, please?" Jason Fields repeated. "We need to get started. Would you all please take your seats? We need to get started."

William and Elizabeth Anne moved from the entryway to the large oval table that filled the center of the library. The Secretaries followed. They were powerful men and women with distinct personalities and concerns. Several were hardcore partisans; some were principled. A few were almost selfless, while some were selfish. While some feared being left behind, others wanted to be left alone. Some had policy concerns, while others had personal agendas. Most were ambitious. All were individuals. None could be taken for granted.

"Ladies, gentlemen, please be seated. Thank you for coming." Vice President Roosevelt stood before his colleagues. "In one hour, at noon, I will deliver our declaration to the Congress. Yesterday, I informed the President I had your support and suggested he consider resigning. While he was adamant that he would not, I gave him until noon today to reconsider."

That the President might not resign was news to several Cabinet members. For HUD Secretary Helen Ramirez it was a bombshell. Elizabeth Anne had convinced her that Stanton was exhausted and wanted to resign. The President, she explained, needed the declaration to convince his staff he had no other choice. She felt betrayed and stupid.

Roosevelt could see Helen simmering and felt she might not be alone. He made a mental note and continued. "Many of us were convinced it would never come to this, but at this hour I am sorry to tell you we have heard nothing from the President. Rather we are aware, as you are, that he has spoken with Secretaries Chadwick and Kruegman."

"Mr. Vice President," Secretary Kruegman spoke up. "I came directly here from a meeting with the President. I can assure you he has no intention of resigning. He stated emphatically to me, he intends to challenge our declaration with his own declaration of fitness."

"Thank you, Harold." Roosevelt looked around the table at the Cabinet members. "You all understand, of course, that constitutionally this requires that we resubmit to the Congress our belief that President Stanton is no longer competent to exercise the powers and duties of his office. We have four days to do that and I suggest we use that time to solicit support from the remainder of the Cabinet."

"Is there any chance of that?" Secretary of Defense Marc Collier   asked.

"Oh yes, Marc. Definitely!" Roosevelt answered. "The question has never been put to them. As soon as we had a bare majority we quit. If we got just one or two additional Secretaries our position with both the public and the Congress would be greatly strengthened."

"But it has to be done in four days?" Collier questioned.

"William," Elizabeth Anne stood, "you'd better be going."

"I'm afraid you're right." The Vice President answered slowly, loading his briefcase. The weight of what he was about to do was oppressive. This was his Rubicon. He looked up at them as he snapped shut his briefcase. "Before I go, I want to thank you all for your courage and patriotism. We have taken this stand together and together we can prevail. I want you to remember, if any of you waver, you put all of us at risk. We've made our decision. It's the right decision. It's the right decision for America. Let us persevere to our goal. God help us and God help America if we fall short."

The library was quiet as Vice President Roosevelt walked to the door. It stayed that way until Elizabeth Anne broke the silence. "Secretary Collins, you asked if our recruitment of the remainder of the Cabinet had to be completed in four days. The answer is, 'yes it does.'"

"The clock starts when President Stanton submits his challenge to our declaration," Jason Fields added. "After that it will be up to Congress."

"Congress will support us," Elizabeth Anne assured them confidently. "They'll listen to the polls and support us."

"Our job today is to make certain it goes to Congress," Jason stated. "While the Vice President is meeting with Speaker Mathis and Senator Albert, we'll go ahead with the individual meetings we've scheduled with each of you."

"We have four objectives for these meetings," Elizabeth Anne stated. "First and most important, we need to have a frank exchange with you. We have to know your hopes, fears, and frustrations if we are to make you feel positive and secure about your place in the new Roosevelt administration."

Not one of the Cabinet Secretaries broke into a grin. They were all serious and restrained, but the opportunists among them recognized that the bidding war had just begun. For the first time all were equal. Each had one vote. They were being asked to reenlist. Bonuses would surely be offered. From their perspective, the President's decision to challenge the declaration was a blessing. The presidency of the United States would be contested. Their support was now critical. The bidding would, indeed, be spirited. While there were limited sellers, the buyers had unlimited resources.

The window of opportunity would be open at least four days, but no more. The fact that most members of the Cabinet would make their decisions based on what they thought was best for the country, meant the opportunists could command a higher price. Still, the game was not without risk. They would have to play their cards right. If they sold to the highest bidder, who then lost, political oblivion or worse would surely follow. Only the winner would pay off. And he would certainly pay both the winners and the losers.

"Second," Elizabeth Anne continued, "we need to define your role with the balance of the Cabinet, the Congress and the media. You must be both comfortable and effective in that role. Third, we will work with you to insure that as a team we stay on message while giving you the latitude to speak honestly about your relationships with President Stanton and Vice President Roosevelt. Finally, we will establish a communication system that is both direct and secure. It must allow you and the Vice President to speak at anytime, night or day, until this issue is resolved."

"Does anyone have any questions?" Jason asked surveying the group. "No?...Okay, then, let's begin. Secretary Chadwick would you join Mrs. Roosevelt in the first reading room; Secretary Collier, you will be with Brad in the second room, the one on the left; and Helen, you and I will be in the reading room at the end of the hall. I'd like the rest of you to work with Estelle and Conrad on interview schedules and Q and A's."

CHAPTER THIRTEEN:

CAPITOL HILL

Noon, Thursday, January 25th.

The Vice President's limousine turned right on Massachu-setts Avenue and headed southeast toward the Capitol. Roosevelt sat alone in the back seat. He reviewed his press release and the talking points they had prepared for the News Hour, but found he couldn't concentrate. It was strange how out of sync he felt with the rest of the world.

The day was pleasant enough, a little warmer than usual, but nothing out of the ordinary. He missed the leaves. Washing-ton had such beautiful trees. Traffic was normal. If anything, he thought, it moved too fast. He had very little time. The joggers, shoppers, and sightseers were all out for the lunch hour. They didn't know; didn't suspect a thing. Yet here he was riding to the Capitol bearing two single sheets of paper that would make him the Acting President of the United States.

The leadership of the world's greatest superpower was about to change, without an election, without war, without an as-sassination or death or resignation, just the application of an un-used provision of the Constitution. It all seemed so implausible. What would people say: "Rules are rules, man has the winning hand?" Was the rule of law that powerful? Could we really be that civilized? Two and a half years ago one hundred and fifty million Americans had participated in the election of the President. Could nine unelected men and women overturn that decision?

Roosevelt thought he knew the answer. The American people would abide by the rule of law in this instance because they believed President Stanton needed to be replaced. They became believers watching Stanton at the State of the Union, seeing and hearing him speak to his dead wife. Many had seen it for them-selves, live and in person. All had seen it in a thousand replays.

What bothered the Vice President was the process. It was constitutional and it favored him, but it was moving so fast that the "peoples' will" would be done before it was half-baked. We're they really ready?

Roosevelt wanted to be elated, but he was not. He was certain the President had to go, but he had nagging doubts. If he were not personally involved he could trust his judgment. But Roosevelt knew he was driven by ambition and that ambition made him suspect his own motives and judgment. While politicians can rightfully be charged with pandering to the public, that pandering was nothing compared with what he experienced from Elizabeth Anne, his staff, and even family friends. It was so hard to know what was right.

There was no solution. He still had to act. Discounting his ambition and self interest as best he could, Roosevelt honestly believed the President could no longer lead the nation, much less the free world. He would proceed with a clear conscience. It just wasn't as satisfying as he had hoped.

Roosevelt knew only the broad outline of this drama had been written. The acts and scenes would be improvised. He'd be flying by the seat of his pants. It would be difficult. There would be a lot of pressure. He had to be guided by his principles.

Speaker Louis Mathis was an impressive man. His background as a professional athlete did not disguise his obvious intelligence. While he wore a Super Bowl ring, he was most proud of the Osborne Trophy he had won as a student athlete involved in community service. As a quarterback he had the spotlight and used it as spokesperson for various popular causes. His role model persona was never tarnished. Two years after retirement from the National Football League he ran for Congress. He won easily. Twenty-two years in Congress and he had never been seriously challenged.

Louis Mathis became Speaker of the House when Andrew Stanton became President. It was a hopeful time; both men seemed reasonable, and both promised, despite their partisan differences, to work together. In time, however, their institutional responsibilities as well as their partisan commitments drove them apart.

While Congressional Republicans still touted Louis as a potential candidate for president his reputation with the public at large had suffered with his service as the Speaker of the House. Leading the opposition to a popular president had cost him dearly. Today the slate would be wiped clean.

"Welcome, Mr. Vice President." Speaker Mathis greeted Roosevelt in the anteroom and escorted him into the Speaker's Conference Room. "I hope you don't mind, but in light of our impending responsibilities, I invited the leadership of both parties to receive the declaration."

"Not at all, Louis, I'm glad you did. It's entirely appropriate. In fact, you might suggest Senator Albert consider having the leadership of the Senate present when I deliver the declaration to him."

"I've already spoken to him," the Speaker responded.

Roosevelt moved slowly about the room speaking quietly to the Majority and Minority leaders, their Whips and the Chairman and ranking minority member of the House Judiciary Committee. This was a historic gathering. The participants were initiating a never before used Constitutional process that could remove and replace the president of the United States.

"Gentlemen, Ms. Roberts, please be seated." Speaker Mathis stood with the Vice President at the far end of the rectangular conference table facing the House leadership. "Mr. Vice President, you requested this meeting."

"Yes, Mr. Speaker, I did." The Vice President spoke formally, but without notes. "Mr. Speaker, in accordance with Section Four of the Twenty Fifth Amendment to the United States Constitution, it is with deep remorse and profound regret that I now deliver to you this written declaration that Andrew Holmes Stanton, President of the United States, is unable to discharge the powers and duties of his office. As required, the declaration is signed by me as Vice President and by a majority of the Cabinet. Within the hour I will deliver this same declaration to the President Pro Tempore of the Senate. At that time I shall immediately assume the powers and duties of the office as Acting President."

With the historical record complete, Roosevelt relaxed and spoke directly to the leadership of the House of Representatives. "Gentlemen, Ms. Roberts, this is a sad day." He paused. "I suspect it was inevitable that one day a president of the United States would be unable to complete his term. Our presidents are human, too. They grow old. They get tired. They can become ill and suffer tragic incapacitating losses. Four years is a long time. President Stanton has served this country well, but try as he might; he simply is no longer able to carry the burdens of his office. We are all aware of the danger. The people expect us to set aside our partisan differences. We must act together to end this crisis."

"Mr. Vice President, will President Stanton challenge your declaration?" Congresswoman Sierra Roberts chaired the powerful Judiciary Committee. If the issue came to Congress her committee would have a lead role in the House of Representatives.

"Ms. Roberts, last September when President Stanton's difficulties were not so widely known, he and I spoke privately about the wisdom of my assuming the duties of his office. We both concluded that the time was not right. From that experience in light of the State of the Union, I had hoped the President would respond favorably to the idea of resigning. I want you to know before coming to Congress, I went to the President and gently suggested he resign. I believed I made a persuasive case, but our meeting was not private. Crayton Langford, his chief of staff was present. When the President refused to resign, I showed him the declaration I've just given to the Speaker and asked him to reconsider." Roosevelt weighed his words carefully and concluded, "I'm afraid President Stanton is a captive of his staff. He has no choice, he will challenge this declaration."

"Mr. Roosevelt, would you support Congressional hearings to resolve this crisis?" Majority Leader Harrison Boggs rarely thought in terms other than partisan advantage. This was no exception.

"Harrison, that decision rests entirely with Congress. I can only say the country would be best served if this issue is resolved quickly and the procedure be seen as governed by only one issue and one concern, the competence of the President and the welfare of the country."

"Thank you, Mr. Vice President," Speaker Mathis cut off any additional questions. "I know you are scheduled to meet with the Senate leadership in just a few minutes. I want you to know that when you conclude there, the President Pro Tempore and I will host a joint press conference to discuss the constitutional foundation of this declaration. For my colleagues here let me thank you for delivering the declaration personally."

Senator Albert Frank from North Carolina was a spry eighty-eight years old. He had been a Republican since Strom Thurman led the Dixiecrats out of the Democratic Party in nineteen forty-eight. After Thurman's death he became the Republican Party's senior senator. As such when his party won control of the Senate at the last election he became the President Pro Tempore of the United States Senate.

Vice President Roosevelt met Senator Frank not in his office, but in the more spacious quarters assigned to Senator Charles Lynch, the Majority Leader. As in the House, the leadership of parties, as well as the chairperson and ranking member of the Senate Judiciary Committee, witnessed Roosevelt deliver his written declaration to the President Pro Tempore of the Senate that President Andrew Holmes Stanton, President of the United States, was no longer able to discharge the powers and duties of his office.

As a well-liked veteran of the Senate, Roosevelt was warmly received. Nevertheless the Vice President came away from the meeting convinced that the Senate leadership would push hearings that would consume most of the twenty-one days before allowing the issue to come to a vote. He understood the rationale, but it seemed so unnecessary since President Stanton had demonstrated his incompetence to both Houses of Congress at the State of the Union.

It was one forty-three p.m., January 25th. Vice President Roosevelt was now the Acting President of the United States.

CHAPTER FOURTEEN:

ROUND TWO

Noon, Thursday, January 25.

As Vice President Roosevelt was presenting the declaration to Congress, Elizabeth Anne and Jason Fields led his efforts to hold and expand their support in the Cabinet. They were in trouble. Shortly, the President would challenge the declaration and declare himself competent – forcing the Vice President to return to Capitol Hill and reaffirm that he and a majority of the Cabinet still believed President Stanton was unable to perform his duties.

"No, I'm not saying I made a mistake. But I am saying that President Stanton was quite impressive. He had had a long day, but appeared vigorous and very much in charge." Secretary Chadwick's summary of his meeting with the President was more than disquieting to Elizabeth Anne. It set off alarms. She couldn't tell if he were still for them or had turned against them. She had to find out. Maybe, she thought, he was just fishing, waiting for them to sweeten the pot.

"Aaron, you know no matter what Stanton said, you're burned with his administration. He's desperate. You must understand...," Elizabeth Anne was interrupted by an insistent knock at the conference room door.

"Excuse me, Elizabeth Anne, Secretary Chadwick." Jason Fields appeared business - like and professional, but Elizabeth Anne knew the interruption signaled a real emergency.

"What is it, Jason?" Her tone carried a significant amount of irritation to let Aaron Chadwick know she considered her meeting with him to be very important.

"I'm sorry, but I need to speak with you briefly. Could we have just a moment, Secretary Chadwick?" Jason persisted.

"Excuse me, Aaron, I'll ask Margaret to bring us some tea." Elizabeth Anne moved to the door and then turned back to Secretary Chadwick. "I won't be long. I promise." She smiled almost flirtatiously and closed the door.

"What the hell's going on?" she demanded.

"Helen Ramirez, she won't wait," Jason responded, moving Elizabeth Anne down the hall to the end conference room. "She believes she was misled. She's adamant. When she leaves here, she's going straight to the White House."

"Good God!" Elizabeth Anne took a deep breath and reminded herself that every battle worth winning is hotly contested. Helen Ramirez was a pious little pain in the ass. She was putting on her scarf when they entered the room.

"Helen, I'm so sorry. I don't know how we could have misled you, but I do apologize. Please give me just a moment; let's talk." Elizabeth Anne put her arm around Helen Ramirez and led her back into the room. "Jason, give us some privacy. We won't be long."

Helen Ramirez, Secretary of Housing and Urban Development, was barely five foot yet, as Jason Fields left the room, she stood tall and confronted Elizabeth Anne. "There was no misunderstanding, only deception and stupidity. You told me yourself that the President was all but a captive of his staff and supporters; that he wanted to resign. You even mentioned the President's daughters. I don't know how I could have been so stupid, but I assure you, Elizabeth Anne, I will not make the same mistake twice."

"Helen, I said I'm sorry. I don't know what I can do. I told you what I thought was the truth. I was either wrong or he changed his mind, but we both saw with our own eyes: President Stanton is no longer capable of doing his job."

"Danny and Andrew Stanton were deeply in love. Of course he made mistakes. The question is how is he now? I plan to find out for myself." Secretary Ramirez had no political ambitions. She was a civil servant, GS-16, filling a late term vacancy at Housing and Urban Development.

"The State of the Union was two days ago. The biggest mistake you could make is to think he has miraculously recovered. He hasn't. His staff wants him to hang on for obvious reasons. But you're a fool if you think they will forgive and forget. Sure, they'll want you back in the fold, but as soon as they feel secure you're gone. You burned your bridges with the Stanton administration, Helen. I warn you, don't do it with us! Do I make myself clear?"

"Elizabeth Anne, your meaning is unambiguous. Now, let me try to be just as clear. I admire your husband, Mr. Roosevelt, and I admire President Stanton. The American people elected President Stanton. If he is competent to serve, he should. If not, he should be replaced. I will interview the President this afternoon and make my own decision. I will inform him and then I will inform the Vice President. I will not lobby my colleagues, the Congress, or the American people. Good day, Mrs. Roosevelt." Helen Ramirez brushed by Elizabeth Anne and then Jason Fields.

Stunned, they stood silently listening to the click of Secretary Ramirez heels as she marched from the library.

"That little bitch may not know it," Elizabeth Anne hissed, "but she just bought the farm. Oh crap, I've got to get back to Chadwick."

"I just checked in with him. He's okay," Jason commented. "I'm sorry about Ramirez."

"Don't panic," Elizabeth Anne cautioned. "We're still in the driver's seat. There are fourteen Secretaries. We only need eight. Assuming Ramirez defects, we still have seven, just one short. I figure Wirtz is beyond reach, but that still says five are up for grabs."

"I think you're right about Secretary Wirtz," Jason agreed. "Do you want me in on Chadwick?"

"No, you take Kruegman." Elizabeth Anne directed. "I think he's solid."

Secretary Chadwick was looking out the window at the Naval Observatory grounds when Elizabeth Anne reentered the conference room. "Did you get some tea?"

"Yes, thank you," Aaron answered. "Margaret is a real sweetheart."

"Yes, she is." Elizabeth Anne hesitated. "Aaron, I don't really know where to begin...You said President Stanton was impressive last night. I believe you, but then you know he was not impressive the night before last. The presidency is not a part-time job. The enemies of the United States are on the job twenty-four hours a day, seven days a week."

"I haven't said I've changed my mind, Elizabeth Anne. I just need time to think. We're modifying the political system of the United States. The Twenty-Fifth Amendment tells us the vice president and a majority of the Cabinet are to make the decision on the president's competence. But our actions are setting the precedents on how that decision is to be made."

As Secretary Chadwick described his concerns he became more and more reflective. Anyone could have seen Elizabeth Anne's growing agitation, but Aaron Chadwick was totally preoccupied.

"We're doing exactly what the Constitution requires," Elizabeth Anne asserted. "What more could we do?"

"Excuse me, what?" Aaron asked.

"I asked, 'what more could we do?'"

"I'm sorry, Elizabeth Anne. I don't know yet, but it deserves our best thinking. Maybe the Cabinet should deliberate like a jury, sequestered from the President and Vice President. After all, they have an obvious conflict of interest."

"The Cabinet is not an impartial jury, Aaron. It can't be. Each and every Secretary has a stake in the decision they make. They win if they back a winner. They lose if they back a loser. It's a political process. The players guarantee that."

"I suppose you have a point," Aaron conceded.

"What you and the others must understand is you've made your choice. When you signed the original declaration you made your choice." Elizabeth Anne was back on message. "You've burned your bridges with one side and curried favor with the other. You'd have to be suicidal to switch now."

"I don't know, Elizabeth Anne. This decision is so incredibly important for the nation; certainly our individual interest should be put aside." The Secretary paused, looking at her. "But maybe you're right. Maybe that's impossible. We're all human."

Initially Elizabeth Anne had been put off by Aaron Chadwick's sanctimonious posturing. Now she understood it for what it was. Secretary Chadwick was trying to up the ante. He wasn't as sharp as he thought. He didn't realize she was already prepared to offer him the Supreme Court. How ironic Elizabeth Anne mused; he almost overplayed his hand.

"Aaron, as Jason stated, one of our goals today was to make sure that you felt positive and secure about your place in the new Roosevelt administration. Frankly, with you that's impossible." Elizabeth Anne paused to insure she had Secretary Chadwick's full attention: "Are you aware the Vice President has been lobbying the Stanton administration to put you on the Supreme Court?"

"No, I was not." Aaron was startled by this unexpected turn in the conversation.

"Obviously," Elizabeth Anne continued, "if he is President he doesn't have to lobby anyone but the United States Senate. Have you thought about your chances there?"

"What?" The question seemed incredulous to Aaron, but he couldn't deny his life long ambition. "I think I'd get a fair hearing."

"You'll be a shoo-in, Aaron," Elizabeth Anne laughed and lightly patted his hand. "Before we adjourn here I still need to know how to contact you day and night until we reaffirm the declaration. You have our number. That's a secure line. It will be manned twenty-four hours a day and those folks are under orders to put you through to the Vice President whenever you call."

"As I told you, Elizabeth Anne, I need time to think. Sharon, the kids, and I are going up to our cabin. It's just off the Skyline Drive near Luray, not far. We'll be back no later than Saturday noon. By that time I will have made my decisions."

"What decisions?" Elizabeth Anne question combined surprise with an unequivocal demand.

Aaron Chadwick looked directly at Elizabeth Anne and answered forthrightly. "As I indicated earlier; first, I intend to revisit my decision on President Stanton's competence and second, I'm weighing the propriety of hosting a meeting of the Cabinet."

"What in the world for?" Elizabeth Anne's tone was now cold and hard.

"I suspect there are many ways the Cabinet could go about determining the competence of the President. We're on the verge of adopting a precedent that has the Vice President and the President lobbying individual members of the Cabinet. That might not be the best way. As I suggested earlier, perhaps the Cabinet should sequester itself like a jury and try to reach a consensus. I know the

Constitution only requires a majority, but the closer we come to achieving consensus the greater the likelihood our decision will be accepted. If we have a badly split decision, it could tear the nation apart."

"God Dammit, Aaron, it's too late for that. We're halfway over Niagara Falls. You can't change the rules."

"Maybe it is too late. Maybe everyone's position has hardened. But even so, such a meeting might set a pattern for the future." Secretary Chadwick would not back down. "The Justices on the Supreme Court always strive mightily for more than a simple majority on critical issues. I think maybe we should do the same."

Elizabeth Anne fixed a steely glare on Secretary Chadwick. "Aaron, I'm warning you. This decision has been made. It's not up for negotiation. We will not allow it to be threatened by a rogue conference. Don't you understand? Think of your family. Forces beyond anyone's control have been unleashed. People are out on a limb. They will not allow it to be cut off by anybody. Period! Leave it alone, Aaron. Do you understand me?"

"I get your drift, Elizabeth Anne," he answered dryly.

The Presidential story broke as Secretary Helen Ramirez was riding to the White House. She didn't hear it; she saw it. All along her route people were congregating in groups that had no rhyme or reason. At crosswalks groups formed that ignored traffic signals and carried on quiet conversations. In front of a busy lunch hour grill, window shoppers, tourists, and professionals listened to a bicycle courier and then to two students with headphones. Just past Twentieth and Pennsylvania, Secretary Ramirez's driver swerved hard to the left as a large car spun out of a parking garage almost hitting them. The driver, a woman with graying hair wearing large glasses, had tears streaming down her face.

"John, let me hear the news."

Helen's driver turned on the radio to CNN's "All News All Day" station and joined the news in progress: "...Vice President William Butler Roosevelt assumed the position of Acting President at twelve thirty-three this afternoon. In a move forecast by much of the media after the State of the Union, Vice President Roosevelt and a majority of the Cabinet invoked the Twenty-Fifth Amendment to the Constitution of the United States and declared that President Andrew Holmes Stanton was no longer able to perform the powers and duties of his office. From the Capitol, Acting President Roosevelt told reporters when President Stanton refused to resign he, Roosevelt, had no other choice but to invoke the Twenty-Fifth Amendment.

Asked if he expected President Stanton would challenge the declaration, Acting President Roosevelt stated that that would be unwise and only prolong the national tragedy."

Secretary Ramirez arrived at the White House shortly after one o'clock. She dreaded her reception. As a career civil servant with no political agenda, she was unlike any other Cabinet Secretary. And unlike any other Cabinet Secretary, she had been genuinely popular with the entire White House Staff. But now as she moved through the West Wing the hostility was palpable. She was a traitor "come for a visit" to those she had betrayed.

"Mr. Langford, a Secretary Ramirez would like to speak with you." Crayton Langford's receptionist was professional but cold.

"Send her right in, Jennie."

Helen took a big breath and marched into Crayton Langford's office. She stood before him like an AWOL private. "I'm sorry, Crayton, I was misled; now I need to know if I made a mistake. My heart was in the right place but..."

"Helen...,"

"Please let me finish. At the New Year's Party, when the President confused Gretchen with Danny, she told me her father had talked seriously to Roosevelt about resigning. Later, on at least two occasions, when I tried to see him, first you and then Howard suggested it wasn't a good time and you'd handle any questions I might have for the President. I thought... I thought you all had... I'm so sorry. I jumped to a conclusion that was incredibly stupid." Secretary Ramirez's fists were clinched and her eye's welled with tears as anger and unhappiness mixed. "When Elizabeth Anne insisted the President wanted to resign, but needed the declaration, I believed her. Crayton, I do not want to make another mistake. I need time with the President."

President Stanton's chief of staff rarely looked back. He wanted to ask her why in the world the President would need the declaration to resign, but he didn't. Secretary Ramirez would be their breakthrough. He was sure of it. Vice President Roosevelt's task had just gotten a lot tougher. His people would have to pick up at least one Secretary from the remaining pool and that pool surely favored President Stanton.

"They caught us sleeping, Helen," Crayton stated simply. "The President has regrets. He should have talked frankly to the Cabinet, but he honestly didn't think it was necessary. I never suggested it, nor did anyone else. Each of you needed to understand that he was aware of his problems, working on them and making progress. You needed to be assured and confident that Danny's death was only a personal problem, that it was never a problem for the nation. I should have seen it. I certainly do now, but then we all have pretty good hindsight, don't we?"

"I'm afraid so, Crayton," Helen smiled.

"Well, you're a little early for your two o'clock, but under the circumstances I'm confident the President will make time for you. In fact, he and I were about to have a late lunch. You can take my place.

Commander Croft was talking privately on the secure line when his executive secretary, who doubled as a bodyguard, told him his daughter was on the home phone. It was shortly after noon. Elizabeth Anne was calling him from the library anteroom. Young Jimmy was by her side.

I'm on the other line, Elizabeth Anne, Commander Croft answered. "What do you need?"

"Just wanted to give you an update, Dad," Elizabeth Anne turned casually to survey the room. She was alone, but ironically Aaron Chadwick was moving her way.

Aaron spotted her from the library as he was taking his leave. Unfortunately he needed his coat. One more exchange, he thought, dreading it. Stalling for a second, he checked his vest pocket for nothing. He hoped she might become fully engaged in her phone conversation. When it worked and she turned toward the wall he went for his coat.

"Hold on, Dad." Elizabeth Anne cupped the receiver and turned to Secretary Chadwick. "Have a safe trip to the mountains, Aaron."

"Why thank you, Elizabeth Anne. Please tell the Vice President I'll call him shortly."

"I will," Elizabeth Anne smiled with a half hand wave. "Give my love to Sharon."

Elizabeth Anne returned to her phone conversation. As Aaron Chadwick left he heard her say, "Dad, could you drop by for Jimmy? We're a little overwhelmed here. Besides it would give us a chance to talk." The message was delivered.

"Helen, how good to see you." The President was obviously delighted. "How are you?"

"Uncomfortable with what I have done. And," she hesitated, "uncomfortable with what I must do."

"You needn't be, Helen. You do what you have to. I believe we have converging interest here. I would like you to reassess your position concerning my competence and I suspect you'd like to somehow assess my competence. What say we have lunch?"

"I'd like that very much, Mr. President."

Vice President Roosevelt, the Acting President of the United States was home later than expected. He had done well. The press was treating him like a patriot who had reluctantly taken the helm from his fallen captain. Instant polls were supportive. Saddened commentators looked into cameras and reviewed President Stanton's remarkable record. They sang his praises while reading his political obituary. They called on the President for one last great service to the nation. They asked him to go quietly and preserve his record of service.

In fact, they predicted he would. What choice did he have after the Vice President and a majority of the Cabinet declared him incompetent? Roosevelt knew; President Stanton could contest the declaration. The other shoe was about to drop.

Huddled in the library with Elizabeth Anne and Jason Fields, Roosevelt learned his Cabinet majority had taken at least one hit and maybe two. Helen Ramirez, Secretary of Housing and Urban Development, was sure to jump ship, and Aaron Chadwick, Secretary of the Interior, had withdrawn to the mountains to consider his options. The good news, after sweetening the pot, the six other Cabinet Secretaries who had signed the original declaration were ready to sign again.

The trio had work to do. Each studied Jason's list of <u>Uncommitted Secretaries, Leaning Toward Stanton</u>

1.   Alan W. Binder, Secretary of the Treasury
2.   Carlos J. Herrera, Attorney General, Department of Justice
3.   James P. Hill, Secretary of Veteran Affairs
4.   Anthony R. Lord, Secretary of State
5.   Nancy O. Pruett, Secretary of Health and Human Services
6.   Helen G. Ramirez, Secretary of Housing and Urban Development
7.   Walter S. Wirtz, Secretary of Labor

They had to rebuild their majority. Depending upon Chadwick's decision, they had to turn at least one and maybe two Secretaries. Time was short.

"Let's line them up according to our chances," Jason suggested.

"We already made an aborted approach to Wirtz. He's where he belongs, last," Elizabeth Anne noted.

"We don't have a chance with Hill either," Roosevelt added. "He and Stanton go back to Vietnam."

"You're right, there's no way we could turn him," Jason commented. "Hill was a sergeant in Nam; he served under Stanton. What about Alan Binder? He'd love the Court. Too bad you've already offered the next vacancy to Chadwick, Elizabeth Anne."

"You what??" Roosevelt was immediately incensed.

"It was just in passing," Elizabeth Anne explained. "I told him that you had lobbied the President on his behalf and hoped to have the opportunity to lobby the Senate. I didn't promise him a thing."

"What in the hell does that have to do with the President's competence?" Roosevelt demanded.

"Not a damn thing," Elizabeth Anne sneered. "But then I don't suppose Secretary Tuckman's suggestion that she'd make an ideal running mate was particularly relevant either. And for that matter Secretary Fong's request that we consider him for State when we dump Anthony Lord was a little wide of the mark, don't you think? We have to respond to this crap. We can't lecture the Secretaries on their unseemly ambition when you're trying to replace an elected President. It's time you come down from the mountain and get a little dirty with the rest of us."

"You're trying to tell me Secretary Chadwick solicited your offer of the Supreme Court? I don't believe it, Elizabeth Anne, not for a minute. I know Aaron Chadwick. He's a man of honor. If you offered him the next vacancy on the Supreme Court, I hope you kissed him good-bye because we won't see him again in our camp."

"Sir, I'm afraid I might be to blame," Jason interjected. "When I lost Secretary Ramirez, I'm sure Elizabeth Anne felt she had no choice but to push Secretary Chadwick hard. He may still be with us, but he's going to make up his own mind in his own sweet time. He's just that way. I really think Secretary Binder is a good possibility."

"So is Nancy Pruett, Bill." Elizabeth Anne's conciliatory tone was obvious, but she couldn't help but mention the Health and Human Services Secretary's ambitions. "Unfortunately, as a well-connected liberal she'll want to discuss her chances of balancing your ticket in the next election. I can guarantee it."

"Mr. Vice President, it's not unreasonable for these folks to believe they are dealing with two separate questions," Jason argued. "They may believe they have answered the first question about President Stanton's competence and now they are trying to answer the question as to what will happen to them in the new administration. Their timing may be unseemly, but they are human and this is their life."

"Look," Roosevelt explained, "I don't mind our responding honestly to real questions. But we must not allow any Secretary to believe, feel, or even hope that there is any linkage, pay off, or quid pro quo, between his decision on President Stanton and his future with us. Do you understand?"

"Okay, dear, we'll play it your way."

Vice President Roosevelt was not naive. Elizabeth Anne's conversion came too quickly. He needed to appeal to their more practical side. "I'm telling you, deals will destroy us. They're counterproductive. Just figure the Washington Post is bugging your conversations. We've got to be squeaky clean. If we're not, it will come back to haunt us."

"We're agreed then; Alan Binder and Nancy Pruett are good prospects?" Jason injected. "What about Herrera and Lord?"

"Ya, I think Binder and Pruett are good," Elizabeth Anne answered, but I don't like Herrera. "We'll do what we have to do, but Justice has never let up on Croft industries, not even after William became Vice President."

"Herrera is a long shot anyway," Roosevelt noted. "Philosophically, he and Stanton are twins."

"How about Lord" Jason asked.

Again Roosevelt answered, "Anthony knows President Stanton gives him a free hand at State. Further he fervently believes that the foreign policy he's crafted is critical to the security of America. Anthony Lords is not a modest man. He doesn't think anybody is competent and he knows that in my administration, I'd be acting as my own Secretary of State."

"Okay, we'll go after Binder and Pruett," Elizabeth Anne summarized. "If we strike out with them we'll reconsider the others."

"We'll do fine," Roosevelt stated. "Jason, I want you to get hold of a report Langford pulled together for Lincoln Smith. The press kept blindsiding Smith about President Stanton's behavior so Crayton conducted a hurry-up internal investigation. It's a bombshell. He asked everybody on the White House staff to report all incidents where the President's behavior was out of the ordinary. All under one cover! Even Crayton was shocked."

"I've never heard of it. It's just what we need," Jason ex-claimed.

"It is," Roosevelt noted. "It deals directly with the President's competence. Even if we can't get our hands on it, we can suggest to Binder and Pruett that they ask for it to help them in their deliberations. I suspect it's so damning the White House staff will refuse to produce it, but that in itself will help convince them the President has real problems."

"That's brilliant, sir. It really is! Either way we win! We'll call Binder and Pruett now and set them up for tomorrow morning."

As President Stanton entered the Capitol he was again surprised by his lack of personal anxiety. Perhaps it was just the positive conclusion of his lunch with Secretary Ramirez, but strangely he found himself quite at ease. If he was worried about anything, it was the absence of anxiety. He wondered if it was normal. After all, the last time he had been to Capitol Hill he had seen Danny and made a spectacle of himself. Now he had the humiliating task of having to declare himself fit for office, but it didn't bother him. It was beyond his control. He was committed only to doing his best - that was all. He had faced his demons and now they were powerless. He wondered whether this was the sort of peace a devoted believer might experience. Whatever it was, he honestly felt for the first time in his life that he could address the problems of the nation unencumbered with himself. President Stanton was liberated; no ego, no image, no reelection concerns. He wasn't concerned with face-saving, credit, or blame. He just wanted to get on with the job. There was so much to be done. If he could mobilize the greatness of the nation and its leaders, there was no limit to what they might achieve.

At four-thirty President Stanton delivered his Declaration of Fitness to both Speaker Mathis and President Pro Tempore Frank. They had agreed to a joint meeting because both were scheduled for live interviews on the evening news. Vice President Roosevelt had been the Acting President of the United States of

American for two hours and forty-eight minutes. Now the issue was joined.

Both Speaker Mathis and Senate Pro Tempore Frank indicated if Vice President Roosevelt and a majority of the Cabinet reasserted their belief that President Stanton was incapable of performing his duties, the Congress would not decide the issue without extensive hearings. The clock was now running against the Acting President. He and his allies in the Cabinet had ninety-six hours, four days, until 4:30 P. M., Monday afternoon. If they reasserted their declaration that President Stanton was unable to discharge the duties and powers of his office, the United States Congress would decide the issue.

It was far from over.

CHAPTER FIFTEEN:

LOSS OF CONTROL

1:25 P.M., Thursday, January 25.

Commander Croft was having an excellent afternoon. He enjoyed a challenge and he enjoyed working with good people. Over the years he had employed very talented people in all professions. He kept the best on retainer. It was a smart move. They had been there for him last night, terms negotiated, contract let and accepted. It was all so simple. The team was in place and on standby. They were good, competent, proven people, give them a task, set the parameters, and he could count it done.

Elizabeth Anne's call launched the operation. His team was moving into position. Croft was delighted. It was expensive, but he knew "you get what you pay for." His time frame would be met. And that wouldn't be easy. It was tight. The accident had to be planned and executed within eighty-four hours. That gave Croft a cushion of twelve hours. For his own peace of mind, Croft authorized a generous sliding bonus for early completion that could actually double the value of the contract. Sooner was definitely better than later.

With a click he made multiple electronic transfers that moved operational funds and an initial payment from his own offshore accounts to others in the Caribbean. Where they went from there he had no idea, but within minutes the vendor confirmed their arrival. Croft would make two additional payments: the first on verification of the hit, and the second when the coroner ruled the death accidental. The latter included a generous bonus if the coroner's judgment was unequivocal.

Croft hated waiting, but in this instance the wait would be short and the rewards great. Others had spent millions just to get access to a president. He would have control. His next call was to Elizabeth Anne. He was buoyant. "Hey, Daughter, you asked if I could come by for Jimmy. Just wanted to let you know, I can. If it's alright I might even be a little ahead of schedule."

"That's wonderful, Dad. I was afraid you couldn't make it. It'll be a big help. We've got a good chance now. Thanks, Dad."

"Chance?" Croft asked. "We don't want to leave anything to chance. You let me know if you need any more help. We've got other resources, you know."

"Thanks again, Dad. We'll see you soon."

When Aaron Chadwick arrived home, Sharon, David, and Nathan were almost packed. Just west of the Skyline Drive and nine miles east of Luray, they had their own Camp David. They left within an hour. More and more, Aaron needed to escape from Washington. The mountains were his sanctuary.

When they left Washington, Aaron had been anxious. His meeting with the Vice President and Elizabeth Anne had been terribly stressful. What a contrast with President Stanton's talk about competence and respecting the people's choice. Over and over he reviewed his conversations. The process was being perverted. Unbelievably he had been offered a bribe, the Supreme Court. It was unmistakable. Even more disturbing, he had been threatened. Given the stakes, perhaps the bribe was to be expected, but the threat was different. It wasn't political - about his career. It was physical and involved his family. Compulsively, he checked the rearview mirror.

Normally, Secretary Chadwick enjoyed driving. He found it relaxing. Now, as he drove, he was lost in thoughts so bizarre he questioned his sanity. How quickly can a hit, if that's what they still called it, be ordered and carried out? He scanned the cars behind him. Do "hit men" always work alone? For that matter, were hit men always men? What could he do? Nothing, he thought. Almost nothing, he didn't have to endanger his family. He checked his mirrors again. It was so foolish. Of course he was being followed. He was on the interstate.

By the time they reached Front Royal, Aaron began putting the danger in perspective. He wasn't dealing with wackos or the mob. He was dealing with the Vice President of the United States and his wife. Besides, they couldn't possibly organize anything this fast and by Monday night it would be all over. But he could take precautions; it was only smart. Yes, he could and would do that. The President had suggested a detailed written account for history. Secretary Chadwick would do it for history and insurance.

He began to relax after they picked up supplies in Front Royal, turned south, and began the climb toward Mt. Marshall. Now he had to pay attention to the road. At the beginning, the shaded switchbacks had only slush. Shortly he had to watch out for ice. As they approached the ridge, the air and smells announced their arrival in a pristine world. The snow glistening in the sun had flocked the trees, and hushed the world. Aaron loved the Skyline Drive and Shenandoah National Park. They gave him needed perspective and were especially beautiful in winter without the crowds. Soon Sharon, David, Nathan, and he would share a spectacular sunset. He stopped at the first pullout. What a treasure, these beautiful mountains.

"Nine eleven Oak Creek Gap Road," Bobby announced. "This must be it, Mr. Reeves." The brown metal address sign protruded from a mound of wet matted leaves next to the asphalt drive. It was topped with a red reflector.

"Drive on, Bobby, there should be a pull-out around the next curve. We'll walk back."

"I hope 911 isn't an omen," Bobby laughed.

Reeves ignored his young associate. He was on the phone. "Chadwick has just left the beltway," he announced. "He's on Highway 66. If he goes by Front Royal we've got at least three hours. If he takes 29 and 211 we've got no more than two. Let's move!"

Kenneth Reeves had been in the business for years. As a former Navy Seal, he had received the best training money could buy. His practicum came in Vietnam. It was there, at the end of the war when desperation hatched the most imaginative projects, that he honed his skills. He became a master of improvisation. He was an artist intent on practicing and perfecting his skills. No matter how bizarre the mission, he volunteered. Time and time again he tested and extended his limits. At first, it was important to believe in the cause, but not for long. He enjoyed the work. Reeves never felt more alive than when he was killing or could be killed.

When the war ended, Kenneth was twenty-five, in his prime, but afraid of losing his edge. Almost immediately he resigned the service and found work as a mercenary. He fought in hot spots around the world, leading insurgents or counterinsurgents; it didn't matter. He enjoyed being a soldier of fortune, but with the passage of time he found his comrades in arms amateurish and unprofessional. They were children (literally in several sub-Saharan wars) and hopelessly immature.

His decision to "freelance" was a natural byproduct of the enjoyment he experienced working alone or with handpicked associates, where only the target could compromise his chances of success. The early years were tough, but his reputation grew until his "celebrated" pro bono hit on a Bin Laden lieutenant put him in a class by himself. His prices were now outrageous, but never questioned. When you're the best, there can be no comparison-shopping. Since he was always booked he was popular among the lesser-known practitioners for his referrals. If he needed a favor he hardly needed to ask.

Robert Hearst, Reeves' driver, while young was also a vet and his most promising protégé. Nevertheless, Reeves tended to micromanage every operation. In this profession you didn't learn from your mistakes. "When you park, Bobby, keep the tires on the pavement."

"Yes, sir."

"More often than not in this profession, Bobby, you don't get to learn from your mistakes, you die, or you learn to regret them serving time. The only tenure you get is five to ten."

"Yes, sir."

"Here's good, Bobby. Pull over, but remember what I told you."

"Yes, sir."

"Get the bag out of the trunk and let's take a look at this place. Put your gloves and shoe covers on. I've got a flashlight."

The Chadwick cabin was pretty much like the others scattered along Big Creek Trail. If anything, it was a little more isolated, sitting back in the woods, well off the road on the upside of the mountain.

"Nice their driveway is paved," Bobby commented.

"Yes it is," a preoccupied Reeves mumbled. Then, turning to his protégé, he explained, "the challenge, Bobby, is meeting the time constraints and insuring that the coroner rules his death to be accidental. With Secretary Chadwick, the coroner's inquest is not going to be a casual affair. Nothing will be accepted on face value. It'll be high profile, extremely thorough. Our client wants an accidental death and that takes time. But he also wants the job done (Reeves checked his watch) in eighty-one hours and forty minutes. We could be tested here. Patience when time is short is the mark of a professional."

Robert Hearst, Bobby, understood Reeves was sharing his thought processes with him as only a true mentor might. He was honored and only answered again with a simple, "Yes, sir."

Reeves continued. "Normally, we would eliminate the target and then stage an accident consistent with the cause of death. The problem is the family. We have to get Aaron away from them or our accident will have to claim four lives."

"It has to be ruled an accident?" Bobby asked. "Chadwick can't walk in on a burglar or be the victim of a carjacking?"

"No, his death will be tragic and untimely, but it must be the result of a simple, even common accident. Nothing exotic; he needs to fall, hit his head in the bathtub. If we do this right, even Chadwick should believe he's had a stupid fatal accident. The answer's here, we just have to find it. The Commander wants an accident and he wants it now."

"Little picky, isn't he?"

"Very picky," Reeves agreed, "but very generous, Bobby."

"Think those wires might help us, Mr. Reeves? They look a little worse for wear." Bobby was squinting at the overhead power lines that ran from a pole at the corner of the lot, alongside the driveway, to an old porcelain insulator nailed to the cabin's ridgepole. The lines were badly frayed from slow dancing with the limbs of several standing dead trees. Under the eaves the lines disappeared into the top of a coverless breaker box. From the bottom of the box six new lines emerged, one for each room in the house. The wires were held together by metal straps and secured to every third log until they disappeared into the crawl space.

"Take a look, Bobby," Reeves directed, handing him the flashlight. "Use that plywood."

Kneeling on the plywood with the flashlight in his right hand, Bobby leaned into the crawl space. He took his time spotting the course of each wire.

"You need to see this, Mr. Reeves," a poker-faced Robert Hearst advised. He stood up, moved out of the way and handed the flashlight to his boss.

Reeves carefully spread a hand towel on the plywood sheet, kneeled, turned on the flashlight and peered into the crawl space. He was astonished. Under the cabin, there was literally a maze of electric, gas, water, and sewer lines. Each of the electrical wires took its own course over and under gas lines, loosely swinging from joist to joist until it reached a wad of old electrical tape that looked like an abandoned mud dauber's nest, but served as a junction box. Inside the wad, hot, neutral, and ground wires were twisted together with smaller partners that stitched between the crawl space and living space, joining outlets and switches into one circuit.

Bobby couldn't contain himself any longer. "Falls a might short of code, wouldn't you say, Mr. Reeves?"

"I think Secretary Chadwick is one of those 'do it yourselfers' you read so much about."

"You mean in the obituaries. This place is a death trap."

"We do have some options here, Bobby. No doubt about it. We have options."

Together for the next hour, Kenneth Reeves and Robert Hearst surveyed the grounds and inspected the cabin. Even to the untrained eye there were a lot of possibilities.

At the end of the drive, off to the left in a small frame garage with a dirt floor, surrounded by shelving loaded with solvents, varnishes, and paints, they found a 1988 Jeep Cherokee, apparently in mint condition. It was covered by a custom car coat, the type normally reserved for Porches, Jaguars, and Corvettes.

In the back yard quite close to the cabin, a five-hundred-gallon propane tank seventy percent full fed a rusted pipe that snaked under the cabin. There, as they had seen, it was teed a half dozen times in order to supply the appliances they found throughout the cabin. Those included a new green enamel Vermont Castings fireplace insert in the living room, an old oversized Wolfe range in the kitchen, two small direct vent heaters (one in each of the bedrooms) and an ancient water heater boxed in the bathroom and vented through a three-inch single-wall pipe that had scorched the ceiling on its way through the attic and out the roof. In addition they found a barbecue grill on the patio. It was fueled through a once flexible, but now dry rotted, gas hose that teed into to the propane line somewhere under the house.

From the patio they explored a well-worn path that skirted along a lush bog area and then split, one branch heading to what appeared to be an outhouse and the other following a tiny stream into a mixed forest of evergreens and hardwoods.

"Think they still use that thing? Long way to go in the middle of the night."

"That's not an outhouse, Bobby; it's a pump house," Reeves answered. "That's where they get their water. See the box in the bog. Water collects there and then gravity feeds a cistern under the pump house. From there it's pumped up to the cabin. That's why it has electricity. Let's take a look."

The pump house didn't amount to much, just a six-foot-tall, four by five box with a door, sitting on a concrete cistern. Its overflow was the source of the stream. Inside, two one-horse electric pumps, one obviously a backup, were plumbed into an inch-and-a-quarter line that supplied the cabin. Two twenty-amp breakers and adjustable pressure switches controlled the pumps. A blue pressure tank kept whichever pump was turned on from cycling continuously.

"Pretty nice set up. I particularly like the breakers and the watermarks. When he brings the water up, I think Mr. Chadwick's got some leaky valves."

"Don't you think we ought to head on back," Bobby asked. "I'll need a half hour or so to plant the bugs."

Reeves checked his watch and then punched the redial button on his cell phone. His call was answered immediately. He listened, smiled, and then confirmed, "Front Royal."

"We have a little time, Bobby. Let's check out the other fork."

"Whatever you say, Mr. Reeves, but I will need some time back at the cabin."

Even in the woods the trail was hard packed and easy going. Within minutes the two men were out of the trees. The trail ended on the neck of a huge rock formation that jutted out of the mountainside to survey Oak Creek Gap and all the country that lay far below and to the east and west. Riding the up drafts, soaring ravens watched them emerge from the woods and move cautiously out onto the rock's smooth surface. The men stopped well before reaching a large log bench that had been rolled into place no more than a few feet from the edge.

"I'll be damned! What an incredible view! This place ought to have a name," Reeves exclaimed, scanning the horizon and then the valley below. "Hey, Bobby, come on up here. Stand on that log. I want to take your picture," he laughed. The pressure of again living up to his reputation and fulfilling the contract had disappeared. To Ken Reeves this was a doable job.

"Yeah, right," Bobby responded. His body language no longer tried to conceal his fear of heights. "I bet this place scares the shit out of a lot of parents."

"You are a sensitive soul. What do you think holds it in place?"

"Holds what?" Bobby asked.

"The log. It looks like it should roll right off the edge. That's a killer drop."

"Damned if I know! But whatever it is, I wouldn't trust it." Bobby held back as Reeves worked his way cautiously to the edge and checked out the log.

"Chadwick's definitely got a death wish," Reeves announced from his knees. "There are just a couple of rocks wedged under this thing. Remove them and it's gone. Be a hell of an accident; don't you think?"

"You thinking of assisted suicide? How would you get him out here? He's a pretty big fella." Bobby wanted Reeves to know he wanted no part of a cliff-top wrestling match.

"We can get him as far as the pump house, easy. Just flip off a breaker and he'll come running. He wouldn't send his wife or the boy. After all he's the electrician," Reeves again laughed. "But you're right; from there it could get a little rough."

"Sure could," Bobby agreed. "Might be better if he just stood in some water and fried himself flipping the breaker back on."

"That's right; that's good," Reeves nodded. "On the other hand," Reeves continued, "a fall from this place would cover up some pretty rough stuff. Hell, it'd break every bone in his body. We could just start with his neck."

"I suppose I could help you get him out here, but to tell you the truth, I'm not real comfortable even here, much less out near the edge," Bobby all but shuddered.

"I never would have guessed. Well, enough of this. We can think about it. Let's head back to the cabin and finish up there."

As Bobby planted bugs throughout the cabin, Reeves did a last walk-through. While he kept his business focus and noted again the electric heater in the bathroom, and the kerosene lanterns in the living room, what impressed him most was the unpretentious comfort and warmth of Chadwick's cottage.

Before leaving, Reeves checked the bugs Bobby placed. Only three were required for full coverage. They had an adjustable service life. Bobby set them for thirty hours. At that time the membrane would dissolve leaving only an inert speck of ash. They were beautifully done. Reeves was impressed. Information spelled options. It eliminated surprises. With patience and a little luck, Chadwick would give them the key and choose his own accident. Patience. Reeves would not act until he could see the entire end game and controlled all the moves. In chess, his opponent would resign. Here, he would die.

"We made it in three and half hours with a grocery stop," Aaron announced pulling up the driveway. "What a difference."

"Feeling better?" Sharon asked popping the trunk lid.

"So much better, Honey. Thank God, you insisted we buy it."

"Well now, I insist on a little help. You two, David, Nathaniel, let's get these groceries put away."

In a matter of minutes both the groceries and luggage were put away. "I suppose it's too late to run down to The Crow's Nest?" Aaron asked.

"Oh I don't know," Sharon answered, "we've got to bring up the water anyway. Just as well make sure all's right with our world. You'll have to light the water heater and furnace when we get back."

Their car was parked in the turn-around just one hundred and fifty yards from Chadwick's cabin. They should have been enjoying a beautiful sunset, but storm clouds had replaced blue skies and darkness would come shortly. The trunk of the car was popped open and an impressive looking refracting telescope stood nearby. While Reeves was a serious amateur astronomer and had won awards for his astrophotography, it was just cover. He enjoyed Bobby's enthusiasm for checking out treetops and cliff faces, but it had turned cold and the men were now sitting in the car, sharing a Subway and a thermos of coffee. The second hour of National Public Radio's "All Things Considered" had just begun.

"Can I change this?" Bobby asked.

"No, Bobby, hold it. They've pulled in," Reeves announced, sitting forward. You did a nice job. Everything is crystal clear." With earphones on, Ken Reeves spoke louder than required. "These things have come a long way since I started in the business," he commented.

"I can wire that right through to the radio's speakers if you like," Bobby offered.

"Maybe, when 'All Things Considered' goes off, okay," Reeves answered. "Those people do a fantastic job. You find yourself interested in some of the strangest thing." They're talking about presidential succession, you know."

"What's Chadwick up to?" Bobby asked.

"He and the whole 'famdamily's' going to the pump house to bring up the water. Then, they say they're going to hike on down to our point. I told you it should have a name. It does. They call it 'The Crow's Nest.'"

"Sticking pretty close together, are they?"

"Yeah, they are," Reeves answered, signaling for quiet. He put his hands on his earphones and pressed them tightly to his head. His brow furrowed as he listened intently until he could hear no more.

"What's the name of that kid?"

"You mean David?" Bobby asked.

"No, the little guy."

"His name's Nathaniel, Nathan. He shouldn't be a problem," Bobby answered.

"Nathan? You sure?" Reeves asked.

"Yes, Nathan's the eight-year-old. Kind of a sickly kid."

"Then, who the hell is Moses?"

"King David, Moses, what are you talking about?"

"The last thing I heard was "Come on, Moses. I'm sure of it," Reeves answered. "Oh Christ, they've got a dog!"

Nancy Pruett had learned lessons the hard way. As a junior at the University of Chicago in 1968, she was a committed, but casual antiwar activist. Three years later when Arden, her husband, was killed in Vietnam she was all but a screaming fanatic. Her activism was moderated, but only slightly, by her baby boy who grew up at rallies and marches. Mother and child became popular symbols of the movement and in Illinois, at least, she became one of its most respected and eloquent speakers. She learned on the job. Two years on Senator Simon's staff, four years with the Chicago City Council, six years in the Illinois state legislature, two years as state treasurer, four years as governor, twelve years as a United States Senator, and now she was Secretary of Health and Human Services. She was a grizzled veteran of public service. Strangely she was attractive – both tough and attractive.

Secretary Pruett had traveled a long, tortuous, switchback road to the top, making tough decisions at every turn. More than once she had rolled the dice. She was known as a gutsy lady, never looking back and always keeping her eye on the prize. The prize for her was the presidency. Nancy Pruett wanted to be the first woman president of the United States. She was not alone. There were other contenders, determined competitors. The summit of American politics was not only in sight, but was now within reach of a half-dozen climbers. Only one would be first.

Secretary Pruett was convinced the winning route was through the office of vice president. Only after the American people accepted a woman as vice president would they be ready to hear "Hail to the Chief" played as she entered a room or "Present Arms" as she reviewed the troops.

In a rare flight of fantasy, when Vice President Matthew Thorn had died, she hoped President Stanton would turn to her. Indeed, she approached Crayton about the job. It had been stupid. In hindsight it was so clear. Like Stanton, she was a liberal. The President needed a conservative who could be confirmed by the Republicans who controlled Congress. William Butler Roosevelt fit the bill. The President did what he had to do.

Tonight at home in Bethesda, she was at yet another crossroads. There would be no more flights of fantasy. At this level, at this time, a wrong turn could be fatal. Nancy Pruett liked and respected Stanton, but right or wrong, his competence was in question and his days as president looked numbered. She had a decision to make, one that might effect the future of the United States and would most certainly effect the future of the Secretary of Health and Human Services.

There was trouble in Vice President Roosevelt's camp. He had gone to Congress with a bare majority and his coalition was fraying; she was sure of it. President Stanton was fighting back and Roosevelt's people were scrambling. She had heard from half the Cabinet, everyone who had signed the declaration except Aaron Chadwick and Helen Ramirez and Herrera and Hill from the President's camp. Nobody wanted to be left out on a limb. Roosevelt was looking for insurance or he had had a defection. She suspected the latter, probably Ramirez. The intensity was too great.

It was time to deal. She might be able to tip the balance and write her own ticket. Politics was about principle, but it also was about timing. She didn't want to jump the gun, but she sure as hell didn't want to wait too long. Her competition was Binder. Alan Binder, the Treasury Secretary, was the architect of the platinum parachute. His timing was impeccable. She was sure he would negotiate a safe and rewarding landing for himself no matter how bloody the battlefield might become.

Secretary Pruett was a realist. She was plowing a mine-field, but she had no choice; she had to choose, Stanton or Roosevelt. If she survived, played her cards right, she would be the next vice president of the United States.

She had no doubt this was her chance. More importantly, she was convinced it was America's chance to take a giant step forward in its long march toward full democracy, where it could take advantage of the talents of all its citizens, men and women.

If she stayed with Stanton, was loyal to the end and went down with the ship, she needed to know that her star would rise again, brighter than before. She needed creditable assurances that she would be the Democratic Party's nominee for vice president of the United States. Those assurances would not come from the President. He didn't operate that way. The question then was simply could the Stanton faction deliver? She had doubts.

With Roosevelt, she had to be convinced that when he assumed the presidency he would send her name to Congress as his nominee to be vice president of the United States. No doubt as president, Roosevelt could deliver on such a commitment. The problem was, the Roosevelt she knew was not likely to make a *quid pro quo* commitment, at least not where his self-interests were so obviously at stake. It was what she admired about him.

If she couldn't make a straight-up deal with the Vice President, the question for the Roosevelt option was how could she be assured that he would nominate her to be vice president? It seemed obvious, at least to Secretary Pruett, that she was the best candidate for the office. Not only was she prepared to be vice president (or indeed president), but also she could bridge the gap between the conservative Roosevelt and the liberal Democratic activists essential to win the party nomination.

How to proceed? Stanton or Roosevelt? She could take but one path. How sensitive were the mines? She needed to feel her way softly, discreetly, and quietly. Without the proper foundation, talking directly to Stanton or Roosevelt could be ruinous. At best it would be a crapshoot. She could speak for herself, but they needed intermediaries, knowledgeable and trusted confidants, who could act as honest brokers. Deniability had to be protected.

If her overtures were to Stanton, she would speak with Crayton. She was comfortable with the President's chief of staff; not only was Crayton Langford a professional, he was the President's alter ego.

On the other hand, if she turned first to Roosevelt, no one truly fit the bill. Roosevelt seemed to keep his own counsel. She considered, and then immediately dismissed the most obvious possibility. Nancy Pruett could not stand Elizabeth Anne. She thought she was a manipulative opportunist. It was visceral. No, she concluded, on Roosevelt's staff, Jason Fields was her best bet. Even he was a gamble. It was time to roll the dice.

"Oh Lord," Sharon giggled, watching Aaron strut about the cabin. "Captain's on the bridge," she piped.

"The water's up. Gas is on. Pilots are lit." Aaron ticked off his accomplishments. He had moved confidently about the cabin executing each of his tasks without a misstep.

"Well done, sir," Sharon responded.

"Takeover, Commander. I'll be in my quarters." Aaron kissed his wife on the forehead. "I have some writing to do, Honey," he explained. "David, you and Nathan help your mom."

"Supper will be ready in forty-five minutes. Can you wrap it up that quick?" she asked.

"Dad, would it be alright if, after supper, I run into town and see Pam." Pam Osgood was David's boyhood chum and latest girlfriend. Her family owned the cedar-shake cabin up the road.

"Sure, that's fine, Aaron answered. "Give her our love."

"What time will you be home, Dear?"

"Not too late, mom. Pam's got an eight o'clock tomorrow."

"Well, I'm off to write. You guys keep it down."

"What's the Brady Bunch up to now?" Bobby asked.

"The Brady Bunch is your generation," Reeves responded. "I'm before the Partridge family. The Nelsons, Ozzie and Harriet, are mine. Ozzie has his chores done; mom's cooking dinner and, I think the boys are getting bored," Reeves replied. "They are going to be down one after dinner. David's going to town."

"That's great. If you decide on the pump house, we can count on Chadwick to do the fixing."

"We still have the dog," Reeves noted.

"Yeah. It's also looking a little nasty. Mind if I turn on the heat?"

"No, go ahead. I'm a little chilled, too. I sure as hell hope it doesn't snow. We can't rig the pump house until after the kid's gone. And even in the dark, that nimrod, Chadwick, could see our prints in the snow. What's the forecast?" Reeves asked.

"Snow."

"God Dam it. We need a little help, here."

"Where's the Big Guy when you need Him, huh?" Bobby laughed.

"Here," Reeves handed Bobby the earphones. "You take over. I'm going to take five. This could be a long night. Wake me if anything happens."

"Mr. President, I know we have to keep looking for converts, but I think you had better keep in touch with your base."

"Who have we missed, Crayton?" President Stanton asked.

"Just Secretaries Hill and Pruett," Crayton replied.

"Jimmy's with us," Stanton smiled and was reflective. "You can count on Sergeant Hill. We go way back. In Vietnam, when the second battalion was being overrun by the Viet Cong, Jimmy and a wonderful little Jewish kid from Yonkers, Davy 'Crocket' Levine, were out on the point of this ridge, running a machine gun that was the target of a ground assault. It was incredible. They just kept coming, right over the bodies of their comrades. We couldn't understand it, thought they had to be pumped on drugs. We were terrified. Some of the kids in my platoon had these wild, unseeing eyes. They'd glance back and forth, up and down the line, if one broke, it was like dominoes; the whole line would start to peel off. They'd drop everything, run like hell. I was screaming and tossing kids back in the trench as fast as I

could. We were just guarding Jimmy's flanks. His machine gun was on fire. We actually held until they started to envelope us. Headquarters ordered us back. About a third of us had, what might be called, an orderly retreat. After that we called Levine, "Crockett, Davy Crocket." Now there was a liberal. I was Tennessee liberal. Davy was from another world. We didn't trust him until the hill. He was always quoting some leftist rag. I remember the banner of one. It had a line drawing of two grunts, one sticking a bayonet through the other. The caption read: 'A bayonet is a weapon with a worker at each end.' Not too subtle. Davy didn't make it, but Jimmy did. I'd trust him with my life. Hell, I did."

"I think," Crayton laughed, "from what you've told me we can call Secretary Hill later."

"You are quick, Crayton," President Stanton teased as Crayton hit the intercom

"Millie, would you ring Secretary Pruett for the President?"

"Nathan, supper's ready. Come on in now." Sharon stood at the screen door, using her hands as a megaphone. She repeated her call twice, covering likely points of the compass. Moses, their golden retriever, appeared first. Nathan, not far behind, arrived at the back door breathless and wheezing. His asthma was exercise-induced and exacerbated by the cold. "Supper's about ready," Sharon repeated. "Go tell your Dad and get washed up."

"Supper's ready, Dad," Nathan panted running down the hall on his way in to the bathroom.

"Nathan, Nathan," Aaron tried to get his son's attention but to no avail. "I'll be right out, Honey. I just need to address an envelope."

David Chadwick didn't need a call. He was anxious to run into Luray and see Pam.

Dinner at the Chadwick household was a family affair. That was particularly true in their log-cabin mountain retreat. Sharon (and Aaron for that matter) enjoyed cooking and took pride in producing simple yet elegant meals even in this rustic setting. Tonight the candles on the antique pine table and the hurricane lanterns on the oak sideboard gave the cabin an especially warm glow.

As Nathan fed Moses, so he wouldn't beg, Sharon, David and Aaron normally had wine. Tonight David passed. He was driving. The senior Chadwicks had a nice Chardonnay, Brie and bread sticks. The crushing problems Aaron had felt in Washington were almost magically swept away by the rich atmosphere. They would not intrude on this gathering. This was home. Here with his family, Aaron had perspective. He knew what was important. With his second glass, as always, he looked at his wife, his boys, their home, and even Moses. He felt extremely fortunate.

"Ready?" Sharon asked, moving into the kitchen.

"You bet, I'm famished," Aaron responded.

"Me too, Mom," David answered. "Can I help?"

"Yes, would you go ahead and take the salads out. Nathan, that's enough now. "Tell Moses to lie down. It's dinner time."

The salad was their favorite; chilled baby spinach with red onions, freshly grated Parmesan cheese, and bacon bits served with a light curry dressing. The meal that followed was David's favorite: stuffed salmon, new potatoes, and steamed asparagus. They all agreed it was delicious. For proud parents the evening was a very special time.

"Well, David, you've been generous with your time, but I suspect Miss Pamela Osgood would like a study break," Aaron's wine had entered the conversation.

"I hope so, Dad. What car should I take?"

"Take the Buick, Dave. It's more comfortable and with front wheel drive, it's really pretty good in snow. I do have one job for you," Aaron continued. "It's important. I have a letter on the hall tree that needs to be posted. Could you and Pam swing by the Post Office and drop it in the out of town box?"

"Sure, Dad," David responded putting on his coat. "You need anything from town, Mom?"

"Nothing, David. Have a good time."

"I'll give you a call from Pam's," David promised.

"Do you have my mail?" Aaron asked.

"I have it."

"Don't forget. It needs to be posted tonight. See you later, son."

"Mr. President, we may have a problem."

"What is it, Millie?"

"I have tried Secretary Pruett three times now," Millie answered. "I waited a couple of minutes between each call, but her phone's still busy."

"I don't understand. What's the problem?" President Stanton asked. "Maybe she's talking to her son."

"The problem, sir, is all the Secretaries, for that matter anyone you might wish to talk to on a regular basis, have 'Call Waiting' and 'Caller ID.'"

Crayton did not try to disguise his concern. "She knows you've been trying to reach her, sir."

"Somebody knows, Crayton, but not necessarily Secretary Pruett." President Stanton was still not sure they had a problem. "Maybe it's an important call or she has an emergency."

"I suppose," Crayton stated, thinking out loud, "if someone other than Secretary Pruett were using her phone, they might not know what to do, or how to reach the White House. But she lives alone, doesn't she?"

"She lives alone," Millie answered. "I've been to her house."

"Maybe I should send a car," Crayton suggested.

"I can have the operator interrupt the call, say it's an emergency," Millie offered. "We do that all the time."

"No, no, we don't have an emergency here," President Stanton was firm. "What we need to know we can learn in the morning. It's not going to change. We'll try again then."

Jason Fields was elated. It had come out of the blue. He wanted to break the news to Vice President Roosevelt and Elizabeth Anne. Jason had just received a phone call from the Secretary of Health and Human Services. Nancy Pruett was ready to join Vice President Roosevelt and declare that President Stanton was unable to discharge the powers and duties of his office. His conversation with Secretary Pruett had gone very, very well. She had talked to him about the vice presidency, but there was absolutely no *quid pro quo*. It was clean; Roosevelt was unencumbered. She would sign the declaration. She only asked for his, Jason's, support. He would give it enthusiastically and honestly.

The Vice President's chief of staff had long considered the problem his boss faced in winning the support of liberal Democratic Party activists. Roosevelt's conservative credentials would insure he could capture the middle in a general election. His problem was winning the party's nomination in the first place. In Jason's mind the answer had always been Secretary Pruett or her twin, a bright, competent, energetic and experienced professional. Nancy Pruett was an attractive savvy politician. She would not only balance the ticket, she would signal Roosevelt's commitment to traditional Democratic Party causes. All the pieces would fall in place. It couldn't get any better. Secretary Pruett was a widow. She had no dead weight. Women would rally to the ticket. Her appointment would not be the last-ditch political gambit of a desperate campaign. Rather, Roosevelt would be performing a constitutional duty.

Jason debated soliciting Elizabeth Anne's help in promoting Secretary Pruett, but he was truly convinced, when Roosevelt became President, Secretary Pruett would be an easy sale. It just made so much sense. No, he decided, he alone would broker this deal. To a conscientious yet ambitious Roosevelt, Secretary Pruett could be sold on merit alone. And if he alone were responsible for her selection, then, with any luck he would be a powerhouse in the next administration.

"Is he better?" Aaron asked. He knew the answer. Sharon was worried. Nathan's asthma had worsened after dinner. It wasn't a full-fledged attack; he wasn't panicky, but he was having trouble.

"Did he use his inhaler?"

"His regular one is empty," Sharon answered. "I thought I packed a backup, but apparently I didn't."

"Don't we still have his old aerosol? He could use it."

"He did. I found it in the medicine cabinet, but it's empty too."

"Are you sure?" Aaron quizzed. "They take a little time."

"No, no, he's used it twice. He's not getting any relief." Sharon was worried. "I checked it and it's practically floating on top of the water."

"What does that mean?" Aaron persisted.

"It means it's empty, dear. The aerosols have no counters. You stick them in water. The canisters sink when they're full. It floated. It doesn't matter how many times he uses it, it's not going to help."

"I'm sorry. What do you want to do?" Aaron asked.

"I tried to reach David," Sharon explained, "but Pam's parents don't expect them home early. Her test isn't until Monday."

"We still have the Cherokee, we can run him into the emergency room," Aaron suggested.

"I don't think that's necessary." Sharon was digging in her purse for her own emergency kit. "I've got the adrenaline if he really gets bad. Could you run into Walgreens? He can have refills."

"Sure, it won't take me long if the car starts. Why don't you go ahead and phone it in. Al, or whatever his name is, can have it ready by the time I get there. Let me go start the car now. It won't take me long. Oh, Sharon, remind me when I get back to call Elizabeth Anne."

"Of course, Honey. Here's your coat; gloves are in the pockets. You'd better get going. Be careful, dear."

"Wake up, Mr. Reeves. Wake up," Bobby nudged his boss. "You awake? We've been living right, sir. The old man is heading to town. Think we can do a rollover?"

"Jesus, how long have I been asleep. When did we get all the snow?"

"It's not that late. Did you hear me? Chadwick is running into town. He's going by himself to the drugstore, some sort of emergency with Nathan."

"A rollover would be great, Bobby, but let's be patient."

"When I was a kid I played a mean game of chicken. I never lost and I never went into the ditch. What do you think?" Bobby was getting pumped.

"Did he keep drinking?" Reeves asked. He was now fully awake.

"I think he had another at dinner. I couldn't tell after that. The house was pretty quiet except for the kid. I could actually hear him wheezing."

"It would be great if he had alcohol in his blood," Reeves commented.

"I didn't put a bug on the jeep, Mr. Reeves. I didn't think of it," Bobby confessed, closing the thermos and tossing his coffee.

"Then we won't have to retrieve it, will we?"

"Do you want to pick him up at the highway?"

"Yeah, that'd be good. We don't want to follow him out of his own Goddamn driveway, could be a little suspicious." Ken Reeves was focused. This is what he lived for. His mind was racing. The Improv Theater was open and he loved it.

"Stop, Bobby!"

"What is it?"

Reeves laughed, "What say you put the telescope in. And let's slow down."

Ken Reeves popped the trunk as Bobby collapsed the telescope, put it in its case and stowed it in the trunk. Before getting back in the car, he slowly checked the area, first with the car in place and then at Reeve's insistence after he had backed up and turned the headlights on. It was clean. The snow that covered the turnaround was already filling in their parking pad and covering their tracks.

In the car, Bobby put on his gloves.

"Do you really need those?" Reeves asked.

"I think they help," Bobby answered switching off the headlights. "Buckle up, Mr. Reeves, it's the law."

The dark sedan moved cautiously down the road toward 911 Oak Creek Gap Road. Snow crunched below the tires and melted slowly on the defrosted windshield. They rounded the curve. Bobby was the first to spot the tracks. "Christ, he's already taken off. Can I turn the lights on?"

"Not yet, Bobby," Reeves directed. "Wait until we get to the highway. He can't be that far ahead."

"Which way will he go?" Bobby asked.

"He'll go left. He's has to be going to Luray. It's the closest."

Within a couple of minutes Bobby spotted Chadwick. "There he is. That's him. See the high profile; that's him."

"Hang back, Bobby."

"You don't have to worry; he's going like a bat out of hell."

"He'll be at the intersection soon. Slow down. Is it slippery?" Reeves asked.

"Maybe a little, not too bad," Bobby pumped his brakes. The second time, they felt the ice. "There are patches."

"It could be worse toward Luray. We'll be going down a north-facing slope."

"He turned left," Bobby noted, pulling on his headlights. "He's still flying."

"Hang back, Bobby. Give him a little room. You don't have to worry; you're not going to lose him. We're the only fools on the road."

Reeves was partially right. Chadwick was cutting new tracks in the snow, but then, at least at this altitude, the snow was not only still falling, it was blowing.

"As we head down look for a good spot. We'll probably send him over on his way back. We'll want the inside bank. Look for a downhill and a good drop off. I want him to have some speed, but remember I need to be able to get to him. One way or another he's going to break his neck."

"I just spotted his taillights. He's really moving out. Do you think he's in four-wheel drive?"

"He might be. It will make him overconfident." Reeves thought of the last ice storm in Atlanta. All the hot shots in their 4-wheel-drive SUV's were whipping by everyone. Channel Five had some great footage of one bouncing off some parked cars and sliding through an intersection with all wheels locked. The guy had just picked up a hitchhiker whose car wouldn't start. He was terrified. Thought he'd take the rest of the day off. Reeves laughed.

"You can go anywhere in one of those things, but you have the same brakes as everyone else. They don't stop worth a damn."

Sharon's first call didn't get through, but in the mountains that wasn't unusual. She kept trying. She had found another inhaler. Nathan was doing better. She didn't want Aaron killing himself going down the mountain.

Aaron saw them as he reached for his cell phone – white-tail, a mother and a youngster. They were looking back across the road. He knew immediately. There were others. He pumped his brakes, nothing but the awful sensation that he was no longer a driver, just a passenger. The phone rang again. He was going too fast, now, sliding broadside down the narrow road. Instinctively he did as he had been told. Resisting his impulses, he slowly turned into the spin. It was too much. He only grazed the first, but when he corrected again he came face to face with a statuesque deer with placid eyes. He braced himself. She didn't have a chance, he thought, but he spun by her. She was only a spectator. He hit the next one in mid-air. He took her legs out from under her and she crashed into the windshield. Together they flew. He held his breath for what seemed like a very long time until the phone stopped ringing.

"Are you seeing this shit," Bobby exclaimed. The distant taillights danced like a child's sparkler.
    "He's lost it, Bobby." Slow down, slow way, way down."
    "Christ, there he goes!" The taillights that had danced now drew a straight line in the night sky and disappeared.
    "He must have gone over the edge, didn't he?" Reeves unbuckled his safety belt and reached for his night glasses. "Slower, Bobby. Remember our tracks. Damn this snow."

"It's an "S" curve, Bobby stated. "Want me to stop? Maybe you can look across and spot him."

"Good, Bobby. Stop." Reeves opened the door, but did not get out. He stood on the frame and leaned forward on the roof, peering into the night. "I see him, I see him, now. He's way the hell down there. I can't see any movement, but we're going to have to stop on the far side."

They rode silently forward, praying no other car was on the road. As they rounded the curve the story was written in the snow. Tracks swung wildly back and forth, and then spun around in a bull's-eye, before exiting straight through the guardrail. With the exception of a little chrome, some broken glass, and the right hind-quarter of a small deer there was no other physical evidence. For them only one question remained.

Bobby cut to the quick. "He's got to be dead," he announced.

"I hope you're right, but I don't know. I've seen some pretty wild things. Drive on, real slow; maybe we can get a better look."

Around the curve, the road straightened out and headed to the valley below. They stopped. Again Reeves trained his glasses on the car and the tree.

"It's totaled," he stated. "Smashed like a beer can. Looks like a weird Grandma Moses. There's even deer in the field. Looks like they scattered a bit. They're still staring at the wreck. Nothing's moving, nothing."

"Let me take a look." Bobby steadied the glasses and focused on the wreck.

"What do you think?" Reeves asked.

Bobby strained to see the slightest movement. He saw nothing. "He's got to be dead," he announced. "No one could live through that."

"I hope you're right, but this isn't getting us anywhere."

"I could check him out," Bobby volunteered.

"No," Reeves was emphatic. "We're not going to hike down through the snow and check him out. We're pushing our luck now. I don't want anyone taking our statement and looking into what the hell two dudes from D.C. are doing in this backwater."

"Headlights coming," Bobby announced.

"Let's get out of here, Bobby," Reeves directed. "If he's not dead now, he can die of 'complications' later."

"He's got to be dead," Bobby repeated.

"At least it ought to be ruled an accident," Reeves laughed. "Let's go home, Bobby."

"Your Mom called, David. She's quite upset. She can't reach your dad. Nobody's seen him. He left the cabin over an hour ago and isn't answering his cell phone." The Osgoods, Pam's parents, met them coming up to the house.

"What was he doing?" David asked.

"Nathan was having trouble, his asthma. He's all right. Your Dad was coming to town for medicine. I hope he's okay. It's such a miserable night." Ellen Osgood rarely saw a silver lining.

"Ah, he took the Cherokee," David stated as though that explained everything. "It's twenty years old and not what you'd call dependable. I'd better be going."

"Should you call your mom?" Ellen asked.

"No, Dad's tough, but I expect he's getting cold. Would you call her for me? He's got to be broken down. Dad's his own mechanic and that might explain a lot. Call you tomorrow, Pam."

"Sure, call me tomorrow, Honey."

David was both embarrassed and thrilled that she was so open with her affection.

In the car he weighed what he should do first. He considered making a pass through town, but decided if his dad was in town he didn't really have a problem. Rather he checked his gas and headed east out of town. If his mom couldn't reach his dad, he was most likely broken down in the mountains.

The ambulance passed him before he was two miles outside of town. He thought about the odds and tried to dismiss them, but he couldn't, not entirely. He saw their lights again when he started the long climb before the switchbacks. The police had traffic blocked just below where the guardrail began to wrap around the curve. Three squad cars and the ambulance were at the scene. The ambulance was backed up to the rail while the squad cars faced it with their spotlights trained below. As soon as he stopped, David was out of his car.

"Can you tell me who it is?" David shouted racing toward the officer

"Wrecker's about ten minutes out, Sam," Officer Dean Jackson talked into his hand-held and signaled for quiet turning his back on David. "Do you need anything else? Yeah, the guys are bringing the jaws down now. How's it look? Okay, okay, yeah, that's right."

"Can you tell me who it is? " David repeated. "My father is missing. He would have been on this road."

"I'm sorry, son, no one has identified the driver. We could barely identify the car." Jackson kicked himself and then continued on a more professional level. "What's your dad's name?"

"It's Aaron Chadwick. We have the last cabin on Oak Creek Gap Road. 911 Oak Creek Gap Road."

"Secretary Chadwick's your dad?"

"Yes, sir, he is. I'm David Chadwick. Can you tell me anything?

"I was about to run the plates. Give me a moment. Officer Jackson headed toward his patrol car.   Uninvited, David followed. "You need to understand, David, this will only tell us who licensed the car, not who was driving."

"What kind was it?" David asked.

"What kind was what?

"The car, you said they identified the car, what kind was it?"

Officer Jackson checked his notes, hesitated for just a moment and then stated flatly, "They think it was a Jeep Cherokee, an old one."

"Oh, God no! Are you sure? A Cherokee?"

"No, David, they are not positive; that's just what they guessed."

"That's what Dad was driving. He had to. I had his car. How bad is it?"

"I don't know, son. I'm sure they're doing everything they can. Let me run the plates."

"Hey Stonewall, they've almost got it out. What a godawful..."

Jackson hit the talk button on his radio and killed the transmission. "I'll check the plates now," he announced. Walking briskly toward his patrol car, Officer Jackson quickly switched his radio to earphones and listened intently. The word from the EMTs and police officers at the wreck was not good. While they were making progress and would have the body out shortly, the EMTs saw no signs of life. Given the condition of the car, they were not surprised.

David walked to the guardrail and stared through tears at the spotlighted wreckage below.

Officer Dean Jackson knew the Chadwicks. He liked them. Despite their prominence, they were not at all pretentious. They were good people. When the Secretary was in Washington, Jackson made a special effort to look after their place. The car was, indeed, a 1988 Jeep Cherokee registered to Aaron and Sharon Chadwick. He called dispatch for another cruiser.

"David, listen to me." Jackson walked to the rail, took the boy by the shoulders and turned him until they were face to face. "I've seen accident victims live where everything and everybody said they didn't have a prayer. I'm sorry, but it is your dad's car down there and I suspect he was driving. I hope to God he'll be okay. He's a wonderful man. For now, you're going to stay right here with me. The Highway Patrol out of Madison County will pick up your mom and brother. When they get here, we'll take you to the hospital. If your dad's going to make it you've got to let the EMTs do their job. The two guys with your dad are real pros."

Waiting was excruciating. David wasn't helping his father nor comforting his mother. He was essentially alone with his thoughts. He didn't have much hope, mainly despair and grief. Grief was such a selfish thing. His thoughts were of himself. Why hadn't he called home? He could have gone by the pharmacy. How could he go on without his dad? Who would he turn to for help? Why had he never told his dad how proud he made the whole family? "Please, dear God," he pleaded, "don't make him suffer. I couldn't stand it."

David Chadwick watched them scrambling up the hill. At one point the bearers almost lost the stretcher. He heard their effort as they strained under the load, but he could do nothing himself except cross his fingers. Surely they wouldn't be so careful with a dead man. As they neared the top he saw his father's lifeless body, strapped to the stretcher. His head, it had to be his head, was a red and black matted ball. It appeared distorted and without features. The EMTs balanced Aaron Chadwick on the guardrail as they prepared to lift him into the ambulance. At least he wasn't in a body bag.

As Officer Jackson attended to his duties, David was drawn closer and closer to the ambulance and the drama. He witnessed everything, but could do nothing. The emergency team ignored him and went about their business. He struggled not to interfere, not to ask the most obvious question. It was frustrating. They were professional. He wanted urgency. To them, his father was business as usual. To David, their movements were methodical, like a drill team. Maybe it was too late.

Stuart Weingardt was the lead EMT on this run and on every run he made. Before moving to Luray and Page County Memorial Hospital, he had been the Operating Room Supervisor at Atlanta General. Weingardt knew trauma. "Jake, have you given Page Memorial our ETA? We're ready to ride back here."

"No, not yet. Do you have him secure? I was waiting until you had him secured. Whenever you're ready, I'll call them." Jake answered. "Could an airbag have saved this dude?"

"He's not dead yet, Jake, but when you call the emergency room, tell them I think this one ought to be on a "Life Flight" to Bethesda. Looks like he has a severely depressed skull fracture. He is in a coma. Without some incredibly skilled intervention, I don't think he'll be coming out of it."

"I've got them on the phone, now. You can talk to them directly. I'm pulling out."

Shortly after the ambulance left for Luray, the Virginia Highway Patrol arrived with Sharon and Nathan Chadwick. To avoid any hassle from his superiors, Officer Jackson went off duty and drove the Chadwicks to the hospital in their own car. When they arrived Doctor Balison, the emergency room doctor, tried to comfort them, but he failed. Nothing he said was reassuring: Aaron was in critical condition. The prognosis was not good. They had done everything they possibly could. He was stable, but Aaron needed Bethesda. The helicopter was waiting. They would not be allowed to see him. There wasn't time.

Sharon could only sign releases. Whatever the medical personnel treating Aaron thought was necessary or advisable they could now do. The Life Flight waiting on the roof to transport what remained of Aaron Chadwick to Bethesda, Maryland was authorized to take off. The family also authorized the execution of Aaron Chadwick's donor card. In case of death his organs could now be legally "harvested."

As they watched the helicopter lift off, only Nathan waved.

CHAPTER SIXTEEN:

THE CHANGING LANDSCAPE

11:05 P.M., Thursday, January 25.

"It's a little late Jason," Elizabeth Anne noted. "I hope this is important."

"It is," Jason smiled. "Is the Vice President still up? I have news, really good news."

"Can you tell me?"

"Let me tell you both."

"That good, huh? Okay. Come with me. William is in the study."

Anticipating his new responsibilities, Vice President Roosevelt had sequestered himself and was diligently reading intelligence reports that he had previously neglected. While his chances of becoming president had slipped with the defection of Helen Ramirez, they were still very real. Roosevelt would be prepared.

"Jason, what brings you out on such a miserable night? Is it still snowing?" Roosevelt was completely comfortable with his Chief of Staff. Unlike Elizabeth Anne, he could be controlled.

"Good evening, sir. I just had to tell you. I've just had the most remarkable conversation with Secretary Pruett. She didn't want to talk to you, just me," he teased. "Tomorrow morning, she will announce that she has concluded that President Stanton is no longer capable of exercising the powers and duties of his office. She will pointedly note that she has not discussed her decision with you, but rather simply placed a courtesy call to me to inform us of her decision.

"That's fabulous. That exactly what we need going into this weekend." Elizabeth Anne was positively gleeful. "I'll take Secretary Pruett over Helen Ramirez any day of the week. Nancy Pruett has one hell of a following. This is just great! We're back in the driver's seat, Bill."

"Not quite, dear. I wish we were, but we're still one short if Aaron bolts. I'm afraid Secretary Chadwick is in the driver's seat," Vice President Roosevelt concluded. "It's wonderful, Jason. It really is. We're very close now."

"Aaron Chadwick is not going to bolt." Elizabeth Anne stated emphatically. "He went on record with you earlier today declaring to the whole world that President Stanton is incompetent. He can't switch. He'd look like an idiot. It's not going to happen."

"I wish I could be so sure," Roosevelt responded.

"Hi Lisa. We're on our way home." Ken Reeves' wife was also his office manager. They had been married thirty-five years. Not only were they grandparents, but they were also partners and neither could be compelled to testify against the other. Their marriage worked. "Honey, this transmission is for CC. It has to be ciphered and sent through secured channels. You ready?"

"Just a second," Lisa responded. "I was getting ready for bed. Let me get something to write with. Cynthia called. She put little Kenny on the phone. He calls me "grandma" just as clear as a bell. She sends her love. Okay, Kenny, I'm ready."

"Okay, Transmission follows: Reference confirmed purchase order 'Charlie,' 'Two,' 'Alpha,' 'Nine.' Order dispatched on day one at 22:07 within optimum time frame. Please remit full payment plus early fulfillment bonus upon third party confirmation as agreed. End transmission. Got it, Lisa?"

"I think so, but let me read it back to you, Kenny."

"Okay." Reeves listened patiently. Over the years he had come to value Lisa's meticulous nature. "That's correct, just as you read it. Can you send it tonight, Hon. I think our client is a little anxious."

"I'll do it immediately. How long before you get home?"

"Two and a half, three hours tops. Bobby and I might pick up a bite to eat, but other than that we'll be straight home. See you soon."

12:30 A.M., Friday, January 26.

Report of Secretary Chadwick's accident had come to FBI Director Parker's attention shortly after midnight. Duty Officer Hank Coe briefed him: Secretary Chadwick had been in an accident. He was in critical condition. Head injuries. No one else was involved – just a single car accident. The Secretary apparently lost control of his car after hitting a deer. He was on highway 211 coming out of the mountains heading toward Luray, Virginia. Although the exact time was unknown, it was well after dark. The weather was lousy, visibility poor, snow blowing. The road had some icy patches. Chadwick's car apparently slammed through or rolled over a guardrail, flew a good distance, and then careened down a mountain bouncing off one thing after another until it slammed into a monster oak. The car was totaled. The lead EMT said he should have died instantly.

The report seemed straightforward. While car accidents are not normally under the purview of the Federal Bureau of Investigation, Parker knew this was no ordinary car accident. It involved the Secretary of Interior, Aaron Chadwick. And Chadwick was the most influential member of the President's Cabinet at a time when that Cabinet was divided – deciding who would be President of the United States.

After years in Washington, Parker knew politics. He had seen the best and the worst. The stakes had never been higher. He could feel it coming. He had felt it before. It made him sick. Here again was the possibility of a high crime. He would be asked to prove a negative, that no crime had been committed. The wedding of conspiracy theorists and congressional opportunists was as certain as the legitimacy they would be given by willing media allies searching for ratings, revenue, and recognition.

All would milk the story. All would demand answers to their salacious speculation and hypotheticals:

"Isn't it possible that this accident was no accident?"

"Isn't it true that 'THEY' would want to make it look like an accident?"

"How do you know the President, or the President's men, didn't order the accident?"

"What are you hiding, Director Parker?"

Director Parker was about to be thrust on center stage. "Inquiring Minds" would never be satisfied, but he could hope others might consider indisputable facts. The first task was to "secure the accident/crime scene." There must be no contamination, breeding doubt and alternative theories. Within seconds of deploying the Bureau's quick response team he was on the phone to Virginia state and local officials requesting they secure the entire area from the Skyline Parkway to Luray. Director Parker would not have taken "No" for an answer. His personal involvement guaranteed a positive response.

The Bureau would take over at eight A.M. Its jurisdiction would not be questioned. Though Parker thought it highly improbable, if Aaron Chadwick's "accident" was attempted murder, it was most definitely a federal crime. Secretary Chadwick was a federal officer, a member of the President's Cabinet. The Constitution of the United States charged that same Cabinet and the vice-president with the responsibility of determining the ability of the president to discharge the powers and duties of his office. If he died, many would suspect he was killed in the line of duty fulfilling his Constitutional duty to determine the fitness of the president of the United States. What a motive!

Parker prayed it was an accident. He had to have the facts. The Bureau would literally leave no leaf or stone unturned. Despite the hour, he called Billie "Doc" Watson. Watson was the obvious choice to lead the investigation. He had spent a lifetime looking at accidents and uncovering crimes. He would have the full resources of the Bureau at his disposal.

6:10 A.M., Friday, January 26.

"Wake him, Hodges, it's important!" Jason had just learned of Secretary Chadwick's accident.

"Good God, Jason, don't you ever sleep?" Vice President Roosevelt hung onto the phone as he sat up in bed and tried to clear his head.

"You need to turn on CNN, sir. Secretary Chadwick is in critical condition. He was in an accident."

"What? Chadwick? When did this happen, Jason?" Roosevelt was stunned. "We were with him yesterday. Is Sharon all right? Was anyone else hurt?"

"Turn on CNN, sir. I'm sorry. I'm just learning about it now."

"Elizabeth Anne, turn on CNN. There's been an accident. Secretary Chadwick's been hurt."

"Hurt?" Elizabeth Anne fumbled for the remote. "Is it serious?" Her concern was palpable.

"We've got it on, Jason," Roosevelt announced. "Let me call you back. I won't be long. No, hold on, Jason. Just come on over."

"It'll take me a few minutes, sir. I'm at Annie's."

"Get here as soon as you can, Jason. We need to talk." Roosevelt's tone had softened. He was often guilty of forgetting Jason occasionally tried to have a real life."

6:18 AM, Friday, January 26.

"Good morning, Crayton. Mind telling me what I'm doing up at this hour? You know early morning is still the only time I sleep worth a damn."

"I tried to wait, but the news is not good, Mr. President." Crayton Langford had never seen President Stanton in pajamas. He couldn't help but notice the "Disney" pattern.

"They were a Christmas present, Crayton, from Devin. I promised him I'd wear them. You wouldn't want me to break a promise to my own grandson?" President Stanton rubbed his eyes and reached for the coffee Crayton had set on his bedside table. "What's your news?"

"Aaron Chadwick has been in an accident. He's at Bethesda in critical condition. I don't think they expect him to live.

"Oh, no! Aaron? Jesus, so many good people . . . How are Sharon and the kids? David was home, wasn't he?"

"They're alright, sir. Aaron was alone when it happened. I don't have any other details."

"Does Sharon have someone to help her? She'll need help. Why don't they expect him to live?"

"I really don't have any details, but apparently Aaron is in a coma."

"Sharon's parents and sister live in Virginia. I think they're close. I need to call Sharon. Is it too early?"

"I'm sure they had a late night. I'll ask Millie to put a call through about seven. That will give me time to learn some details," Crayton paused.

"Is there something else?"

"Yes, sir, there is. Secretary Pruett has scheduled a press conference for eleven. She called me late last night so we wouldn't be surprised. She intends to join the Vice President and sign the declaration."

6:30 A.M., Friday, January 26.

Elizabeth Anne found them in the study. She was still wearing her white bathrobe, but had been up long enough to make a phone call and bring them a pot of coffee. They were in opposite corners, backs to each other, left hands covering an ear and right hands holding phones.

"You're okay on the House side, Charlie? All right then, let me ask you to set it up with Louis. Call me if eleven won't work." Roosevelt paused, and then responded to an apparent question. " Yes, in fact Jason is talking to him now. Thomas is the expert and he's there because of you, Charlie." He listened again and then continued. "That's right, there must be no question. We'll talk it over, but right now my inclination is to go with his opinion, whatever it is. We simply must have consensus. See you there, Charlie."

"Charles Lynch, the Senate Majority Leader? Speaker Louis Mathis?" Moments before Elizabeth Anne had been convinced all the dominoes were falling in place. Now she had questions. "What's happened? Pruett's still on board, isn't she?"

"Pruett's not a problem; at least I hope not. The problem is Aaron. I know that's horribly insensitive, but he's the problem. We can hardly expect him to sign the Declaration of Incompetence while he's in a coma, but the fact is as long as he is alive we have a fourteen person Cabinet. A majority of fourteen is eight. Even with Secretary Pruett, we still need another convert."

"You can't be serious?" Elizabeth Anne exclaimed. "Thursday, yesterday, Chadwick joined you, in writing mind you, to declare President Stanton incapable of fulfilling his duties. It's Friday! For god's sake, William, nothing has changed!"

"You are only half right, dear," Vice President Roosevelt responded with controlled condescension. "You see one thing has very definitely changed, and one thing has remained the same. First, the change, since we submitted the declaration and I became Acting President, President Stanton has asserted that he is competent. That effectively limits my 'Acting Presidency' to four whole days. Maybe you missed that."

"William, I..."

"You will let me finish," Roosevelt commanded quietly. "What has remained the same throughout this crisis is the United States Constitution. It still requires a majority of the Cabinet to reassert their belief, you know, a second time, that the President is unable to discharge the powers and duties of his office.'"

"You know, William, you have a classic approach-avoidance complex. It's not uncommon in," Elizabeth Anne gained partial control of her anger and "losers" remained unspoken, but it was understood. "Oh William," she continued. "When the presidency is beyond your reach, you want it desperately, but when it is within your grasp, you can't quite seem to close the deal."

"You're wrong, dear. Take a deep breath. I will close the 'deal' as you call it, but I will close it in a manner that will guarantee my presidency legitimacy in the eyes of the American people." As Roosevelt continued his tone asked for understanding. "This is all new. I am assuming the presidency through a method never before used in the history of this great land. The American people must see our actions as an absolute necessity and absolutely in accordance with both the spirit and the letter of the Constitution. It is not a *coup d'état*. It is not a backroom deal. We are following Constitutional procedures. Understood?"

Elizabeth Anne remained silent, sullen and thoughtful.

"I'm sorry, dear. Shortly, Jason and I are going to the Capitol to meet with the Congressional Leadership and the Solicitor General. You have my word, Elizabeth Anne; before we adjourn we will have a common understanding of what in the hell the Constitution requires in these most unfortunate circumstances. I need you to take charge of the staff here and continue our efforts to woo additional Cabinet support. If you need me, buzz Jason. He'll know where we are in the meeting and whether we can be interrupted."

"We'll do our best." Elizabeth Anne saw no percentage in continuing the squabble. "Maybe another Cabinet member will join us and we'll have our majority by any definition."

"That would be great." Roosevelt responded. "You know I'd love for the question of what constitutes a majority to be purely academic, or moot, but if we can't convince another Cabinet member to join us, as long as Secretary Chadwick lingers between life and death, it has to be resolved."

"Are you ready, Jason?"

10:00 A.M., Friday, January 26.

"Ladies and gentlemen, before I take your questions I have a brief statement." As promised, Nancy Pruett, Secretary of Health and Human Services, began her regularly scheduled Friday press conference with the announcement that she believed the President Stanton was no longer capable of performing the duties of the President of the United States. She stated that in light of her personal relationship with the President and his monumental contribution to the nation, that her decision had been the most difficult she was ever required making. She noted that President Stanton had always put the nation first and she hoped that he would do so again. The nation could be spared the trauma and uncertainty that would inevitably result if President Stanton were to continue his challenge to the declaration before the Congress.

"I agreed completely with President Stanton's judgment last February when he selected William Roosevelt to be his Vice President," Secretary Pruett paused gaining the attention she wanted. "You will recall that the President stated then that he was selecting Senator Roosevelt to be his Vice President because he was a conciliatory figure in American politics who was ready and able to assume the powers and duties of the presidency if ever that were required. Unfortunately, I believe that it is required today. I am happy for the nation that President Stanton chose Vice President Roosevelt to be his successor. Are there any questions?"

"Secretary Pruett, Adam Shaw, NBC News. Given your experience, ability and rumored ambition, can you tell me and the American people, that there was no *quid pro quo* offered you by Vice President Roosevelt in exchange for your support?"

"Adam, I can tell you I have not even spoken to the Vice President about my decision. As a courtesy I did alert the President's chief of staff, Mr. Langford, as well as the Vice President's chief of staff, Mr. Fields, that I would be making this announcement. There is no *quid pro quo* here. Adam, the American people must know that only one factor influenced my decision and that was the fitness of the President to continue in office. Sadly, it is my belief that he is no longer able to perform his duties. It is therefore my constitutional duty to join with others to make Vice President Roosevelt the Acting President of the United States."

"You were not offered the Vice Presidency in a Roosevelt administration?" Sandra Bullock of ABC News shouted her question from the back of the auditorium.

"Sandra, if you were listening you would know that I just answered that question. I have had, as I said, no discussions with the Vice President of any sort concerning any position in his administration, including the one I currently occupy. Now let's move on."

Despite Secretary Pruett's protests, a few more questions followed in the same vein. But she was well rehearsed for them, as well as those that probed for specific evidence of presidential incompetence. She was not prepared, however, for the vast majority of questions which concentrated on her reaction to Secretary

Chadwick's untimely accident and the impact of his condition on the ability of the Vice President to achieve the majority of Cabinet officers as required by the constitution. Indeed it was obvious she had thought of it as only an accident and had not considered more sinister possibilities; that played almost as an attractive innocence, or so she thought.

The fact that the world was round took centuries to circumnavigate the world. The fact that Aaron Chadwick was in critical condition went around the world instantaneously at 6:07 A.M. Eastern Standard Time. CNN broke the story. President Stanton, Vice President Roosevelt, their chiefs of staff all learned of the accident from the same source at essentially the same time. By 8:00 A.M. all the networks carried the story and CNN's coverage included live interviews with Officer Jackson, and EMT Stewart Weingardt. While the automobile accident was now described in great detail and enhanced with photographs, Secretary Chadwick's condition was guarded in every sense.

At 11:00 A.M. the curtain lifted, but only slightly as Dr. Margaret Di Linzencio, Bethesda Naval Hospital physician/spokesperson, met the press in the hospital's main auditorium. Measured by microphones, lights, cameras, and media notables, a major news event was anticipated. "I have a brief statement concerning Secretary Chadwick's condition," Dr. Di Linzencio announced. "When I have concluded I will entertain your questions. Since information concerning the accident is still under investigation, I will limit my answers to medical assessments and facts known to this hospital. There will be no speculation from this podium."

Doctor Di Linzencio had just made news. Reporters were scribbling feverishly and kibitzing among themselves as to the implications of these announcements. Reading between the lines and interpreting what isn't said is a finely honed reportorial skill. Apparently speculation concerning Secretary Chadwick's accident was widespread and not simply limited to an ever-cynical media. Further, Chadwick's accident was being investigated. Who was doing the investigation? How wide ranging was that investigation?

Dr. Di Linzencio waited for silence. Only then did she begin: "Secretary Aaron Chadwick is in critical condition. He arrived at Bethesda Naval Hospital's heliport at 0:37 this morning. Medical crew aboard Virginia's Life-Flight helicopter eleven had successfully stopped his bleeding and stabilized Secretary Chadwick. The transfer documents provided reported he had been removed from a 1988 Jeep Cherokee off U.S. Highway 211 approximately six miles east of Luray, Virginia. The Secretary had experienced multiple fractures, including a severely depressed skull fracture. Within minutes of Bethesda's receipt of the patient, staff determined that surgical intervention was required. The operation was necessary to relieve intra-cranial pressure. It was successful to the extent that a skull fragment was lifted exposing a large subdural hematoma. That hematoma was suctioned and a shunt inserted. Currently Secretary Chadwick is in intensive care. He is in a coma, but appears to remain stable. Questions?"

"What's his prognosis?" The question erupted from a half-dozen reporters simultaneously. The answer would be their lead.

"Secretary Chadwick's injuries are life-threatening. He is in critical condition. His vital signs have been all over the place and continue to be of great concern. He is receiving the best care available."

"Doctor," Gerald Holder struggled with Dr. Di Linzencio's name and then gave up. "Doctor, how would you characterize Secretary Chadwick's coma."

"My colleagues call me Doctor 'D'; you may also. Unlike Doctor Kevorkian, my 'D' is not disparaging, just convenient. Secretary Chadwick responds to no stimuli. I suppose that could be described as a deep coma, but you should understand – as of now his coma is actually helpful. It limits both movement and brain activity and consequently it minimizes bleeding, pressure and additional injury. We are not now trying to rouse Secretary Chadwick. In fact we are supplementing the coma with some drug therapy."

"What drugs are being used, Doctor 'D'?" Holder followed his first question.

"I'm sorry; I don't have that information for you. Perhaps I can have it available at our next briefing." Doctor Di Linzencio turned to a colleague and apparently confirmed the schedule.

"That briefing is tentatively scheduled for 1100 hours tomorrow morning here in the auditorium."

"Valerie Flowers, Fox News, two questions. Had Secretary Chadwick been drinking and if the Secretary survives do his injuries suggest that he will be impaired, mentally impaired?"

"The transfer document noted that Secretary and Mrs. Chadwick had had wine with dinner. The alcohol levels we found did not affect treatment decisions. At this time, the answer to your second question would be pure speculation."

"You don't have an informed opinion?"

"I have answered your question, Mrs. Flowers." Dr. Di Linzencio was emphatic. "Are there others? I have time for two more."

"Doctor 'D', John Wolfson, ABC News. Is the Secretary's family with him?"

"No, Mr. Wolfson, The Secretary is in intensive care. I met with his family just before coming here. They are staying nearby and we have staff members on call for them. One more question."

"Randy Mulberg, NBC. Are Secretary Chadwick's injuries entirely consistent with an automobile accident?"

As live coverage of the news conference ended, Fox News returned to its midday anchors, Brian Valentine and Julianne Shepherd. Shuffling papers, a "stunned" Brian Valentine took a moment to compose his thoughts and then read from the teleprompter. "Well, Julianne, there you have it. Secretary Chadwick is in critical condition, just hanging between life and death. Tragic."

Julianne seem similarly affected, but still professional. "I suspect, Brian," she read, "we should recap the breaking news from Bethesda Naval Hospital for those viewers just joining us. Moments ago, a spokesperson from Bethesda announced to the world that Secretary of the Interior Aaron Chadwick was in a deep coma, in intensive care and in critical condition. He was found last night, alone in a totaled automobile. His injuries are life-threatening. The cause of the accident is a mystery."

"It's a very consequential mystery," Brian intoned with solemnity, "perhaps as consequential as the bullets fired by Lee Harvey Oswald."

"It's incredulous," Julianne ticked off the facts. "Yesterday, Aaron Chadwick, Secretary of the Interior, joined seven other Cabinet members and declared President Andrew Holmes Stanton incompetent. Their declaration removed President Stanton from power and made Vice President Roosevelt the Acting President of the United States. Today, Secretary Chadwick lies in critical condition at Bethesda Naval Hospital, the victim of a near fatal automobile accident, and President Stanton is positioned to regain the Presidency."

"Well, that's the story we are to believe, Secretary Chadwick has suffered a very timely, consequential and coincidental accident – a remarkable turn of events. And remember, Julianne, Secretary Chadwick was the dominant player in the Cabinet. Now he's not a player at all. He's incapable of joining his colleagues to reassert the President's disability as required by the Constitution."

"What a difference a day makes," Julianne mused.

"President Stanton appears to be living a charmed life," Brian commented. "What a difference, indeed. Of course, there's the unspoken question. It's on everyone's mind. Here at Fox News we cut to the quick. Did Chadwick's accident involve foul play or was it just a fortuitous turn of events for the President of the United States as he fights to stay in power?"

"'Foul Play' or 'Fortuitous Event' that's the question and Fox News wants to know your opinion. Phone in your vote to 1 800 Fox News or vote at our web site at www.foxnewsknows.com We'll have preliminary results at the end of our 'midday program' and you can learn final results tonight when the polls close on 'Fox News Night.' Remember your call is free on Fox."

The suggestive media was in full swing "connecting the dots." As always there would be more conspiracies hatched after the fact than before. The absence of factual information was liberating to freethinking conspirators.

Late in the day The Insider, a "leading" grocery store tabloid, got the jump on its competition with a special edition. Their 70-point headline question, "ACCIDENT?" capped a vivid photograph of Secretary Chadwick's demolished Jeep Cherokee. The subtitle asked another: "Presidential Foe Victim of Foul Play?"

Noon, Friday, January 26.

Four men and one woman sat in a semicircle around Acting President Roosevelt's desk in the Vice President's House side, U.S. Capitol Office. Their small talk seemed incongruous with who they were, where they were and what they were about. The Acting President of the United States, his chief of staff, the Speaker of the House of Representatives, the Majority Leader of the United States Senate, and the chairmen of their respective Judiciary Committees were waiting impatiently on Thomas B. Pickering, the Solicitor General of the United States. As Jason announced to the group that he had called Pickering's office and been told the Solicitor General was out and would not be back until midafternoon, Pickering arrived. He was breathless and cold.

"I'm sorry I kept you waiting, but I think you'll find I am well-rehearsed. I was with Attorney General Herrera until about ten minutes ago. He kept a group of us at Justice, meeting on this same topic all morning. By the way, that man is not only my boss, he is also one hundred percent behind President Stanton. I'd just as soon my presence here did not make the evening news."

"Thank you for coming, Thomas. Maybe the delay will serve us well." Roosevelt's demeanor was sincere and serious as he opened the meeting. "Thank you all for coming. Gentlemen, lady, I need your best counsel. Secretary Chadwick's critical condition raises a most troublesome question: simply put, we need to know what constitutes a majority of the Cabinet when one of its officers is incapacitated. Specifically, there are fourteen Cabinet Secretaries, but with Secretary Chadwick in a coma, is the Constitutionally required 'majority of the principal officers of the executive departments' reduced from eight of fourteen to seven of thirteen, or is it not. Incapacitation is again the problem."

Solicitor General Pickering spoke not only from his position of legal authority, but as a recognized constitutional scholar on leave from his position as Dean of Vanderbilt University's School of Law. "I'm sorry, sir, but there is no definitive answer or even a consensus answer to your question – not among practitioners, academia, or for that matter any place else. What we discovered this morning with Attorney General Herrera, is that the question has simply never been asked, therefore it has never been answered either in theory or in practice, with authority or without authority."

"But isn't it obvious," Speaker Mathis spoke with an abundance of confidence, "that in the real world, the House and Senate would make that determination. After all the declaration of incapacity comes to us, so we will determine if it carries the requisite number of signatories. If it does, we proceed. If it doesn't, we don't. I would think our decision would be final, just as the Constitution makes us the sole judge of our own elections. It's not as if we don't work with majorities and pluralities around here twenty-four hours a day."

"Me thinks the Speaker defends the prerogatives of his legislative branch too much," Pickering announced to the others. "Of course, you might be right, Louis, but I believe that such a controversial decision would inevitably be appealed to the Supreme Court. After all, not only could it result in ousting a popularly elected President, but also every citizen in the country would have standing to bring suit. Any one of them could bring suit," Pickering laughed.

"First," Speaker Mathis replied, "I don't believe when there are only thirteen Cabinet officials capable of making a decision that the American people would find a congressional judgment that seven constitutes a majority of the thirteen to be particularly controversial. Second, while every American might have standing, I would argue that the Judiciary does not have jurisdiction."

Pickering's rebuttal gave no quarter. "While that position would carry the day here among your colleagues, Mr. Speaker, if that day truly comes you would be arguing your 'jurisdiction case' not here, but before the Supreme Court and their decisions can not be predicted much less appealed.'

"Slow down, gentlemen," Roosevelt interrupted. "What do you think, Charles?"

Senate Majority Leader Lynch was unflappable and unequivocal. "Well, while I believe the American people would initially accept a congressional decision that seven cabinet secretaries constitute a majority, I also believe that the decision would be appealed. It would be appealed in the Judiciary Committees, on the floor, and in the press, as well as to the Supreme Court. With all that discussion, in time people would learn that the U. S. Constitution does in fact distinguish between majorities of membership, and majorities of those present and voting. At that point some percentage of the American people will conclude and never be dissuaded, that since the authors of the Twenty-Fifth Amendment did not use the phrase "a majority of the officers present' they in fact meant a majority of the entire membership. For us to argue that our distinguished predecessors and three fourths of all the State legislators just screwed up would not be well received. I believe your Presidency, Mr. Roosevelt, would be compromised."

"Ms Roberts?"

Sierra Roberts, Chairperson of the House Judiciary Committee, had earned influence even beyond her powerful position by an uncanny ability to anticipate public opinion. She spoke easily. "Mr. Vice President, I believe you need eight cabinet members in your camp. Not because it is constitutionally required – that is unclear – but because it is clearly politically required. The people understand that some decisions, some important decisions, must be beyond a reasonable doubt. If we choose to remove a popularly elected president, all of our actions must be constitutional beyond any reasonable doubt. You must have a minimum of eight cabinet members support the reassertion that President Stanton is no longer capable of performing his duties."

"Senator Talbert, how do you see this unfolding?" Roosevelt already had his answer, but he listened patiently.

"Mr. Vice President...huh...Acting President Roosevelt, I could take the heat. We all could. We could go with seven, run over the opposition, but I, too, believe your Presidency would be compromised. Now as a Republican that's not a great concern for me, but as an American it is. Mr. Roosevelt, my committee will hold exhaustive hearings on this matter. If you prevail in the Congress, the legitimacy of your Presidency would best be served if your reassertion of the inability of the President to perform his duties was supported by an undeniable majority of eight." And then as an uncomfortable afterthought he added, "Of course, seven would be sufficient if Secretary Chadwick doesn't make it."

"Thank you, gentlemen. Thank you, Ms. Roberts. I appreciate your candor. You have confirmed what my better inclinations have been telling me. I know now which course is best. I

will not proceed without a clear, indisputable, majority of the Cabinet."

Just a few hours later, listeners of National Public Radio's "All Things Considered" and viewers of the Public Broadcasting System's "Jim Lehrer News Hour" received much the same information that Acting President Vice President Roosevelt had heard in his Capitol Office. This time the information came from the academic community's legal scholars. Both programs as well as "Washington Week in Review" devoted major portions of their broadcasts to the examination of the impact of a comatose Cabinet Secretary on the "Cabinet majority" requirement of the Twenty-Fifth Amendment.

Margaret Warner conducted the interview, which offered the most succinct explanation of the requirements of the Twenty-Fifth. She spoke with Richard Thurman, professor emeritus Stanford University, and Harry Shapiro, Chairman of the Political Science Department at Rutgers University. They were two old friends whose lifetime interest had, until now, been of great interest to no one but themselves.

"So," Margaret began after the setup piece, "tell us why there is so much confusion as to the meaning of this Amendment, Doctor..."

Shapiro was off. It wasn't just his fifteen minutes of fame; this was his life's work. "Margaret, you must understand, Section Four of the Twenty-Fifth Amendment has never, never been invoked. This is the first time; the first time the Amendment has confronted the clarifying test of reality. We knew there were problems, but we also knew they would only be resolved in practice and in court."

"That's right," Thurman interrupted with John Madden-like enthusiasm. "Up until Thursday, just yesterday, Section Four existed only on paper; black ink on white parchment. For forty years it sat on the bench waiting to play. Now it's in the game and we will see how it works. All of the Constitution is defined by use in case law. Even terms as simple as the word 'no' in 'congress shall make no law. . . abridging freedom of speech' has had to be clarified again and again. You can abridge slander, you can limit libel, you can prohibit perjury, and you can limit incitement. Even the free exercise of religion has been limited. Parents cannot endanger the lives of their children in the name of religion. A group of consenting adults can do damn near anything but get married; polygamy is prohibited. All the passages have to be interpreted against the realities of the times. We are about to learn what majority means in Section Four..."

As Thurman paused for a breath, Shapiro took over. "Taken quite literally the Constitution requires a majority of the fourteen-member cabinet, in other words, eight. The Twenty-Fifth Amendment does not admit to the lesser requirement of a majority of 'those present and voting' found elsewhere in the Constitution. Nevertheless, this is its first time out of the box. Certainly we know what a majority is, and isn't, at the extremes. Fourteen of fourteen certainly constitutes a majority and one of fourteen certainly does not. Now as it is tested with Secretary Chadwick lying in a coma, reality is about to define majority at the margins. The question is simply this: If eight is solid, is seven sufficient?"

Before Margaret Warner could reclaim the floor, Thurman exclaimed, "Oh, I love this man. He does have a way with words," and News Hour control cued her, "Let him go. It's good."

"Yes, indeed, you do have a way with words. But, Harry, academically the real question is not what a majority is, but what is the universe. If the universe of cabinet members is fourteen, then a majority is eight. If the universe is thirteen, a majority is seven. The real question is the size of the universe of Cabinet members.' Thurman turned to his friend and took over the interview, "Does the incapacitation of a Cabinet member reduce the size of the Cabinet?"

"Well, Richard, if it does, then that fact might encourage foul play - if not now, then in the future." Dr. Shapiro should have quit with that insight, but in his enthusiasm he continued, "We could have Cabinet Secretaries dropping like flies."

"Yes, gentlemen," Margaret interrupted, "but would you now address the political question."

"Well, that is the real question," Dr. Thurman acknowledged. "Will anything less than a clear majority, obvious to all, be accepted by the American people? I don't think so. I think if Mr.

Roosevelt and the Congress try to sell his Presidency on the cheap, it would be severely compromised from the get-go."

"Get-go?" Shapiro laughed. "What my learned colleague from the hills of west Texas is trying to say is this. A Roosevelt presidency based on a declaration of incompetence supported by only seven members of the Cabinet would lack legitimacy. It would be impotent from the outset, or the 'get-go' as he so quaintly observed."

"Well, thank you, gentlemen," Margaret smiled. "It's been entertaining and informative. We'll be seeking your analysis regularly over the next few weeks until this situation has played out."

Before Margaret Warner could introduce the next segment of the News Hour, Dr. Thurman continued his analysis. "It should be 'played out' in no more than twenty-four days. Vice President Roosevelt has three more days to reassert President Stanton's incompetence and then the Congress must decide the issue within twenty-one days. That's a total of twenty-four days."

"Ah, but are those calendar days, work days, or legislative days?" Dr. Shapiro asked. "So many questions, so little time."

"Another time," Ms. Warner asserted emphatically. "Thank you again, gentlemen."

While the audiences for these programs were relatively small, they included a significant number of influential opinion leaders or so, at least, each program's promotional demographics reported. For this program and particularly Margaret Warner's interview with Doctors Shapiro and Thurman there would be hard evidence. Commander Croft and Elizabeth Anne Roosevelt were regulars and tonight they were especially interested in the scheduled, "What's in a Majority" segment. They split a bottle of iced chardonnay

"You know, he may be right, Dad." Elizabeth Anne's report preceded the "News Hour." She had just come from home and a disagreeable exchange with the Vice President. She had learned directly from her husband that he would not challenge President Stanton unless he had "eight Secretaries, a clear majority of the Cabinet, willing to rebut the President and declare Stanton incapable of exercising the powers and duties of his office."

"God Damn it!" Roosevelt had argued angrily, "A questionable majority will doom this country to an ineffective President. How is an ineffective President any better than incompetent one? I will not be that President, Elizabeth Anne. I will not!"

At that juncture, Elizabeth Anne reported she had responded calmly (patronizingly, Roosevelt surely thought), "I understand, Dear." There was in fact no point in arguing. As always, she would do what she had to do.

"He didn't leave it there, Daddy," Elizabeth Anne continued, "No, my dear husband concluded his raving with: 'As long as Secretary Chadwick lives,' she mimicked a pompous Roosevelt, 'we must have eight. Binder's our only chance. It's all up to Secretary Binder.'" Elizabeth Anne paused, sighed with exasperation. "All up to Binder, my ass."

"Your husband does seem a little passive in his pursuit of the presidency," Croft noted sarcastically.

"It's his: 'All right, if you insist, I'll serve' posture. My god, it's pathetic," Elizabeth groaned. "You know he really thought Stanton would plead with him to take over and save his Presidency."

"Your Bill can be just a little naïve," Croft agreed.

"I've said it before. He wants to be President, but he wants to be squeaky clean."

"Maybe that's best, Elizabeth Anne. We can be big about it. You and I, we'll do what we must. Just remember, it will be our presidency. We'll let William believe he earned it flying on an angel's wings. It will make him a more credible president. Later, when he's into the office a bit, we might have to tell him the truth. Then he can choose either healthy denial or disgrace and destruction of the office."

"Hold on, here it comes, Dad." Elizabeth Anne reached for the remote and increased the volume on the "News Hour." They listened together until it was nearly over.

"God Dammed eggheads." The Commander was not impressed with the analysis of Shapiro and Thurman. "What do they know? They analyze the news. We make it. We could ram seven through the Congress. Then it's a *'fait accompli.'* Twenty-four hours, forty-eight tops, and 'the people' would be back to 'Days of our Lives.' That was bull shit."

"I don't know, Dad, maybe William's right."

"It doesn't matter, Elizabeth Anne. That bastard Chadwick is going to die. And dead makes seven an obvious majority, even to the dumbest son of a bitch."

"What do you hear, Dad?' Are they still in the field?"

"Nothing," Croft answered, "but they know what's got to be done and when it's got to be done. We'll know it, when it's announced. That's billing day and our payday." Croft took a sip of wine, smiled and patted his daughter's hand. "You know, Honey, these people trying to report the news don't understand. Hell, they don't have the foggiest idea. The events they are trying to analyze are controlled by the politics we control. We will do damn well what we want."

"I suppose. Still I wish I knew what Bethesda's using to keep him sedated." Elizabeth Anne laughed.

"Don't worry, our contractor knows," Croft's conviction was absolute. "He's incredible."

"I guess I should dust off the family Bible?"

"Of course, we'll need it for the swearing-in ceremony." Croft finished his wine in grandiose fashion.

The day ended with "Nightline's" host emeritus, Forest Sawyer, again walking the media tight rope pursuing both professional reportage and ratings. His guests, Sierra Roberts, Chairperson of the House Judiciary Committee, and her counterpart, Senator Richard Talbert, Chairman of the Senate Judiciary Committee, were scheduled to talk about Congressional hearings on President Stanton's competence. Sawyer's producers expected him to see that the discussion strayed to President Stanton's culpability in Secretary Chadwick's accident. Sawyer hoped he would play only a minor role in the show's run for ratings.

"Congresswoman Roberts, Senator Talbert, welcome to 'Nightline.' Your committees will share the lead roles in the Presidential drama now playing in Washington. Would you explain to our viewers the focus of your hearings? Let's begin with you, Ms. Roberts."

"Thank you, Forest. Your listeners might believe that Chairman Talbert and I are leading a partisan rush to judgment," Sierra Roberts looked directly at the camera, "but that is not the case. It is true we have scheduled hearings starting Tuesday morning even though we have yet to receive the required reassertion of Presidential incompetence. Scheduling hearings is not being partisan. It is being prudent."

"You mean," Sawyer interrupted, "your actions could be considered premature since President Stanton has asserted his competence and the Acting President and a majority of the Cabinet have yet to resubmit their assertion that President Stanton is no longer able to execute the powers and duties of his office."

"Yes, that's exactly right. However if the second shoe does drop, the decision we will be required to make is momentous and the time frames extremely tight. We simply have to be prepared for the possibility that hearings will be required. You realize, Forest, our committees will have no more than two weeks to determine the competence of the President of the United States. That will leave only one week for the issue to be debated in the full House and Senate. We must be prepared."

While each insisted that the primary focus of their committee hearings would indeed be to determine the competence of President Stanton to continue in office, without prompting, they both solemnly assured Sawyer and the American public that they were also engaged in an exhaustive investigation of the conduct of not only President Stanton and Acting President Roosevelt, but also their staffs.

"If there were foul play it will be exposed and will undoubtedly weigh heavily on our deliberations," Ms. Roberts volunteered.

"Forest, I say to you and to the American public it is a sad, sad day in the history of our great Republic that we are forced to consider the real possibility that the President of the United States might be compromised in the tragic accident that now threatens the life of Secretary Aaron Chadwick." Senator Talbert, in addition to being Chairman of the Senate Judiciary Committee, was also the majority Whip and therefore a leading Republican partisan. It came with the position.

"Nightline" was again not just covering the news; it was making the news. Fortunately, this time no baiting had been required, just everyday "take no prisoners" partisanship. Sawyer, a pro, now cemented the headline and strived for at least the perception of balance. "Senator Talbert, you and Ms. Roberts have made a credible case for preparing for hearings, but surely it is premature to be talking about 'the real possibility' of President Stanton's involvement in Secretary Chadwick's tragic accident. What makes this a 'real' possibility, Senator?"

"Please, Forest, I certainly did not mean to suggest that President Stanton was, in any way, personally involved in the Chadwick tragedy. What we all must understand is the stakes in this contest are enormous for many people, people who are not only the 'die-hard' supporters of the administration, but those are the 'enemies within' this administration."

"But Senator, again I ask, what evidence do you have?" While Sawyer pressed, he worried that even pursuing the question gave credence to its premise.

"Forest, our investigations are just beginning, but let me tell you there are important, powerful, people within this administration who are now threatened with the loss of everything they hold dear. We will leave no stone unturned in our investigation of the untimely coincidence of Secretary Chadwick's 'accident.' We will find the truth."

Philip Lamb   158

CHAPTER SEVENTEEN:

PROFESSIONALS

11:05 P.M., Friday, January 26.

The Commander's message traveled tens of thousands of miles as it bounced between the earth and a dozen satellites. Each time it was relayed it was translated again into another one-time randomly generated language. It arrived almost instantly in another Washington suburb. Un-ciphered the Commander was clear and direct: Coma does not meet contractual requirement or constitutional need. Contract requires accidental death within thirty-seven hours.

Reeves's response was immediate. It traveled a similarly convoluted path back through cyber space. "Bethesda Naval Hospital information office will make sad announcement no later than Sunday night at midnight, 2400 hours."

Reeves had worked hospitals before. He was personally familiar with the Bethesda Naval Hospital. Indeed, both he and Bobby, though years apart, had been patients there. Hospitals provided some challenges, but not many. Death was common there. Infections ran rampant. Mistakes with meds, and diets, and dosages were commonplace. President Stanton's own Secretary of Health and Human Services, Nancy Pruett, had, in fact, labeled the problem "a national disgrace." Her department tracked accidental deaths by hospital and published the results annually. The patients most vulnerable were those, like Aaron Chadwick, who were incapable of interacting with their health care providers. Reeves was confident he and young Robert could engineer Secretary Chadwick's demise consistent with Bethesda's "HHS Report of In Patient Hospital Deaths."

9:00 A.M., Saturday, January 27.

"Good morning, Mrs. Wilson." Robert Parker, Director of the Federal Bureau of Investigation, was not a stranger to the White House, but his unscheduled appearance Saturday morning was a surprise to the President's secretary. "I gather I didn't make the right list," he smiled.

"Is he expecting you, Director?" Even though Robert Parker was an obvious favorite Millie was always on guard against the bureaucratic end run.

"He called me, himself, Millie. I thought it a bit unusual, but he is my President." He smiled easily radiating a combination of charm, confidence, intelligence, and athleticism that Millie, like others, found both faintly annoying and quite irresistible.

"President Stanton, Director Parker is here. He says you called him direct; that you needed to see him immediately."

"That's right, Millie. Please send him in. Give us ten minutes undisturbed," President Stanton directed. "And, Millie, I'd like you to forget his appointment."

"Well, yes, sir. Of course, whatever you say, Mr. President." Millie's puzzlement was obvious even as she turned away from the Director and back to her monitor. "Go on in, Mr. Parker. He is expecting you."

Robert Parker had achieved his lifelong ambition early. He had risen through the ranks and now had served as Director longer than anyone but J. Edgar Hoover, himself. Under his leadership, the Bureau had achieved in reality the excellence his predecessors had regularly claimed. Even rival organizations routinely sang his praises. He had been tested, time and time again, and hindsight regularly confirmed his foresight.

President Stanton met his Director as he was shown into the Oval Office. "Robert, please have a seat," the President motioned toward two high back leather chairs separated only by a small Queen Anne table. "As you might imagine, I'm rather busy," he stated dryly, "so I'll get right to the point."

"Thank you, Mr. President." Parker was surprised.

For all of his troubles President Stanton seemed almost unburdened. He moved purposely to the far chair, sat down, leaned forward, adjusted his glasses and picked up a clipboard. He handed it to his Director. "Take a look, Robert."

"Yes, sir." Director Parker scanned several pages consisting of a collage of headlines from around the nation.

"I have two jobs for you, Robert. As you can see, it has been widely reported that Secretary Chadwick's accident was no accident..."

"Mr. President, sir," Director Parker tried to interrupt.

"Let me continue, Robert," President Stanton insisted. "In fact, as you will note it is also being reported that I, or members of my administration, have the most to gain from his death and may have ordered the 'accident.' I want you to ..."

"Mr. President, I'm sorry, sir, but please say nothing more until you hear me out. The Bureau is already aggressively investigating the circumstances surrounding Secretary Chadwick's accident. Because of the allegations against you, this conversation cannot continue. Even without malicious intent it could and would be misconstrued and then misrepresented."

"I understand your concern, Robert, so I will be as circumspect as I know how. I want you to write an executive order for my signature requiring the cooperation of every member of my administration with your investigation. There will be no claim of executive privilege. Additionally, the political Schedule C appointees must understand they have no right to employment in this administration. They serve at my pleasure. Of course, they retain their constitutional right against self-incrimination, but if they invoke that right, I will not be pleased and they will not be retained. Make it as explicit as you believe appropriate."

"Yes, sir, I will." Parker was impressed. This was executive privilege of a very different order. The President apparently believed Secretary Chadwick's accident was just that, an accident, but his next comments revealed more than a little doubt.

"Just as important, Director, "President Stanton stopped, collected himself, and took a deep breath. He leaned forward, clutching his hands together, his eyes fixed on Parker, commanding his attention. "Just as important, Director, you are to consider the threat to Secretary Chadwick's life as real. You and the Bureau must ensure his safety. You are to do whatever is required. You have blanket authorization. You need ask no one and you need tell no one. Secretary Chadwick's safety, his security, is in your hands. He is your responsibility. You are to leave nothing to chance. Do you understand?"

"Yes sir, I do. But I must ask, Mr. President, do you suspect the threat is real?"

"No, Robert, I don't, but it doesn't matter. You must consider it real. You must consider it imminent. We cannot take chances with the Republic. Whatever the odds, miniscule, infinitesimal, they are too great to put our democracy at risk."

"You have no information?" Director Parker persisted. "No basis for suspicion?"

"I do not, Robert." President Stanton spoke slowly picking his words with care. "The conspiracy theorists are not all wrong. This nation is confronting a constitutional crisis. The stakes are incredible. There will be winners and there will be losers. For such a prize, not everyone can be expected to play by the rules. Political history is more a tale of blood than ballots. Secretary Chadwick is the most influential member of my Cabinet. This accident is untimely. I know nothing, I suspect nothing, but I also reject nothing as impossible. I am uneasy, so very, very uneasy. You must leave nothing to chance."

"I understand, Mr. President, and I assure you we will do all we can to protect Secretary Chadwick. Unfortunately, as I hope you will understand, sir, this is the only assurance I can give you. We must have no further contact and that, of course, extends to our respective staffs.

Stanton nodded, "Of course, it has to be that way. The people's confidence in this process has already been shaken. Any impropriety, real or imagined, will destroy it." Then, more reflective, President Stanton added, "Another 'coincidence' like Secretary Chadwick's and neither Roosevelt nor I will be able to govern."

"I'm afraid you're right, Mr. President." Robert Parker stood. "I wish you well, sir."

His concern was very real, greater than President Stanton imagined. Director Parker's job was to assume the worst. Secretary Chadwick was just one of fourteen Cabinet Secretaries; all would require twenty-four-hour protection. If one was at risk, they all were. He considered, just for a moment, discussing their safety with the President. He chose instead to excuse himself. "I'll do my best, Mr. President."

9:10 A.M., Saturday, January 27.

Ken Reeves met Bobby Hearst at Bethesda's South Gate. Hearst had driven while Reeves had taken Metro's Redline to the Medical Center Station. Both men were enrolled in the Department of Defense's TRICARE program and had been to Bethesda many times. Nevertheless, they needed to scout out the mission; the National Naval Medical Center at Bethesda, Maryland is a huge place. What they found would dictate the "final solution."

While a number of vehicles were backed-up at the gate being randomly searched, the pedestrian line was short and moving right along. First Reeves and then Bobby completed the entry ledger. They knew the routine and had their military identification cards ready when the guard asked for them. The young man made a quick visual check and then passed the card across the scanner. There was no "heightened security," the procedures hadn't changed.

Reeves and Hearst passed on to the "Campus" and headed toward the Intensive Care Unit (ICU). It was on the third floor of Building Ten. The Navy's user-friendly web site included directions, visitor hours and guest procedures. Reeves had printed them out, as well as a Metro map. From the gate, he and Bobby walked to the Visitors' Garage, took the second skyway on the far left to Building Ten and then the elevator to the third floor. The web site was right on; there it was. Even after six years of terrorism, his country had not forgotten it was a democracy and these facilities belonged to the people.

Bethesda's ICU was obviously a large unit. Wandering the third floor corridors they discovered several entry points. Deathwatch reporters milled around each. Reeves found them boorish and insensitive. On pay phones they dictated stories in whispers, but with each other they talked in tones that announced they were oblivious to their surroundings and wanted a larger audience. Apparently, because of fire regulations, all of the entry points including that from the visitors' waiting room had oversized double doors wide enough to accommodate gurneys, fluids and side walkers.

Reeves had found his staging area. The waiting room was spacious, had limited traffic, fewer reporters, and immediate access to the ICU. He took it all in at a glance. It was nearly perfect. In addition to the waiting room there were nearby bathrooms and three consultation rooms. Each of the latter had a narrow vertical soundproof window guaranteeing that doctors and patient families would not be needlessly interrupted. Reeves smiled. In the bathroom he would become a doctor and as a doctor he would commandeer a consultation room. Through the window a doctor would be seen discussing the dismal prospects of his patient with a distraught relative. He and Bobby would not be interrupted. They would not be rushed. How convenient, he thought. They could observe the ICU at their leisure and pick just the right time.

Whether the reporters were preoccupied by Chadwick or just self-absorbed, Reeves and Hearst took corner seats in the waiting room without causing the slightest stir. They needed to get a feel for the ICU. Tomorrow they would join the staff and Reeves wanted to be in sync with its professional rhythms. Thumbing through a magazine, Bobby tried to concentrate and make mental notes of everything; tomorrow would be his graduation. Reeves scribbled cryptic notes in flowered sympathy cards. Tonight he would check his memory and repeatedly visualize variations of the end game.

Occasionally the men talked quietly. Neither used the other's name. Reeves needed less than a minute; he would enter the room with a drawn syringe in his lab coat, make the injection and leave. It was a question of timing–like jumping rope or a comic routine with actors coming on and off stage through a dozen doors, but never seeing each other.

Reeves and Bobby patiently observed the trickle of doctors, nurses, anesthesiologists, lab techs, pharmacy techs, orderlies, maintenance, and sanitary personnel that passed by and in and out of the ICU. Tomorrow they would slip into that stream. While there were no consistent patterns, it was slow and doable. Reeves wouldn't count on luck; Bobby would be ready with an inconsequential, but sufficient diversion.

Early on, an attractive nurse stepped out of the ICU and conferred with a couple of reporters. Within minutes they all broke for coffee.

"They've got an insider," Reeves noted.

"She must think he's going to live a few more minutes," Bobby observed. "When are you thinking?"

"Midmorning, Bobby, I'll have the meds tonight. Tomorrow, before the break, we'll be stationed in that nearest consultation room. Then we'll play it by ear."

"Will I be going in?

"You'd need a good cover, but I'd like you with me. If I'm interrupted you could buy me a moment or two with Chadwick."

"I'd like to help, sir."

"Sure?"

"Yes, sir, I'm sure."

"You've seen the exchange carts?" Reeves checked his protégé.

"Yes, sir, from Central Supply. Young fellow about my age pushed one into the ICU just after we sat down. He came out with a different one. The load had shifted and it happened pretty fast."

"Good, Bobby. Okay, then, you'll be pushing or pulling one of those carts. You'll park it near the doorway ready to push it forward or pull it back to block any interruption. If you have to you'll dump some sterile supplies and buy me some time."

As they talked only a door separated the would-be killers from Aaron Chadwick. Still in critical condition and dependent on a half dozen life-support systems Chadwick had been stabilized in a coma. At the Friday afternoon briefing, Dr. Leon Starling, Secretary Chadwick's primary physician, described Chadwick's history of allergic reactions and the combination of IV drugs used to sustain his coma. It included sub lethal therapeutic doses of pentobarbital. Reeves would change the concentration using Chadwick's injection port, a simple *coup de grace* ending the Secretary's suffering.

A single minute, probably less, that was all he needed. Reeves understood things could still go to hell, but compared to a lot of his jobs, Chadwick's "degree of difficulty" looked like a cakewalk.

The autopsy would confirm the obvious. It would concentrate on the accident, clearly the cause of death. The medical examiners would consider whether it was rigged, but it wasn't. Reeves was there. It was an accident. They would find pentobarbital and all the other therapeutic drugs used at Bethesda, but those would be expected and even the high concentration would be dismissed as kidney or other organ failure. They certainly would not find Bethesda's desperate efforts to save Chadwick to be the cause of death when the accident was so clearly responsible.

"Do you need any more time here, Bobby?" Reeves asked.

"No, I'm okay with it." Hearst tried to contain his pleasure. He was being treated as a full partner. "I'll be ready."

"Good. Tomorrow is Sunday; it will be just as slow as today. We won't go in until we're comfortable."

"I'll be fine," Bobby responded.

"Okay, then." Reeves tucked away the sympathy cards and stood up. "Let's go work out the details."

11:15 A.M., Saturday, January 27.

After his meeting with the President, Director Parker returned to his office. Lead investigator Billie "Doc" Watson was waiting for him.

"How'd it go, boss?" Watson asked.

"Good, very good, Doc," Parker was obviously upbeat. "I didn't know why the President wanted to see me, but I was worried."

"Then, the investigation continues?" Watson probed. "You don't have to 'recuse' yourself?"

"No, Stanton was good. As far as I could tell he just wanted to be assured we were on the case. If he was trying to influence the investigation, it was imperceptible to me. When I told him the Bureau was investigating Chadwick's accident as a possible attempted murder of a federal officer, he seemed genuinely pleased that we were already pushing ahead."

"Could he be that good an actor?" Watson asked.

"I don't think so. I was straight with him. I told him in light of all the allegations swirling around the White House, any additional contact concerning the investigation would have to be at our initiation and according to our rules."

"How'd he take that?"

"Fine. He was in complete agreement. Gave me his personal assurance we would have his administration's total cooperation."

"He wasn't blowing smoke?"

"I don't think so, Doc. He called me in to insist on a complete investigation. Once he was assured it was ongoing, he asked me to draft a memo for his signature to be sent to his entire staff directing their full cooperation and implying severe consequences for any one who failed to give us that cooperation. It wasn't an act, Doc, I'm sure of it. It doesn't matter anyway, we're going to let the chips fall where they may." Director Park paused.

Watson hesitated and then asked, "Is there something else, sir?"

"Yes, Doc, there is. The President gave us full responsibility for the protection of Secretary Chadwick. He told me to do whatever it took. He was very insistent." The Director moved around his desk, sat down and pulled out a legal pad and pen. "You know for all the pressure he's under, the President was impressive, really quite impressive."

"You think this whole thing is just a power grab?"

"No, no I don't. I've known Roosevelt for years now. He's a pretty standup guy. Stanton has had his troubles; that's a fact. I guess the question is whether he's got them behind him. But, Doc, that's not our problem, others get to wrestle with that one. I need to know what you've learned about Chadwick."

"You know, Director, before I joined the Bureau, in the real world I was a claims investigator for accidental death benefits."

"You are modest, Doc. I know the story. You were New York Life's Chief Investigator for Accidental Death Benefits. You unmasked some of the most imaginative, hideous scams I've ever read about – that Longmont woman was the best – incredible work."

"Why thank you, sir."

"It's why you're in charge of this investigation, Doc. If Chadwick's 'accident' was no accident we have to know who was responsible. Now, tell me what you know. And call me, Robert, Doc."

"Yes, sir. You know, sir, this is preliminary."

"Of course, Doc."

"Thus far, Director, there is nothing about the scene of the accident that suggests it was anything other than an accident caused by the conjunction of conditions and circumstances beyond human control. However, at this stage that's not surprising, sir. Accidents look like accidents and well-crafted homicides made to appear like accidents look like accidents."

"Where do you begin?"

"We begin with what we know, or think we know, and then work back. On its face, what we know is this. Chadwick's trip to the mountains was a spur of the moment decision. The accident occurred at night, during a snowstorm, on a mountain road. Secretary Chadwick was making an emergency run for asthma medicine in an old Jeep Cherokee, a vehicle he rarely used. He encountered a small herd of deer, hit one or more, lost control of the Jeep, smashed through a guard rail, was airborne, and flew down the mountain landing nose first, plowing into the legendary old oak tree."

"If that's a homicide, Doc, we're dealing with pros, mission-impossible type pros," Director Roberts commented. "How could it be done?"

"I don't know, sir, but that's the job. We have to be able to design a murder consistent with all of the known facts. If this 'accident" was man-made it can be replicated. If it cannot be replicated it was not murder."

"Okay, I understand that," Parker injected. If it can't be replicated then the accident is just that, an accident."

"Right. Now, for investigative purposes we assume it was attempted murder and look for the answers to a number of corollary questions. For instance, since the Chadwick's plans to travel to their cabin were almost spur-of-the-moment, the killer or killers had to get on site fast. They had to be situational opportunists stationed near the cabin, ready to improvise. If they had time they would have bugged the cabin. So the question is where did our killers hunker down until opportunity knocked? Since its unlikely they were locals where did they come from? Anybody notice them? This is not the tourist season on the Skyline Drive, there's nobody there now that doesn't belong there. Did our guys buy gas or supplies coming or going? There's a lot of field work to be done."

"Are you asking for additional resources, Doc? If you are, they're yours. This thing is going to tear the country apart until we get the facts, indisputable facts. There are no higher priorities. Do you need additional resources, Doc?"

"No, no we have everything we need, Director. What we need, you can't give us. We need time, not much, but some. At the beginning of these investigations what we produce are questions, lots of them. Fieldwork produces fieldwork. Interviews lead to more interviews and lab tests suggest the need for more lab work. But each time our questions get better and better. They are more refined and focused until finally they produce answers, conclusive answers that will satisfy all but the hopelessly irrational."

"I hear you, Doc, but if you find in the future, you need something, anything, you tell me and I'll get it for you. I swear I will. Understood?"

"Understood."

"Okay, then, tell me what you're working on."

"Yes, sir, let me summarize. Since we know Secretary Chadwick was not murdered and then placed in the car, we have to determine whether he was mugged/drugged or incapacitated in some way allowing the accident to be staged. If it wasn't staged, was his Cherokee sabotaged, guaranteed to crash, or was an explosive device used? If an explosive device was used, was it remotely controlled, timed, or just a disguised mine. If the vehicle was sabotaged or exploded, was a second vehicle involved? Was Chadwick forced to swerve off the road to avoid a head-on collision? Or was his Cherokee rammed from the rear and pushed through the guardrail?"

"Good God. Any progress?"

"A little bit. Most of the answers are going to come from our labs and those at Bethesda Naval. The Jeep, what's left of it, is at our Virginia facility. They're going to tell us whether it was rammed or sabotaged and confirm that it was not hit with an explosive device.

"Why are you ruling out an explosive device, Doc, and what's Bethesda looking for?"

"Our people have been all over the crash site, Robert. There's hardly a stone out of place on the highway until the Jeep hit the guardrail. An explosion is no way to hide a homicide. It's pretty crude. If you're going to blow a car off the road, the roads going to take a hit as well as the car. Our folks didn't find any indications at the crash site and I'm betting the lab is not going to find any traces on the Jeep. As for Bethesda, they are doing their own thing, way over my head, all sorts of scans and tests on Chadwick, his blood, urine, hair and anything else they think might indicate unrelated trauma or the introduction of drugs or toxins."

As Watson was speaking he leafed through the latest field and lab reports. "There is one thing here that's of interest." He waited to insure he had Parker's attention.

"I'm with you, Doc. Go on."

"Assuming it was murder, or an attempted murder, the killers had to be in place. Chadwick's have the last cabin on a dead end road. Beyond their cabin there's only a turn-around with a spectacular view of Pinnacle Mountain and a cliff face called the Crows Nest. There was a car out there Thursday. It arrived before the snow fell and left shortly after Chadwick headed to town. State Patrol saw the tracks when they went to pick up the family."

"Did you get impressions?"

"Maybe. The conditions weren't real great and the State guys missed Chadwick's tracks. When they drove out to the turnaround they obliterated most of them. We may not have enough, but there's more. It's beautiful up there; it's a parking spot for kids from Luray. You'd think it would be littered with beer bottles, condoms, and trash; but the cabin owners take great pride in keeping the whole area pristine. Their association has a man who walks it every Monday picking up trash. When our team went over the turnout, it was spotless except for a large lens cap."

"For a camera?"

"No," Watson replied. "A telescope, a very expensive telescope."

"Sounds traceable?"

"There's a good possibility. The cap is from a new model, and as I said, very expensive. The number is molded right on it."

"Why would killers have a telescope?" Director Parker questioned. "If they could use it to see the Chadwick's place, couldn't they be seen?"

"Yes, but it could have been cover," Watson noted. "But that's not all. We have partials, a finger and thumb."

"I'm afraid you're going to spend a lot of energy identifying an amateur astronomer or lovers, but I understand it has to be done. Anything else, Doc?"

"Yes, but one more thing on the telescope, Thursday was an awful day for stargazing – first impenetrable clouds and then snow."

"Couldn't the cap have been there for a while?"

"Maybe, but it's big. They found it right in the center of the turn-around. We're interviewing people. Nobody saw it. Owners of the first cabin, an old couple, walked down there earlier in the week; they couldn't remember when, but they didn't see it. The sheriff's department drives it daily, they didn't see it either."

"You said you had something else?"

"Just a problem, the deer. The deer wouldn't be a problem if the killers had time, but if Chadwick's decision to go to the country was as spontaneous as we believe, then time was really tight. We are doing our best to determine when the deer died. If they died simultaneously with Chadwick's accident, then the accident was either that, an accident, or an incredibly fortuitous attempted murder enhanced by the presence of deer."

"Incredible is an understatement. You know, Doc, we need to put this thing to rest. Chase down the loose ends, but do it quick. I pray this thing was an accident. If you can put the deer, alive and well, squarely in Chadwick's headlights just before they went to meet their maker, we'll be able to prove it was an accident. Right?"

"I hope so, sir. Our difficulty is the deer were not considered part of a crime scene. They were plowed off the highway. Forensics is looking at deer hair, blood, and body parts on the Cherokee, the highway, the guardrail, and down the mountain to the jeep's final resting place. You're right. If their death was simultaneous with the accident it is one element of the crime scene we cannot even imagine duplicating. Barring other evidence to the contrary, we'll have to conclude that Chadwick was the victim of a tragic, but common accident."

"What 'evidence to the contrary' could possibly dissuade you that this wasn't just another accident?" Considering the deer, Director Parker was all but ready to close the case, but he understood that Doc Watson had considerable experience in unraveling creative murders and might still have some doubts.

"Maybe I'm just guarding my backside, but I want to know whether anyone tampered with the jeep, I want to know the results of Chadwick's blood work, and I want to know who was stargazing on a starless night in the dead of winter one hundred and fifty yards from Chadwick's cabin. I'll have the answers soon. The labs and our guys are busting their tails.

"That's what I need, answers real fast. In fact, Doc, I need you back here this afternoon. You've got to give me tentative conclusions, at least a range of probabilities; I've got decisions to make. The President laid a pretty heavy trip on me this morning; I don't want to do anything rash, but I don't want to be blindsided either."

"I'll give you everything I've got and I'll do my best to draw defensible conclusions. How much time do I have? I need all you can give me."

"I'll be out much of the afternoon. Make it seven, Doc, no later." Director Parker was emphatic and then a little obscure as he led Watson to the door. "It's all a gamble; there is no way to play it safe."

"Yes, sir. I'll see you tonight at seven, Robert."

CHAPTER EIGHTEEN

DEADLINES

2:30 P. M., Saturday, January 27.

Secretary of the Treasury Alan F. Binder was in the driver's seat. He was the last holdout, the only member of the Cabinet who had not publicly announced his intention to stand with the President or join the Vice President. Commentators, pundits, academicians, they all knew what he intended, they just didn't agree. They did agree generally, however, on his character and described it with clichés. They pissed him off. They said he had the Midas touch, was the author of the platinum parachute and was an opportunist who never looked back and worse he never looked out for anyone else. It irked him.

It was true that time and again in Alan Binder's corporate career he had made the right move at the right time. As Secretary of the Treasury he had been a spectacular choice. The business community had been reassured. A man who understood self-interest would be the President's chief economic adviser. Labor leaders simply dismissed him as "All For Business" Binder. They gave him no credit for the country's robust economy or for its declining trade and budget deficits. He was just another big business Republican, jobs were still going to China, and Wall Street was at an all-time high.

Friday morning, standing in his living room, Secretary Binder had watched Secretary Pruett's news conference. She was an astute politician and she was making her move. For a moment he thought she had made the game-winning shot and that he had waited too long. He ran his options like a computer chess program, searching for the best move. Suddenly without thought he clapped his hands, then looked around to make sure he was alone. The game was going into overtime. He would have the last say after all, and he was going to make the best of it. Two eggheads confirmed his analysis later that evening on the News Hour. As long as Aaron Chadwick was alive, Roosevelt needed eight. It seemed ludicrous. This was democracy? Never in his wildest dreams could he have imagined that he, a lifelong Republican, would be deciding between two lifelong Democrats who would be President. He admired both men, but the decision was his. He would visit the President this afternoon and the Vice President tonight. He still had time. Unless he learned something he had failed to consider, he was ready to make his move. The nation would thank him. He could not fail.

3:00 P. M., Saturday, January 27.

Aaron Chadwick's condition was unchanged. Sharon and David, gowned and gloved, stood at the foot of his bed. They did not recognize him nor did he show any signs of recognizing them. He was comatose, though Dr. Starling insisted Aaron's vital signs were somewhat improved.

"I know it seems like a lifetime, but it's been less than 48 hours, Sharon. Don't give up hope, not yet."

"I don't understand," Sharon murmured. "He's so..." She stopped. No words would come. She looked toward David for help, but found none. He only squeezed her hand and then looked away hiding his own tears. "He's so still," she blurted.

"He is alive. There is a battle raging before you. You can't see it, but it's there. Aaron hasn't given up and neither should you." Dr. Starling was insistent now. "His body has hung on, fought off death for two days. It has marshaled auto systems with healing powers we barely understand. The body is a machine like no other. You can break it, burn it, bleed it, starve it, but given a chance it will come back. We just assist; he's the healer."

"How long? When will we know?" She spoke through hands that covered her mouth.

"I don't know, Sharon. I think the battle is far from over. His body is struggling mightily to put its house in order, but it has to fight on so many fronts. I just don't know. I'm sorry, but I don't know."

"What about his mind, Doctor?"

"Mom, don't."

"Let's go back to my office. We can talk there." Dr. Starling took Sharon's arm and started to usher her into the hallway, when an ICU nurse indicated they might want to go the back way. "She's right, Sharon. I don't think any of us want to face the press right now. It's not far." He turned her. They moved again by the foot of Aaron's bed, hesitated uncomfortably, said nothing, and moved down the corridor.

As they entered his office, Pam Wilson, Dr. Starling's receptionist stood. "Excuse me, Mrs. Chadwick, David. Dr. Starling, you have a visitor."

"A visitor? Now?"

"Yes, sir. It's FBI Director Robert Parker. He says it's urgent. He came by helicopter. I told him you were with the Chadwicks. He said that he'd like to see them as well. I didn't know what to do. I ask him to wait in your office. He's in there now. He's on the phone, I think."

"I'm sorry, Sharon, David. Can you give me just a moment?

"It's alright, Doctor. Robert Parker and I are good friends. He's practically a neighbor."

"That's fine, but you must know Aaron is our first concern; you and David are next. I've never met Robert Parker, but if this visit is about his investigation, it's ill-timed. I need to answer your questions, not his."

"Honestly," Sharon continued to assure Dr. Starling, "Bob is a dear family friend. I hope he's here to hold my hand."

"Okay, it's you're call. Pam would you see that we are not disturbed."

Director Parker was standing with his back to the door talking on a cell phone as they entered. They heard only: "Move quickly, Doc. I'll see you tonight," before he hung up and turned his full attention to Sharon and David. "I'm sorry, Sharon, so sorry," he said, hugging her with the warmth of a longtime friend. "You and David must try to be strong. Aaron's incredible. I saw the Jeep at our lab. Aaron is tough, he's alive and he has so much to live for, I can't help but believe that he's going to recover." Then turning to Dr. Starling he continued. "These guys at Bethesda work miracles." He extended his hand. "Doctor Starling, I'm

Robert Parker, a friend of the family. As I'm sure Ms. Wilson told you, I'm also Director of the FBI."

"Sharon said you were a good friend," Dr. Starling commented. "We were just with Aaron, but thought it would be easier to talk here. Sharon and David naturally have a number of questions."

"I understand. I need only a moment. I have some decisions to make concerning security and I need to know what my options are. As of now, I think the threat is imaginary and I don't want to do anything that would compromise Aaron's chances or stress you in any way. I just need some help."

"Shouldn't you be talking to Bethesda's security people?" Dr. Starling asked.

"We are talking to them, but while they know security and we know security, our security procedures can't compromise his treatment. Pure security means lockdowns. Patients are locked in and threats are locked out. Everything is screened. It's either approved or denied, but always delayed. It doesn't matter whether it is specialists, treatments, movement to surgery, x-rays, dialysis, drugs, testing equipment, everything; it's all delayed, even when there is a distraction like a medical emergency. Lockdowns don't allow the flexibility that unimpaired treatment requires. I hope we can do better or there's a middle ground. I've got some ideas I need to check out with you."

"I have time," Dr. Starling stated. "Are you and David up to this?"

"Certainly, but we do want to see Aaron again before we head home," Sharon responded, motioning to David to join her on the large leather couch to the right of Dr. Starling's desk.

"Thanks, Sharon. Do you mind if I close the door, Dr. Starling?" Director Parker assumed the answer and moved to close the door. "This won't take long, but could be very helpful."

3:24 P. M., Saturday, January 27.

Looking out from his upstairs sitting room, Secretary Binder could see many of the newsmen and camera crews stationed at his home to monitor and report his every move. Shortly there would be pandemonium. He would move through them to a waiting limo and though he would acknowledge he was on his way to the White House he would politely tell them nothing more, at least nothing that they would believe. Nevertheless, broadcasts would be interrupted, commentators interviewed, and panels polled all to report and speculate upon the "Breaking News: Secretary Binder to Visit the White House."

Alan Binder was disciplined. The press closed in on him as he left his home. His space was more than violated. Flashes blinded him and microphones were shoved in his face. Reporters formed a loud, abrasive, and unintelligible chorus. All demanded his attention with a "Secretary Binder" and then without a breath they went for broke, asking their questions hoping the others would back off. They did not. The bedlam continued as he forced his way to his car. Once there, he turned and faced them.

"Listen! Listen Up!" He was a commanding figure as he called for quiet. "Listen!" He waited. Those in front called for quiet from those behind them. The word spread. They needed the story. He waited until there was silence. Booms with microphones silently stretched forward until they hung over his head. "Please do not interrupt, he began. "I am on my way to the White House. I have asked to see President Stanton and his chief of staff, Crayton Langford. Later this evening or tomorrow morning as time permits, I will meet with Vice President Roosevelt and his chief of staff, Jason Fields. I am not involved in negotiations. I am involved in decision-making. I will not be rushed by anyone or anything but The Constitution of the United States. It dictates the time frame and I will honor the Constitution."

Before the press realized that was it, Binder said "Thank You" and got into his car, shut the door and told his driver: "Don't kill anyone, John, but get us the hell out of here."

3:30 P.M., Saturday, January 27.

Doc Watson was pushing his team hard. The dam was beginning to burst. Each piece of information now generated dozens of questions. He needed answers. Already his team was being buried by random information. It needed to be sifted, strained, filtered and sorted. There was so much to be flushed out; so much to be pulled together. As of yet, he had no conclusions, but he had facts, disturbing facts and a link he didn't like.

The fingerprints on the telescope lens-cap found in the snow just beyond Chadwick's place belonged to Robert Derby Hearst. Hearst was a twenty-seven-year-old ex-marine. He was unemployed, yet on Thursday, January 24th he was a hundred plus miles from his home, high in the Appalachian Mountains. He was stargazing, but it was snowing. The telescope he used was a Mead 10" (254mm) f/10 LXD200R with Advanced Ritchey-Chretien Optics, top of the line. Stripped down it would retail for well over five thousand dollars. Maybe the apparent inconsistencies could be explained: the prints had to belong to someone, maybe Hearst's family had money or the telescope belonged to a friend. Still it was snowing. Even the Mead didn't see through snow.

There was more, a very simple frightening fact. The same Robert Derby Hearst had checked through the South Gate at Bethesda Naval Medical Center at 09:17 this morning. What were the odds? Again it could be innocent. Maybe Hearst knew the Chadwicks, met them in the mountains, heard the news, and wanted to pay his respects, but what were the odds.

Watson was uneasy. He had a lot of experience. Before a case would break open you could smell it.   Thursday, Robert Hearst had been at the end of Oak Creek Gap Road just yards from where Aaron Chadwick and his family were having dinner in their log cabin hideaway. Saturday morning, less than thirty-six hours later, Robert Hearst was again just yards away from Aaron Chadwick. This time Aaron Chadwick lay near death, but not dead, in the intensive care unit at Bethesda Naval Hospital.

Though he didn't understand the accident, Doc Watson was on a scent and it was rank. He had all the techs digging. If Robert Hearst was alive he was leaving a trail. Even in private practice he could access "purchaser profiles," but now leading the FBI's investigation he and his lieutenants were armed with emergency national security warrants. They had access to everything. Watson's immediate subordinate, Randall Cummins, was heading up the "Consolidated Mining Group," the data processors exploring the life of Robert Hearst. Every database, large or small, recording everything done between life and death was open to their investigation. A very experienced, intelligent, and imaginative staff entered searches and managed the information. Their computers scanned the world, collating, sorting, and crosschecking hits. They were under orders to deliver an executive summary of whatever they had by 5:30.

Watson's second in command, Shelly Carrie, was working with Mead Optics and its distributors to identify owners of the LXD 200R. Unfortunately on that front, it was Saturday and many of Mead's people – those who could access manufacturing, sales, and warranty files were "out" until Monday. They would be found and brought "in." Media speculation on the "accident" all but guaranteed full cooperation. Watson also had people on the ground. OIC Ralph Dean and much of his Washington Field Office staff supplemented with specialists from surrounding offices were now assigned to the investigation. He hoped for quick answers, but could only wait. He had a professional staff. They knew the stakes.

Doc also had other irons heating in the fire, but he had little hope they would be ready for his meeting with the Director. The timing of the accident and the deer still seemed impossible, but they were looking hard at everything. Bonnie O'Neil, one of his favorites, a strange little bird specializing in detonators, was working on the premise that Chadwick's own cell phone was the trigger. Finally, Jennifer Watson, no relation, was working with the balance of OIC Dean's field office staff on a digital video recorded timeline. Shortly, Doc would be able to rewind Chadwick's life to Wednesday morning when he announced his decision to join the Roosevelt faction. Then he would watch, and re-watch, Chadwick's every move through Thursday night when for whatever reason he launched his Jeep Cherokee from the Luray highway into a massive, two-hundred-year-old oak. Seen in context, Watson hoped to understand what the Secretary was doing and who would be affected, both positively and adversely.

Watson had everything he needed but time. He needed more. He had only a couple of hours before his meeting with Parker. The Director was counting on him. Unless he caught a break, he was going to let him down. Parker needed solid intelligence. All Watson had was his gut.

3:42 P.M., Saturday, January 27.

Despite popular opinion Secretary Alan Binder was not a weather vane. He was confident he knew what he should do. He was also certain his motives would be suspect and his decision challenged as self-serving. He needed to be more than confident; he needed to be positive. He was determined to reserve his final decision until both sides had tested it. At that point it would be defensible, at least in his own mind, and he could be resolute in the storm that was sure to follow. A lover of British understatement, Binder knew this visit would be awkward, very awkward, indeed. "To thine own self be true" he repeated silently as he approached the White House.

"Alan, thank you for coming." Crayton Langford greeted Secretary Binder in the West Wing of the White House. "These are tumultuous times, Alan. The President is pleased you have not joined in the rush to judgment. I cleared his schedule. He's eager to spend time with you."

"That's wonderful. I do want to do that, Crayton, I really do. But first, before I see the President, I want to see the 'Incidents File.'" He said it firmly, but without malice.

"The Incident Report?" Langford hesitated imperceptibly, but could not suppress his defensive response. "You know I could refuse. It is privileged. Certainly, if executive privilege covers nothing else, it applies to a report I produced for the President." The report flashed before Crayton's mind. He remembered every damning word and his own initial reaction to its cumulative mass.

"You can win a battle on a technicality, Crayton, but not a war. I'll be happy to review it in your presence, in chambers if you will. I will make no copies, take no notes, but I believe I must see the report before I go public with my decision."

"I don't like this, Alan." Crayton did not use the term 'blackmail,' but given the stakes it did seem appropriate.

"Do you need to speak with the President, Crayton?" Secretary Binder tried not to be offensive, but he was not backing off.

"No, President Stanton has already made his decision." Crayton allowed Binder a moment to weigh that fact before continuing. "While my Incident Report shows a man personally crippled with overwhelming grief, it also demonstrates emphatically that this President's grief never compromised his performance as President of the United States. You can see the report, Secretary Binder. You can see it now. Take as much time as you like, but when you are done I have another report I would like you to see. Then, I would hope that you would have time to meet with the President. It is his judgment and competence that should resolve this challenge to our democracy and the decision the American people made at the last election."

Crayton's lecturing did not truly explain the decision. It was simple: neither he nor the President could know how Secretary Binder would react to the report, but they were convinced that the facts found there were not nearly as damning as those that would be imagined if access to the report were denied.

"Thank you, Crayton."

"It's okay. I understand your position. Come with me you can use Virginia's office. She's working with Lincoln. I'll bring you the report. You won't be disturbed. When you're through bring it to my office.

5:00 P.M., Saturday, January 27.

They had spent much of the afternoon together working out the details and equipping themselves for the day to come. The mission had begun. Bobby was in awe of Reeves, his preparations and contingencies. Reeves was guarding against possibilities he had never considered. Indeed even when considered, they seemed so remote they were all but impossible. He assumed he was wrong and had much to learn. Reeves understood the opposition. He came from their world and was its best and brightest alumni. Bobby saw only the tip of the iceberg. Reeves saw it all and knew the sea was also dangerous.

"Improvisation is done best when you are prepared," Reeves stated giving Bobby his new identity. "Bobby Hearst is dead, long live Robert Harris. You're a professional. This isn't a job; it's a life. You've got to be flexible."

Reeves, or so he called himself, Bobby thought, had provided everything. Robert Harris had an abbreviated life story that paralleled Bobby's life. It would be easy to learn. His "new" wallet came with a driver's license, military identification, credit cards, cash, and glasses. Bobby barely recognized himself. Not only was Harris wearing glasses, he didn't have Hearst's mustache.

"That's not a mistake, is it," Bobby asked?

"No, You'll use a different gate tomorrow, but there is still a chance you'll run into the same guard who checked you through this morning. The glasses are clear and the mustache will grow back. Mine always did. Unfortunately, the last time it came back it was gray and I got rid of it for good."

"You sure you'll recognize me?"

"Oh ya, I did your licenses." Reeves gave Bobby a prepaid cell phone and an embossed Wells Fargo checkbook showing a balance of $5,175.20.

"You're already checked in at the Regency," Reeves stated, handing Bobby a plastic room key. "You're in room 212. Go straight to your room."

You are something else," Bobby laughed. Go straight to my room?"

"Yes, Bobby, and don't go out. It's important. Nobody will remember you making reservations, checking in, or checking out. A young lady made your reservations not just for tonight, but the rest of the week. You'll be on the road. And Bobby, just answer your cell phone – don't use it. No outgoing calls.

"Am I going to be wearing an ankle bracelet too?" Bobby joked.

"No, I trust you," Reeves responded. "And who knows I might be in the next room." Reeves waited just a fraction of a second to make sure the message was received and then smiled. "We meet tomorrow in the cafeteria. Just go to the coffee bar. I'll spot you."

"Should I take the Metro to Bethesda?" Bobby asked.

"No," Reeves responded, "I want you to drive. We need the option, but not the truck. You drove it the last time. They have cameras scanning the parking areas. I really do trust you, Bobby. You'll find a new Camry in the Regency's guest lot, in space 12, level B. It has your luggage." Reeves handed Bobby a set of keys attached to a zipped leather notebook. "Consider it a bonus. You'll earn it tomorrow." Always compulsive Reeves couldn't help but add, "Give yourself plenty of time, Bobby, leave the Regency before 8:00. Okay?"

"Sure. What's the notebook about?"

"It has your itinerary for the next five days, Bobby. You're traveling first class. You'll be visiting smaller State capitals in the D. C. area, thinking of setting up a security business for State governments. You'll start in Delaware at Dover, and then spend a night each at Annapolis, Harrisburg, and Charleston. On your way to Richmond make sure you take the Blue Ridge Parkway. You love that area. In fact, if any one should ask, you were in the same area last Thursday on the Skyline drive. Stay on schedule, and keep the cell charged. I may need to reach you."

"How do I reach you?" Bobby asked.

"You don't. I told you. I do the calling. It's simple, Bobby, if you are caught you could cut a deal and give me up. If I'm caught there's no percentage in giving you up. I'll get life, that's it. So I call you. Understand?"

"Yes, I guess. I just feel a little hung out."

"Don't. I'll call you. Your notebook has the schedule. Don't panic if I miss a call. I'll reach you at your motel or leave a message. Your money will be deposited to your Wells Fargo account in two installments, the first just a down payment on Monday with the balance no later than Thursday. Your money will have traveled around the world with a dozen stops, splits, and unions but it well end up just down the street from where it started. It will arrive in small deposits just below bank reporting requirements. You can check it on line. You are going to be rich, Bobby, but rich doesn't make you smart. Use your head. Pull most of it out and split it into a number of smaller accounts. Think long term. If this thing ever dies out I'll give you an all clear.

"Are you pretty confident about tomorrow, Mr. Reeves?"

"Yes, but this isn't routine, Bobby; far from it. There is a lot of nasty speculation that Chadwick's accident was not an accident but attempted murder; that means they have their guard up if for no other reason than to cover their asses. It could be tough, but I'm betting they are just going through the motions. In any case we're prepared and in this instance the rewards are more than commensurate with the risks." Reeves turned into the Regency and stopped under the canopy. "Try to get a good night's sleep, Bobby. I'll see you in the morning."

Bobby opened the car door, but was slow getting out. A white limo pulled up behind them. "Just one more question, Mr. Reeves."

"What's that?"

"Is Reeves your real name?"

"It works for me," Reeves answered. "Don't worry. It's all set up, Bobby. You can count on me and we're ready."

Robert Harris, a.k.a. Bobby Hearst, saw Reeves turn right into the flow of traffic from the Regency lobby. He took the stairs to his room. It wasn't a prison, but he felt confined. He needed to get out. Lying on the bed he thumbed through his biography. It all looked good, but he felt uneasy. The cocky, decorated ex-Marine was out of his league. Reeves, or whoever he was, was the director and had cast him in a supporting role. He had his part, he knew the first act, but he wasn't sure he knew the plot. Alone in the silence of his surroundings he had time to think the worst. He needed distraction. He decided to check out the car. Surely the parking garage wasn't "going out."

The car smelled new and had 117 miles on the odometer. If he was going out, he was going out in style. It was loaded. The glove box had his title, registration and insurance. The trunk, his leather luggage embossed with RH.

Reeves said the job was all set up and Bobby trusted him, believed him, but he also knew Reeves was a pro. Maybe he was being set up. Despite his fear, Bobby had his pride and tomorrow, partner or patsy, he would play his part.

5:20 P.M., Saturday, January 27.

"Crayton, I can't stand this. It's obscene. Here we sit, the President and his chief of staff waiting, speculating what others might be doing while we do nothing." President Stanton moved around the Oval Office toward some conclusion, energized and focused. "My good friend, Aaron Chadwick, is in a coma and the country is paralyzed and vulnerable." Crayton had no time to agree or disagree. "I can't win on a technicality, what constitutes a majority; and I certainly can't govern on a technicality. I need the American people behind me. The Congress must respect my mandate. A stalemate won't do."

"That all may be true, sir, but the ball isn't in our court. We're not in a position to hit an ace when we don't have the serve. I don't see that we have any options."

"If it's not in our court now, where do you think it will be in forty-eight hours when Roosevelt reasserts my incompetence? He may be Acting President, but we have got to take charge and define the terms of the Congressional debate."

"You think Binder has already decided to sign on?" Crayton's question was more statement than question. "Is his visit just a charade?"

"I don't know, but I think Alan Binder has the weight of the world on his shoulders and we should lighten his load. Let's get him in here, now."

"Are you sure?"

"Yes," the President laughed, "I think I am. We need to lead, Crayton. Seven or eight cabinet members, it doesn't matter. In this world perception is reality. Before the Vice President drags me before Congress I'm going to demand a full Congressional hearing. If I don't regain the confidence of the country, I can't govern. In the words of the Twenty-Fifth Amendment, I won't be able to discharge the duties and powers of this office. Roosevelt will be right." Stanton paused. "Strangely, Crayton, I think I need Congressional hearings every bit as much as Roosevelt."

Crayton stood and walked to the President's desk. "May I, sir?"

"Please do!"

Crayton pressed the private intercom to Millie's desk.

"Yes, sir. What can I do for you?"

"It's Crayton, Millie. The President wants to see Secretary Binder. I believe you'll find him in Virginia's office.

5:29 P.M., Saturday, January 27.

Randall Cummins, Watson's immediate subordinate, was early, not by much, but early. He handed Doc Watson the "Consolidated Mine Group's Preliminary Report on Robert Derby Hearst. It was massive.

"What in the hell is this?" Watson asked fanning through the spiral bound report.

"It's less than meets the eye, Doc, Most of it is appended material, but the executive summary has some bright red flags."

"Walk me through it, Randall."

"Okay, You know the basics. We've been looking hard at Robert Hearst because he not only left his prints near Chadwick's cabin Thursday night, but he also visited Bethesda this morning. That's a hell of a coincidence, but then Robert Hearst is a helluva guy. He's an unemployed ex-Marine. His service record is outstanding, but a little over the top. He was more than gung-ho. Two years ago he effectively ended the May Day war games when his squad blew up the opposition battalion's green zone. Really creative shit, but then, strangely, he didn't re-up. Just called it quits. He still doesn't have a job, yet he makes deposits, not regularly, but he does have money. It's not a huge amount, but he spends it easy like more is coming in. He lives in a nice upscale apartment complex near Bethesda and drives a big 4 X 4. We have it under surveillance. His neighbors say he stays pretty much to himself. They don't seem to know much about him, but they all seem to think he's a really neat fellow."

"So where are the bright red flags?" Watson asked with some impatience.

"Sorry, Doc, there are two flags. First, no one has seen Robert Hearst for several days, but his truck hasn't moved from his assigned parking spot. Second, get this, a Robert Harris, not Hearst, just bought a new Camry using Robert Hearst's address.

It's crazy. He paid cash, but he is not Hearst and not even a Hearst look alike, an old guy with thinning hair. Sales manager said he was in good shape, looked like he pumped, thought maybe he was a runner or a swimmer. We haven't found the car, but have learned that Robert Harris is going out of town. He has single night guaranteed reservations for the next week. Tomorrow night he's registered in Delaware at the Dover Downs Hotel and Casino."

"A new identity?" Watson asked.

"Maybe. Maybe just a new roommate," Cummins responded.

"Or maybe a coconspirator," Watson noted.

"Can I join you, Doc?" Shelly Carrie carried her report in a Mead Products catalogue. "Hi Randall."

"Sure, Let's hear what you got."

"Well, the Mead people have been great. They dropped everything to give us a hand. Fortunately the LXD200R has been on the market only a couple of years. They have sold nine in our area, none to a Robert Hearst. Eight were easy. The buyers used credit cards, bought extended warranty contracts and completed sales questionnaires that we could use for a full field investigation. We'll do more, but they all check out. Number nine's our problem. All we have is a name, Kenneth Reeves. He paid cash and then completed the warranty information using an Arlington P.O. Box. We've got nothing even the P. O. Box isn't his anymore. We've crosschecked his name with related magazines, catalogues, astronomy clubs, observatory guest lists - the works. We still have nothing. Our only break was Mead's Arlington sales manager. Cash sales are unusual. He remembers the guy; older fellow looked more like a retired running back than an amateur astronomer."

"You've got more than you know, Shelly." Doc Watson was animated. "You heard that, Randall? We've got work to do. Randall here has a Camry, cash-only purchase. The buyer wasn't Robert Hearst; it was Robert Harris, but he used Robert Hearst's address. But get this; the car dealer described him as an older athletic fellow. I don't know what the game is, but we have three names, at least two players, and it's not a conventional game."

"If it involves Chadwick, I suspect they've got a deadline, Monday at 4:30 P.M.," Shelly announced. "Either Vice President Roosevelt has a majority of the Cabinet and it goes to Congress and extra innings or he doesn't and President Stanton reclaims the office."

"You're right," Doc Watson continued. "Monday's the latest; but they can't bump right up against it. Assuming the worst, Robert Harris's reservation in Dover tomorrow night suggests they are going to make their move in the morning. We've got to be ready."

"For what?" Cummins asked.

"I don't know, but maybe we can shake things up a bit and throw a wrench or two in their plans." Watson liked the idea of being proactive. He felt better about his upcoming meeting with Director Parker.

CHAPTER NINETEEN:

THE BEST OF INTENTIONS

5:40 P.M., Saturday, January 27.

"Any word from Secretary Binder?" Roosevelt asked. He knew the answer. If Jason Fields had heard anything Acting President, Vice President Roosevelt would have known.

"No, sir. He is still at the White House. Maybe they are still haggling over the 'Incidents File.' He assured me he'd call us by 6 if he was running late and needed to move the meeting to tomorrow morning."

"This is wild," Roosevelt exclaimed. "We have a President, an Acting President, and now a *de facto* President, Secretary Alan Binder."

"I didn't read the '*de facto*' clause." Jason responded.

"Must be that fine legal print you hear so much talk about." Roosevelt mused. "Wonder what else we missed?"

"I hope nothing; but you, President Stanton, the Cabinet, and the Congress are in new territory setting precedents with every move. With the stakes so high, it's a wonder that you've chosen the high road."

"I've tried to heed the President's warning. He was convinced our dispute would unleash forces neither of us could control. I'm afraid he was right."

"I think so too, sir." While Vice President Roosevelt and President Stanton were often above the fray, Jason and his counterpart Crayton had been in the thick of it. Both had dealt with the subtle and not so subtle *quid pro quo* suggestions of a number of Cabinet Secretaries.

"Jason, I need to talk to the President. If Secretary Binder joins our ranks this contest will go to the Congress and the Congress is filled with capable and ambitious men and women. They may confuse their personal interest with the interest of the nation. To avoid a bidding war President Stanton needs to resign."

"He never will, sir. He was elected and he'll fight to the end."

"Then somehow the President and I need to help the Congress with some ground rules so they can focus on what is in the long-term interest of this country."

"You and President Stanton do share a very important common interest. Whoever prevails must be able to govern. That interest is the basis for an agreement. Unfortunately the opposition party does not share your interest. They will want to embarrass you both and win the next election."

"You may be right, but twenty one days, 100 Senators, 435 Representatives, this could be a horrible debacle." Roosevelt paused momentarily and then continued. "We have got to try. I think if it could be done privately, with no advantage seen for either side, President Stanton will work with us to focus the debate."

Jason hesitated and then plunged ahead countering the Vice President. "Sir, I doubt that it could be done privately. Publicly, we will be arguing that President Stanton is incapable of discharging the powers and duties of his presidency; privately we would be asking him to do just that in the interest of the nation. I don't think we can have it both ways."

"Christ!" Roosevelt exclaimed. "We're going to make this up as we go?"

"I'm just saying Stanton's people will go public," Jason explained.

"Then it's going to escalate. It sounds like mutually assured destruction," an exasperated Roosevelt declared.

"Yes, unless someone surrenders." Jason noted. "And that's not going to happen."

5:45 P.M., Saturday, January 27.

Secretary Binder felt it as he approached the President in the Oval Office. This was a historic moment in a majestic place. He was not a religious man, but he felt the presence of the past and prayed his decision was right for the nation. He was confident it was, but the stakes were so monumental that even the slightest chance of error was terrifying. Andrew Holmes Stanton was the people's choice. His service had been selfless. He had honored the office and the best of his predecessors with his own perfor- mance, but he could no longer discharge the duties and powers of his office.

"Alan, are you alright?"

"Yes, Mr. President. I'm okay. How are you, sir?"

"Well, in fact, Alan, I am much better. I've made some decisions. Crayton's counsel was, as usual invaluable. As things stand today, with my competence challenged by the Vice President and seven and, with your decision, perhaps eight members of my Cabinet, I cannot discharge the duties and powers of my office."

"Mr. President, you're not considering resigning?" Secre- tary Binder's interruption was incredulous and forceful. "You mustn't! There is another way. You need vindication. You need to challenge the Congress to look at your decisions, your leader- ship of the American people, and the world community and then demand they tell the American people where you failed them. You have not. I never thought you had. The 'Incidents File' proves only that you loved your wife. Even in your grief you attended to the nation's interests."

President Stanton's delight was obvious. "Let me finish, Alan. I, too, believe Congress must vindicate me. Only then will I be able to effectively discharge my duties as President. Whatever you had decided, I have decided to ask Congress, in light of Aa- ron's condition, to consider seven as the majority of the Cabinet necessary to call for a decision on my fitness. I will urge Congress to hold exhaustive hearings and I will insist that I be allowed to testify under oath about my decisions and actions since Danny's death."

"My God, Mr. President, I came here today to convince you of the wisdom of the decision you have just described. I want to join you in implementing that decision and convincing Congress of your competence."

"Thank you, Alan, thank you." Crayton held Secretary Binder's forearm and pumped his hand enthusiastically. He could no longer maintain his silence. "The President campaigned on his record for a second term and he won and he can campaign on his record of the last two years including the last four months and he will win again. I've worked with him every day since Danny's death and he has never taken his eye off the ball. He served with pain and distinction. Those that think otherwise need to know the facts. We can win this fight."

"In this instance, winning is not enough. We have to run up the score." President Stanton was deadly serious. "The Constitution requires that I retain the support of only one-third of the Congress to stay in office. That may be good enough to stay in office, but it is not good enough to govern. I must have the support of at least fifty percent of both Houses of Congress. If I fall short, I shall resign."

President Stanton had not discussed the possibility of resignation with Crayton. He was stunned. "Excuse me, sir. I know you want vindication, but Vice President Roosevelt does have some support and we are dealing with a Republican Congress. Surely we can let the Constitution govern."

"You might be setting the bar too high, Mr. President," Secretary Binder agreed. "We would need significant defection among Republicans to achieve a majority. I don't know whether that is possible."

"We only have twenty-one days," Crayton added.

"I assure you both," Stanton laughed, "this is not a matter of incompetence. I have given my decision a great deal of thought. If nearly two-thirds of the membership of each House of Congress believes I am incompetent I will not be able to govern, no matter what the Constitution says. I need a vote of confidence."

"You'll still have the veto," Crayton asserted.

"Yes, the President acknowledged, "but like Andrew Johnson, who survived impeachment by only one vote, I won't be able to sustain a veto."

"What about Clinton?" Secretary Binder asked. "He was effective his last year in office despite impeachment."

"You're right, he was effective," President Stanton answered. "And that's my point. Johnson survived by one vote; Clinton survived by twenty-two. He had a majority, maybe not a comfortable majority, but still a majority. He was able to get things done. I still have a lot of things to do. I, too, need a majority. I won't accept less."

"Neither will Vice-President Roosevelt," Alan Binder interjected.

"What are you saying, Alan?" Crayton found equating Roosevelt's decision with the President's both unintelligible and insulting. "Since the President can resign any time he wants, he obviously can insist on more support from Congress than the Constitution requires, but that hardly suggests the Vice President can require less. He still has to have the support of two thirds of both Houses of Congress."

"No, no, Crayton, you misunderstand me. That's not what I'm saying. Vice President Roosevelt is insisting on an unqualified majority of the cabinet, eight of fourteen, before he will resubmit the declaration to Congress." Secretary Binder paused to ensure the President and his Chief of Staff understood the implications of Roosevelt's position. "If you want Congressional vindication, Mr. President, I must join the Vice President in declaring you incapable of discharging the powers and duties of your office. Do you understand?"

President Stanton understood immediately and was emphatic. "Yes, of course. That is what you must do, Alan. The country does not need a procedural debate; it needs to know it has a competent, experienced president."

"Yes, Mr. President!" Secretary Binder was immensely relieved. "Wonderful! We need time to prepare, sir. Monday morning I will announce that I am joining the Vice President not to end your presidency, but to revitalize it with the truth. I will emphasize that any 'incapacity' you suffer is due solely to the misperception that your grief affected the discharge of the duties and powers of your office."

"What about the 'Incidents File'?" Stanton asked. "You don't think it documents problems?"

"It documents grief," Secretary Binder responded. "I think you should release it. With your permission, I will assure the nation that I have read it carefully, cover to cover. It is exhaustive and conclusive: never did you let your grief distract you from the national interest. The opposite is true. You focused on the nation's interest to avoid your grief."

"That is a sympathetic reading of the file," Crayton cautioned, "but since it is bound to come out, I agree, we should break the news. We should also be realistic. The polls are badly against us. The opposition controls Congress. They are not going to roll over for us."

"You know, Alan," President Stanton continued in the same vein. "Roosevelt wasn't my first choice. We went with him because he was an easy sale. He had support across the aisle with the majority party. And he's still popular with them."

"I suspect that's all true," Alan agreed, "but it is equally true that while everybody is entitled to their own opinion, they are not entitled to their own facts. The facts support you. We are obligated to make them known."

"You know I agree," the President said, "but I'm afraid you are preaching to the choir. The people do know one thing: they saw it with their own eyes. At the State of the Union, a Constitutionally prescribed duty, before the Congress and the country I saw and spoke to my dead wife. That's the fact that won't go away."

"Yes, but I saw her too," Secretary Binder announced. "I saw her just after you did. She was in her place, wearing her State of the Union dress. Even her body language was classic Danny."

"You saw her? Or did Crayton show you the tapes?"

"I saw her. I was standing with the Cabinet. The whole chamber had exploded. I was trying to feel what you must have been feeling – the triumph. I followed your gaze around the gallery and that's when I saw her. She waved, they were all clapping, and she continued to wave, and then blew you a kiss. I'm sorry, sir. I don't believe that it was a coincidence. I think it was a deliberate impersonation and I think it speaks for itself."

"You'd use it?" the President asked. "It still makes me look crazy."

"Yes, sir, if the State of the Union is introduced to impeach your competence, I would use it." Secretary Binder was positive. "It would help people understand."

"A blue dress and a necklace don't constitute a conspiracy," President Stanton stated. "I don't believe Roosevelt would have been a party to such a charade. Do you?" President Stanton's statement reflected hope; his question suggested doubt.

"I don't know. I've never been married, but it was his wife who blew you a kiss. I come from the world of business where ambition is often a family affair. I suspect in politics where power and profit mix it can be even worse. Maybe they play good cop bad cop."

"Either Roosevelt's declaration came from an anguished patriot or an ambitious politician," President Stanton observed. "I suspect the right hand doesn't know what the left hand is doing."

Crayton, too, was willing to cut Roosevelt some slack, but not his wife. "Elizabeth Anne is a work of art. There's one dog that will hunt. She's Croft's creation and he was in a league all by himself until she grew into long pants. Now there are two in that league. I can see Roosevelt being in the dark, but not Elizabeth Anne and not Croft. Roosevelt was just another one of their acquisitions."

"That may be," President Stanton observed, "but Roosevelt is his own man. They can manipulate pawns, bishops, knights, and rooks, but Roosevelt comes from a family of giants. I guarantee you when Roosevelt decided to give me twenty-four hours to resign rather than face removal, it was over strenuous objections. He may not be able to call all of their shots, but my bet is he is still calling his shots. We need to deal with him, only him. He wasn't my first choice, but he has his strengths. We need to use them. Any suggestions?"

"Just one, Mr. President," Crayton responded. "I believe that we should invite the Vice President and Jason Fields here to the White House after Secretary Binder's news conference. We need to establish some common ground rules for the Congressional hearings. At the end of this process, the country needs a president who can, in fact, discharge the duties and powers of his office. He needs to be able to perform the constitutional responsibilities our founding fathers envisioned and the times demand. If the hearings emasculate the Presidency, then neither of you, whoever is left standing, will be able to govern or serve as a check and balance on the Congress and the courts."

"Why not before?" Secretary Binder asked.

"What?" President Stanton and Crayton asked in unison.

"Why not meet before my news conference? I'm meeting with Roosevelt this evening. I can lay the groundwork. For that matter I can delay my news conference until midafternoon or even Monday so Crayton and Jason can negotiate an acceptable statement. Roosevelt won't refuse. He wants to be able to govern, too."

"If you can do it, then do it," President Stanton directed. "Crayton and Jason go way back. Roosevelt trusts Jason and I trust Crayton. We can do this."

"Wonderful!" Secretary Binder exclaimed.

"As for your news conference, Secretary Binder, I'd love to introduce you, but I believe it would diminish your effectiveness. You are an independent player and you need to be seen that way."

"You don't want me to clear my statement with Crayton?"

"No, of course not, but I would ask you to tell the people that we, you and I, came to this same conclusion, independently. And I'd also like you to tell them that I am eager to work with Congress. The Constitution assigns them an awesome responsibility. They will have to decide who will be President of the United States. I pray it will be done honorably."

7:00 P.M., Saturday, January 27.

Saturday night, normally a slow period in the news cycle, found an unruly mob of newsmen and women with attendant lighting, sound and cameramen hanging out at the White House, hungry for news. They were a leaderless pack of alpha males and alpha females ready to fight over raw meat. They had been waiting hours and patience was never their virtue. There had been false alarms, but this time it was Secretary Binder. With pent-up fury they set upon him, shouting for attention in a chaotic chorus. Sound and cameramen recorded the mayhem that Binder tried to ignore as he bulled his way toward an approaching limousine. Media madness reflected resentment, anger and desperation. A few questions gained momentum, broke out from the pack and became a competitive chorus. They could be heard above the rabble, but they were still mixed with strident challenges hurled like Molotov Cocktails.

"Secretary Binder, what have you decided?"

"What's the deal?

"Who's going to be our President, Stanton or Roosevelt?"

"Is the Congress going to choose our President?"

"Mr. Secretary, will the Supreme Court be involved? Do they have to decide what constitutes a majority?"

"What did you get, Binder?

"Can Roosevelt match Stanton's offer?

"Who is the highest bidder, Mr. Secretary?"

The last question hung in the air. Secretary Binder spun on his heels and searched the mob for his accuser. "Enough! That's enough." His anger was apparent, but controlled. "President Stanton and Acting President Roosevelt are both well-intentioned decent men. They disagree, but their disagreement is honest. They want what is best for our country and so do I. There are no deals - only extremely difficult decisions. You will learn of mine soon enough. Now, you will excuse me. I'm late for a meeting with my good friend, Acting President Roosevelt."

With that said, ignoring another barrage of questions, Treasury Secretary Binder moved swiftly to the departmental limousine, joined his driver, left the White House and drove to Roosevelt's residence at the Naval Observatory.

7:28 P.M., Saturday, January 27.

"In sum, Director, while we have no idea how the accident could have been staged, we believe that Secretary Chadwick may have been and still is the target of an assassination plot." Doc Watson had hedged, but only slightly. He wanted the Director and the FBI to be far more aggressive in protecting Chadwick and prosecuting the investigation. He continued with the same self-assurance. "We believe at least two individuals are involved. One is Robert Hearst, a.k.a. Robert Harris. His prints were found on the lens cap of the telescope the other fellow purchased. The second guy, probably in charge, is an older athletic man who used the name Kenneth Reeves when he purchased the telescope. With the exception of Hearst's appearance at Chadwick's cabin and Bethesda, both disappeared shortly after midnight Thursday just after Hearst received a phone call from Reeves' area code."

"This Thursday?" Parker asked.

"The day Chadwick went off the road," Watson replied. "While we don't know where they are now, Harris has telegraphed his trail for next week. Starting tomorrow night he has one night reservations in four-diamond hotels all within a day's drive of D.C."

"What's that about?" Parker asked.

"I don't know. He certainly didn't know we'd have his prints, but our geeks have cross- checked his data profile with every conceivable computerized transaction and that's what they've found. I think it means they are going to have another go at Chadwick in the next twenty-four hours."

"Jesus Christ! Okay, Doc, you've told me what I need to know about Chadwick. Now I need to know what Binder's doing."

"Binder?" Watson questioned. "Am I missing something? Chadwick's the one in danger. It's time to throw out the rulebook. There must be something we can do."

"Look, Doc, I agree, but for now, my hands are tied. You continue your investigation working within the law. Chadwick's injuries are his greatest threat. He has the best care at Bethesda and our own protective services are responsible for securing and defending Secretary Chadwick."

"Are you talking to a recorder?" Watson questioned. "I've just told you Chadwick may be the target of an assassination plot. These people could be nuts. If planes can go into the twin towers, nobody can protect Chadwick playing by the rules."

"I understand what you are saying and I agree. Do you hear me? I agree, but listen. I'm constrained. The FBI cannot tip or even touch the Constitutional scales. This dispute is between President Stanton and Acting President Roosevelt. It must be settled with complete transparency according to the Twenty-Fifth Amendment. If Acting President Roosevelt can keep his majority of the Cabinet and reassert President Stanton's incapacity, the Congress will decide who will be our President. If he fails to keep his majority, President Stanton will reassume his Presidency."

"I know all that. Give me a break. Tell me something I don't know." Watson pushed hard.

"God dammit, Doc, trust me." Director Parker hesitated momentarily and then plowed ahead. "I have a plan, but it has a hair trigger. If I jump the gun, conspiracy theorists will have a political murder mystery to milk into a majority. They will have more than enough arsenic to poison our democratic well, permanently. Roosevelt or Stanton? It won't matter. Governments have to have legitimacy." Again Parker hesitated and continued. "There's no recording here, Doc. Keep pushing. Get us answers, rock solid unequivocal answers. The nation needs answers. I'll do everything I can, when I can."

"I'll do my best, Director. I just hope Secretary Chadwick doesn't die before you trigger your plan."

"I understand your report, Doc. Chadwick is the target. He needs us, now."

8:15 P.M., Saturday, January 27.

Though they had been together for over an hour, William Roosevelt and Alan Binder were shaking hands as Jason Fields entered the library. "You have my word, Alan, I'll do what I can do, but as you know, events may be in control."

"Excuse me, should I come back later?"

"No, no, of course not, Jason. Secretary Binder and I have just had a very productive discussion."

"Hi, Jason, it's good to see you again. I know you've been very busy." Secretary Binder smiled and extended his hand.

Jason responded automatically, but with some caution. "A productive discussion? You're not going to make me guess, are you?"

"No, Roosevelt answered, "However, Jason, what I am about to tell you must be held in strictest confidence."

"I understand," Jason responded.

"Monday morning," Roosevelt continued, "Secretary Binder will announce his decision to call upon Congress to determine the competence of President Stanton to continue in office. As you know, with the other commitments we have, his decision gives us an indisputable majority of the Cabinet and guarantees that the issue will go to Congress and be resolved in accordance with the Twenty-Fifth Amendment."

"That's wonderful, sir."

"Yes, it is. But, Jason, as I told you, until late Monday morning only President Stanton, his chief of staff, you and I, no one else, will be aware of Alan's decision. One more thing, Jason, while Secretary Binder is going to join me and seven of his colleagues Monday morning calling for the Congress to determine who will be the President for the next two years he will also argue that that person should be President Stanton."

"What? How does that make any sense? Surely, Secretary Binder, you can't have it both ways. Either President Stanton has or does not have the ability to discharge the duties of his office."

"As I suggested to the Acting President," Secretary Binder explained, "I believe President Stanton is incapable of performing his duties only because of a gross misunderstanding. After the public and the Congress understand that he never allowed his grief to effect his performance and is still perfectly capable of performing his duties, I believe the Congress will give him a vote of confidence. Their vote and the public's understanding will in fact restore his ability to govern."

"I'm sorry, Mr. Secretary, but that's crazy." Jason's tone was both respectful and adamant.

"Time will tell, Jason. Time will tell. But look at the upside. My decision means you have an indisputable majority of the Cabinet supporting Acting President Roosevelt's assertion. He will have his days in Congress, twenty-one I suspect. And by delaying my announcement, I am buying you 'insiders' time to negotiate a set of ground rules that might allow President Stanton or Acting President Roosevelt, whoever prevails, to govern."

"Ground rules," again Jason was all but incredulous. "It seems to me the Constitution gives the Congress free rein other than to require a two-thirds vote of both Houses to replace the President."

"Jason," Roosevelt interrupted, "the Secretary has convinced me. We need ground rules; we have no precedents, we are making this up as we go. The most powerful nation on the face of the earth is flying by the seat of its pants. That's no good, and with five hundred and thirty five members of Congress about to climb into the driver's seat it's going to get worse."

"Much worse. Unless President Stanton and Acting President Roosevelt can come together and assert control over the ship of state, it is headed for the rocks." Alan Binder knew Jason Fields was as important to William Roosevelt as Crayton Langford was to President Stanton. "Jason, you know Presidential elections drive our politics. The Republicans have been out of power for ten years. They smell blood. As of now they will support Acting President Roosevelt and he will complete President Stanton's term."

"Is there a problem here?" Jason asked.

"Yes," Roosevelt responded. "They want me as a straw man they can blow over at the next election. Unless we can rein in this process, I will be asked not only to destroy the legacy of President Stanton, but also my own chances of winning the Presidency."

Secretary Binder followed. "You both know I was appointed because I am a Republican. I assure you I am still very well connected in my party. Unfortunately, its leadership includes a number of ambitious men who are perfectly willing to see the nation go to hell for a mere twenty-four months. They believe that would be a small price to pay to return America to its core values and, by the way, to propel them to the White House.

"To be blunt, Secretary Binder, why do you care?"

"To be just as blunt, Jason, you are missing the point. My motives would be relevant if I were telling you something you do not already know or could not independently verify, but I am not. These are dangerous times. Two years is an eternity filled with infinite opportunities for major screw-ups - irreversible errors. The nation needs a president that can govern. That's why I care."

"Roosevelt or Stanton?" Jason questioned.

"Either, that's my point. They share a common interest. I have my preference, but in either case we must insure the winner is not so damaged by the process that he cannot govern."

"I'm sorry, Secretary Binder. I understand. I only wish you were going to be in our corner as we go to Congress." In a more reflective mood, Jason continued. "Forty-three years ago I sat with my best friend in the House gallery and watched President Johnson address a joint session of Congress. Behind him we saw Speaker McCormick and Senator Pro Temp Carl Hayden and we knew the country needed the Twenty-Fifth Amendment. Do you know who that friend was?"

"What a small world." Secretary Binder exclaimed. "So was I! I wasn't always in politics, but I was always a junkie, especially when I was at Georgetown."

"Really? It is a small world, but you didn't ask about my best friend. Mr. Roosevelt knows. My best friend was Crayton Langford. We were both on the Washington Semester Program at American University."

"That's why I told you, Alan," Acting President Roosevelt injected, "Jason and Crayton can draft ground rules consistent with the original intent. They just need to get started."

"Can I call the President?" Secretary Binder asked.

"Of course," Roosevelt answered. "Tell him he was right. He did warn me. We need to get this jack back in the box. Do you want to be involved in the negotiations?"

"No, that's for you guys. I'm going into hiding. I just hope Director Parker will be able to put me up in a safe house until Monday when I go public."

"Will we be able to reach you?" Roosevelt asked.

"Yes, I'm sure I can work out the details with Parker. I'll let you know." Binder replied. "For you, time is short. By your actions you and the President may be able to insure the Twenty-Fifth Amendment is not a threat to our democracy, but the safeguard it was intended to be."

"If we fail?" Roosevelt asked.

"I trust you both to give it your best effort, but my decision is not conditional. On Monday I will join you and the decision will be sent to the Congress. I hope immediately thereafter, you and the President will be able to release a joint statement defining the boundaries that you both believe should govern the Congressional decision. I pray it will focus entirely on the President's ability to discharge his powers and duties."

CHAPTER TWENTY:

A LIFE OR DEATH GAME

8:27 P.M., Saturday, January 27.

"Bobby, where have you been? I just called."

"I'm sorry, Mr. Reeves. I just ran out to the car. I left my cell in the room."

"Keep it with you, Bobby, always. I've got a hell of an imagination and I don't like to worry."

"I understand, sir."

"Good," Reeves responded and moved on. "Now, how are you doing? Any questions?"

"Fine. I'm doing fine. I'm ready, sir."

"Then we're ready."

"Mr. Reeves, I do have one question. What happens if he dies? I mean what happens if he dies without us?"

Reeves laughed, "That's not a problem, Bobby. Hell, I'd call it the perfect crime. The feds will rule Chadwick's death an accident and the Commander will be so impressed he'll probably want to put us both on retainer."

"So it wouldn't make any difference?"

"It would make a big difference. It would make our lives a hell of a lot easier. Even if the feds put this whole bizarre plot together and charged us with conspiracy to commit murder, we'd argue we just conned an evil old bastard intent on subverting our democracy. He's the big fish. We have options. He'd have none. Before I'd spend a day in prison, I'd roll on him.

"Jesus, you're a few moves ahead of me."

"That's why they pay me the big money. Tomorrow is payday, Bobby. It doesn't matter whether God plays God or we do."

"So all I have to do is worry about going to hell."

"You're in the wrong business, if you're worried about hell. What you need to think about, Bobby, is now. Worry about prison. Down the road, if you're still worried about hell, you can always play it safe and have a death bed conversion."

"I don't think it works unless you're truly sincere," Hearst suggested.

"If you're scared when you're dying you'll be sincere, truly sincere."

"Is this supposed to help me sleep?"

"I suspect I could have done better, but I'll be there for you tomorrow," Reeves responded. "I'll keep my fingers crossed and hope he dies during the night. In any case I'll touch base with you in the morning before you head out."

"I'll have my cell with me. Talk to you then."

Saturday, 9:00 P.M., January 27.

"Good evening, Director Parker," Secretary Binder obviously enjoyed surprising his friend at FBI headquarters.

"Alan, what are you doing here? For that matter how did you get in? Has our security gone to hell?" Robert Parker was still puzzled, but back in charge. "Welcome, Alan, how can I help you?"

"I had the help of an insider. Benjamin Brode is an extremely competent young man. Thank you for assigning him to me. I know you're busy with the Chadwick investigation and Cabinet security so I'll try to be brief."

"Brode, get in here," Parker commanded. "You need to hear this." He wasn't long. "Alan, in all humility, the Bureau is loaded with extremely competent men and women. Brode is just one of a cast of thousands. He does have a certain rising star power. If it doesn't go to his head he could have a future here. He needs to be a little more sensitive to his Director's need for privacy, but only time will tell. Now again, Alan, how can I help?"

"Excuse me, Director Parker."

"Yes, Brode, what is it now?"

"May I be excused, sir?

"Yes, of course, very good, Ben."

"Robert, "I have an unusual request. Feel free to say, 'No.' I'd like to spend tonight and tomorrow night in a safe house."

"What's this about, Alan? Have you been threatened?"

"No, no, Director. I am perfectly safe, particularly with Brode. It's just that I am the only Cabinet member who has not announced his decision and I don't intend to, not Monday. The press and paparazzi are hounding me."

"You've made a decision?"

"Et tu, director? Yes, I have, but I have given my word to both President Stanton and Acting President Roosevelt that I will not announce my decision until late Monday."

"But you've told them?" Parker asked.

"Yes, I have," Secretary Binder answered.

"Is it conditional?" Parker persisted.

"No, Robert, it is not!" Secretary Binder bristled. He had been hammered all day with the accusation that he had made a deal. "I simply want it to remain confidential so that the President and Acting President have time to agree on some ground rules."

"Alan, I wasn't suggesting anything, but you are telling me that you will announce Monday that you are joining Mr. Roosevelt and sending the issue to Congress."

"No, I'm not telling you that. They might need time to establish ground rules for the exchange of power."

"Alan, you and I are friends. I met with President Stanton earlier today. He has no intention of resigning. I understand your desire to buy them a little time. You don't have to worry. I would love confirmation, but your decision is safe. I will share it with no one, absolutely no one and Brode can take you to a safe house not far from your home."

"Why do you want confirmation?"

"I can't tell you much, other than it would help me protect you and the rest of the Cabinet."

"Oh, Robert, you are clever. How the hell can I say 'No' to that? Are you serious?"

"I am serious, Alan."

"That's it then," Secretary Binder announced. "On Monday I will join Roosevelt. There will be no debate about what a majority is with Aaron Chadwick clinging to life. The issue is going to Congress, but, Robert, I am joining Roosevelt to save Andrew Stanton's Presidency. He can't govern without Congressional vindication. I am going to do everything in my power to convince the Congress that he needs and deserves a mandate to finish the term Americans elected him to serve."

"Thanks, Alan. I won't breathe a word. I understand what you are doing and you have been a big help."

"Can you tell me how?" Alan asked.

"No. Maybe in time, but not now."

"Do you owe me?"

"Ya, I owe you big time," Director Parker responded.

Sunday, 6:45 A.M., January 28.

"How'd you sleep?" Reeves asked.

'Okay, I guess. I had some weird dreams so I must have been asleep. How about you?

"Okay. I'm a little early so you can take your time. Be through the gate by 8:30. I'll meet you at the coffee bar in main cafeteria no later than 9:15. Don't screw up. Drive like an old lady, but don't park in a handicap spot. Don't call attention to yourself. Understand? You're the invisible man."

"Yes, sir. No waves, coming or going."

"See you there, Bobby."

Sunday, 7:30 A.M., January 28.

Jason came through the tunnel from the Old Executive Office Building. They were meeting on Crayton's turf in the White House. It was to be private. No one but the principals knew. Jason was sure that despite their opposing positions, Crayton was still a good friend and could be trusted. They could work with each other.

Together in 1963 after the assassination of John Kennedy, they witnessed the inception of the Twenty-Fifth Amendment. It took three and a half years for the nation to adopt the amendment that attempted to address the inevitability of an incompetent president. Now, forty-three years later, Jason Fields and Crayton Langford, two political professionals, were charged with defining the rules of engagement. They had no time for games. Ready or not, the battle would be joined no later than four-thirty Monday afternoon. They had thirty-three hours.

"Thanks for meeting me more than halfway, Jason. I need to be here. President Stanton has a very full schedule. Today, he and Danny would have been married forty years. He has lots of well-wishers."

"I'm sure he does," Jason responded. "They were a wonderful couple."

"Yes, they were. How do we proceed with this, Jason?" Crayton asked. "I have to tell you, I'll try to compartmentalize, but if the truth be known I am a candidate for anger management."

"I understand, Crayton, but the issue is going to Congress and Secretary Binder is right. We all agree. Whoever Congress chooses must not be marginalized in the process. The nation needs a president who can govern."

Crayton could barely contain himself. "Of course we agree, Jason, but we are playing with fire. The process is inherently political and the higher the stakes, the dirtier the game. Friday, President Stanton, the most decent man I've ever known, was accused of directing the murder of Aaron Chadwick. That's where we are. The world has gone mad and now the issue moves to Congress where the Republicans are in control. I assure you they will give us just enough rope to hang ourselves."

"Aren't you being just a little pessimistic?" Jason asked. He had never seen his friend so despondent. "This isn't like you."

"The Republicans are counting on our party to self-destruct. And it will. As it stands now the process will martyr the President, marginalize the Acting President and guarantee a Republican landslide. It's simple, Jason, I fear for the country and for our democracy when elections are overruled."

"Elections still rule, but we both know presidents can become incompetent. It's a fact of life. It's American history. They shouldn't have to be impeached to be removed. That's adding insult to injury. You and I were there. The Twenty-Fifth Amendment gave the nation a way to remove presidents without charging them with high crimes and misdemeanors."

"The Constitutional standard is that the president must be 'unable to discharge the powers and duties of the office.' It is the only standard. That is not the case here!" Crayton was insistent.

"The amendment makes Congress the judge of that, not you or me or even the Cabinet."

"Then let the Congress judge using the Constitutional standard." Crayton was emphatic. "The only question Congress must address is whether President Stanton is able to discharge the powers and duties of his office. Nothing else."

"Crayton, it may surprise you that Vice President Roosevelt insisted that we discuss only that question with members of the Cabinet. It was not always easy, particularly with several Cabinet members who had more than an unseemly interest in upgrading their situation in a Roosevelt administration. But that is not our problem. We are charged with going forward and coming up with ground rules that will focus Congress on fulfilling its Constitutional responsibilities."

Crayton was surprised, pleasantly surprised. "Then, we have a good start, Jason. I can't believe it," he confessed. "But if we are agreed on the principle governing the end game, then we can devise ground rules that could work now, and in the future. I am convinced it can be done."

"The problem is enforcement," Jason stated. "The Vice President has a relatively small staff and he has had difficulty, but the White House has a cast of thousands. How do we stop the deals? It's what we all do. We divvy up a three-trillion-dollar budget - what goes in and what stays out. We write policies that affect millions. We locate hospitals, highways, bases, and dams. We promise support and we threaten opposition. We hire, fire, promote, and demote every day. How can it all be controlled?"

"I've thought of nothing else since Secretary Binder defined the issue. There may be a way. I think it's the high road. I assure you it is the road less traveled. The solution is like a cease-fire. It's in everyone's interest, but one shot will blow it all to hell. It will be war, a war without winners. We have dirt too, Jason." While it was President Stanton's call, Crayton still felt exposing

Elizabeth Anne's masquerade at the State of the Union was a viable option.

"You have my attention."

"Okay, this is the best scenario I can envision. We'll have to flush this out, but I would have President Stanton and Acting President Roosevelt hold separate, simultaneous news conferences. They would each announce, first that the only question before Congress is whether or not President Stanton is able to discharge the duties and powers of his office, second that no one is authorized to speak for them in any capacity, and third that they and they alone will speak for themselves and whatever they say and do will be on the public record. That's essentially it."

"We might have a starting point, Crayton. That's very interesting. I need to give it much more thought, but my first response is positive. It seems to be straightforward. It just might work. Has President Stanton signed off on this?"

"No, but he would. Do you know how Roosevelt would respond?" Crayton asked.

"No, but I think he'd go for it. It might be a hard sell to a few of his supporters, but he's a pretty tough guy. If he signs on, it's a done deal no matter who objects."

"Even Elizabeth Anne?" Crayton couldn't resist.

"Yes, Crayton. As I said, William Roosevelt is a tough guy. He doesn't flinch when he knows he's right. He practices what he preaches. Why not make it a joint conference?" Jason asked, trying to turn the tables.

"I thought about it. I wouldn't rule it out. There are advantages and disadvantage. It's true Roosevelt would look young and vigorous, but I assure you President Stanton would appear both competent and presidential. I'm sure we could work out the details," Crayton challenged.

"That's probably enough. Let's slow down. I suggest we check with our respective Presidents and ensure we are on the right track."

"A good idea, Jason. Are you comfortable calling Roosevelt from here?"

"I'd like to speak with him in person. Give me a couple of hours and I'll join you back here.

"You know, Jason, we have never been involved in anything so important.

"I know. And I fear there are players and events we will never anticipate, much less control."

"We will do our best. See you soon."

Kenneth Reeves sat alone reading the Washington Post while picking at his half-eaten breakfast. The gate had been no problem. He occupied a small two-person table pushed tight against one of the large pillars that marched across the main Bethesda Naval Hospital cafeteria. His coat was hung on the opposite chair obliquely facing a still full cup of coffee. Over his paper he could easily see the coffee bar and cashier lines. He watched for Robert. He needed him. Reeves liked Robert. He was a competent young man, dependable, respectful, and anxious to learn. While Reeves was comfortable with his plan, he needed Robert – not only as a potential diversion, but also as a fall guy if things went to hell. He'd never worked without one.

"Robert, here," Reeves stood signaling his young friend who had just paid the cashier in the far line. "I've got cream and sugar, ketchup, and Tabasco at our table. Do you need anything else?"

"No, no. That's fine," Robert Hearst (now Harris) replied. "Have you been here long?"

"Not long," Reeves removed his coat from the second chair and placed it on his own. The two men sat and melded into the still crowded cafeteria. "How was the gate? Anything unusual?"

"I don't think so. They all but waved me through. I think they might have had an extra man there. The gate guy checked off to him before he let me through, but it didn't take but a moment. Must be my new clean-cut look. What do you think?"

"Could be, but I think I'd let the mustache grow back," Reeves answered. "You look like a raw recruit."

"No, say it isn't so. Even with the glasses?" Bobby asked. "I think they give me a certain gravitās."

"Gravitās? Oh, my lord, a grunt with gravitās. Brawny and bright, will wonders never cease to amaze?"

"I do try harder."

"Yes, you do, Bobby. For now just finish your breakfast. I thought we should go to work during the Chadwick briefing when the reporters would be out, but it's been delayed. I'm going to check it out. I won't be gone long. Don't even go to the bathroom without leaving me a note."

Leaving his coat, but picking up a small attaché case, Kenneth Reeves joined a small school of big and little medical fish heading toward the exit. He didn't look back. The Intensive Care Unit wasn't far, just a couple of long corridors to the skywalk to Building 10, then up the elevator to the third floor, and you were there.

Bobby Hearst, a.k.a. Harris, sat alone. He checked his watch. It was 9:30. Together with Reeves he felt confident, now he felt conspicuous. His breakfast was cold and tasteless. The Post demanded to be read, but he couldn't concentrate. It was just a prop. He turned its pages and scanned the cafeteria. Only the headline, "Chadwick Condition Critical" caught his attention. The article barely considered the possibility of assassination, but he continued to look for plainclothesmen and reviewed the evidence against him. There wasn't any, none, yet he was uneasy. Even in the military he wasn't good at waiting especially when he sensed a setup. He checked his watch again. Reeves should be back. He wondered how long he would wait and then dismissed the thought. He had never run before. He wouldn't now.

Reeves also worried about Bobby. He couldn't be gone too long. In Building 10, slapped on walls above the call buttons for both banks of elevators, he saw the crude signs announcing that the briefing on Secretary Chadwick's condition had been postponed until 10:00 and had been moved to the main auditorium. When he had arrived at the ICU waiting room, it was all but empty. There were no visitors, no staff, and only two reporters looking like stranded travelers at an airport.

"What's the deal with Chadwick?" asked one, sitting up on the couch he had claimed.

"Are you talking to me?" Reeves responded.

"You're the one with the white coat. Lady with his fluids didn't show this morning. What do you suppose that means?"

"Sorry I can't help you fellows. I'm not on the case," Reeves answered. "You do know there is a briefing on Chadwick at eleven. They moved it to the auditorium."

"You don't get a scoop at a news conference," the second reporter volunteered as he got up and stretched. "Something is amiss just behind that door. It's Sunday and they're slow getting their act together. Somebody's going to jump the gun. It's all about being first. If I had the guts I'd do it."

"Sounds pretty risky," Reeves responded. "The medical mantra is 'do no harm.'"

"Ours is 'get it first.' Sure you can't you help us, doc?"

"Sorry. You know your business better than I do. There's a story here somewhere. Good luck."

"Thanks, Doc."

They were right, Reeves thought. Something was amiss. The normally busy ICU appeared to be in lockdown. No doctors, nurses, or orderlies were coming or going. The fluids Chadwick needed to live were no longer delivered through the waiting room. The briefing had been postponed. Reeves was sure that Secretary Chadwick had been moved – either for security reason or because his condition had changed. If he were moved for security reasons he would still need ICU type care. If he were moved for medical reasons then there were three options. He was sent back to surgery, up to a floor, or down to the morgue. Reeves had seen the accident. He headed downstairs to the morgue with his fingers crossed.

The autopsy on President Kennedy had been performed at Bethesda. Reeves was only fifteen then, but Kennedy had been his hero. It was Kennedy who had created the Navy Seals. Reeves still thought of those years as his best. Could it be the same morgue, he wondered.

As soon as he opened the stairwell door he saw them. Two men were planted in front of the morgue. They were FBI. They spotted him immediately. He was living right. Chadwick was dead and they didn't have a clue.

"Another doctor, I suppose," the agent on the right observed. "Don't you guys ever give up?"

"This isn't original?" Reeves laughed.

"Not hardly," the other agent responded. "Let me make this simple. You can't come in, we can't talk, and you need to get to the briefing. It starts in ten minutes."

Reeves made it back to the cafeteria in ten minutes. He cut through one of the reserved dining rooms. Bobby was at the coffee bar where he could observe the whole room. Reeves sat down at their table as Bobby approached with a refill.

"Sorry I'm late," Reeves announced to anyone who might have been curious. "They were pretty well backed up." Then in more hushed tones he told Bobby what he had learned. "We're through here Bobby. He's dead." Reeves waited to let Bobby absorb what he had said.

"Did you?"

"No, it was the accident, but we still need to be cautious. Nothing's changed there, nothing at all. The FBI and the press are going to try to solve an accident and make it murder. Every conspiracy nut in the country is going to join in the hunt. They'll demand the answer they want, not the truth. We may not be out of the woods."

"What do we do?" Bobby asked.

"Stick to the plan. Tonight, you're at the Dover Downs Hotel and Casino. Spend the day like a tourist. Look over the city; visit some residential neighborhoods as well as the capital. Maybe take in a museum. Remember your cover, you're windshielding five small state capitals looking for a place to relocate and establish a business. Enjoy yourself, but always consider the possibility that you're under surveillance."

"That makes it a little tough."

"Yes, it does, but you can do it. You're good, Bobby," Reeves added, standing. "Now, shake my hand. We've got to get the hell out of here. I'll call you tonight or tomorrow morning at the latest. Don't worry. This is looking good. Real good."

Sunday, 10:30 A.M., January 28.

At last those on stage seem to organize themselves behind the podium. Then Bethesda Naval Medical Center spokeswoman, Ms. Cheryl Hynik, stepped forward to the microphone, introduced herself, spelled her last name and read the announcement: Aaron Chadwick, Secretary of the Interior, died early this morning. He remained in a coma until a cardiac infarction took his life. In accordance with his living will, no additional extraordinary measures were taken. He was pronounced dead at 6:43 A.M. While attending physicians were ready to certify the causes and circumstances of his death to be the direct result of massive trauma suffered in an automobile accident, at the request of Robert Parker, Director of the Federal Bureau of Investigation with the concurrence of Mrs. Sharon Chadwick a full medicolegal autopsy will be performed. The Director noted that Mrs. Chadwick's concurrence was required in his mind because the Bureau has no evidence to suggest the accident was anything more than just that - a tragic accident.

Following the announcement, Ms. Hynik and her medical panel answered questions for nearly an hour and a half. They had little new information. The session ended when she was asked again, "Did Secretary Chadwick have any last words?"

CHAPTER TWENTY-ONE:

MISSION ACCOMPLISHED

12:12 P.M., Sunday, January 28.

The news of Chadwick's death was overshadowed by its consequences. The press, unaware of Secretary Binder's decision, announced that Aaron Chadwick's death meant that Acting President Roosevelt finally had the clear majority he needed to reassert his declaration that President Stanton was no longer able to discharge the powers and duties of his office.

Anchors, White House correspondents, syndicated columnists, and pool reporters all sought interviews with President Stanton and Acting President Roosevelt. Seven of the thirteen surviving members of President Stanton's Cabinet had already announced their decision to join Roosevelt. The issue was definitely going to Congress. Ironically, newscasters noted, a Republican Congress would decide which Democrat, Stanton or Roosevelt, would lead the nation for the next two years.

The announcement that a full autopsy had been ordered to quell speculation that Aaron Chadwick's death had been anything but accidental ignited speculation that his death was the result of foul play. Given the Secretary's signature on the first declaration to Congress that President Stanton was no longer fit to perform his duties led conspiracy theorists to pronounce the obvious: President Stanton, or at the least the Stanton White House, was behind Chadwick's timely death. It was a better story than the truth. Instant polls showed public approval of President Stanton in a free fall. 'Right Think,' the patriot news network, piled on with public push polling:

"Would you be more or less likely to urge Congress to remove the President if the White House staff was involved in Secretary Chadwick's death, even if the President claimed he had no knowledge of their involvement?" To register their vote, viewers were instructed to call 1 800 Remove Y or 1 800 Remove N. Ratings spiked.

Media competition was most ferocious in the gutter media, but spread to the mainstream as the latter, in good conscience, felt compelled to report on what was being reported in the gutter. It had a liberating effect on their reporting which for a time had been constrained by the truth.

While "responsible" newscasters still shied away from the "murder story," they uniformly announced the battle for the Presidency of the United States had been joined. Then, following slightly different paths, all downhill, they went from descriptive analysis, to speculation, and then to full rank hyperbole.

The stakes were in fact enormous. Congress would not only choose the President for the next two years, but it would also set the stage for future elections. Five hundred and thirty-five Congressmen would make the decision. The Presidency of the United States was the tip of the iceberg, the trophy that could be seen. The annual budget of the United States was approaching three trillion dollars. The President proposes when, where, and how that money will be spent. He is the leader of the free world and commander-in-chief of the most lethal force in world history. He can bring troops home or he can send them abroad. The threat can be real or imagined; it doesn't matter, because the Presidency is all about power.

In pursuit of such power politicians might pay any price. With the Presidency held hostage they had no choice. It would be a bidding war. Everything was on the auction block. Senators and Representatives might describe their conditions in terms of principles, programs and policies, but that could be far from the truth. Real power brokers would want a puppet. Strangely, most commentators, perhaps concerned about future access, felt neither Stanton nor Roosevelt fit the puppet profile. They did, however, add the caveat that it was still early in the game and desperate men were known to take desperate measures. It was Armageddon.

Since facts were scarce and opinions plentiful, the networks went with opinions. They interviewed Washington insiders, academicians, and elder statesmen, as well as "the man on the street". They then turned to their regular reporters and commentators for opinions about the opinions they had just heard. The airwaves were full.

Sunday, 3:00 P.M., January 28.

"Hey Jimmy, how's my boy?" Commander Croft braced himself, then caught little Jimmy Roosevelt in midair and swung him up onto his shoulders. "We've still got it, 'J-Man.'"

"You're the best granddad. The best."

"Can we go inside now? It's cold." Elizabeth Anne moved past her father into the foyer of Castle Croft. Carl took their coats.

"Will you be in the den, sir?" he asked. "I have a fire going and Winston's waiting for Jimmy."

"That will be fine, Carl. Thanks." Commander Croft lowered Jimmy to the floor. His legs were in motion when he hit the ground. Winston, a nine-year-old golden who smiled, was Jimmy's best friend.

"I don't know how Winston knows, but he does," Carl remarked.

"I think Dad gives Jimmy away. He gets excited, too."

As they moved down the hall toward the den, Elizabeth Anne couldn't wait. "When did you learn?" she asked.

"Thursday," he answered with a smug chuckle.

"No, you know what I mean."

"I got a 'mission accomplished' billing statement this morning. Just early enough so that I had time to turn on the television and wait for the breaking news. I've paid the first installment. After the autopsy I'll make the last. How'd William react?"

"Strangely," Elizabeth Anne reflected. "He's been in a different world since Binder left last night."

"What do you mean?"

"When the news came on this morning every network had the same lead: 'Chadwick dies, Congress to choose the President.' William only reacted to Aaron's death. He talked about the tragedy, wrote Sharon a note, asked if I would order flowers, and then sequestered himself back in his office. William didn't even mention Congress, not a word."

"What's the deal with Binder?" Croft asked, muting the television that was still rehashing the news. "He's supposed to be a deal maker. Why did he wait?"

"I don't know, Dad. It doesn't make sense. He was in the driver's seat, he could have named his price, but you did the right thing. He could have come out against us. Now it doesn't matter. Will we win?"

"You've seen the polls. Congress will milk the hearings, but Stanton is dead meat. Unless he's a captive of his staff, he'll resign rather than force a vote." Commander Croft spoke with authority – as he always did.

"Why hasn't he?" Elizabeth Anne's question was a mixture of frustration and anger.

"He was grasping at straws. He thought he could turn Aaron. He knows better now." Croft moved back of the bar and got two glasses. "Like a drink?"

"Sure, the sun will be setting shortly."

"Scotch on the rocks?"

"Great."

Croft handed Elizabeth Anne a crystal glass with two fingers of single malt scotch. "To the sun setting on Stanton and rising on the Roosevelts."

Flush with victory, warmed by the scotch, Elizabeth Anne and Commander Croft shared their dreams for the future. Neither saw nor heard the breaking news playing on the muted television in the opposite corner of the den.

Sunday, 5:00 P.M., January 28.

While the initial audience was small, reporters, commentators, and partisans of all stripes were astonished. At precisely 5 P.M. spokesmen for President Stanton and Acting President Roosevelt released a joint statement to the American people. Apparently the combatants in the much-ballyhooed "Presidential Wars" were talking. Reluctantly, networks aired the statement.

------- Statement -------

of

Andrew Holmes Stanton   &   William Butler Roosevelt
President of the United States   Acting President of the United
                                   States

President Stanton and Acting President Roosevelt want to express their sincere condolences to Aaron Chadwick's family. Aaron will be sorely missed, particularly now when his thoughtful and selfless counsel would again help point the way through new territory. Nevertheless he will lead us by example and we are pledged to adhere to his principles.

While these are difficult times, Americans must understand that their democracy is not in danger. There is no threat to the nation or to the rule of law. Invocation of Section Four of the Twenty-Fifth Amendment is not a Constitutional crisis; it is a Constitutional process. President Stanton and Acting President Roosevelt are both sworn to preserve, protect, and defend the Constitution of the United States, as are the Senators and Representatives of the United States Congress.

Tomorrow, in accordance with the Constitution, both houses of Congress will begin the process of deciding whether President Stanton is able to discharge the powers and duties of his office. Their decision must be made within three weeks. If they determine President Stanton is unable to discharge the powers and duties of his office, then Acting President Roosevelt will continue to perform those duties. If they determine President Stanton is able to discharge the powers and duties of his office, he shall reassume those powers and duties.

Written to counter the "Presidential Wars" being hyped by media mania, the statement was a good trial run for Crayton Langford and Jason Fields. Though hastily prepared, both President Stanton and Acting President Roosevelt signed off with only one change. They added the phrase "as are the Senators and Representatives of the United States Congress" to emphasize that Congressmen, too, were "sworn to preserve, protect, and defend the Constitution."

After a little hesitation, initial television reporting was predictable. The regular banter of dual anchors was interrupted with "Presidential Wars: Breaking News." Shortly thereafter the theme music announced to well-conditioned listeners that the news was now. Producers switched to narrowly framed, breathless senior correspondents planted at twelve-foot intervals in front of the White House. Mostly respectful tourists watched "correspondents" fumbled with their earpieces. The latter were told they were 'live,' and began to read the release they had just been handed in the White House Briefing Room. To the tourists, it sounded like a round, not of "Row, Row, Row Your Boat," but rather a poorly coordinated one with each reporter trying to get to the front of the verse. To viewers at home each network appeared to have an exclusive; "First with the news you need to know."

Back at the studio, experts from around the country were being summoned to perform. They were on retainer and like emergency medical personnel they were on call. Within minutes they sat in front of cameras against impressive backdrops portraying their location. As makeup was being applied, they were briefed on the specific area of their expertise to be probed; then they too were 'live.' Opinions were spontaneous and conflicting. Some found the statement suggested a negotiated settlement was in the offing, some took issue with its premise that invocation of Section Four was just another Constitutional process. Others suggested the statement had been unilaterally issued by one or the other of the alleged signatories who understood that it would be political suicide for his opponent to challenge the reassuring content of the statement. Most argued that the statement was simply incredulous. Of course the "Presidential War" would be fought, too much was at stake. It would end only when it was won.

Into the night, the run-up to war continued. At three in the morning, the language was adjusted and listeners heard "the genie was way out of the bottle and anyone who thought otherwise was simply pissing in the wind." Armageddon was back and it was being milked.

CHAPTER TWENTY-TWO:

PEOPLE OF INTEREST

9:12 A.M., Monday, January 29.

"Alan, you can come out of hiding. We have our ground rules." President Stanton's enthusiasm was obvious even over the phone.

"Wonderful! I was beginning to think they had blocked my calls. These FBI guys take their work seriously. So you're pleased?"

"Yes, Alan. Both Roosevelt and I are pleased. It is a little frightening. Makes me think I'm missing something."

"What's next?"

"First, while Aaron's death gives Acting President Roosevelt an indisputable majority, I still believe, Alan, you must join his majority in sending the issue to Congress. You've earned great credibility with both of us; you need to keep it. Similarly, of course, I hope when you make your announcement you will emphasize your belief that as soon as the facts are known Congress should decide that I should resume my duties."

"Of course, Mr. President, that's exactly what I intend to do."

"Good. The timing is tight, Alan. We need you to go first, soon. At noon, Mr. Roosevelt will formally deliver the rebuttal declaration to Congress and then at two, Crayton and Jason will hold a joint press conference. They will begin by acknowledging the very positive role you played in helping us contain a potential threat to our democracy."

"That's not necessary Mr. President, but I do appreciate it. Saturday night when I left you I had to plow my way through a media mob. It got ugly. The last three questions yelled at me were: 'What did you get, Binder?' 'Can Roosevelt match Stanton's offer?' and 'Who is the highest bidder, Mr. Secretary?' They are burned in my mind. How did I get such a reputation?"

"I'm sorry, Alan." President Stanton's empathy was easy. He knew abuse. "People have not just lost their innocence, they are hopelessly cynical. You can understand some of it. A lot of people aren't playing by the rules and then we're all painted with that same brush."

"It is so destructive," Binder lamented. "Good people are being driven from public service. The cycle of cynicism is self-fulfilling. It is terribly lazy. It is not skepticism. There's no critical objective thinking, and worse yet, cynicism seems to be confused with intelligence and sophistication."

"Alan, we've got to get you out of that safe house. You're going sour. It's still morning in America, my friend." President Stanton was still upbeat.

"You're right, Mr. President and I do think with this announcement you and Mr. Roosevelt are exceeding all expectations and setting a new absolutely wonderful standard."

"Crayton and Jason were at it all night, but what they produced is really straightforward. The people will understand what we are doing. And they will know it is for the good of the country."

"So at three, what will Crayton and Jason have to say?"

"First they will make it perfectly clear they are speaking for Mr. Roosevelt and me. Then they will share our view of the Constitutional issue before Congress and our great fear of the vicious forces of ambition, greed, and zealotry that the issue has unleashed. When that is understood they will present the rules of engagement we have adopted to ensure the process is in no way corrupted."

"Will your ground rules really work?" Alan asked.

"It's the sunshine theory with teeth. I can give you a quick summary, but then you've got an announcement to make."

"Please do, Mr. President"

"As I said, Alan, it is the Sunshine Rule taken to its logical extreme. First, Roosevelt and I have agreed the only question before Congress is whether I am able to discharge the duties and powers of my office. Second, in resolving that issue no one is authorized to speak for either of us, and no one will; we will speak for ourselves. Third, whatever we say and do will be on the public record. Fourth, a member of Mr. Roosevelt's staff will be assigned to me and a member of my staff will be assigned to him and we will have a pool reporter assigned to each of us night and day."

"So you are trying to undercut or eliminate side deals. That's great!"

"If it holds, Alan, I think this could truly be a positive legitimate Constitutional process."

"I hope so. I was convinced this whole procedure might just be a sealed auction where the highest bidder buys the Presidency."

"It's not going to happen, Alan!"

"Will you give the Congressional leadership a heads-up?" Secretary Binder asked.

"Yes, Crayton and Jason are with them now. We'd like them to endorse the agreement, but we're not waiting. We're trying to reclaim control of this juggernaut."

"No more surprises?"

"I could hope, Alan, but I've lived too long. I suspect we are still in for a few surprises, but maybe they won't all be bad.

9:40 A.M., Monday, January 29.

Associate Justice Steven Holt was in his fourth year on the Supreme Court. While he was still its most junior member and not fully vetted, he was already highly respected by his colleagues. His writing was exceptional and he was often instrumental in finding middle ground that made majorities possible. For Holt, however, a simple majority was not enough. He wanted consensus. He worked for opinions that settled issues, that would last and allow the court and the country to turn its attention elsewhere.

This morning he had not wanted to be alone. The time he would have normally used to find common ground, he used to talk about a common friend. Both he and his mentor, senior Associate Justice John Paul Stevens, loved Aaron Chadwick. Chadwick had clerked for Stevens years ago and before that he had been Holt's roommate. They had been best friends. Now he was dead. Both had tales they had not shared until now. There had been no occasion.

With oral arguments just twenty minutes away, Holt returned to his chambers to robe and collect his case brief. In the center of his desk where it could not be missed he found a note clipped to a large envelope:

Justice Holt,

> This came in today's mail.
> It was postmarked Friday and
> was sent from zip code 22835.
> I looked it up. That's Luray,
> Virginia.
>
> Let me know if you need
> anything.

Barbara

Removing the note Holt saw the legal sized envelope was addressed to him at the Supreme Court. Written boldly on both sides was the directive: To be Opened by Addressee Only!! There was no return address on either the front or back of the envelope. He checked his watch. He still had fifteen minutes. Looking back at the note he read again, "That's Luray." It had to be from Aaron. He ripped open the envelope and found a cover letter wrapped around a smaller envelope sealed with scotch tape.

Dear Steve,

> I hope to see you Tuesday afternoon and reclaim the enclosed letter. I'll explain everything then, including my fleeting bout of paranoia. In the meantime I have an unusual favor to ask. If I should die before Tuesday, I want you to immediately, personally deliver the enclosed envelope to our mutual friend Robert Parker.
>
> Don't worry – this is just an insurance policy to mitigate a very unlikely event. Thanks, Steve.
> We'll talk Tuesday.
> Aaron

"Barbara, Get in here quick, please. I need your help. The letter is from Aaron."

"What did you say?" Barbara asked racing toward his office.

"The letter is from Aaron Chadwick. I have no time. You must call Robert Parker, the Director of the FBI. Use my name. Speak to no one but Parker. Tell him I must see him here at noon. It concerns his investigation."

"But what if he's not in, or can't..."

"Barbara, I'm late. Stay in my office. Speak to no one but Parker. I don't know what we have here, but it could be critical." With that, Justice Holt, still struggling with his robe, bolted down the corridor toward the right door. Since he had the least seniority he would be seated last. Maybe he wouldn't be late.

10:00 A.M., Monday, January 29.

Saturday, the press had mobbed Secretary Alan Binder. The entire nation was focused on what he might or might not do. His every utterance was breaking news. Even when he went underground his whereabouts was the lead story, yet now it was over. He had hoped his press conference would jump-start his effort to convince America that President Stanton was fully capable of leading the nation, but he was yesterday's news.

From the stage of the Department of the Treasury's auditorium, Binder could see only a handful of reporters. Even with a short notice, the turnout was embarrassing. Apparently, since the announcement of Aaron Chadwick's death had already guaranteed Congress would decide the issue of President Stanton's competence, it was thought that the Secretary would have little new information. The fact that he had joined the Roosevelt coalition and was also supporting Stanton only suggested he was trying to have it both ways.

Secretary Binder was quick to realize the futility of his efforts. The nation's attention was now being focused on the hard news to come. At noon, Acting President William Roosevelt and a clear majority of the Cabinet would again deliver their written declaration that President Andrew Stanton was unable to discharge the powers and duties of his office. There was no bigger story; there was no other story except the one to follow.

Noon, Monday, January 29.

The Supreme Court is just over a mile from the J. Edgar Hoover FBI Office Building. Less than three blocks from his office, Director Parker sat in the back seat of a Bureau car checking his watch, offering suggestions to his driver, and debating walking to the Court. He did not have time for this. He was receiving equal treatment in a nation that preaches, but does not always practice, equality. It doesn't matter who you are, or how well you know a city, you can still experience gridlock. Inevitably that experience occurs when you are in a hurry, late, or on a fool's errand.

Robert Parker was fairly certain he had better things to do with his time than "race" up to the Supreme Court to discuss his investigation of Aaron Chadwick's alleged death. Unfortunately he had not been able to talk to Justice Holt and gauge for himself what the Judge had to offer. Rather he spoke only to an adamant clerk who would say nothing other than Justice Holt was insistent that what he had was critical to the investigation of Aaron Chadwick's death and that he was honor bound to speak to no one other than Director Parker.

"Hell, it's Roosevelt," his driver Tim explained.

"What about Roosevelt?" Parker questioned.

"That's why we're stopped. He just went by in a motorcade heading toward the Capitol. We should be moving soon, sir."

"It's another historic day, Tim. We're living in interesting times. Our country is cutting the ribbon on a road it's never taken. It's a little frightening."

"He's early; isn't he?"

"Yes, he is; he had until 4:30."

"I'm afraid we're late, sir. Do you think you should call?"

"Not yet. Try the backside of the Court, Tim. We'll be OK."

"Thank you for coming, Robert." Justice Holt, struggling with his robe, moved by the Director.

"No problem, Justice Holt, Director Parker responded. "How have you been?"

"Alright, fine, I guess, so hectic. I miss Aaron, but fine. As soon as I get out of this robe, I'll be Steve again, okay? You know I was a good friend of Aaron's?"

"Of course."

"It's in my office. I really don't know what I have, but it's from Aaron and I think it must be important." Justice Holt had too much on his mind. "I found it right there in the center of my desk. My clerk put it there. It came this morning, postmarked 'Luray.' This is the cover letter."

"I see. Give me just a moment, Steve." Robert Parker studied the postmark and then the cover letter, itself. "It's postmarked around the time of the accident. He never made it to Luray. Was the letter to you wrapped around the envelope?"

"Yes, it was. I don't think I even touched the envelope. If I did it was just lightly as I unfolded his note to me. I can't be sure. I was in hurry. I do know, once I had read his note, I didn't touch the envelope and neither did Barbara, my clerk."

"Do you have a letter opener?" Parker asked.

"Yes, in the center drawer."

"Do you mind?" Parker asked

"No, help yourself."

Using the letter opener, Robert Parker slit the bottom length of the envelope and removed a three page single spaced typewritten letter.

"Should I leave?" Justice Holt volunteered.

"I'm sorry, Steve, could I use your office for a few minutes? I do think this is important."

"Of course. I'll be right outside if you need anything."

Sitting at Justice Holt's desk, Robert Parker thought of Aaron Chadwick. Saturday afternoon he had seen what was left of his friend. Now he saw him again. Aaron had an almost photographic memory. His letter, like his conversation, was direct and persuasive. It was sequential. First, he described his Wednesday evening meeting with President Stanton. He was obviously impressed with the President and believed that he was "thoughtful, vigorous, and in charge." Then he reported how he learned of Elizabeth Anne's masquerade at the State of the Union. And finally he wrote of his Thursday meeting with her at the Vice President's residence. He was convinced he had not only been offered a bribe, a seat on the Supreme Court, but that he and his family had been threatened. He made each case quoting and paraphrasing Elizabeth Anne. "Are you aware the Vice President has been lobbying the Stanton Administration to put you on the Supreme Court? ... If he is President he doesn't have to lobby anyone, but the U.S. Senate...You'll be a shoo-in, Aaron." For Director Parker the threats were more damning. "You'd have to be suicidal to switch now...Aaron I'm warning you...forces beyond anyone's control have been unleashed...think of your family...leave it alone, Aaron...Do you understand me?"

In closing, Aaron wrote there was no mistaking Elizabeth Anne's words. He just couldn't believe she was serious. The problem was she was so intense and perfectly clear. His insurance, he thought, was both prudent and silly. What he regretted was telling her that he was taking his family to the cabin.

Robert Parker looked away from the letter. He had much to consider. The Aaron Chadwick he knew so well was a very reasonable man. He was not an alarmist, but his letter reported a death threat. And contrary to widespread speculation, Aaron stated that threat came not from the White House, but from Vice President Roosevelt's camp. Parker was worried that despite the Bureau's efforts to maintain objectivity, the investigation had been looking in the wrong direction. He needed to get back to the Bureau.

"Steve, I've packed up Aaron's letters and I'm heading back to the Bureau. Thank you so much for insisting I come. I still hope our investigation proves that Aaron's accident was just that, but I can tell his letter has advanced our investigation and narrowed its focus. With any luck we will have answers soon. It's obvious that Aaron knew you were a friend he could trust."

"He didn't give me a lot of choice," Justice Holt smiled.

"No, but he did choose you. Thank you again," Parker added. "Maybe this will all end well."

Commander Croft was at his desk when Elizabeth Ann stormed into his study slamming the door behind her. What is it now?" he asked.

"I am so angry I could just scream."

"You are screaming, Elizabeth Anne. What in hell is going on?"

"It's William. Today, at three, Crayton Langford and Jason Fields are holding a news conference. President Stanton and my Bill, the Acting President of the United States, have agreed to suspend reality. It's crazy. For the next three weeks as Congress makes the most important political decision imaginable they will engage in no politics."

"You knew nothing about this?"

"No. Ever since Secretary Binder stopped by, William has seemed preoccupied. When he left for the White House I checked his office and there they were, Jason and Crayton, buddy-buddy, preparing for their news conference. Those guys are unflappable. They brought me up to speed as though William had kept me informed. It's bullshit and they knew it. He consciously left me out of the loop."

"How did you do?" Croft asked.

"What do you mean?"

"Were you unflappable?"

"I was controlled. There was no percentage. I just smiled and did a slow burn until William came home. Even then it was water over the dam. I just suggested there was an obvious discrepancy in asserting to Congress that President Stanton is incompetent and then announcing that the two of you have co-authored a landmark agreement."

"To which he responded?"

"William argued it was no big deal and it brought Binder on board."

"So William did make a deal," Croft laughed.

"In his defense, he didn't know Aaron was going to meet his maker."

"No, he didn't. I'm afraid we left him out of the loop on Aaron."

"William did try to calm me down with some poll numbers. Have you seen them? He says Congress is just going through the motions. They have already decided Stanton has to go."

"Yes, I heard the same newscast but Stanton is still a sympathetic character. He could rally a lot of support." Commander Croft did not like leaving anything to chance. "You know, Elizabeth Anne, we could put the last nail in his coffin if we connect him to Aaron's death."

"Could you do that?" Elizabeth Anne asked.

"I think so. The problem is my contract instructed the vendor to make it look like an accident. I'd have to contact him and get something solid we could feed to the Bureau."

"It sounds risky, Dad."

It is, but those guys are so cocky they'd convince themselves it was just their top flight detective work," Croft grinned.

"We don't have to make a decision now, do we? Can't we play it by ear?"

"Sure. William is right here. Congress is going to extract its pint of blood, but all we have to do is run out the clock. If things go to hell, we can play the joker and tie Aaron's death to a member of the 'Stanton Gang.'

"I hope it doesn't come to that. I'll be back this evening. We can relax, watch the late night news and sing each other's praises."

"Sounds wonderful, Hon, see you then."

Doc Watson was waiting impatiently in the Director's office. "Where have you been?" he asked before Robert Parker could close the door. "I have news, big news."

"So do I," Parker countered. "Really, big news, but I'd like to hear what you have first."

"Okay, it is your office." Watson glanced at his notes. "Yesterday, at 8:20 A.M. Bobby Hearst, a.k.a. Robert Harris, checked through the gate at Bethesda Naval Medical Center. Shortly after nine he met an older fit guy, who we assume was Kenneth Reeves, in the main cafeteria. They talked for a short while and then Reeves left Hearst in the cafeteria, went to the ICU, talked to two reporters, one an undercover FBI agent. From there he checked out the morgue where he spoke to two additional 'un-uniformed' agents and then returned to Harris in the cafeteria. After just a couple of minutes they split, exiting Bethesda from different gates."

"Where are they now?"

"We lost Reeves on the Metro. We had him on the red line from the Medical Center Station to Metro Center where he may have switched to the Blue line or Orange line. We had a sighting at Federal Triangle, but the agent was unsure and in any case he lost whomever he was following as soon as he left the station. We still have Harris. He's easy, driving his new ruby red Camry and staying on schedule. He stayed in Dover last night and now appears to be heading to Harrisburg, Pennsylvania and the Hilton."

"So that's it." Parker summarized. "These two guys traveled separately to Bethesda and had coffee, then Reeves leaves Hearst, checks out the ICU, and then the morgue where he presumably learns Chadwick has died. From there he returns to Harris and they split.

"There's more," Watson insisted. "This morning, the first banking day after Chadwick's death, Harris's Wells Fargo account received quite an impressive infusion of cash. Since eight this morning he has received ten electronic funds transfers totaling forty-five thousand dollars. Since leaving the Marines, Hearst before he became Harris never had a bank balance that exceeded a couple thousand dollars."

"Do you still think Reeves is in charge, Doc?"

"Well, yes, Hearst works for Reeves, but Reeves is still just a contract killer. He's probably very good, but he was given the target. There could be several layers. We want the man who hired Reeves to kill Chadwick and is now paying for the hit."

"Do you have anything on the accident?"

"I'm sorry, sir, nothing yet."

"It still looks like an accident?"

"Yes, sir," Watson admitted. "We don't have a smoking gun, but we do have smoke.

"Well, I don't know whether I can shed any light, but I can stoke the fire. I just came from the Supreme Court." Director Parker paused to organize his thoughts. "Just before his 'accident' Secretary Chadwick wrote a letter to me in care of Justice Holt. He insisted the Judge deliver it to me personally, but only if he, Aaron, died before he could retrieve his letter on Tuesday, tomorrow."

"This isn't a suicide note?" Watson asked skeptically. "How do we know it's truly from Chadwick?"

"No, no. Slow down, Doc. It's not a suicide note. It's an incredible letter. Let me give you the highlights. On Wednesday evening Aaron met with President Stanton and was quite impressed with him despite the incident during the State of the Union. On Thursday he and the other Cabinet members who signed the declaration met individually with Roosevelt's wife or one of his chief advisers. Chadwick met with Elizabeth Anne. Have you met her?"

"No, but I've picked up vibes."

"Well, she's not the 'little missus.' She's every bit as tough as her father, Commander Croft. Aaron told her that he was having second thoughts about replacing President Stanton. Evidently, she took that as a negotiating posture and out of the blue suggested that Roosevelt would nominate him to fill the next available position on the Supreme Court. Aaron was flattered, but felt it was an obvious bribe. More important, when he stayed on the fence, Elizabeth Anne threatened him and his family. He had no doubt; he quotes her."

"So you're telling me either camp could have hired Reeves and Hearst?" Watson asked.

"No, Doc," Parker responded incredulously. "Oh, I'm sorry, I didn't tell you at the conclusion of their meeting, Aaron assured President Stanton that he would reconsider his position. Aaron writes, 'Stanton was delighted.'"

"What about the President's staff, did they know Aaron was considering returning to the fold?"

"Good question, Doc. I didn't consider that, but I am confident his top staff would have known. As for others in the administration, they might still have considered Aaron to be in the enemy's camp."

"Anything else?" Watson asked.

"Yes, two things. One, Aaron wrote that his biggest regret was telling Elizabeth Anne he needed time to think and was taking his family to their cabin. That could answer a lot of logistical questions. And two, Aaron's letter suggests we need to compare tapes of Stanton's State of the Union addresses for the last couple of years. It could be Elizabeth Anne Roosevelt triggered Stanton's flashback by masquerading as Stanton's wife Danielle."

"You know, sir, I'd really like to be able to conclude Aaron's accident was just that, but we have a lot of circumstantial evidence that points toward murder. We need to get to the bottom of this quick. You're going to be called before Congress and they need answers. They have to make a decision."

"There was no murder," Parker stated emphatically.

"I don't think you can say that yet, sir. I know we can't explain the means, how it was done, but our suspects have skill sets that make anything possible. We have obvious motives – greed, ambition, and power. And we have opportunity; the killers were at the scene of the crime. In addition, we have aliases, payoffs, flight, and an incredible collage of coincidences that suggests intelligent design. I'm not talking about God, Director; I'm talking about a top dog, the paymaster and chess master, the guy who controls all the pieces."

"I'm sorry, Doc, you're not up to speed. I'm afraid I applied 'the need to know' restriction too literally. I have something to tell you."

Watson's reaction was intuitive, "Just don't take me off this case, Director. I'm a bit of a bulldog and..."

"No, never, Doc," Parker interrupted. "I'm counting on you. You're simply the best."

"So what's this about?"

"First, remember," the Director began, "I haven't seen you since Saturday night when you told me Chadwick was still the target and I needed to throw out the rulebook. I told you then I had a plan, but it had a hair trigger and I could not jump the gun. Well, later that night Secretary Binder told me he was joining Roosevelt and calling on Congress to determine the fitness of Stanton to continue in office. That was my trigger; at that point our hands were no longer tied. Whether Aaron lived or died would not change the Presidential contest. The issue was going to Congress. I had long felt Aaron would be easier to protect if he were thought to be dead and so it came to pass."

"Robert, you're telling me you staged Secretary Chadwick death. Aaron is still alive?"

"Yes, he is."

"That's absolutely great!" Watson exclaimed. "You really can think outside of the box. Makes me proud to be working for you. How's he doing?"

"Sharon tells me they'll know much more shortly. When Aaron arrived at Bethesda he had severe, life-threatening, head injuries, but he was in a coma and that, apparently, was good. It gave him time to recover. In fact, his doctors put him on a drug therapy to sustain the coma. Now they're starting to wean him off those drugs. They hope he will regain consciousness in a day or two. Then they'll be able to evaluate his condition and hopefully address the outstanding problems."

"It's incredible isn't it?" Watson commented. "We both saw the reports. You didn't have to read between the lines to conclude he didn't have a chance."

"It really is," Parker replied. "Fortunately, Aaron didn't have a chance to read those reports. His body simply went into an autocorrect mode. Dr. Starling said Bethesda's primary job was simply to assist Aaron's own healing powers."

"I gather Dr. Starling was willing to be more proactive when it came to protecting Aaron from human predators."

"He was tremendous. He has an elite team caring for Aaron. Counting everybody, Sharon, David, Starling's team, the chief medical examiner and two members of her staff who would normally be aware of any autopsy, you, and me, only sixteen people know Aaron is alive. Unfortunately that number will grow if we don't get to the bottom of this shortly. Can we accelerate the investigation? Congress needs answers."

"We are at a crossroad, Director. We can proceed cautiously, or go for broke and pick up Hearst. As you said, Congress needs to know if Aaron was the target of an attempted murder or perhaps a conspiracy to commit murder. If he was, they need to know who ordered the hit and they need to know now. Congress is picking our President; they have to get it right."

"Doc, can you imagine what would happen if we ended up charging their chosen President with conspiracy to commit murder. Who would lead the country, a presumed innocent man charged with murder?"

"Can we bring Hearst in?" Watson asked.

"Do you have enough to turn him?"

"That depends on him. We should be able to convince him that 'Kenneth Reeves' is an alias for the contract killer who set him up. We'll be straight with him. When we are through he'll know that contract killers like Reeves regularly have an assistant that they also use as an expensive patsy if anything goes wrong. He'll know Reeves gave us his address, his car, his bank account, his itinerary, everything we needed to know to make him the scapegoat for both Reeves and his client."

"You have to convince him that he is going to be charged with and convicted of murdering Aaron Chadwick in a plot to overthrow the government of the United States. His crime carries the death penalty. He's going to help us now, or he's going to die by lethal injection."

"What about legal counsel?" Watson asked.

"Do it by the book. You give him his rights the moment he's apprehended. Any defensive attorney worth his salt will advise Hearst to take the deal."

"What if he chooses to remain silent and wait for his attorney?"

"I'd go ahead and tell him what we have, what his options are, but I'd also tell him that he has only a twenty-four hour window of opportunity to exercise those options. When his attorney arrives repeat everything verbatim. He'll sell the deal to Hearst."

"One more thing, Doc. Both Hearst and his attorney must understand that Hearst's 'get out of jail free' card comes with an inviolate condition: if Reeves or his client are tipped off in any manner, both Hearst and his lawyer are going directly to jail."

"That's the great concern," Watson agreed. "When we pick up Hearst we may be alerting Reeves and his client."

"You're not suggesting we wait, are you Doc?"

"No, but you said it, Director. We have to resolve this case so Congress has what it needs to make an informed decision. Hearst has to give us actionable intelligence so we can get to the real culprits."

"What kind of help do you need?" Parker asked.

"The death penalty is our stick, but he has a big stick too, bigger than ours. If he refuses to cooperate, our country could be thrown into chaos; without legitimacy our President could only lead us to anarchy. I need an irresistible carrot."

"Be more specific, Doc," Parker directed.

"Sir, we are confronting a twenty-one day ticking bomb. Even with solid information, it could take weeks to disarm it. Given the stakes and the time constraints, we can't afford to be penny-wise and pound-foolish. I think you should authorize a generous 'stimulus' package; whatever is required. Given the stakes, if this guy plays his cards right and can give us the kingpin, I think he could walk into the witness protection program with a lifetime pension."

"You're making me nervous, Doc. It's all how you play your cards. Lead with the death penalty."

"Don't worry," Watson assured Parker. "We've had your interrogation team with us from the outset. They have reams. I suspect they know more about Hearst than he does. If he has buttons to push they know where they are. They're good, I've worked with them."

"Bring him in, Doc. Assume Reeves could be watching, so let Hearst check into the Hilton and get into his room. Have your people pre-positioned there. One more thing, have one of our people stay there tonight and keep Hearst's reservations down the line all the way to Richmond. Have him check in about the same time everyday. Maybe he'll get lucky, get a call or have company."

"I'll get moving. We should have him here this evening," Watson stated. "Given the urgency, I'm convinced you've made the right decision no matter how it plays out."

"Doc, you told me early that Aaron's killing had to look like an accident. It seems to me the client, the guy who ordered the hit, would give the contractor some earnest money up front and a down payment when Aaron was killed, but the bulk of money owed would be withheld until Aaron's death was officially determined to have been the result of an accident. Is that the way you see it?"

"That's exactly how I see it. There's one other scenario; I don't think it's realistic. It's possible that the client might specify the killing be made to look like an accident but prove to be a murder committed by the client's opposition. For instance, let's assume Aaron's letter is authentic, then the client supporting Roosevelt might want Aaron killed with some evidence left to cast suspicion on the Stanton administration."

"Why don't you think it's realistic?" Director Parker asked.

"I think for a murder, the accident itself was too perfect. There is no evidence pointing at either the Roosevelt or Stanton camp. In fact, thus far the evidence suggests it was just an unfortunate accident. Nevertheless, I am convinced our suspects were in the area to cause Aaron's 'accidental death.' Mother Nature just beat them to it."

"So you think their Saturday morning visit to Bethesda was to locate Aaron, case the area, and develop a plan to finish what Mom Nature started?"

"Yes," Watson responded, "and Sunday morning they were back at the hospital to finish the job. When they learned that Chadwick had died, they simply took credit for his death and today they got the down payment."

"Then we are together," Parker announced. "Pick up Hearst, and offer him death by lethal injection or the good life with a golden parachute, anything to give us the name of the man who ordered the hit. I'll have a judge standing by with warrants ready for names. They will be as broad as he will allow. Given the circumstances, that shouldn't be a problem."

"Just as long as we can trace electronic funds transfers. Are you ready with an autopsy report?" Watson asked.

"Yes, the chief medical examiner and I are prepared to announce that Aaron Chadwick died in a tragic accident as he was driving to Luray. We'll take questions and suggest that the full report will be posted on the Bureau's web site."

"Then, we'll wait and watch."

CHAPTER TWENTY-THREE:

NEWSMAKERS

3:00 P.M., Monday, January 29.

Jason Fields and Crayton Langford retreated to the office of Louis Mathis, Speaker of the House. Their news conference had lasted nearly an hour. They were both exhausted, but pleased. Initially, the questions reflected the instinctive skepticism of seasoned reporters confronting politicians claiming the high road. In an attempt to challenge the realism of ground rules in a high stakes brawl, they repeatedly tried to drive wedges between Fields and Langford. They failed. They were dealing with professionals. Each attempt was met with solidarity and tightly reasoned conviction, but the reporters were also professional. They began looking for the "devils in the details." Again Crayton and Jason were impressive. The only "detail" they did not attempt to answer was how the Congressional leadership would respond. That they suggested was a question the leadership would have to address, noting that Speaker Mathis and Majority Leader Boggs had scheduled a news conference at the same venue starting at four-thirty. Their performance was flawless.

"Mr. President, Jason and I are already practicing the 'sunshine rule'; you're on my speakerphone," Crayton announced.

"I'll be very careful." President Stanton responded. "Hi, Jason."

"Good afternoon, Mr. President. Did you watch the news conference?"

"Yes, Jason, I did. We may be back on track. That went well, very well. You and Crayton were superb. Do you know anything about the Congressional response?"

"No, we haven't had much feedback, but we won't have to wait long," Jason responded. "I think most Congressmen will be pleased that we have framed the issue tightly. It looked like they were about to be pressed into competition with their colleagues. If a few Senators and Representatives were able to sell their votes, others would think they were foolish not to cash in, at least for their states and districts, not to mention themselves. Maybe we've avoided a silent auction. That would be crazy."

"It could be dangerous as well." President Stanton added. "Bribes can be both carrots and sticks, promises and threats, and even life and death. Impartial juries, free and fair elections, and the rule of law are exceptions in world history."

"Well, I think we may have dodged a bullet with this agreement. Look on the bright side, sir" Crayton laughed. "The Republican leadership is in a terrible bind. Who would believe we Democrats have taken the lead as strict constructionist. They have to fall in line. I love it."

"Mr. President," Jason injected, "I have a text message from my boss. He must have sent it during the conference. He wants to know what you would think of suggesting to the leadership of both parties that they make this vote a matter of conscience. If Congress divides solely along party lines, whoever prevails will have a difficult time governing."

"I believe you're right, Jason. Making this a vote of conscience would be consistent with what we have tried to do with our ground rules. You guys see if you can persuade the Congressional leadership."

"Of course, Mr. President."

"One more thing, Jason. I hope you understand how much I appreciate your help. We've done a good thing."

"Thank you, Mr. President. Hold on just a moment sir, Crayton has something else."

"Mr. President, this is Crayton again, if you have no objections, we're going to stick here for a few minutes and see if we can corner Speaker Mathis after his news conference and get his private take on Congressional reaction.

"That's fine. Millie just passed me a note, Crayton. CNN is flashing they have 'Breaking News.' I'm reading the scroll now. 'CNN will be switching to Capitol Hill for a statement from Louis Mathis, Speaker of the House, and Harrison Boggs, Majority Leader of the Senate.' They have my attention. Check in with me as soon as you're back."

"Yes, sir, see you shortly."

4:00 P.M., Monday, January 29.

The Congressional news conference was held in the House Judiciary Committee Hearing Room in the Rayburn Office Building. It was full. Seated at the center of the arced members' rostrum were, from left to right, House Judiciary Committee Chairwoman Sierra Roberts, Speaker Louis Mathis, Senate Majority Leader Harrison Boggs, and Senate Judiciary Chairman Richard Talbert. Each had a live mike and all felt comfortable supplementing the answers of their colleagues.

"Thank you all for coming." Speaker Mathis led off. "Senate and House hearings will begin tomorrow. We will be brief. Majority Leader Boggs and I want this conference to be carried on the evening news so the American people will understand the Constitutional responsibilities assigned to the Congress in determining who will be the nation's President for the next two years."

In a seamless transfer, Majority Leader Boggs continued. "Let me bring you all up to speed with today's events and then with the help of House Judiciary Committee Chairwoman Sierra Roberts and Senate Judiciary Chairman Richard Talbert we will answer your questions."

Boggs spoke without notes. "Today at noon, as required by the Constitution, Vice President William Butler Roosevelt again delivered his written declaration that President Stanton is unable to discharge the duties and powers of his office. This rebuttal declaration to President Stanton's assertion of competence had the support of eight of thirteen members of President Stanton's Cabinet. The Declaration meets all Constitutional requirements and the issue now moves to the Congress of the United States."

Majority Leader Boggs paused, and took a drink of water. "As required by the Constitution, the Congress – the peoples' representatives – will determine who will serve as President for the remainder of President Stanton's term. That decision will be made no later than noon February 28th, within twenty-one days of our receipt of the declaration. If both Houses of Congress affirm the declaration by a two-thirds vote, Vice President Roosevelt will continue to serve as Acting President of the United States. If not,

President Stanton will resume the power and duties of his office."
Boggs paused again. He wanted viewers of the nightly news to
understand the gravity of this unprecedented moment in American
history.

"Senator Boggs, will Congress investigate Chadwick's
death in determining..."

"Hold your questions," Speaker Mathis directed with a nod
to his colleague to continue.

"I should note that Secretary Binder's support for the declaration was announced before Aaron Chadwick's death. While Secretary Chadwick signed the initial declaration, his untimely accident and subsequent coma prevented him from making known his
position on the rebuttal declaration. Secretary Binder signed the
declaration to ensure it had a clear majority of the Cabinet and
would go to Congress. He was confident that when all the facts
were learned President Stanton would receive a mandate from
Congress to complete his term of office. We intend to learn those
facts and they alone will dictate our decision. Now to your questions. Hamilton."

"Acting President Roosevelt and President Stanton have
agreed upon ground rules to govern their interactions with Congress. Can you live with them?"

"Yes, we can," Boggs replied. "We have no problems with
their rules. They are designed to stop backroom deals negotiated
by folks who claim to speak for them and others who claim to
speak for us. President Stanton and Acting President Roosevelt
warn not only Senators and Representatives but also their staffs
that only they will speak for themselves. They also warn anyone
trying to sell their vote to either 'candidate' that all their communications would be on the record. Their rules are both reasonable
and transparent."

"You must understand," Speaker Mathis added, "our rules
are also reasonable and transparent, but the focus is quite different.
We are directed by the Constitution to determine the ability of
President Stanton to discharge the powers and duties of his office.
The Congress is judge and jury in this deliberation. The powers of
the Presidency are awesome. The duties of the Presidency are
overwhelming. Ours is a very broad mandate. The President of
the United States is Head of State, Head of Government, Com-

mander-in-Chief, Chief Executive Officer; it goes on and on. The American people have our assurance that both the House and the Senate will examine all areas of alleged inability."

"Brian Valentine with Fox News. Will you investigate the role of the White House in the death of Aaron Chadwick?"

Majority Leader Boggs was back in the driver's seat. "The Congressional investigations and hearings will be led in the Senate by Judiciary Chairman Richard Talbert and in the House by Judiciary Chairwoman Sierra Roberts. They can speak for themselves." Then with an ironic smile he added, "Chairwoman Roberts, ladies first."

"Thank you, Harrison." She paused. "While the evidence to date suggests that Secretary Chadwick's death was a tragic accident, the House and Senate Judiciary Committees and the American people are deeply concerned with the fortuitous timing and nature of his accident. Let me be perfectly clear – if the administration was in any way involved in Aaron Chadwick's death it would show a complete collapse in President Stanton's judgment and ability to perform his duties as President."

"In that regard," Richard Talbert added, "we will take testimony from President Stanton's staff as well as the staff of Acting President Roosevelt. Their testimony will be under oath. If anyone commits perjury they will be prosecuted and imprisoned."

"Additionally," Speaker Mathis noted, "I believe FBI Director Robert Parker will testify before our Judiciary Committees as early as Thursday of this week."

"That's correct," Majority Leader Boggs stated.

"Doug Nelson, LA Times, two questions. How will you know the President is unable to discharge the duties and powers of his office? And two, are you equating unable with incompetent?"

It was Chairman Talbert's turn. "I'm afraid, Doug, there may be as many answers to your questions as there are Representatives and Senators. I can speak only for myself. I believe past performance is the best predictor of future behavior. Of course, inability can be of a temporary nature or more permanent. If the President's difficulties are behind him, he should continue in office. If there is a possibility they are not, and may be incapacitating, then the nation is at risk and I will vote that he be replaced. As far as equating incompetence with inability, I do not. I see incompetence as the propensity to make bad decisions, while I see inability as the incapacity to make any decision at all."

"Arnold Bradley, New York Times. Can you tell us who or what your sources are that document the President's inability to do his job?"

"Certainly," Sierra Roberts responded. "We have witnesses whose testimony we will have to evaluate. The most obvious are the Cabinet Secretaries who signed the declaration, but there are many other witnesses who worked for and with the President who will be questioned. Additionally, we have an exhaustive supply of Presidential documents, records, schedules, minutes, and reports. In fact we will have 'The Incidents File' prepared by the President's chief of staff documenting incidents noted by the President's staff that they felt might suggest President Stanton was having difficulties performing the duties of his office."

"Stephanie Grant, ABC News. "Since President Stanton re-appointed FBI Director Parker, can you trust him to conduct an independent investigation?"

Majority Leader Boggs responded. "Based on past performance, Ms. Grant, I believe Robert Parker's loyalty is to the truth. I am confident he would resign before compromising an investigation.

"You got the last question, Ms. Grant." Time was up and Speaker Mathis was calling the conference to an end. "As I announced at the outset we want this information to make tonight's evening news. In fact, all of us on the panel are scheduled to appear on one or more of the network and cable programs to discuss the news. Thank you all for..."

"Are you aware, Speaker Mathis, that Director Parker met with President Stanton after Secretary Chadwick's accident?"

"You can be assured, Ms. Grant, our hearings will be gathering and analyzing all the facts."

CHAPTER TWENTY-FOUR:

CASE BREAKERS

4:15 P.M., Monday, January 29.

He had had a wonderful day, traveling back roads and scenic highways all the way from Dover to Harrisburg. The whole world was open to him. He followed whims, backtracked to historical sites and city parks. Periodically he stopped for a snack or parked in range of a wireless Internet signal and checked his Wells Fargo account. From Dover to Wilmington, Delaware, just forty-four miles, his bank balance grew by ten thousand dollars. North of Wilmington he traveled on scenic Route 322 through the Pennsylvania countryside, stopping only to take photographs and check his bank balance. As he neared Harrisburg he entered his user name and password one last time. He now had a balance of sixty thousand dollars, just as Reeves had promised.

He couldn't believe it. He really hadn't done anything and yet there was more to come, much more. When the autopsy confirmed Chadwick's death was accidental, his bank account would grow again. By the end of the week, Bobby calculated, he would receive another ninety thousand dollars. He could go anywhere and do anything his heart desired. It was almost too much freedom.

Bobby remembered Reeves's counsel. He wouldn't do anything rash. He'd take his time; make good sound choices. Maybe a security service was the right move. He still had a lot of contacts, former Special Forces talent. They could deliver security even in the most hostile settings. His people could be defensive and offensive, conventional and nonconventional. Bobby was confident he could assemble a dream team. He'd play with it tonight at the Harrisburg Hilton. In the meantime he programmed his navigation system and took pleasure in how far he had come.

Less than a block from the Hilton, Kenneth Reeves was in his room on the eighth floor of the Crowne Plaza. His payday had been much larger than his protégé's. In fact, because the routing system to his various accounts was far more complex and defied tracing, he was still receiving payments. Nevertheless Reeves was upset and angry. Shortly after he had received his first payment Reeves also received an e-mail from his client asking how the accident had been staged. Now, he had received another – perhaps threatening, but most certainly condescending. His client wanted "info-nuggets" that could be used to direct suspicion toward the White House. It was outrageous and dangerous. It violated their agreement. Chadwick was to die naturally or in an accident. How Reeves executed the contract was his business and only his business, just as the Commander's motives were none of his business. Both knew there were to be no communications, only payments. The latter were dangerous, but necessary. The former were stupid; they put everybody at risk.

Reeves responded cryptically: "Contract fulfilled. 'Accident' will be determined to be an accident. With announcement of autopsy results payment will be required in full. This e-mail account is now closed. Any further communication will be rejected."

More upsetting then the risk posed by the Commander's desire to know his *modus operandi* was the fact the lens cap to his telescope was missing.   The last time the Mead had been out of his trunk was when he had helped Bobby set it up at Chadwick's turnaround. Now he had it trained on the living room of Bobby's Harrisburg Hilton suite and projecting a live picture on Reeves's laptop. The lens cap was nowhere to be found. Reeves knew they had been careless trying to stay with Chadwick as he left for Luray. Odds were the FBI had it. He had wiped it clean before the job, but Bobby had taken his gloves off to plant the bugs. He was barehanded when he put on his driving gloves.

Reeves was sick. He liked Bobby. He wasn't just another patsy. Bobby was his protégé, he wanted to learn, he asked questions, and best, he listened. Reeves enjoyed working with him, but Kenneth Reeves was a professional and professionals take precautions. He always had a "Plan B," a misdirection play that included a patsy. If he felt threatened he could trigger it simply by helping his pursuers find the trailhead. There they would pick up the trail he had carefully laid leading to the fall guy. In this instance the trailhead was Bobby's identity, but Reeves hadn't triggered "Plan B." Maybe it wasn't even in play, but if the FBI had the lens cap and pulled even partials they would have made Bobby and be on his trail. They would place Bobby at Chadwick's cabin, then Bethesda; they'd learn his address, and realize he had a handler who had bought him a new car, paying cash, and had given Bobby an alias, a new name, and bank account using his old address. They would run transaction searches and find his new name on credit card reservations at luxury hotels. And today, after the report of Aaron Chadwick's death, they would watch Bobby's bank account grow incrementally by sums below the known bank reporting requirements until it totaled nearly fifty-six thousand dollars. Had the FBI made Bobby? Reeves would know shortly. The Bureau had to be working feverishly. Congressional hearings to determine the President of the United States would begin in less than eighteen hours.

4:52 P.M., Monday, January 29.

"This is Hoffman. Let me speak to Doc."

"Where are you, Paul?" Watson was impatient. Hearst's countryside tour through Pennsylvania's rural Lancaster and Lebanon counties had thrown him way off schedule. He had hoped to be in Washington with Hearst no later than six. He wasn't likely to roll on Reeves and his client without some time consuming persuasion.

"Our guy is just a couple of lights from you. He should be turning into the Hilton's parking garage within the next five minutes unless he decides to take a tour of the Capitol."

"Oh, God, I hope not," Watson responded. "Just stay on the line and keep me posted."

"Sure, Doc. We're moving again. He's the ruby red Camry. He's going to make the next light. We still have him in sight. He's signaling to move into the right lane. It looks good.

You're in luck, Doc. He's still got his turn signal on. He should be joining you shortly."

"We see him. Will he make you if you follow him in?"

"No, we're back a ways and half the cars in this lane are signaling to turn into the garage. We'll stake out the car. Let us know when we can take possession."

"We'll be down with keys," Watson responded. "You guys did a nice job, Paul. Thanks"

4:57 P.M., Monday, January 29.

While Ken Reeves had trained his camera on Bobby's room, he had seated himself where he had a clear view down North 2nd Street. If the FBI had found his lens cap and made Bobby they'd have him in custody or have him under surveillance. He'd know shortly. He prayed Bobby arrived alone and had a wonderful night.

At 4:57 Reeves saw Bobby's ruby red Camry turn into the Hilton parking garage. At least he wasn't in custody yet. Reeves looked at his television. The telescope playing through the digital video recording showed nothing but a closed curtain. He backed up his recording five minutes and hit 'play." At 4:53 the curtain moved. He paused and zoomed in. Not only had a hand carefully pulled back the curtain ever so slightly, just above the hand and to the right he could make out a man's forehead. He was squinting into the sun and looking at the highway below. He paused the recording, backed it up and played it again. There was no doubt. They were in his room. Watching for his arrival. At 4:57 the hand disappeared and the drapes were closed.

Reeves knew instinctively what he would do. This was his fault. He was the pro, yet he left his lens cap at the crime scene. Bobby was to be the patsy, but he had become a friend who admired and trusted him. He'd have to wait, but Kenneth Reeves had never abandoned a friend on the battlefield.

5:12 P.M., Monday, January 29.

"You have a call, sir. It's Watson."

"Put him through, Sally." Director Parker was impatient. The Bureau needed to bait the trap, announce the autopsy results, and follow the money. But before he could do any of that he needed a suspect and he needed a warrant. Time was running out. In less than seventeen hours the most important hearings in the history of the nation would begin. At 9 A.M., Judiciary Chairs Sierra Roberts and Richard Talbert would gavel their committees to order and they would march blindly forward. In his worse nightmare, the Congress would choose as President a man they would subsequently be compelled to impeach for conspiracy to commit murder.

"We have him, sir. We're bringing him in."

"Thank God! What are our prospects, Doc? What's Hearst like? We're running out of time, damn it"

"I understand, Director. We're following your script. We've read him his rights, and told him he needs a lawyer. Kenny and I will be riding with him back to D.C. Kenny will tell him what we have and that he's facing the death penalty. I'll describe his options and our time constraints."

"What do you think? Will he break?"

"It's too early to tell, but he's a professional. I see it in his eyes, and hear it when he speaks. He's not showing any fear. He has strong bearing and quick intelligence. He'll understand he's been betrayed and he'll understand his choices. They're clear cut."

"Will he understand he's not protecting God and Country? There's no honor at stake here. Robert Hearst is just the sacrificial lamb in a contract murder." Director Parker wanted to hear he was right, but even more he needed to know the truth.

"I know that, sir, but there is such a thing as honor among thieves. This could take longer than we can afford." Doc Watson was all about facts; he rarely varnished the truth.

"We need a break, Doc, or we need to create a break."

"Yes, sir, we do."

As Doc Watson's team was rushing Bobby Hearst to FBI Headquarters in Washington, Washington and the rest of the country tuned to the nightly news. The nation was engaged. Talk radio, Cable, and Network News, foreign and domestic, all were focused exclusively on the Presidential dilemma. Most outlets saw "The Crisis" not only as a great opportunity to enhance their viewer demographics and advertising revenue, but also as a great threat to their current market share and advertising revenue. They were all in the hunt, some would win and others would lose. With slight variation the strategy adopted by most was driven by dollars - the story was hyped, the content was dumbed down.

Reasoned conversation and analysis were rare but treasured. Despite their obvious differences, the players at The White House, the Naval Observatory, and Commander Croft's headquarters all listened to NPR's "All Things Considered" followed by the PBS "Jim Lehrer News Hour."

Jim Lehrer's lead was familiar and comforting. "Good evening. This is the News Hour. And in the news tonight we'll spend the entire hour examining the nation's struggles to judge the competence of its elected President. First we will have extensive excerpts from a joint press conference held by White House chief of staff, Crayton Langford, and Acting President Roosevelt's chief of staff, Jason Fields. In that news conference Langford and Fields defied conventional wisdom, announcing rules they say will govern both President Stanton and Acting President Roosevelt as the evaluation process unfolds. Then Ray Suarez interviews presidential historians Michael Beshloff and Doris Kerns Goodwin on the case for the Twenty-Fifth Amendment. Judy Woodruff follows with the political analysis of the News Hour's own David Brooks and Mark Shields. They look at prospects of both President Stanton and Acting President Roosevelt and what's at stake for the nation. Then Margaret Warner interviews House Judiciary Chairwoman Sierra Roberts and Senate Judiciary Chairman Richard Talbert on what we can expect at tomorrow's Congressional hearings. Finally on the news tonight, Jeffery Brown talks to Andrew Dugan of the Pew Opinion Research Center to learn how Americans are reacting to this Constitutional, but most unconventional manner of selecting a President.

At the White House President Stanton was joined not only by his regulars, Crayton Langford, Howard Lipsack, and Virginia Hastings, but also Jean Thorn, Vice President Mathew Lee Thorn's widow and the President's lifelong friend. Despite the news, which was devastating, their mood was still upbeat. The President, reflecting his age, said they were all cockeyed optimists, but he also felt if the American people learned the truth they would force the Congress to give him the vote of confidence he needed to assume the leadership of the nation. The problem was time. Truth and lies compete like the tortoise and the hare. If the course is long enough the truth will out, but too often vindication comes well after the immediate race is won. Nevertheless President Stanton was comfortable with himself and pleased with the reaction of those whose opinions he valued most.

At the Naval Observatory, the Vice President's residence, Acting President Roosevelt and his immediate staff - Jason Fields, Estelle Cohen and Conrad Tate – also assessed the news. They were particularly pleased with Margaret Warner's interviews with Sierra Roberts and Richard Talbert. Both announced they had received the "Incidents File" from the White House and found it quite disturbing. Further, they were concerned about the death of Aaron Chadwick and would be calling FBI Director Robert Parker and anyone else who could shed light on his untimely death. They were also delighted with the Pew Research polling. When asked their preference: (1) Should Acting President Roosevelt withdraw his challenge to President Stanton; or (2) Should President Stanton resign his office; or (3) Should the Congress decided the issue in accordance with the Constitution. A sizeable majority of Americans (63.4%) felt President Stanton should resign and allow Acting President Roosevelt to serve out his term. Only twenty-one percent (21%) felt Roosevelt should drop his challenge and less than sixteen percent (16%) felt the issue should go to Congress.

The polls also showed that people still cared for President Stanton. They didn't want him hurt, but they did want him to resign and end the crisis. Brooks and Shields were not "preaching to the choir" when they counseled that the public should watch the hearings play out before drawing any conclusions. Most people had already formed their opinions. They wanted the trauma to end and end now. Despite their warm feelings for Andrew Stanton, they wanted their government to get on with the business of governing and address their problems.

At Croft headquarters, Elizabeth Anne and Commander Croft had mixed emotions. The closer William Roosevelt came to winning the Presidency the more distant he became. While he had never been close to the Commander, he and Elizabeth Anne were at least allies. Since their marriage he had rarely made a move without having her on board. Now he seemed withdrawn. He and Jason spent hours and hours together in deep conversation that seemed to lighten whenever she came into his study. She worried she was no longer his confidant. His agreement with Stanton had surprised and infuriated her. She wanted to jerk him back to reality and let him know the facts of life. Though patience was not her strong suit, that was what James Croft counseled. She knew he was right. After the Congress had anointed Roosevelt President then, if she had to, she'd let him know the truth. Chadwick had been murdered. At that point Roosevelt would have no choice. His Presidency might be a sham, but if he resigned the country would descend into utter chaos. Roosevelt would never let that happen. Rather, he would serve out his term on a leash, a very short, tight leash.

10:00 P.M., Monday, January 29.

They met in the observation gallery associated with Interrogation Room 7. "Where have you been, Director?"

"I've been on the phone, Doc, important people," Parker smiled. "It appears the Roosevelt camp has organized a 'call-in' campaign. They want to make sure Chadwick's autopsy leaves no stone unturned. My callers are pretty convinced he was murdered and they have no doubt that, if he were, someone on President Stanton's team pulled the trigger. I just wish I could have shared Secretary Chadwick's letter to Justice Holt. That would cut them off." Director Parker took a deep breath and changed his tone. "How's it going here, Doc?"

"Well, Hearst has his lawyer, the fellow on the left, and they have both been briefed on what we have and what options they have. They both seem to accept our version of the facts, but while we believe the lawyer is counseling Hearst to live out his life on easy street, Hearst is all marine, *semper fi*. He's ready to die. He hasn't told us a thing."

"Good God! Doesn't he understand he's betraying his country to protect his buddy? Is he an idiot?"

"Give us some time, Director. He might still come around."

"Excuse me, Director, Doctor Watson." Parker's deputy had given a perfunctory knock and entered the observation room. "You have a call, Director. It came in on 5022."

"My private line?"

"No identification, sir. He wanted to talk to you and Mr. Hearst."

"Anyone know we have Hearst here, Doc?"

"No sir, everything has been in house. Unless we have a huge breach in security the only person who could know he's here is Kenneth Reeves. He set Hearst up as his fall guy. He must have observed the arrest. I would have thought he'd go underground, but our Mr. Reeves is quite the operator. Take the call, sir, but let him know we are on top of our game as well."

"Okay, Doc, but you listen in."

"Yes, sir. Give me just a second. Okay, Director, whenever you are ready."

"Mr. Reeves, how can I help you?"

"Oh, well done, Director Parker, but it is I who can help you. I need to talk to my associate, Mr. Hearst; you may know him as Robert Harris. You arrested him in Harrisburg just a few hours ago."

"I can't, as you might imagine, guarantee you any privacy, Mr. Reeves. The entire conversation will be recorded. Indeed, both ends of the conversation will be delayed so it can be edited if we suspect coded messages."

"I understand the recording, Director, but the delay is a mistake. Robert is bright and he's a soldier. You won't break him. If he suspects anything's amiss, he won't listen to me any more than he is listening to you. Let me suggest that you and Watson join him. Put us all on your speakerphone. You'll earn his trust and I won't have to repeat myself."

"Give me a moment," Parker turned to Doc Watson just as he finished scribbling a note: "He's right. Hearst is stonewalling us. Think you should do it." They moved quickly into the interrogation room. "Okay, Mr. Reeves, we are here with Bobby. Go ahead. We're listening."

"Bobby, I don't want you to say a word. Just listen."

"Hold on a moment, Director. I want it understood and acknowledged by you that my client's silence is not to be construed in a manner as acknowledging the veracity of anything this caller, whoever he may be, has to say."

"Of course that's understood and now it's publicly acknowledged," Director Parker's frustration was obvious. "You'll get both a tape and a transcript of this conversation, Daniel. Now, let's hear from Mr. Reeves."

"Bobby, you've done well. Daniel Berman is a wonderful lawyer. When we wrap up here listen to him, but right now listen to me."

Bobby Hearst nodded ever so slightly before Berman's hand cautioned him, squeezing his knee. Watson saw it all.

"I'm sorry about your predicament," Reeves began. "I needed your help. You were good and I like you, but you were also my fall guy if things went to hell. I never thought they would. It was just a routine precaution, but when Chadwick made his run for Nathan we got in a hurry. That's never smart. We left my lens cap in the snow. That's where things unraveled. The FBI pulled your prints from that cap. I'm truly sorry."

"We have told Mr. Hearst the same story, Mr. Reeves." Parker paused. He was now convinced Reeves was calling to tell Bobby to save himself. "We have also told him he has a choice. For a very short period, if he cooperates and gives us what we need, he can walk away from this a free man."

"Bobby, listen to me." Reeves voice was caring and commanding. "You don't owe me a thing and you can't hurt me. You're in charge now, not the FBI. You dictate the terms of your cooperation. Tell them nothing until they accept every condition. Berman can write it up. Have a Federal District Judge witness and seal the agreement. Then, and only then, should you tell them everything you know. Director Parker is right, but he hasn't told you the whole truth. You can walk away from this not only a free man, but also a very rich man.

"What about you, Mr. Reeves? Watson asked the obvious. "Why don't you help us? I'm sure we could make it attractive."

"I'm already a very rich man, and I'm hardly in the same position as Bobby, but if I were I wouldn't hesitate, not for a moment. Bobby, Director Parker is only going to make one deal. He's not going to buy the same information twice. You need it. I don't."

"Look, Mr. Reeves, we need to move fast." Director Parker was just as commanding and even more insistent. "We can't allow Congress to make their decision based on misinformation. We don't have time to negotiate a deal from scratch. Mr. Hearst was ready to go to prison. He hasn't given any thought to alternatives; you obviously have. Berman here can guarantee Mr. Hearst remains a free man. But what are you talking about, making him a rich man? We don't normally reward coconspirators in murder cases. You say you want to help him. Now is the time!"

"He's right, Bobby. I have given this a lot of thought and while you have a lot of options I believe this is the best for you and the government. It won't cost you a dime, Director. The crime boss pays the whole price."

"You have my attention, Mr. Reeves."

"Once you accept Bobby's deal, officially and formally, he will tell you everything he knows. I assure you it's enough for the Bureau to put the pieces together and get the warrants you'll need. At that point, you and Bethesda will announce the results of Secretary Chadwick's autopsy; his death was the result of a tragic accident. That announcement will trigger my client's balloon payment. You must have everything in place, Director, because his payment will be made within minutes of the announcement. I will route the payment around the world a couple of times but it will end up in Robert Harris's (a.k.a. Bobby Hearst's) Wells Fargo account. Since the payment will include exact expenses it will be a nine-digit sum, exact to the penny. It will leave my client's account and arrive to the penny in Bobby's account over the space of an hour or two. A statistician would have to tell you the odds, but off the top of my head I think it would be one in nine hundred million. If our client adds the bonus, which theoretically we are due, I think it would be one in nine billion. In either case, Director, Congress will have the information it needs to make an intelligent decision and you will have an ironclad case to convict my client of conspiracy to commit murder."

Bobby's lawyer, Daniel Berman, was not satisfied. "How can Mr. Hearst be assured the payment will be directed to his account?"

"That is the right question, Bobby," Reeves responded. "Do you trust me? If I were you, given your present circumstances I'd have some doubts. But remember I was asleep when you heard Chadwick was going to town for Nathan's asthma medicine and I stayed in the car while you put the telescope in the trunk. Neither of us remembered the lens cap."

"I was caught up in the chase," Bobby announced. Berman, without words, again signaled him to remain silent.

"Take your time, Bobby," Reeves cautioned. "I'm going to do what I'm going to do. However, you need a Plan B just in case I cross you. That plan must include a guaranteed commitment by the FBI to place you in their witness protection program with a very substantial monthly stipend."

"I think we could live with that," Berman volunteered. "What do you think, Director?"

Director Parker only nodded his agreement.

"I didn't hear your response, Director," Reeves prompted. "If your answer is 'yes' it seems to me we have an agreement in principle. All you have to do is negotiate the stipend."

"My answer is 'yes,' Mr. Reeves."

"That's great. If I screw you, Bobby, the government will guarantee you a monthly stipend for the rest of your life. You don't need to trust me. Just have Berman negotiate an airtight contract."

"Thank you, Mr. Reeves."

"That's enough, Bobby. Not another word! I'll walk." Berman was trying to protect his client and he didn't like getting direction from a third party – particularly a contract killer.

"He's right, Bobby. Listen to him." Reeves had done what he felt he could. "I'm proud of most of what I've done in my life, but this has been a nightmare that needs to end. I hope to hear the autopsy announcement tomorrow, Director. Bobby, I've already changed the full payment's routing so when it's made it will be deposited in your account. I made the changes shortly after I saw you arrested. Good luck, Bobby."

With that the line went dead.

CHAPTER TWENTY-FIVE:

THE FOURTH QUARTER

3:30 A.M., Tuesday, January 30.

Bobby Hearst had his contract with the witness protection program option. The monthly stipend he had negotiated was in fact modest, but Bobby had every confidence that he would never exercise that option. He was sure Kenneth Reeves would transfer his client's entire payment into his Wells Fargo account. What that would amount to he didn't know, but Reeves's assurance that it would be at least nine digits "exact to the penny" meant he should receive between one and nine million dollars; even more if the client sent the bonus Reeves felt they had earned.

Once the agreement was formalized, around 1 A.M. Bobby relaxed. Under Robert Parker and Doc Watson's direction, with Daniel Berman's concurrence, his interrogators skipped all background and preliminary questions. "Mr. Hearst, you understand we are on the same side now and we are under severe time constraints. Tell us everything you know about Mr. Reeves's client."

"I actually know very little, but as you heard, Mr. Reeves is convinced that you can put together what I know, and what you know, and identify his client."

Despite his modesty, Bobby Hearst proved to have a remarkable memory. His attention to detail reflected an unconditional admiration of Reeves and a desire to one day be considered in his same class.

"Yes, go on please."

"I know Mr. Reeves had been on a retainer to his client for some time, and this job simply came out of the blue. Through some sort of complex channels his client informed him that he wanted Secretary Chadwick killed, but he wanted his death to appear to have been the result of an accident. The problem, Mr. Reeves explained at Chadwick's cabin, was his client not only wanted it to appear to be the result of an accident, but the accident had to occur within the next 'eighty one hours and forty minutes.'

He was very specific. I thought it was obvious that the hit was timed to the Twenty-Fifth Amendment.

"What the hell do you know about the Twenty-Fifth Amendment?" Watson laughed.

"I follow the news. I read the papers."

"What else do you know about Reeves's client?"

"Reeves said he was a very picky man, but a very generous man. The way he described the communication and payoff system, I'm sure his client lived in Washington. He said the payoffs would zigzag, split, crisscross, merge around the world, and end up just a few miles from where they started. Reeves lived in Washington, so I think his client does too."

"Did he ever describe his client or refer to him in any other manner other than his client?"

"Just once. He called him 'The Commander.' We're both military so I thought he was just referring to him as the ranking officer, but maybe it was a nickname. I'm not sure."

Director Parker hit the intercom. "Are you sure Reeves called him 'The Commander?"

"Yes, sir. I remember it exactly. He said, 'The Commander wants an accident and he wants it now.'"

"That bastard!" Parker erupted.

Doc Watson flipped off the intercom. "You know him, sir?"

"Unless Hearst is feeding us a bunch of bullshit, I know him. He's James Croft, William Roosevelt's father-in-law."

"How do you figure that?"

"I got to know Croft in Secretary Kelly's investigation. But long before that, for as long as I can remember, Croft has delighted in referring to himself as 'The Commander.' He lives in Washington so Reeves' description of routing his payoffs around the world only to end up down the block makes sense. The James Croft I know is extremely wealthy, and holds himself above the law. His wealth is based on purchasing and peddling influence. He has a huge stable of fixers, lobbyists, and politicians in his pocket."

"A lot of wealthy folks do," Watson commented.

"They're not in his league. Croft makes classical Faustian bargains. Once he hooks you there's no escape. You do his bidding for as long as he likes. When Elizabeth Anne snagged Roosevelt, Croft described him as his finest acquisition. Croft's ambition has no limits. With Roosevelt as President and Elizabeth Anne his de facto chief of staff, the Commander could sell influence and play with the purse strings. The Federal budget is over three trillion dollars. Croft must be salivating. He's so close."

"But," Doc interrupted, "Elizabeth Anne saw an obstacle – Secretary Chadwick. He had to be neutralized or eliminated."

"Yea, what a team, Croft and his daughter."

"Do you think Roosevelt is involved?" Watson asked.

"No, I don't think so. I hope not, but we need to cast our net wide enough to find out, Doc."

"Can we get warrants with that kind of latitude?"

"I think so. Judge Nathan Burke is waiting. I've briefed him in general terms. He understands the stakes. He should give us what we need, but you make sure."

"Me? You want me to get the warrants?"

"Yes, Doc. Just make sure we can get everything that moves in and out of Croft's household. Don't limit us. Make it open-ended. Our warrants have to open lots of doors – banks, Internet providers, mail, phone, radio, broadband, whatever. We intercept it all."

"Where will you be, sir?"

"First, I'll be on Capitol Hill trying to explain, without telling them anything, why I can't testify at this morning's hearings. I'm not going to break our cover, but it isn't going to be pretty. Second, at 10:30 the Bethesda's medical examiner and I will be live on national television lying to the world. We'll announce the results of Aaron Chadwick's autopsy. They will be unequivocal – Secretary Chadwick died in a tragic accident. There was no foul play. The press, who by and large, believe he was murdered by White House operatives, will react with disdainful and vociferous skepticism. We'll stick to our guns and escape behind a black curtain, exiting Bethesda through a little known basement passage that leads to a service entrance. Then I pray, Doc that James Croft will play his part and we can follow the money."

8:15 A.M., Tuesday, January 30.

"Good morning, Daughter! How is the Acting First Lady of the United States?" Commander Croft was ecstatic.

"You've been watching the Congressional Hearings Preshows, Daddy."

"It's better than the Super Bowl when your team is heavily favored."

"Don't believe everything you hear, particularly about the home team. They're just hyping the hearings."

"Yes, they are, Elizabeth Anne, but they're all saying the same thing, every network. It doesn't matter whether you tune in Fox, CNN, CNBC, ABC, or PBS; they are saying it would take a bombshell, a 'Hail Mary' completion for Stanton to stop the Roosevelt juggernaut. Your William is about to win the first constitutionally required Congressional vote of confidence. He has a chance of becoming the second-longest-serving President of the United States. Only Franklin Roosevelt will have served longer. William could be the longest-serving President since the passage of the Twenty-Second Amendment."

"Don't jinx us, Dad."

"Don't worry. We didn't leave our fortunes to chance, Elizabeth Anne. Winners don't take odds."

"Did you hear Bethesda has scheduled a news conference for ten-thirty?"

"Yea, my guess is everything we needed will be bought and paid for by eleven. No need to keep your fingers crossed."

"Call me when it's done, Dad."

"Sure, Honey. Plan on having dinner here tonight. We can have cocktails with the nightly news."

"And then while we're in the mood we can work on the supplemental budget," Elizabeth Anne suggested.

"To the winner goes the spoils, Daughter," Croft laughed. "We might also start outlining William's presidential campaign."

"Remember to call me. I'll see you tonight, Dad."

"I'm so glad you suggested breakfast, Andy. I wanted to be with you." Jean took another sip of coffee. She liked it black and nearly scalding. "You need somebody like me, Andy, who thinks of you not as the President, but as her best friend."

"How do you drink that stuff?" President Stanton asked doctoring his coffee with cream and sugar.

"You know I'm tough," Jean laughed.

"Oh yes, I do, Jean." President Stanton and Jean Thorn went way back. With her husband and his wife, years ago, they camped regularly in East Tennessee, in the Smoky Mountains. They spoke easily. "Thank you for being here, Jean. Occasionally, I just need to be myself and that means I need you."

"It going to be an interesting day, Hon." She patted his hand before taking another sip of coffee.

"Yes it is."

9:00 A.M., Tuesday, January 30.

At precisely 9:00 A.M. Judiciary Chairs, Representative Sierra Roberts and Senator Richard Talbert, gaveled their committees "to order." All members were in attendance and the hearing rooms were packed. After remarks from the chairs, all members in seniority order alternating between the two parties would be given five minutes for opening remarks. While all the major networks were carrying the hearings live, the mood of several of the members was not the expected, sober and somber. Rather, it was nasty and sour. Committee members had just learned from their Chairs, in executive session, that the hearings would have to recess in an hour and a half. The networks were announcing they would be going live to Bethesda Naval Hospital to cover FBI Director Parker's and Chief Medical Examiner Debra Chapin's news conference. Fox News was already promoting the news conference as: "Live at 10:30 from Bethesda: Aaron Chadwick's Death, a Crime or a Coincidence? The FBI Weighs In."

House and Senate Judiciary Committee Chairs, Sierra Roberts and Richard Talbert were very upset with Director Parker for choosing to release the autopsy results at Bethesda. They were insistent that the results be released first before their committees. Fortunately for Parker, Senator Talbert and Representative Roberts were at loggerheads. Each wanted Parker to testify before his (or her) committee first. Neither would give an inch. The only compromise they could agree upon was to delay the announcement. Parker could make it before a joint meeting of both the House and Senate Judiciary Committees. It could be scheduled for later in the week. Parker insisted he could not reschedule the conference without opening a Pandora's box of speculation that would feed conspiracy theorists for years to come. They saw his point and reluctantly agreed on a joint meeting to be held Thursday. Parker tried to hide his relief and prayed that by Thursday he could testify under oath, and tell the truth.

While the Democrats on both committees had always intended to let the hearings play out before taking sides, their Republican colleagues knew they wanted President Stanton out, leaving a wounded Roosevelt head of a caretaker government. They knew Roosevelt. He was an ambitious but conservative Democrat. He would run for President in his own right but he would undoubtedly be challenged from the left in the Democratic primaries. Whoever won those primaries and the Democratic nomination would be severely weakened, giving the Republicans a good chance of recapturing the White House while building their majorities in the House and Senate.

Unfortunately the senior Republicans scheduled to speak first were in a quandary. They didn't know how to handle the question of Aaron's death. The most partisan had intended to suggest White House complicity in his death. But without knowing what Parker intended to announce, they had to hold their fire.

The hearings began with both Chairs taking the high road. Both described the gravity of the questions facing the nation and matter-of-factly announced the change in their previously announced schedule. They gave a brief history of the Twenty-Fifth Amendment, the current question of President Stanton's competence, and their intention to be though, meticulous, and objective. They then called upon their senior members for their opening comments. There were no surprises, only a few complaints that Director Parker had chosen a news conference rather than the

Committee hearings to discuss the autopsy findings and the Bureau's progress in investigating Aaron Chadwick's death.

10:25 A.M., Tuesday, January 30.

It had been a long night and a longer morning. Director Parker was working on adrenalin. He and Debra Chapin, Bethesda Chief Medical Examiner, stood together, stage left, waiting to be introduced by Bethesda's Public Relations Officer.

In the last two hours, Director Parker had been reamed by Judiciary Chairs Roberts and Talbert. The former suggested that a number of her colleagues would accuse him of being a White House pawn and a couple might go so far as to recommend he be charged with complicity in the murder of Secretary Chadwick. Similarly, Senator Talbert warned him he should expect demands for his resignation.

On the brighter side, he had just heard from Watson. The warrants had been issued and his field teams were already in place.

Now, after an introduction that included short biographies of both Director Parker and Doctor Chapin it was time to release the report and trigger Croft's payment. As agreed, Chapin went first, reading an executive summary of Aaron Chadwick's autopsy. She was brief and to the point. "In sum, Aaron Chadwick died as he raced to Luray, Virginia to pick up asthma medicine for his youngest child, Nathan Chadwick. He was driving a little-used Jeep, down a steep grade, in a snowstorm that had resulted in some accumulation on the north-facing slopes. When he approached the last steeply graded 'S'curve he encountered both ice and deer. He tried to slow down and turn but slid directly into several deer and then through an outdated guardrail. The Jeep landed forty yards below the highway and careened down the mountain through a small meadow into a large oak tree. His Jeep had no air bags. His head smashed into the steering wheel and, while he had many other injuries, that blow ultimately proved to be the cause of his death.

Dr. Chapin was asked several questions concerning the presence of drugs or alcohol that might have impaired Secretary Chadwick's judgment. She responded with an extensive review of the toxicological portion of the autopsy, concluding that the short answer to the question was simply, "No." Similarly, she overwhelmed her questioners with details when she was asked about treatment decisions. She concluded her response by referring the reporters to Appendix A of the autopsy report. It was entitled: "A Chronological Review of Secretary Aaron Chadwick's Medical Care from Thursday evening January 25th, through Sunday morning, January 28th. It began with EMT Stuart Weingardt's arrival at the Luray accident scene and ended Sunday morning at 6:43 A.M. at Bethesda's ICU when Aaron Chadwick was pronounced dead. (With one significant exception, Dr. Chapin's statements were correct. The exception, of course, was that Aaron Chadwick had not died at 6:43 A.M. and was now, in fact, expected to live. The question still unanswered was whether he had suffered permanent irreversible brain damage.)

On the other hand, Director Parker told only the truth, not the whole truth, but the truth. Under grueling questioning he insisted that there was absolutely no evidence that Secretary Chadwick had been murdered. Indeed he demonstrated that every single shred of evidence supported the fact that he had not been murdered. There were no questions about a conspiracy to commit murder.

By noon, the trap was baited.

12:15 P.M., Tuesday, January 30.

Within minutes of the Parker/Chapin news conference, the Congressional hearings resumed. The remaining opening statements referenced the autopsy report. Democrats uniformly championed the report's findings. They argued that it had always been ludicrous to suggest that President Stanton or his staff could ever be involved in any way with the death of Aaron Chadwick. They admitted there were legitimate questions concerning President Stanton's competency, and assured the nation they would reserve judgment until they heard all the evidence. Republicans, on the other, hand questioned the autopsy results and noted the Medical Examiner had made her determination in less than forty-eight hours after Aaron Chadwick was declared dead. They asked "why the rush to judgment?" and promised the American people the autopsy would be put under a microscope.

Instant polling showed a large portion of the public agreed with the Republicans. They, too, were skeptical about Chadwick's death – and politicians in general. They maintained President Stanton's FBI Director could not be an impartial investigator. They wanted an independent investigation.

12:30 P.M., Tuesday, January 30.

Commander Croft felt both worthy and blessed. He had been prepared, decisive and lucky. Not only had Aaron Chadwick been eliminated and his death ruled accidental, but also, to his delight, even that ruling failed to lift the cloud of suspicion that had hung over Stanton's White House since Aaron's "accident." Coming less than two days after Secretary Chadwick joined Roosevelt in declaring President Stanton incompetent, many Americans continued to believe his accident was no accident.

For Croft it was the best of all worlds. He sat in his office reveling in his success. He swiveled around in his desk chair and faced "the grand console." There was one last job to do. He booted up his computer and double-clicked on "My Bank." The menu was extensive. Commander Croft scrolled down to "UTEFT," Untraceable Electronic Funds Transfers and double-clicked. Again the menu was extensive. He double-clicked on "Retainer Accounts" and then again on "Covert." He entered the agreed amount, including the bonus for a clean autopsy. He didn't want an unhappy contractor. The money would be drawn from eight different accounts in three decimal portions that totaled one. He was proud of the system and completely confident his payments could never be traced. He double-clicked the "Send" button. It would be done in seconds.

Commander Croft felt immense pride.

1:00 P.M., Tuesday, January 30.

"We have it, Director. That smug bastard didn't even bother to stagger the payments. All of them were made at exactly the same moment."

"What are you saying, Randall?"

"We have Croft," Randall Cummins reported. Parker's head of the data processing unit was in the 'intercept van' parked less than two blocks from the Croft residence. He spoke excitedly, yet confidently. "He does his banking on line. He's clever, but this time he was careless; all of his transfers to Harris were made simultaneously. If Croft had staggered his payments, like he did last time, they would have been difficult, maybe impossible, to trace back to him."

"I think last time we were dealing with Reeves," Director Parker suggested. "He's clever and cautious."

"Yes," Randall acknowledged, "If Reeves handled Harris's payments that would explain a lot, but there could be another explanation, sir. Croft obviously believed your report or he would not have made the payment. I suspect hearing the all-clear whistle made him careless. In any case, sir, we have traced every dollar and cent deposited in Robert Harris's account to money leaving Croft's accounts. Can we arrest him, sir?"

"Don't do it yet, Randall. Let's give Commander Croft a little time to share his success."

"Whatever you say, sir, but we are not going to have the element of surprise for long. Croft has a security system in place that would make the Pentagon proud."

"I want to know who shares his secret, Randall."

"Yes, sir. I understand we need the whole story; I'm just afraid if our cover is blown everything will be shredded."

"I appreciate that, Randall. You be ready to move in quickly and seal the compound."

"Yes, sir, but sir, Croft has a real fortress here. In addition to Dobermans roaming the grounds he has night vision cameras, infrared scanners, and movement sensors. We don't know what all is in the house, but you can bet he has safe rooms and at least one escape route that surfaces outside the compound."

"Are you serious?"

"Mr. Parker, we've already found a garage apartment that borders the compound. It's on a huge lot and is built into the hillside. The apartment has never been rented, but there's a BMW in the garage that's plugged into a battery charger. I've got two men watching that place and dozens more checking the ownership of all the properties bordering Croft's and all the cars parked on the bordering street. It's hardly foolproof. Croft knows all about aliases."

"Randall, I won't wait long. Let's just give him a few minutes, no more than a half-hour, to spread our net. If he chooses to move out of the compound, pick him up and read him his rights."

"It's your call, but a half-hour is a lifetime when you're holding your breath."

1:30 P.M., Tuesday, January 30.

Since reconvening, the Congressional hearings had been going on for over an hour. In the last twenty-five minutes they had been dealing with Crayton Langford's "Incidents File." Each committee's chief counsel led their committee members through the White House report describing staffers' recollection of embarrassing incidents where Stanton's grief left him incapacitated. They gave no context and failed to explain that many of the descriptions were of the same event. That was the minority party's responsibility. It would come later.

"Director, it's been a half-hour. We're taking quite a gamble here, sir. This is a quiet, upscale neighborhood. Every home has at least a couple of acres and I've got so many undercover agents roaming around in service and delivery trucks they're likely to have an accident."

"I understand your point, Randall."

"I'd like to arrest Croft now, sir, before our cover is blown. His home is his office. It has to be loaded with records and files and prints. Let our crime scene folks take his place apart. Give them a little time. They'll find what we need."

"I'm sure they would, but Congress needs the truth now. They could screw up so badly that faith in our government would be destroyed for a quarter-century. Hang in there, Randall. Keep me posted if you learn something or your cover is broken."

"Are you sure, Director?"

"Yes, Randall."

1:45 P.M., Tuesday, January 30.

It had been well over an hour. Croft's payments had been sent and received. He craved feedback from his only confidant. When Elizabeth Anne called, he was delighted.

"Hey, Honey, how are you doing?"

"Good, Daddy. I had a hard time reaching you. Were you on the phone? I got a bunch of static and a busy signal."

"Yeah, I was on the phone earlier."

"Have you been watching the hearings?"

"Yes, indeed, and I'm convinced that your William is going to be President."

"I think so too, Dad. We'll need to give him a little space, but you know he owes us; he's our President, yours and mine."

"When the time is right we'll rein him in, Elizabeth Anne. We'll be in charge."

"Thanks for all your help, Dad."

"We did it, Honey. The bills are all paid, we're free and clear, and on course to the White House."

"The bills are paid?"

"Yes, just over an hour ago. I told you I was on the phone."

"That's wonderful, Dad. No problems?"

"None! Aren't the hearings spectacular? Langford's 'Incidents File' documents so many more problems than the few you engineered I'm not sure they were necessary. Stanton's toast!"

"We did it, Dad. The game is over. Can I come by tonight and share the glory?"

"I was hoping you would. I'm so proud of you, Honey. See you tonight"

1:55 P.M., Tuesday, January 30.

"Director, I think we can move in now."

"What's changed?"

"Croft just got off the phone with Elizabeth Anne. We have it all. It nails Croft and leaves very little doubt that Elizabeth Anne was his coconspirator. While both of them gave Roosevelt a clean bill of health, it is obvious they intend to control him. They had him cornered. He would either have had to submit to blackmail or resign as the most disgraced, naive President in history, leaving the nation in shambles."

"Randall, are they getting together tonight?"

"Yes, sir, they are."

"Could we learn more by listening in on their celebratory evening?" Parker asked.

"I'm sure we could, Director, but we'd be pushing our luck. We are playing with a pro. Our presence here is becoming more conspicuous with each passing minute. Roosevelt is clean. Let me grab Croft before he starts covering his tracks. We can get Elizabeth Anne at our leisure. The first-lady-in-waiting is not a flight risk."

"Okay, Randall, bring him in."

"We'll do our best, sir. We are entering Croft's catacombs."

"Stay in touch, Randall. Keep someone on line with my office until you have Croft in cuffs."

"Yes, sir."

2:27 P.M., Tuesday, January 30.

Parker was running out of patience. Something was wrong. Too much time had passed. "Get Randall for me, Helen. I need an update."

"Yes, sir. Just stay on the line. I'll buzz him."

"This is Randall, Director. I'm sorry, sir, the news is not good. Croft has either left the compound, escaped, or is in one of his vaults."

"Find him, Randall. Rip that place apart. Thursday, I'm going before Congress. We have to wrap this thing up. I'm way out on a limb. I don't want to apologize. I don't want to make excuses, and tell them about my suspicions. I want to present facts, arrests, and indictments."

"I understand, sir. We're not out of the woods but we're not lost. We have Croft's right hand man, Ronald Hodges. He's cooperating fully. If Croft is in one of the vaults we'll have him out shortly. If he left the grounds, he's on foot and we'll pick him up on infrared. We're scanning the entire area. We'll get him, sir."

"I hope so, Randall. I hope so. This country needs to have confidence in its leadership. We need to give the American people answers that they can accept because they are obviously and indisputably true."

"Yes, sir. We are doing our best, sir."

"I know you are, Randall."

"Thank you, sir."

"Keep me informed."

"Yes, sir."

2:36 P.M., Tuesday, January 30.

"Elizabeth Anne, just listen to me. I don't have much time." She understood his warning; his message was unmistakable. "I'm sorry; I've made a terrible mistake. I was wrong, but Honey, I was so very afraid for the future of our country that I took matters into my own hands. I arranged Aaron Chadwick's accident to insure Congress would judge the competence of President Stanton. I didn't tell you or William because I knew you, Elizabeth Anne, would have tried to convince me I was wrong, and William would have tried to have me arrested."

"Oh, Daddy."

"I'm so sorry, Honey. You and William must keep fighting for America. I only pray I have not jeopardized the future of this country I love."

"Daddy, what are you saying?"

"I'm saying goodbye, Baby. You must be strong. Keep fighting for our country. You know Stanton must be replaced. I love you, Elizabeth Anne. Goodbye, Honey. I love you."

"Daddy, don't! Please, please don't!"

Croft, with a lump in his throat so large he could barely talk, whispered once more, "I love you, Honey" and hung up.

2:40 P.M., Tuesday, January 30.

Elizabeth Anne waited no more than five seconds and then misdialed 911 two times. A minute had passed and she dialed it correctly. Speaking breathlessly, she described at length a very disturbing call from her father. She wanted to be taken seriously; she feared he might be suicidal and begged the police to send an ambulance to her father's home.

She had covered herself and bought him a little time to do whatever he needed to do. She needn't have worried, but nevertheless prayed he had left a good note. He did. Croft had already drafted his suicide note, several times. When he had it right, he transcribed it in his own hand. Then he deleted the draft from "Word" and emptied his "Junk Box." Finally he pushed back from his desk, walked to his wood stove, opened the door and tossed his laptop into the blazing fire. He had one job left to do.

3:00 P.M., Tuesday, January 30.

"Croft is dead?" Director Parker responded incredulously.

"Yes, sir. I'm sorry. We found him quickly. His dog was sitting outside a guest room closet. It was literally a vault. Hodges got us in after the local police arrived. They had received a 911 call from Mrs. Roosevelt. She feared her father was suicidal. We monitored that call."

"How did he die, Randall?"

"He shot himself. We didn't even hear the shot. I guess the dog did."

"Did he leave a note?"

"He not only left us a note, he made a phone call. I'm sure he knew it was being monitored. He called Elizabeth Anne and confessed that he had arranged Aaron's accident. Then like Nixon's "but that would be wrong" tape, Croft noted, on a line he knew was tapped, that he had not informed either Elizabeth Anne or William – knowing, and I quote: 'you, Elizabeth Anne would have tried to convince me I was wrong, and William would have tried to have me arrested.' He tried to absolve them of any responsibility."

"Christ, he wants us to think he was just a patriot acting in splendid isolation. Christ! What changed? Less than two hours ago Croft was on top of the world. Then he calls his daughter, confesses to arranging Chadwick's accident, writes a suicide note, and blows his brains out. What changed, Randall?"

"Croft learned the game was up. I'm not sure how but I suspect he learned that we had monitored his electronic funds transfers and further that we were on the grounds. He was nailed. The only thing he could do to win the game was to insulate Elizabeth Anne and Roosevelt from his actions. He went to his grave hoping the public would still consider replacing President Stanton with Vice President Roosevelt and more importantly Elizabeth Anne Croft Roosevelt. He never gave up. This was his last hurrah."

"Thanks, Randall. I just needed some help understanding this insanity. I've been battling conspiracy theorists ever since I joined the FBI. Now we are about to expose a conspiracy as ambitious and cynical as any ever imagined." Director Parker was at last relaxed. "I tell you, Randall, James Croft had an unquenchable thirst for power and money. You know, when all is said and done, I believe James Croft will have in fact determined who will be the President of the United States for the next two years."

"Yes, sir. Director Parker, I..."

"Ironically it won't be his son-in-law. Roosevelt is an honorable man. I consider him a friend, but his career is trashed. Croft's daughter, his only child, may face prison time."

"Director Parker, you'll have to excuse me, sir. I have to go. I have a situation here that requires my attention."

"What's that, Randall?"

"Elizabeth Anne, sir. She's here."

"I understand, but you remember your counsel, Randall; she's not a flight risk. You're in control. You've got a crime scene to protect. Stay cool. One more thing. Randall, thank you and thank your team."

"Mrs. Roosevelt, I'm so sorry." Randall mumbled.

"Is he dead? Mr. Cummins?" Elizabeth Anne demanded of the man she was told was in charge.

"Yes, I'm afraid so."

"How did he die?"

"We can't say for sure but we believe he committed suicide. There is a note."

"May I see him, please?" Elizabeth Anne's tone mixed insistence with grief.

"Not just yet, Mrs. Roosevelt. This is a crime scene. In his note your father confessed to arranging the death of Aaron Chadwick. This is a large home and your father had many friends and associates. We must leave no stone unturned."

"I appreciate your telling me that," Elizabeth Anne changed tack. "He in fact called me just minutes ago and told me the same thing. I can't believe it, but I still need to say goodbye. You're in charge. Can't you let me see him?" she pleaded.

"I don't think that's a good idea. You should remember him in the best of times, not this way."

"I must insist," her voice was now icy hard.

"Then you will give me your hand and I will take you into the vault but you will leave as soon as I direct you to do so. Give me your word."

"You have my word, Mr. Cummins. Thank you." Elizabeth Anne spoke with what she hoped was obvious sincerity. "Can we go now?" She took his hand and gave him an appreciative smile. Elizabeth Anne understood she needed to cultivate a high placed "friend" in the Bureau to whom she could feed and solicit information.

Randall led her to a walk-in closet in Croft's second guest bedroom. "Oh, Winnie, what are you doing here," Elizabeth Anne knelt and gave Croft's nine-year-old golden retriever a hug. Winston was seated staring at the rear wall of the closet. He acknowledged Elizabeth Anne only briefly with his eyes, a short side-glance, that ended when he resumed staring at the rear wall of the closet.

"That's how we found your dad so quickly. This wall is really a large pocket door, but maybe you knew that." There was no response. Randall turned a coat hook and the wall slid into the left end wall revealing a well-furnished but windowless vault. The room smelled of gunpowder and smoke. It was quite warm. A direct-vent stove with its loading door wide open was still smoldering. A burned out lap top had been retrieved from the firebox and lay in a pile of ashes piled on the floor heat shield.

James Croft was still seated at his desk. His head lay on its left side on a neatly folded towel drenched with blood. His right arm stretched out to the northeast corner of his desk. There just beyond his reach was a long hand-written letter and a gold-capped pen. Between his head and hand lay a Ruger SR9 semiautomatic pistol.

Elizabeth Anne stood frozen in the doorway. Silently she took in the whole scene quickly. She paused, just for a second, to look at her dad. Her eyes welled with tears. "Can we go now," Elizabeth Anne whispered, "I've seen enough."

CHAPTER TWENTY-SIX:

BRIEFING THE PRINCIPALS

5:00 P.M., Tuesday, January 30.

Ever since Bobby Hearst unknowingly fingered James Croft, Director Parker had been preparing to brief the principals. They included President Stanton, Acting President Roosevelt, the Republican and Democratic leadership of the Congress, as well as the Senate and House Judiciary chairmen and their ranking minority members. While the Bureau's investigation was far from complete, Parker was certain much of its implications were already clear.

He was beginning with a one-on-one meeting with Acting President Roosevelt, simply because he would have to decide whether he would continue his pursuit of the Presidency. There were still issues of Stanton's competence, but no one on the President's team had engaged in a conspiracy to commit murder. Congress would look to the FBI and Parker specifically for the information it needed to resolve the Constitutional dilemma facing the nation.

Parker needed answers and he needed them quickly. Had Croft masterminded the conspiracy on his own initiative or was he acting at the bequest of Jason Fields, Elizabeth Anne, Acting President Roosevelt, or all of the above? Given the politics of the situation it probably did not matter. All would be painted with the same brush. Guilt by association was not a matter of law; it was a matter of fact. He would learn as much as he could from Roosevelt, then he would brief the President, ending his evening with a meeting on Capitol Hill with all the Congressional leaders.

"Director Parker, Acting President Roosevelt is here to see you."

"Show him in, Betty."

"William, thank you for coming on such short notice."

"You gave me no choice, my friend. Your request was like a fire alarm. Is it really that serious?"

"I could hope not, but I'm afraid so. William, you are a good friend, but the information I have for you is not good. For Congress it might well be a deal breaker."

"You will have to be more direct, Robert. What in the world are you talking about?"

"Have a seat. I really don't know where to begin. I just need answers." Robert Parker picked up a file from his desk and sat down next to the Acting President. "William, your father-in-law engaged in a conspiracy to murder Aaron Chadwick."

"What! What are you saying???" Roosevelt was on his feet confronting the Director. "Aaron signed the first declaration. He was supporting me. My father-in-law and I rarely see eye-to-eye, but he too supports me and he is not stupid. He wants me to be President so bad he can taste it. He wants power and money and he thinks I'm his ticket. If he did what you say, he'd be helping President Stanton. Hell, he'd be cutting his own throat. There's just no way, Robert. That's crazy."

"I'm so sorry, William. Please sit down. I thought you had spoken with Elizabeth Anne."

"About what?" Roosevelt suddenly felt very uneasy.

"William, James Croft is dead. He committed suicide shortly after talking to Elizabeth Anne a little over two hours ago. She called 911 and arrived at Croft's home shortly after the police had arrived."

"Is she okay? She must have tried to reach me. I don't understand. Where is she now?"

"She's at home, William. I'm not sure when she arrived, but she's still there." Director Parker tried to be reassuring, however his last comment set off more alarms for Roosevelt.

"Is she under surveillance, Robert?"

"Randall Cummins, my onsite officer-in-charge of the Croft watch was concerned about her. He believes she may have the answers to a number of important questions raised by our investigation."

"Is that a 'yes'?" William pressed.

"Yes it is," Parker responded.

"Before we go there, Director, would you answer my initial objections? As I told you, for his own reasons, James Croft desperately wanted me to be President. He knew Aaron Chadwick supported me. By what convoluted logic would he have targeted Aaron Chadwick?"

"William, I want you to read this letter. Aaron Chadwick wrote it at his cabin Thursday evening to his good friend, Associate Justice Steven Holt. He asked the judge to release it only if he died before returning to Washington. David, Aaron's son, posted it that evening from Luray at eight P.M. Take your time, William."

Director Parker sat down and waited for Roosevelt to take the seat opposite him. As he did, Parker handed him Aaron's letter. "Take your time, William."

Roosevelt read it twice. When he had finished he set the letter on the coffee table that separated them and shoved it toward Director Parker. He sat silently trying to absorb what he had read.

Gently, quietly, Director Parker summarized: "When Aaron left the Observatory he was no longer in your camp, William. He was leaning toward the President. Aaron was convinced Elizabeth Anne had offered him a bribe and it sickened him. When he still remained non-committal Aaron was convinced that she had threatened not only him, but also his family. He was frightened. He anticipated his death and thought this letter would protect him. Unfortunately, before he could alert Elizabeth Anne that he had an insurance policy that would be made public if he were to die, Nathan had an asthma attack. The call was never made."

"Elizabeth Anne was in the heat of battle when she was talking to Aaron. She went over the top and put her foot in her mouth, but that's all." Roosevelt was increasingly defensive, but still on the attack

"You still haven't answered how Croft would have known any of this!"

Parker was restrained. "There's an obvious answer. You read the letter. Elizabeth Anne was on the phone with her father when Aaron left for the mountains. He told her he was going to his cabin off Skyline Drive near Luray. It was a last-minute decision. Nobody knew but his family and Elizabeth Anne. She could have told her father."

"She could have told anyone, Robert. This is a house of cards built on a lot of 'she could have,' and 'he could have' long shots. You're asking me to believe that Croft organized a last- minute murder and executed it in less than eight hours? I just don't believe it."

"I'm sorry, William. I have much more to tell you. James Croft left a suicide note. He knew we were on to him. In the note he specifically confessed to arranging Chadwick's accident and then just as specifically he absolved you and Elizabeth Anne of any responsibility for his actions."

"What else should I know?" Roosevelt asked with obvious frustration.

"You should know that we have been able to follow the money. There is no doubt Commander Croft paid his hired killers in accordance with their agreement. Croft was to make the final payment only when Bethesda's autopsy reported Aaron Chadwick's injuries were the result of an accident. We issued that report at a press conference that ended at noon. Within minutes eleven million, one hundred fifty seven thousand, four hundred and eighty three dollars and twenty-two cents left Croft accounts and that exact amount was deposited in Robert Hearst's local Wells Fargo account. We have Robert Hearst in custody and he has confessed to his involvement in the conspiracy."

"If what you say is true, then I could accept that you've proved your case against Croft. He was an evil son-of-a-bitch. When I married Elizabeth Anne he came with the package. But, Robert, you haven't made a case against my wife. She talked to her father all the time. It drove me nuts but you don't know what she said. He was always a loose cannon. He probably had Chadwick under surveillance."

"William, I said I couldn't yet prove Elizabeth Anne was part of the conspiracy. I ask for a separate meeting with you so I could tell you what else I know that you need to know."

"There's more?" William sighed.

"Yes, a few items I think you should be aware of. I don't want you to be blindsided, William. I won't share them with any of the other principals unless they are fully substantiated. I am sure you understand that considering only Croft, you are going to be severely tarred with guilt by association. However, if Elizabeth Anne is involved you will be mortally wounded by that guilt."

"I appreciate your discretion, but please tell me what you are talking about?"

"Croft absolved you and Elizabeth Anne of any responsibility after he was aware we were on to him. Before that, just after he made his payment to Robert Hearst, he had a more candid conversation with Elizabeth Anne. This will tell you where we are coming from," Parker said handing Roosevelt a one-page highlighted transcript:

Highlighted Transcript of Phone Conversation Between Elizabeth Anne Roosevelt and James Croft - 1:45 P.M., Tuesday, January 30.

"Hey, Honey, how are you doing?"

"Good, Daddy. I had a hard time reaching you. We're you on the phone? I got a bunch of static and a busy signal."

"Yeah, I was on the phone earlier."

"Have you been watching the hearings?"

"Yes indeed and I'm convinced that your <u>William is going to be President.</u>"

"<u>I think so too, Dad. We'll need to give him a little space, but you know he owes us; he's our president, yours and mine.</u>"

"<u>When the time is right we'll rein him in, Elizabeth Anne. We'll be in charge.</u>"

"Thanks for all your help, Dad."

"We did it, Honey. The bills are all paid, we're free and clear, and on course to the White House."

"The bills are paid?"

"Yes, just over an hour ago. I told you I was on the phone."

"That's wonderful, Dad. No problems?"

"None! Aren't the hearings spectacular? <u>Langford's 'Incidents File' documents so many more problems than the few you engineered</u> I'm not sure they were necessary. Stanton's toast!"

"We did it, Dad. The game's over. Can I come by tonight and share the glory?"

"I was hoping you would. I'm so proud of you, Honey. See you tonight"

\-\-\-\-\-\-\-\-\-\-\-\-\-\-

"The bad news here for you, William, is this transcript implicates Elizabeth Anne, not only in a conspiracy to commit murder, but also in a long term organized effort to discredit President Stanton's competency. Then there's her statement concerning you 'but you know he owes us.' My initial interpretation of that phrase is they believed they could blackmail you and control your Presidency. But, William, I have to explore the alternative that they delivered for you and you owe them."

"I understand that, Robert, and I know I have decisions to make, but I could use your counsel." Acting President Roosevelt was not desperate, but he knew he was personally immersed in a criminal conspiracy and he lacked objectivity.

"William, I am your friend and I must tell you, you are in serious trouble. First, you should hire the best attorneys you know and second, you should seek the advice of people you trust implicitly."

"Who can I trust?" Roosevelt wondered. "This has all been so disillusioning. My confidence has been shaken, my trust betrayed. Who can I trust?"

"I'm not sure I can help you with that, William. I can tell you if I were you I would begin with the presumption that James Croft was working with someone in your inner circle who was privy early on to Aaron Chadwick's change of heart. While I think Elizabeth Anne is the most obvious candidate, particularly in light of the transcripts, Jason Fields certainly was in a position to know about the leanings of all the Cabinet members. Could he have been Croft's confidant?"

"Hardly," Roosevelt grunted. "Jason thought Croft was a scumbag. I shared his opinion. I could see Jason leaking information to Crayton, they're good friends, but not to Croft. Jason couldn't stand him. For that matter he was not fond of Elizabeth Anne. He never said anything to me, but I knew and I suspect he knew, I knew."

"If you think you can trust him, I can't think of a better confidant. He knows what's going on and he has both your, and the nation's, interest at heart. In the same vein, William, if I were you I'd trust President Stanton. You can talk to him and you should before you talk to the Congressional leadership.

"How much time do I have?" Roosevelt asked.

"Not much. In the next two hours I'll brief the President and his chief of staff, and then the Congressional leadership – including the Judiciary Committee Chairs and their ranking minority members. I'm telling you and everyone I brief that any leaked information could compromise our investigation. With the hearings resuming tomorrow at nine, I think that gives you at most fifteen hours, William, to decide how you wish to proceed with your challenge to President Stanton."

"Fifteen hours," Roosevelt repeated. "Do you think the Congress would delay their hearings?"

"I don't believe so, but I think you should talk to Jason. The Republican leadership is looking forward to the 2008 Presidential elections. They don't intend to do President Stanton, you, or the Democratic party any favors."

"I can talk to Jason?"

"I think so, but you need to give us time to interrogate him. We need to be assured he was not in Croft's pocket. I'll let you know, but William I warn you I will hold you responsible. If our investigation is compromised you will be prosecuted."

"I understand but I'll need to talk to Elizabeth, as well."

"There's no problem there. You can't tell her anything she does not already know."

"Thank you, Robert. You have been very helpful. Please excuse me now. I have much to consider and much to do."

"Certainly, William. Again, I'm sorry and wish you well. Please keep me informed. The nation still needs your help."

"Thank you, Robert."

"One last thing, William. This is Doc Watson, my lead investigator on the Chadwick case. I have asked him to show you several abbreviated State of the Union addresses delivered by President Stanton. I think you will find them informative. Oh, one more thing, William, it may not be my place, but can I tell the President you'd like to speak with him?"

"Yes, Robert, please do. Let him know I'd like to meet with him at his earliest convenience."

"I'll call you from the White House, William. I hope you can speak to him tonight."

6:30 P.M., Tuesday, January 30.

"Director Parker, welcome. Please come in. The President and Mrs. Thorn are in his residence. He asked me to bring you up."

"Thank you, Crayton," Robert Parker had not been in the Presidential residence for many years. He was surprised how unpretentious and comfortable it appeared.

"Robert, I'm sure you remember Mrs. Jean Thorn. She's here to give me moral support."

"Of course, it is good to see you again, Mrs. Thorn. Just by your presence you and Danielle brought much needed civility and good cheer to the whole nation. We've missed you. I hope you'll be staying a good long while."

"You're very kind, Robert. I'll check in on the kitchen, Andy, and ask them to hold dinner." As she reached the door, Jean Thorn turned back to Director Parker, "I know they could set another plate, Robert, if you'd care to join us."

"Oh, no thank you, Mrs. Thorn. You're very kind, but when I finish here I have a meeting back at the Bureau." As soon as she had left, Robert Parker turned to President Stanton, "I'm sorry to interrupt, sir, but I have important information for you."

"Have a seat, Robert. Take as long as you like. You have my full attention."

Robert Parker sat on the edge of his chair leaning forward toward the President. "I hardly know where to begin." He paused and then launched into a non-stop, step by step record of the Bureau's investigation of Aaron Chadwick's accident. He recounted in some length and detail their Saturday morning meeting when the President directed him to do whatever was required to protect Secretary Chadwick. He then cited the evidence suggesting that there had indeed been a conspiracy to murder Aaron Chadwick. At that point Parker confessed to the President that Aaron Chadwick's death had been staged.

"Aaron's alive!" Stanton exclaimed. "How is he?"

"He's still in a coma, sir, but until this morning that coma was partially sustained by drug therapy. Now they have taken him off those drugs. Thus far he's holding his own. He still has a chance. Even a full recovery is not impossible."

"And Sharon?"

"She's anxious, frightened, and tough as nails. She's also very much in love."

"What about the autopsy, Robert? Couldn't you have low-keyed it."

"That's really why I am here. Aaron Chadwick was in fact the target of a conspiracy to commit murder. The conspirators wanted to insure that Congress would resolve Roosevelt's challenge to your Presidency."

"William would never have permitted any such thing. Your mistaken, Robert. It was an accident."

"You're right, Mr. President. William knew nothing about the plot and it was an accident, but there was also a conspiracy. It involved at least three individuals, two contract killers and the lead contractor, James Croft."

"James Croft! Commander James Croft!" President Stanton sneered. "I can believe anything about that bastard. How do you know?"

"The autopsy was a ruse. It triggered Croft's payoff to the would-be killers."

"Can you prove that?" President Stanton was astonished.

"Yes, we traced the payments," Parker responded, "but given his suicide note it is hardly required."

"Suicide note! My God, Parker, the implications of this are incredible. We don't have to wait years for proof. Does anyone else know?"

"Yes, sir. In addition to the agents involved, I informed Acting President Roosevelt and I will shortly brief the Congressional leadership including the Chairs and ranking members of both Judiciary Committees."

"How's Roosevelt?" President Stanton asked.

"Even though our investigation, including phone taps and the suicide note, strongly suggests he was in no way involved, Roosevelt knows he will be found guilty in the court of public opinion. He's struggling with how he should proceed with his challenge to your Presidency. I suspect he's still concerned about competency."

"I understand, Robert. I gave the entire nation cause for concern. That's over now. You know, I believe Vice President Roosevelt was sincere, but I also believe that his wife and ambition colored his judgment."

"You could be right, Mr. President. Elizabeth Anne's role in this whole affair still needs to be sorted out. I just hope there is an honorable way through this mess and that you, Mr. Roosevelt, and the Congress can give our country back the leadership it needs."

"I'm sure we can." President Stanton replied.

"In that regard, sir, Mr. Roosevelt asked me to convey to you that he would like to speak with you at your earliest convenience. I told him I would call him from the White House with your reaction."

"Tell him I want to see him now, Robert. And tell him to bring Jason Fields," President Stanton directed. "And, Robert, when you have finished your Congressional briefing I'd like you to alert the Congressional leadership that Mr. Roosevelt and I might like to see them here at the White House to arrange a joint appearance before a joint meeting of the House and Senate Judiciary Committees. And, Robert, if that flies, I will suggest to Mr. Roosevelt that you appear with us."

"Thank you, sir. I'm on my way to brief the Congressional leadership. Some of their members who had all but convicted you of murder need time to consider how they wish to eat crow. Good night, Mr. President."

"Good night, Robert."

Acting President Roosevelt sat alone in his living room at the National Naval Observatory. He was more than despondent. His lifelong dream to lead the nation he loved was now a nightmare. He watched the evening news and listened to commentators report the Presidency was his. Public opinion favored him over Stanton by more than three to one. Coverage of the Congressional hearings concentrated on the "Incidents File." Polls of Senators and Representatives left no doubt that Congress was just going through the motions. Roosevelt had the votes; the Presidency was his, but it wasn't. An evil old man, who Roosevelt despised, aided and abetted by Elizabeth Anne, who had shared his dream, had endangered the nation and destroyed their dream. He was sure she was involved. That hurt more than anything else. He was guilty too. He recognized their unprincipled ambition, yet did nothing. Maybe he shared it. He had soiled the Roosevelt name by his flawed judgment and ineptitude. There was no way out.

Lost in his misery, Roosevelt didn't see or hear Elizabeth Anne come into the room. She startled him when she dropped to her knees dropped her head in his lap and sobbed, "My dad's dead, William. He's dead. He killed himself."

"I know, Honey. I'm sorry."

"You know?" she asked.

"Yes," Roosevelt answered. "Director Parker told me everything."

"I guess Daddy thought he was helping the country. No matter how misguided his actions were he believed in you, William. You must continue the fight for the good of the nation."

"Oh no, Elizabeth Anne, please, please don't. Parker told me everything." Roosevelt held her head, looked at her and with tears welling in his eyes he repeated, "Everything."

"What do you mean, William? I don't understand."

"Give it up, Elizabeth. They have a case, a solid case."

"What are you saying?"

"Just before Aaron died, he wrote a letter to Judge Holt. He called it his insurance policy, but before he could call you and activate the policy Nathan had a medical emergency. Nevertheless the letter was sent. You offered him a seat on the Supreme Court. When he refused your bribe, you threatened him and even his family. The FBI has the letter."

"That's not true. I told him he had burned his bridges with President Stanton. He had to stick with you. It wasn't a threat."

"Well, when the public learns that Aaron thought you threatened him, and then your dad confesses to hiring his killers, it's hard not to conclude that one plus one equals two. You were the one who provided your father with the information he needed to target Aaron."

"I had nothing to do with it. It was stupid. I know my dad confessed. He phoned me just before he committed suicide, but that doesn't implicate me, any more than it implicates you. I repeat I had nothing to do with it. You must believe me, William, and you must fight on. Nothing James Croft did or did not do made President Stanton competent. The country needs you."

"Elizabeth, listen to me. The FBI is looking at you as your father's coconspirator in the murder of Aaron Chadwick. They not only recorded your last conversation with your dad when he knew they were listening; they also taped your earlier conversation. They let me read the transcript. You might remember it. You cautioned your dad to give me a little space and he assured you that, 'When the time is right we'll rein him in...We'll be in charge.' Then you went on to delight that the payoff to the killers had gone smoothly, without a hitch. Elizabeth, you're guilty and I'm guilty by association and failed judgment. We both need lawyers, different lawyers," he added. "They shouldn't have a conflict of interest."

"You think that they can convict me for humoring a senile old man. I had no idea he was serious. When he counseled you to "take no prisoners,' you didn't take him seriously. You didn't alert the FBI. He was all bluster. You know it."

"Are you saying you were the kingpin; he was all bluster, a senile old man. You hired the killers, Elizabeth?"

"Of course not, William   Take a deep breath. You're country needs you."

"You are crazy, Elizabeth Anne. That's your best defense. When a jury reads Aaron's letter, listens to the phone tap about paying the killers and engineering incidents sabotaging President Stanton, and then watches you in action as you mimic President Stanton's dead wife at the State of the Union, they won't need to consider a verdict. They'll shout it, 'GUILTY!' Hell, insanity might be your only defense."

"You're the one who's crazy, William. First, I confess I humored my dad, but I did nothing more. His deathbed confession expressly stated I played no part in his plot to kill Aaron. Second, apparently you have forgotten that after Danielle's death President Stanton asked me to be First Lady, and before the State of the Union he told me how comforting it would be to see me in Danny's place. I went the extra mile and dressed the part. Like half the people in the visitor's gallery, I waved and blew him a kiss. I hardly think I set him off. Everyone who worked with him knew he was having trouble long before the State of the Union. He lost his best friend and then his wife in just a matter of months. He couldn't handle it. That's tragic but it's not my fault. I tried to help."

"My God, you are a clever woman, Elizabeth Anne, and if I don't testify, you might win and be acquitted."

"You'd testify against me?"

"I don't know. I don't know what I'm going to do about the Presidency, our marriage, or custody of Jimmy. I do know you should reject a trial by jury. You'll have a better chance before a judge. Judges require proof beyond a reasonable doubt to convict; juries are more persuaded by the emotions of the case. The emotions in your case will send you to prison."

Before Elizabeth Anne could respond, Jason Fields was knocking insistently at the door. "Mr. Roosevelt, Director Parker is on the phone. He said you were expecting his call."

"Yes, thank you, Jason. Tell him I'll be right with him." Without saying another word Roosevelt left Elizabeth Anne, moved to his office, and took the call. When he returned he went to the closet and got his winter coat and then announced with finality that he and Jason were going to the White House to meet with President Stanton and Crayton Langford. "I'm sorry, I could be late. Don't wait up."

"William, for God's sake, think! Nothing has changed. You, the Cabinet, the American people, and now the Congress believe President Stanton is incompetent. What my dad did changes nothing. The country is still in danger. You must do what's right for our country." Elizabeth Anne's command sounded more like a plea.

Roosevelt stopped at the door to respond, "Elizabeth, I know what I know. And I know what I must do and what you must do."

"And just what is that, Dear?"

"I need to see President Stanton and you, Elizabeth, need to see a lawyer."

CHAPTER TWENTY-SEVEN:

PUTTING THE GENIE BACK IN THE BOTTLE

8:00 P.M., Tuesday, January 30.

They met in the Oval Office – President Andrew Stanton, Acting President William Roosevelt, and their chiefs of staff Crayton Langford and Jason Fields. Last to arrive was FBI Director Robert Parker. It was uncomfortable and clumsy. All had acted honorably and done their duty. All had abided by both the letter and the spirit of the Constitution, yet the process was corrupted. Murder, even "just" a conspiracy to commit murder, can do that.

On its face, Congress confronted an impossible choice. They would decide who would lead the United States for the next two years – a man implicated in a conspiracy to commit murder or a President judged incompetent by his own cabinet.

"Gentlemen, we're all here," President Stanton announced. "No one else was invited. Please be seated. We have precious little time," President Stanton stated as he took the last chair just to the right of Acting President Roosevelt. William, I briefed Crayton and I assume you briefed Jason?"

"That's correct," Roosevelt replied.

"As the oldest man in the room," President Stanton continued, "I want to clear the air and save us some time. I want to stipulate that I sincerely believe that Acting President Roosevelt's motives and actions in invoking the Twenty-Fifth Amendment have been entirely honorable. It was my behavior, no one else's, that called into question my competence. Though I sincerely believe my personal difficulties never affected my ability to perform the powers and duties of my office, I understand that's a minority opinion. If I am to govern, the American people must see my competence and believe as I do that whatever difficulties I had are behind me."

Acting President Roosevelt, normally a self-confident even commanding presence, was embarrassed and humiliated by the position in which he found himself. "Mr. President, you are very kind. I desperately want to believe your assessment of my motives and actions. Just a few hours ago I might have smugly agreed. I should have listened to you. You warned me our contest would 'unleash forces no one could control.' It is now apparent to me that others felt my ambition was unleashed and could be exploited to their advantage. It was they who killed Aaron Chadwick."

"William," Director Parker interrupted, "I need to correct the record with you. Everything I told you about the conspiracy was the truth; it was however, not the whole truth. James Croft did hire killers to murder Aaron Chadwick. He guaranteed them a million plus dollars on two conditions: The murder had to occur no later than midnight, Sunday, January twenty-ninth and it had to be ruled an accident. This morning when Dr. Chapin and I announced the results of Aaron's autopsy it was a hoax designed to smoke out the conspirators. It worked and to top it all Aaron Chadwick is alive. His accident was nearly fatal, but with a great deal of luck, he could have a full recovery."

"He's alive?" Roosevelt exclaimed in disbelief.

"Yes, he is," Parker confirmed.

"How wonderful; how absolutely wonderful. I am so pleased. You have lifted a crushing burden from my soul. You just can't understand. I am so relieved. Excuse me." Roosevelt took just a moment to compose himself. "Help me. Do I have this right; Aaron's killers were stalking him when he had his accident and Croft credited them with pulling off the perfect murder?"

"You're close, but you're missing a few pieces. The killers also went after Aaron at Bethesda. When they 'learned' he was already dead they called off their efforts and simply notified Croft of their success. We triggered Croft's payment when we announced Aaron's death had been the result of a tragic accident."

"Extraordinary times require extraordinary measures," Roosevelt stated.

"They certainly do," Parker agreed. "President Stanton had ordered me to do whatever was required to protect Aaron and that's what we did. Thank you for your understanding, William."

"Croft was an audacious bastard. Worse than even I suspected," Roosevelt confessed. "His plot was devoid of any hint of a moral justification. They were just greedy for power and money. God, it's just horrific."

"They intended to blackmail you, William. How foolish," President Stanton remarked. "They didn't have a chance. I know you. They would have failed."

"President Stanton, earlier this evening at Director Parker's insistence, I reviewed your last three State of the Union addresses."

"That is still embarrassing for me," the President complained.

"No, no. That's not my point at all, Mr. President. Without any doubt your address last week was your best. The message was perfect. It was incredible. It was logical, inspirational, powerful, and persuasive. Being a New Yorker, your timing and delivery reminded me of Mario Cuomo's 1984 Democratic convention keynote address. It proclaimed your competence as well as leadership and decency. You were back in command until Elizabeth Anne startled you with her impersonation of Danny," Roosevelt stated, looking directly at President Stanton. "I'm so sorry. It was sick, mean, and devious. I don't understand why I didn't see it for what it was. I must have been blinded by ambition."

"William, I stated before I believe your motives were entirely honorable. It was my behavior that called into question my competence. Nevertheless one of us must lead. I believe with your help and the help of the cabinet and the American people, Congress can be convinced of my competence and give me the mandate I need to govern our country for the remainder of my term."

"Mr. President, let me state the obvious so we can move quickly. My father-in-law, and perhaps my wife, engaged in a conspiracy to commit murder to advance my chances of replacing you. That fact alone would condemn my Presidency to failure. If I continued to pursue the Presidency it could only be justified if you were dangerously and hopelessly incompetent. That is not the case. Even if it were, a Roosevelt administration would never be accepted. It would be seen as a necessary evil. If the American people tolerated it at all, it would still be despised and ridiculed as a caretaker government indebted to criminals. We must assure the American people that you are again the extraordinary leader they elected and you are fully capable of leading the nation for the next two years."

Crayton Langford and Jason Fields, who had been huddled together, now took center stage. Crayton led off. "Mr. President, Acting President Roosevelt, Jason and I have listened to you both and we have cobbled together an action plan that needs your input and approval. First, the Twenty Fifth Amendment makes no provision for the withdrawal of the second declaration. Rather it states once it is delivered 'Congress shall decide the issue.'"

Jason continued: "In making their decision the Senate and House Judiciary Committees have already announced their intentions to call President Stanton, Acting President Roosevelt and every member of the Cabinet. We need to call them first and get our act together."

"Mr. Roosevelt, would you be willing to join the President and Director Parker in a meeting with the entire Cabinet?"

"Yes, of course I would. They need to know my situation and they need to know my family exploited the President's grief. They distorted his service and sabotaged his reputation. When they understand the strength and leadership he has shown in this crisis, I am confident that even those who signed the second declaration will conclude that President Stanton is perfectly competent to lead our nation."

"In all honesty, William, I believe I could say the same about you." President Stanton's sincerity was obvious. "Unfortunately, while we both have crosses to bear, mine is more easily understood and forgiven. People have walked in my shoes. They've had loved ones die. They were inconsolable, they grieved, and they survived. Your experience is different. You suffered betrayal. Your trust was violated. People have less experience with that. I suspect they will look at it more like divorce. They don't know who's to blame, but they assume no one is without fault."

"I think you're right," Roosevelt acknowledged. Certainly my judgment can be faulted. I fault it myself. But, Mr. President, I do take great comfort in the fact that I believed I was doing what was right for the country. I am also very thankful that I have this opportunity to make amends."

"Robert, this means you have two more briefings. The first will be tomorrow morning at eight with the Cabinet. While I will be in attendance, Acting President Roosevelt will chair the meeting and call upon you to summarize your findings. Following your briefing, Mr. Roosevelt will state our positions, his and mine, and invite questions."

"As chair," Roosevelt smiled, "we will not adjourn until we achieve consensus and the Cabinet agrees to join the President and me in persuading Congress that he is capable of performing his duties. Indeed, I will argue that his performance during this Constitutional challenge is obvious proof of his judgment and abilities. I am aware, Mr. President, that you were informed early of my wife's performance at your State of the Union address. I truly admire you for resisting temptation and leaking that footage."

"Thank you, William," Stanton responded. "I was just demonstrating to my staff that I could control my emotions."

"You should know, Mr. Roosevelt, that the President's inner circle did not applaud that decision." There was a slight edge to Crayton's comment. "We felt we were fighting this battle with our hands tied behind our backs."

"Back to the business at hand," President Stanton directed. "Robert, your second briefing, midmorning or early afternoon should be before a joint meeting of the Congressional Judiciary Committees."

"Mr. President, the cumulative effect of all of these briefings could be to compromise potential prosecutions. Maybe my second briefing tomorrow should be presented in an executive session."

"An executive session? I don't think so, Robert." President Stanton did not mince words. "If we are to win public support for this about-face, the people will need to hear the unvarnished truth. I feel strongly about this, but make your case."

"I'm sorry, Mr. Roosevelt, this is delicate, but everyone here has heard the tapes." Director Parker was hesitant, but continued. "You are aware that as of yet we do not know the full extent of this conspiracy. Our phone taps do, however, suggest that Elizabeth Anne Roosevelt was a coconspirator with her father. In my opinion, she at least had prior knowledge of the conspiracy. If that is true she is almost certainly guilty of complicity. Public hearings could taint the jury pool."

Acting President Roosevelt visually checked the others; apparently it was his turn to weigh in. He began slowly. "Like President Stanton, I too believe that public hearings are in the best interest of the country. However, Robert is correct. After public hearings carried live by every network and milked by every broadcaster, blogger, and rag for months to come, my wife's attorneys will argue correctly that no change in venue could possibly assure her of a fair trial by an impartial jury of her peers. Strangely, given the evidence, she does not want to win on a technicality. Nor, does she want to be tried in the court of public opinion. She would much prefer to be tried in Federal District Court. She believes she has a credible defense even against her own words. I've heard it. She maintains she thought she was just humoring a senile old man that she loved very much. She maintains she never took him seriously. I have serious doubts. James Croft was evil, but he was neither crazy nor senile. Nevertheless, I guarantee you she can make a very good case."

"Robert," Crayton injected, "as far as prosecuting Mrs. Roosevelt, it doesn't matter whether your Congressional testimony is public or private. It will be public within a week. Nobody likes a surprise. I think you should deliver your brief in executive session and then let the committees determine if and when they want you to repeat all or a portion of your testimony in a public session. They have a big stake in this. We will be asking a number of committee members to make a U-turn. They will want the public to understand and even applaud their about-face. We want to make it easy for them to give President Stanton a mandate to govern. On the other hand, in all candor, I don't give a damn about those partisan bastards who accused us of murder. I hope the voters in their districts and states remember and send them packing."

"Unfortunately, those guys come from districts that are even more rabid than they are," Jason commented. "Hopefully, with the President, Acting President, and the entire Cabinet presenting a unified front we will give reasonable Senators and Representatives all the cover they need to give the President the mandate he needs."

"I have just one comment," Roosevelt stated. "As far as I am concerned, we could suffer the loss of either Secretary Kelly or

Reynolds, or both in fact, without damaging our case one iota. Those two have no standing. They're poison."

"We are indeed of one mind, William," President Stanton laughed. "The only undeniable evidence of my incompetence occurred before Thorny's or Danny's death when I appointed those two bozos."

"You didn't marry them," Roosevelt quipped.

"Don't be hard on yourself, William. I gave you legitimate cause for concern. You did your duty." At that, President Stanton concluded the meeting. "Thank you all for coming, particularly you, William. I think we are done here. As always Crayton, Jason, your labors have just begun – work your miracles. We meet here tomorrow at eight with the Cabinet."

8:05 A.M., Wednesday, January 30.

President Stanton was visibly irritated. Director Park was late. While President Stanton and Acting President Roosevelt waited in the Oval Office, the Secretaries had assembled in the Cabinet Room. Rather naturally they had divided into two respectful, but opposing camps. Crayton Langford and Jason Fields were still huddled together at the first hall entrance to the Cabinet Room where they had greeted the Secretaries. Now they waited 'patiently' checking the time until they quietly agreed that Crayton should visit the Oval Office.

"What's the delay?" Crayton asked before he realized Millie was on the phone.

"The President's secretary smiled and indicated she would be just a moment. "He's on line one, Mr. President. Go easy, sir."

"Where are you, Robert?" Stanton asked, though reading between the lines his question was more accurately understood to be "Where the hell are you, Robert?"

"I'm under escort, sir. I'll be there in just a couple of minutes."

"We'll have to make that work," Stanton muttered. Then lightening he added, "You had us worried." However, Parker responded President Stanton brightened remarkably ending the phone call with, "Wonderful, Robert, I can't wait."

"What was that all about?" Roosevelt asked.

"Patience, my friend." Stanton smiled. "It's a wonderful surprise."

Roosevelt's smile indicated he had been the last to know too often in recent days.

"Oh, you shouldn't have to wait, William. He's your friend as much as mine. Parker has Sharon Chadwick with him. She brings good tidings from Aaron. He asks the Cabinet to listen to our counsel and then inform them through Sharon that he intends to stand by our agreement."

"My God, Mr. President, we are going to get the genie back in the bottle."

"Yes, we are, William. Yes, we are. Crayton, is the Cabinet assembled?"

"Assembled, but not seated, sir."

"Get them seated, Crayton. Shall we join them, William?"

Acting President Roosevelt took a big breath and exhaled before responding. "No time like the present, sir."

"I guess that means we're ready," President Stanton replied. "Remember, you're chairing the meeting. I'd recommend we hear from Director Parker and Sharon first. Then you and I can do a shared *mea culpa* followed by our request that they join our unified front. At that point we'll open the floor to questions."

Roosevelt laughed. "Remind me again, Mr. President."

"Remind you of what, William?"

"Who's in charge?"

"You are, William. Oh, I am sorry. Old habits die hard. Just be assured I'll be ready to step in if you need help... or even if you don't."

8:13 A.M., Wednesday, January 30.

In the West Wing only the office of the President's secretary separates the Oval Office from the Cabinet Room. As President Stanton and Acting President Roosevelt emerged from the Oval Office, a smiling Millie Wilson stood and spoke quietly. "They're a little unruly but they are in their assigned seats. Even better, the front desk just called. Director Parker and Sharon Chadwick are here. Do you want me to send them right in?"

"Yes, thanks, Millie. Are you ready, Mr. Roosevelt? We better set the stage."

"Yes, Mr. President, but in keeping with our 'Sunshine Rules' may I suggest Ms. Wilson and two pool reporters join us."

"Yes, of course. That's excellent. Millie would you ask Lincoln to check in the pressroom and bring a couple of pool reporters to the Cabinet Room.

"Of course, Mr. President."

"Shall we go?" Roosevelt asked. "Your Cabinet awaits."

The Cabinet was indeed waiting but their patience was stretched. The nation was in crisis. This was an emergency meeting of the entire Cabinet, members of both sides. They were anxious. Within the next forty-eight hours each would sit alone before Congress and the nation. Some would claim executive privilege, risking prison sentences for contempt of Congress. Others would reject that claim and testify about private meetings with President Stanton. They would be forced to draw fine lines between public and private grief, mourning and madness, competence and incompetence. They were sitting on a powder keg. All hoped to hear the nightmare was over. Maybe President Stanton would resign.

At the Cabinet Room door they heard the room abuzz with both public and private conversations. The Secretaries exchanged reports and rumors, facts and fiction, reasoned theories and rank gossip at par value. The unannounced appearance of President Stanton and Acting President Roosevelt brought silence in quick stages until the last comment, "He's got to resign," stood alone filling the room.

"Let me clear the air." Acting President Roosevelt enunciated each word authoritatively and emphatically. "President Stanton does not have to resign. We are here at his invitation because we are all involved in a Constitutional process that has now moved to the Congress. All of us, President Stanton and myself included, have been called to testify as to his competence and by inference my own. In no way did the authors and adopters of the Twenty-

Fifth Amendment intend to replace a sitting President with a less competent Acting President. The competence of both must be judged. In that regard the President and I have new information that has radically altered our positions. You need to have that same information if you are to advise Congress intelligently."

"Just a little foreshadowing," President Stanton commented. "You should know that Acting President Roosevelt and I are now of one mind as to implications of this information."

"Not only are we of one mind, but we also believe that if you join us the Congress will heed our collective advice and the nation can move forward."

Acting President Roosevelt's statement was greeted with an uneven smattering of applause until President Stanton put his left hand on Roosevelt's shoulder while shaking his right hand with obvious enthusiasm. With that the Cabinet Secretaries came to their feet and applauded both men as they proceeded slowly to their seats opposite one another. The sense of relief was palpable. With Roosevelt and Stanton working together the nation might indeed get back on track.

"Thank you, thank you all. Mr. President I believe this bodes well for our future. Would you do me the favor of outlining our agenda?"

"Certainly. Momentarily, FBI Director Parker will bring you up to date on the Aaron Chadwick investigation and its spinoffs. Sharon Chadwick will join us for his briefing. She will be hearing all but the medical information for the first time. Although Director Parker is scheduled to brief a joint executive session of the Judiciary Committees, he should have sufficient time to answer all your questions. Finally, Acting President Roosevelt and I will share our thoughts with you in the hope that we all can come to a consensus that will guide the Congress in its deliberations."

"Jason, have Director Parker and Mrs. Chadwick join us, please."

As Jason opened the door to Millie's Office, Robert Parker's poorly hushed voice was clearly heard by those in the adjoining room. "Watson, I don't have time for details. Just give me names. Who was on his payroll?....I understand....Any Cabinet officers?....Take your time....This is important....Okay, that's it then. Doc, I'm going to put you on hold. I'll get Millie and she

can give you her personal line. Call that number if you have anything else.

8:23 A.M., Wednesday, January 30.

Robert Parker had already briefed Acting President Roosevelt, President Stanton, and the Congressional leadership. He had
two more to go, the Cabinet and then the Judiciary Committees.
This would be the toughest. Two members of the Cabinet were on
Croft's payroll when they signed the declarations that President
Stanton was unable to discharge the powers and duties of his office.

"Acting President Roosevelt, Mr. President, ladies and gentlemen, I am so sorry to keep you waiting. The Aaron Chadwick
investigation is ongoing. While we are flushing out more and
more details every day, I can now share with you the basic ele-
ments of a murder conspiracy designed to overthrow the government of the United States.

With that introduction the Cabinet was riveted by Director
Parker's every word. From his earlier presentations he knew the
questions that needed to be answered so his audience could follow
the facts just as the FBI had. Even so they were stunned when he
revealed that Aaron's death had been declared to save his life.
When he announced that Aaron's autopsy report was simply a successful ruse that allowed them to follow the contract killers to
James Croft they were astounded. As all eyes turned toward Acting President Roosevelt, Croft's son-in-law, Parker distributed the
transcripts of Croft's phone conversation with Elizabeth Anne
Roosevelt. He pointedly read the paragraphs where they described
their intention to hold the nation hostage and blackmail the Acting
President. He also read that portion of the transcripts that indicated
that a number of the episodes cited in Crayton's "File" had been
setups meant to discredit President Stanton. As proof, Parker
asked Crayton and Jason to play the tapes of President Stanton's
most recent State of the Union – announcing that during the showing he would like to meet briefly with both Acting President Roosevelt and President Stanton.

As they entered the Oval Office, President Stanton was the first to speak. "You're doing beautifully, Robert, but what's this about?"

"We are learning more about the conspiracy every minute," Parker began.

"More about Elizabeth Anne?" Roosevelt asked almost mournfully.

"No, no, William, more about Croft. I'm sorry I have to make this quick. You two have major decisions to make. Croft Industries is a Goliath, but it may be just the tip of an iceberg. We have already uncovered a network of moles throughout our political system. Let me generalize. Croft paid them all a handsome monthly retainer; they are ambitious, strategically located, and I suspect completely unscrupulous. Now, today, get this; Doc Watson's 'Mining Group' has found regular monthly payments have been made in the last two years to thirteen Representatives, three Senators and most importantly two Cabinet members."

"Oh my God," Roosevelt exclaimed. "Those two bastards joined Elizabeth Anne and insisted it was my constitutional duty to assume the Presidency to avoid the certainty of a national calamity. Their concerns supported the old adage that the last refuge of a scoundrel is patriotism."

"One of you needs to tell me, who are you talking about?" President Stanton demanded.

"Just a guess," William responded. "Secretary of Transportation Robert Kelly and Secretary of Commerce Paul Reynolds."

"You're right on the money," Parker acknowledged. "The question is how do we proceed? "

"Director, just a couple of quick questions."

"Certainly, Mr. Roosevelt."

"Were the payments ever declared in the disclosure process or on tax returns and did they involve any *quid pro quos*? In short were the payments illegal?"

"Yes, they were illegal; they were never disclosed and according to Croft's notes they all were payments for services rendered."

"Let's not make this too difficult," President Stanton injected. "Cabinet officials serve at the pleasure of the President or in this case the Acting President. I suggest you invite them into the

Oval Office one at a time, confront them with the information against them. If they have no satisfactory explanation take the appropriate action, require their written resignation effective immediately. They can use my desk."

"In the meantime, Mr. President, while Director Parker and I confront Reynolds and Kelly, you could call upon Sharon Chadwick to update the Cabinet on Aaron's condition. We should not be long and as soon as we are through we will join you and finish the briefing."

"And then we move to the end game," President Stanton stated. "Strangely we have options; we just don't have much time to consider them."

"Good," Roosevelt responded. "I'll ask Jason to bring Reynolds first and then Kelly. Let's go."

When Jason arrived with Paul Reynolds he informed Acting President Roosevelt and Director Parker that the Cabinet was still reviewing President Stanton's last State of the Union. Next they would go through a side-by-side, frame-by-frame comparison of the last full minute of each address. "We'll be ready for you in about five minutes unless President Stanton calls on Sharon Chadwick. Then you'll have an additional ten to fifteen minutes."

"Keep your eye on the door, Jason; I'll signal you when to bring Kelly in."

"Yes, sir. I don't think the Cabinet is restless. They're all dumbfounded about what they have learned. I think they feel duped just as we did."

It was not long before Roosevelt signaled Jason that he was ready for Secretary Kelly. After notifying Kelly that Acting President Roosevelt would like to see him in the Oval Office, Jason moved quickly to have a few words with Acting President Roosevelt. He couldn't resist. "Where's Reynolds?" he asked.

"Secretary Reynolds has resigned. He denied any *quid pro quo*. Then just before he lawyered-up, he "confessed' that Secretary Kelly made him do it, led him down the path of 'sin and perniciousness.' I think that's from 'Elmer Gantry,' but it fairly reflects his statement. Does Kelly have a clue?"

"I think so. He's green and he's packing up."

As Secretary Kelly left the Cabinet Room for the Oval Office, President Stanton called on Sharon Chadwick. Unlike Parker's depressing presentation of the facts, Sharon was a breath of fresh air. She was upbeat and positive. She described Aaron's mood after meeting with Elizabeth Anne, their flight to the cabin, Aaron laboring on his letter to Justice Steven Holt, their dinner, and then Nathan's asthma attack. "Aaron did what he always does. He dropped everything for his family. He didn't wait for me to search for another inhaler, he didn't notify Elizabeth Anne of his letter, he tramped out in the snow, got in that old Jeep and headed out into the night."

Before Sharon could report on Aaron's progress, Acting President Roosevelt and Director Parker rejoined the Cabinet. Secretary Kelly was not with them. All were delighted when Sharon announced Aaron and his doctors anticipated that he would make a full recovery and could resume his duties within three to four weeks. She ended by reading a short message from Aaron: "While I had hoped to be treated at least as well as a rowdy courthouse defendant and sequestered in a nearby room watching you all on a closed-circuit television, Director Parker refuses to release me from my 'safe house' until Watson blows the all-clear whistle. In the meantime Sharon is keeping me well informed and I can tell you, I intend to support the plan offered jointly by President Stanton and Acting President Roosevelt. If that changes I will let you know and give you my reasons. I've missed you all and hope to be working with you soon."

"Thank you so much, Sharon. If there are no objections, President Stanton and I would like to ask Sharon Chadwick to stay with us through our deliberation so Aaron can make an informed decision as to how he believes the Congress should proceed." Roosevelt waited momentarily and then announced, "Without objection it is done."

"Thank you all," Sharon responded. "This is great. I am a witness to history."

"We are indeed making history," Roosevelt commented. "Aaron's accident was the beginning of a remarkable chain of events that derailed a *coup d'état* that was posed to destroy our democracy.   The chain had many links: a vigilant FBI, partial prints on a lens cap, security at Bethesda, a Presidential directive, an imaginative Director, and a most unusual contract killer all played critical roles.   Director Parker will bring us up-to-date on his investigation and then President Stanton and I will make our recommendations and call for your comments and questions.   Director Parker."

"Gentlemen, ladies you know I was late. My excuse was that I was picking up Sharon and briefing Aaron, but in fact I was also in constant contact with chief investigator William Watson. 'Doc' Watson is a remarkable man and another link in that chain Mr. Roosevelt described. Throughout the night and continuing this morning Doc Watson's investigators have been reviewing James Croft's 'payroll' expenditures. As I told our 'Presidents,' James Croft had a network of moles throughout our political system, but he also had parallel and cooperating networks among media moguls and the nation's economic elite. Fortunately for our investigation, Croft was remarkably well organized and apparently had no fear of ever being caught. His spreadsheets were organized by year, by category and subcategory with the payees alphabetized. On the national political level, regular monthly payments have been made in the last two years to thirteen Representatives, three Senators, and two Cabinet Secretaries."

In the general clamor that followed, questions that were directed at anyone and everyone went unanswered.

"What the hell did he say?"

"Did he say 'two Cabinet Secretaries'?"

"Who are they?"

"Surely you're not serious?"

"Are you serious or just seeing if we were paying attention?"

"Who are they?'

"Oh my God, Did they sign the declarations?"

"Could there be others?"

Instinctively Acting President Roosevelt made eye contact with President Stanton, saw his nod, and took charge. "Hold on, everybody. The repercussions could be complex but the answers to your questions are straightforward and complete. Croft's only agents in the President's Cabinet were Secretary of Transportation

Robert Kelly, and Secretary of Commerce Paul Reynolds. Tragically I must admit to you that these two men and my wife were the first to insist that I use Section Four of the Twenty-Fifth Amendment to save our country from potential dangers they saw so clearly. Sadly, I regret my own ambitions may have made me an easy mark. In any case now, with the concurrence of President Stanton, I asked for and received their resignations. Both men have now been arrested and are in the custody of the FBI. As to the question whether there may be other Croft agents among us, Director Parker assures me the answer is 'No.'

"It is very simple, Parker explained, "if ever you sold your soul to Croft he owned you for life. He listed all of his acquisitions whether or not they were currently being paid a monthly retainer. Croft didn't accept resignations. Let me give you just one example of his tenacity and reach. Before I do, I want to apologize to Acting President Roosevelt for not telling him first what I am about to tell you, but it is very instructive. You need to hear it. Fourteen years ago, when the Roosevelts moved to Washington, they hired Ronald Hodges to head their household staff. They paid him handsomely but not nearly as well as James Croft. For all these years he was another paid informant keeping Croft abreast of all that was happening in the Roosevelt household."

Roosevelt again questioned his judgment. How could he have been so blind? Fourteen years of deceit and betrayal and he was oblivious. "Thank you, Robert. We must all remember that judgment is a critical component of competence. Mr. President, it is time we open up the discussion. Would you lead off?"

"Of course, William," President Stanton looked about the room at his Cabinet. "In the absence of Secretaries Kelly and Reynolds I can honestly say I consider all of you my friends. We have had many disagreements over the years, but they concerned policy; this disagreement concerns my fitness to serve out the remainder of my term. Yet, even here our disagreements have been honest and honorable. Unfortunately, I gave you cause to doubt my competence. My grief did adversely affect my performance. I hoped you would forgive my performance and look only at my decisions, but they are inseparable. The question for us today is whether my grief and perhaps my age is still affecting my performance sufficiently so that the nation would be better served by Acting President Roosevelt."

Almost before the President invited comments, James Hill, Secretary of Veteran Affairs, was standing and confirming his continued support of President Stanton. "While I care what the rest of you are thinking, I must tell you I believe firmly that President Stanton must be returned to power. The nation needs him now. I have known him since the Vietnam War. What I have learned today from Director Parker confirms the President's competence and challenges Mr. Roosevelt's judgment if not his culpability. When I testify before Congress, I intend to demand that they return to the American people their elected President."

In a calmer vein Secretary of State, Anthony Lord, spoke briefly of his continued confidence in the President and the need for continuity in foreign relations.

Nancy Pruett, Secretary of Health and Human Services, was the first supporter of Roosevelt to speak. She had thought of him as her ticket to the White House; now she knew better. As always she was quick and decisive. "With what I have learned today, I am ready to reverse my position. What troubles me most is the conscious conspiracy to overthrow President Stanton's Presidency. Lord knows when it began, but it surfaced with the death of Vice President Mathew Thorn and the campaign to fill his vacancy with then Senator Roosevelt. It gained momentum when Danielle died and, excuse me, Mr. President, the opportunity to exploit your grief presented itself. It was all so cynical, so methodical, and so well, so damn well, executed that Elizabeth Anne's masquerade at the State of the Union was never exposed as the tripwire it was. I cannot support replacing our elected President with an Acting President whose candidacy was promoted by such outrageous tactics."

Fast on her heels was Charlene Tuckman, Secretary of Energy. She recognized that Section Four of the Twenty-Fifth Amendment addressed a very real problem, but she lamented that the process came dangerously close to a political auction with the Presidency going to the highest bidder. At that point, she, too, announced that she would urge Congress to reinstate President Stanton with a vote of confidence. "I am convinced President Stanton needs to complete his term of office."

Lee Fong, Secretary of Education, was far less committal. He stated only that he wanted to hear from his colleagues and consider their opinions.

Walter Wirtz, Secretary of Labor and a Stanton loyalist, was next. He was not sitting on the fence and he minced no words. "This whole Constitutional crisis was manufactured. I'm shocked by the exploitation of President Stanton's grief, but I am absolutely appalled by the actions of Secretary Kelly and Secretary Reynolds. James Croft, who tried to murder Aaron Chadwick for reconsidering his support of Mr. Roosevelt, hired those two thugs to rig our political system. I'm outraged."

"They didn't act alone, you know." Helen Ramirez, the diminutive Secretary of Housing and Urban Development, was determined to be heard. "I signed the first declaration only after Elizabeth Anne convinced me that President Stanton was a captive of his staff and needed an excuse to resign. She conned me. She looked me straight in the eye and lied repeatedly. When I went to the President I learned the truth. He was completely honest. He admitted to problems. We talked about Danny. He told me he could now think of her with joy. His grief was under control. I believed him then and I believe him now."

Attorney General Herrera was just as blunt as he spoke to his colleagues. "The first declaration was completely bogus. Without even considering the deception of Helen Ramirez, if we simply discount the signatures Croft bought, Reynolds and Kelly, the declaration never passed the Constitutional test for submission to Congress. That means that all that followed has no legal standing. Congress can simply state that fact and rule that President Stanton is to 'resume the powers and duties of his office.'"

"I agree with everything that has been said here," Harold Kruegman, Secretary of Agriculture, admitted, but I would like to add a very personal note to my dear friend President Stanton. I was wrong, very wrong. I did compare your situation with that of my father's. After his wife died he had nothing, you had Danny's wishes, your children and the nation. In the last month you have been tested like no other president. Your decisions, actions, judgment and composure have been flawless. I should have known. I'm sorry I let you down."

"Harold, we have all been making decisions on incomplete information. The better the information, the better our decisions. At the very least I gave you all legitimate cause for concern. I should have addressed those concerns earlier. We need to do our best now. Secretary Collier, can you help us?"

"I'd like to think so, Mr. President. We've all made mistakes. I'm sure you are aware of many of mine. Surely you remember I once called you a Pollyanna. I was wrong, sir. You're tough as nails. In the last hour we all watched Elizabeth Anne at the State of the Union, but I want you to know, Mr. President, I also listened to you. I hope my colleagues did as well. The whole nation knew of your troubles and waited to see if you could still lead our country. Without doubt, your State of the Union was the best I have ever heard or read. It was magnificent in substance, sentiment, and delivery. The State of the Union is one of your constitutionally mandated duties. You executed it flawlessly. Only when you had concluded and were accepting the adoration of the audience and saw the image of your beloved Danny did you appear to slip. But you didn't. How did we miss it? You told her and all of us you were better. I wrote down your words. 'Thank you, Danny. Thank you for being here for me. I'm all right now.' And then you whispered 'Goodbye, Goodbye, Danny.'" Collier paused wiped his right eye and continued, "You're all right, Mr. President and we need you to lead this country."

"Well," Acting President Roosevelt began, "if public tears disqualify us from public office we might as well turn in our resignations en masse. I have a few important facts that you all have been too kind to mention, but must be presented to Congress and the American people. Last week President Stanton and his staff were steady under fire. They dealt only with questions of competence. No deals were offered, no promises were made. At considerable risk, President Stanton did contact Director Parker to draft a letter to his staff requiring that they cooperate with the Bureau's investigation or resign. He also authorized Parker to take whatever measures were required to protect Aaron and the rest of the Cabinet. On the other hand, in that same week, to advance my chances of becoming Acting President my wife offered Secretary Chadwick the next seat on the Supreme Court and when Aaron rejected that my father-in-law plotted his murder. I have huge crosses that I cannot bear. While guilt by association should not send me to prison it most certainly should deny me the Presidency. As President Stanton proved himself wise, I have proven myself naïve. I believe we should go to the Judiciary Committees and speak with one voice."

"Secretary Binder, you have given wise counsel to both Acting President Roosevelt and myself throughout this process. How do you believe we should proceed?"

"President Stanton, Acting President Roosevelt, my great fear has always been that in our circumstances, the Twenty-Fifth Amendment mandates a process that almost guarantees the very condition it seeks to avoid – a President so weak that he is in fact unable to discharge the powers and duties of his office. I now think we can dodge that bullet. As best I can tell, we are of one mind. There may have been a time when invoking the Twenty-Fifth Amendment made sense but that time is past. Not only do you, President Stanton, believe you are able to lead the nation so does your Vice President and the entire Cabinet. What we need is a unanimous or near unanimous vote by the Congress reinstating President Stanton to his office. The question is how do we achieve such a mandate?"

"Congress will give President Stanton the same vote of confidence we have when it learns the truth," Roosevelt insisted. "The Judiciary Committees and the public must hear what we have heard. They are already scheduled to hear Director Parker's briefing. Our testimony should follow."

"I don't believe we should be to structured in our testimony, but I believe I should follow Director Parker," President Stanton suggested. "I want the Committee and the American people to understand that Acting President Roosevelt and all but two members of my Cabinet were acting honestly and honorably. I gave them cause to be concerned. My behavior was erratic. I'd like them to know the devastation I felt following the deaths of Mathew Thorn and my own Danny. I'd like them to understand my only real consolation was my country. It still needed me. Even with hindsight I believe my decisions were solid. Working on the nation's problems held my grief in check, but when the decisions were made and I again confronted Danny's death that's when my grief recaptured my heart and mind and I was inconsolable. They should know that I was doing much better by Christmas. I celebrated that fact New Year's Eve toasting my friends and dancing with my daughters. Then I moved into the twilight zone and introduced Gretchen as Danny and sowed doubts everywhere. That made the State of the Union address absolutely critical. The people believe I failed that test."

"Mr. President?"

"Yes, Secretary of Defense Collier."

"You did not fail that test, sir. The State of the Union was your Super Bowl. You passed the test. We have the replays to prove it. We need to show the Committees and the nation how you smashed that test. Mr. President, I'd like to present the tapes and tell the Committees my evaluation not only of the address but also Elizabeth Anne's charade and your statement to Danny. Coupled with your conduct during this crisis I don't believe there is a more compelling argument that you are ready to resume your duties. I would conclude by letting everyone know that as Secretary of Defense, a crusty old military type and lifelong Republican, I believe national security and the military needs you as its commander-in-chief."

"Any objections, Acting President Roosevelt?"

"None, Mr. President. I think Secretary Collier will be a powerful spokesman for reestablishing your Presidency."

"Mr. President, I know you don't want the Cabinet's testimony to be scripted, but maybe before the rest of the Cabinet and Mr. Roosevelt testify, the Committees could hear from Aaron."

"What are you suggesting, Sharon?" President Stanton asked.

"I know that Aaron would like to speak on your behalf. If he can't do it in person, he can tape a statement. He still feels a great deal of guilt for his initial decision to sign the declaration."

"Mr. Roosevelt, are you okay with that?"

"Certainly, I would only suggest that we allow the Committee to call upon the remainder of the Cabinet in whatever order they desire."

"Director Parker, you have some question about that?"

"Yes, President Stanton. I'm convinced that the Committees will insist upon hearing from former Secretaries Reynolds and

Kelly. If they are 'encouraged' to tell the truth, they might make it impossible to vote against you."

"Surely they would just assert their Fifth Amendment rights," Attorney General Herrera stated. Director, are you suggesting that we encourage Congress to grant them immunity from prosecution?"

"I'm suggesting we should have a position on the question. It's bound to come up. We don't want to go off on a dozen different paths," Parker stated.

"If the hearings are going badly," President Stanton conditioned, "we could encourage the Committees to grant both Secretaries immunity and then encourage them to probe Croft's conspiracy to remove a democratically elected president. We can keep it in reserve."

"I have another option that you can keep in reserve, President Stanton." Acting President Roosevelt was deadly serious. He wanted the President and his Cabinet to know his commitment to righting the wrong he had made possible was unconditional. "With the information that we will be giving to Congress, this should be a very easy quick decision. If Congress chooses to embarrass you and milk this issue for partisan advantage, I'll nail them. I'll resign. You will resume your Presidential duties. The Congress will confront a *fait accompli*."

"I understand and appreciate your offer, William, but we should all pray it doesn't come to that. We are going to win this battle," President Stanton proclaimed, "but we dare not lose the war. This country has problems. We need to work with this Congress."

"You're right, Mr. President. I'm learning. Most importantly, I learned that we conclude our meetings by dumping on Crayton and Jason to do whatever is required by what we have decided. In this instance I would ask the two of you to work with the Judiciary Committees to bring this process to an expeditious conclusion."

"In that spirit," Director Parker added, "I need Crayton and Jason to join me on Capitol Hill in briefing the Congressional Judiciary Committees. Much has happened here today. They need to know in an executive session not only about the Bureau's investigation but also about the positions you all have agreed to this morning. They must not be surprised in the public hearings. Someone will go off half-cocked and grab the headlines with a sensational charge of conspiracies in high places. The story that President Stanton has received an overwhelming vote of confidence not only from his Cabinet and Acting President Roosevelt but also the Congress of the United States will be buried in the back pages. We can't let that happen. This should be a wonderful story, a real American moment."

"Mr. President, with your permission I will amend our directive to Crayton and Jason to work with Director Parker to ensure the executive briefing of the Congressional Judiciary Committees includes the decisions we have taken this morning."

5:45 P.M., Wednesday, January 30.

The hearings had gone on for two bathroom breaks and five-and-a-half hours. An exhausted Senate Chairman Richard Talbert was already standing when House Chairwoman Sierra Roberts took up the gavel and stated, "If there are no more questions for Director Parker, chief of staff Crayton Langford, or Acting President Roosevelt's chief of staff Jason Fields, this hearing is officially adjourned." The gavel struck the sound block simultaneously with "adjourned."

It was over. The chairs and ranking minority members met quietly at the north exit with Crayton, Jason, and Director Parker. All had gone exceedingly well. Thursday morning at ten, following a brief executive session, joint public hearings of the House and Senate Judiciary Committees would begin.

CHAPTER TWENTY-EIGHT:

THEREUPON THE CONGRESS WILL DECIDE THE ISSUE

10:00 A.M., Thursday, January 30.

Like faculty members at a commencement address they marched into the chamber by seniority through two doors, the left for Representatives, the right for Senators. At the conclusion of the processional, Senate Chairman Richard Talbert and House Chairwoman Sierra Roberts stood together, centered in the upper arc of desks and chairs.

By prior agreement Chairman Talbert opened the session noting that the joint committee had held a marathon executive session Wednesday. Today's hearing, he announced, was to provide not only that same information in abbreviated form to the American people, but also to take testimony from President Stanton, Acting President Roosevelt, and members of the President's Cabinet. After outlining the rules that would govern the hearings Chairman Talbert called the first witness, Director Robert Parker. It was 10:20 A.M.

Without a break for six hours and forty minutes the joint committee heard electrifying testimony. A mini-series about honorable men, death, grief, drugs, alcohol, conspirators, constitutional law, contract killers, promises, threats, bribes, lies, a fall guy, protection programs, money laundering, payoffs, phone taps, surveillance, suicide, and resignations. The nation was mesmerized; all the networks had live coverage, and streaming feeds. Viewership grew throughout Director Parker's testimony. It grew again as Secretaries Kelly and Reynolds repeatedly invoked their Fifth Amendment rights. It peaked with a live feed of the testimony of Secretary of Interior Aaron Chadwick, a man previously pronounced dead. It remained off the charts as President Stanton and Acting President Roosevelt testified. Their candor and civility was startling to a nation that had been bombarded with talk of Armageddon. They were in complete agreement except when Roosevelt spoke of resignation and President Stanton emphatically stated that Roosevelt had acted honorably and he would not accept his resignation unless he was absolutely convinced that the Vice President needed to resign for personal reasons. From coast to coast Americans remembered why they were so taken with Andrew Holmes Stanton.

At 5:00 P.M. Committee Chair Richard Talbert announced the Joint Committee would take a short recess to consider whether both the House and Senate Committees were ready to announce their recommendations to the full House and full Senate.

Despite the recess news coverage continued unabated. So much had been revealed that rather than mirror one another, each network had their own collage of replays and expert analysis. The audience remained huge and hungry for news. They were hopeful, yet anxious about the return of their President. They wouldn't tolerate commercial breaks; they didn't want to miss anything and news was everywhere.

At 5:50 P.M. both Committees returned to the chamber. Chairwoman Sierra Roberts had won the coin toss and made the announcement. "Chairman Talbert, with your permission I would like to announce the decisions of both the House and Senate Judiciary Committees. Our committees, unanimously and independently, have concluded that the declaration of President Stanton's inability to discharge the powers and duties of his office was illegally and decisively influenced by an attempted *coup d'état*. While the full extent of the conspiracy is not yet known, without a doubt it did involve two of the Cabinet signatories to the declaration. Without those signatures the declaration did not meet the Constitutional requirement of the Twenty-Fifth Amendment that a majority of the Cabinet determine that the President is unable to perform the duties and powers of his office. Therefore it is our Committees' unanimous decision that President Stanton has been and continues to be the President of the United States. Tomorrow, we are informed there will be a proforma vote in both Houses of Congress and President Stanton 'shall resume the powers and duties of his office.'"

EPILOGUE

On Friday, January 31st, both Houses of Congress followed the recommendations of their Judiciary Committees by overwhelming margins. A handful of Senators and Representatives vented long held anger with President Stanton but their votes were immediately ridiculed and then dismissed as irrelevant. President Stanton had his mandate.

The story with legs centered on Elizabeth Anne Roosevelt. Was she cochair of the conspiracy to murder Aaron Chadwick? Would she be charged? Speculation and unflattering portraits were daily fare. Elizabeth Anne tried to take the offensive with appearances on news shows and late night television but she was only partially successful and that was short-lived.

On Valentine's Day Director Parker informed Elizabeth Anne that the FBI had completed their analysis of her father's papers and computer files. He told her that she was not only a suspect in the conspiracy investigation but now she was a suspect in the death of her brother and two companions. Elizabeth Anne was outraged and adamant. She loved her brother and still mourned his death. "How dare you," she cried.

"Mrs. Roosevelt," Director Parker responded firmly. "In a safe within your father's vault room we found a detailed report by a private investigator hired by your father that implicates you in the death of James Croft Jr. and his two companions."

"I don't believe you. Where's the report?" she demanded.

"Mrs. Roosevelt, when you are charged, you and your attorney will receive all of the information we have relevant to the charges."

Looking directly at Robert Parker, Elizabeth Anne stood and confronted the Director of the FBI. "Get out of my home and don't come back unless you have a warrant. Get out. Now!"

"I have a court order here, Mrs. Roosevelt. Read it carefully. I will leave as soon you surrender your passport."

****

BIOGRAPHY

My fascination with politics began high atop my father's shoulders as I saw Harry Truman "Give'em Hell" at a whistle stop in Grand Island, Nebraska. My mom and dad worked nearby at  Hastings College. Mom was the College Nurse. Dad chaired the Economics Dept. My memories of that time not only include my mom campaigning for sanitary drinking fountains and vitamin D in milk but also my father leading the boycott of the town barbers who refused to cut the "kinky hair" of blacks who had served in WWII and attended Hastings College on the G.I. Bill.

I received formal training in political science at Carroll College in Wisconsin, Vanderbilt University in Tennessee, and American University in Washington, D.C. I have taught political science for twelve years at the college level and served in the administrations of four presidents.

At American University I became a committed activist. My first march was to Lafayette Square after the Bombing in Birmingham. Later that fall I was an eyewitness to history as President Johnson in the aftermath of the Kennedy assassination addressed a joint session of Congress. President Johnson had no Vice-President. He did have a long history of heart disease. Speaker McCormack and Senate Pro Tem. Carl Hayden sat behind the President. They were next in the line of succession. Both were relics of a by-gone era. McCormack, the younger of the two, had served in the House since 1928. Hayden born in 1877 represented Arizona since its statehood in 1912. Both suffered from serious dementia and both were sound asleep.

That scene witnessed, by the world, gave birth to the Twenty-fifth Amendment. Unfortunately rather than a real solution to Presidential disability it could be a frightening prescription for a *coup d'état*. This novel exploits that fact and gives you a political thriller with intrigue, mayhem, and murder.   Have a good read!!!

www.ingramcontent.com/pod-product-compliance
Lightning Source LLC
Chambersburg PA
CBHW061325170626
46817CB00001B/318